Hungry Women

KU-629-878

"What we need is a menu of men that we could order from. That would make things so much easier."

"Absolutely," Dixie says. "With guys listed according to their appeal. Like some guys are merely appetizers, some are desserts."

"And some," Diva says, grinning lewdly, "are full-course meals."

"How about something like this," Trina says. "Beef Ribs à la Jack: Huge slabs of meaty ribs that take all night to finish."

Barcelona laughs. "With juicy, buttery corn on a stiff cob. On the side."

"That's the way I like it best," Diva says.

Diva lays a twenty in the middle of the table. "Let's do it for real."

"Do what?" Barcelona asks.

"Make this menu. With men on it."

"That's crazy."

"No, it's not," Diva says. "We all know and meet lots of men. Some of them you're interested in, but some of them you're not. Maybe one of us would be."

"This sounds a little like high school," Barcelona says.

"Not today's high school," Dixie says.

"It doesn't sound like high school," Trina says. "It sounds like business."

"Be careful when you pick up this novel, because you won't be able to put it down. Laramie Dunaway's women aren't just hungry. They're funny, raunchy, brave, and deeply human."

Elizabeth Villars, author of *Lipstick on His Collar*

Hungry Women

LARAMIE DUNAWAY

NEW ENGLISH LIBRARY
Hodder and Stoughton

Copyright © 1990 by Laramie
Dunaway

First published in Great Britain in
1990 by New English Library

First published in the USA in 1990 by
Warner Books, Inc.

*A New England Library Paperback
Original*

Eighth impression 1992

*The characters and situations in this
book are entirely imaginary and bear
no relation to any real person or actual
happenings.*

The right of Laramie Dunaway to be
identified as the author of this work
has been asserted by her in accord-
ance with the Copyright, Designs and
Patents Act 1988.

This book is sold subject to the condition that it shall not, by way of trade
or otherwise, be lent, re-sold, hired
out or otherwise circulated without
the publisher's prior consent in any
form of binding or cover other than
that in which it is published and without a similar condition including this
condition being imposed on the sub-
sequent purchaser.

No part of this publication may be
reproduced or transmitted in any
form or by any means, electronic or
mechanical, including photocopying,
recording or any information storage
or retrieval system, without either
the prior permission in writing from
the publisher or a licence, permitting
restricted copying. In the United King-
dom such licences are issued by the
Copyright Licensing Agency, 90
Tottenham Court Road, London W1P
9HE.

Printed and bound in Great Britain for
Hodder and Stoughton Paperbacks, a
division of Hodder and Stoughton
Ltd., Mill Road, Dunton Green,
Sevenoaks, Kent TN13 2YA (Editorial
Office: 47 Bedford Square, London
WC1B 3DP) by Clays Ltd., St Ives plc.

A CIP catalogue record for this book
is available from the British Library.

ISBN 0-450-53471-5

PART ONE

Live Wires

In Which the Differences
Between Sex and Death
Are Finally Revealed

1

Barcelona Lee sits at the wobbliest table in Hamburger Hamlet waiting for her best friend to arrive so she can lie to her. Lying makes Barcelona anxious. She thinks of the radio news report she heard on the drive here that claimed each year more women than men attempt suicide, but more men actually succeed. She wonders if that means women are more incompetent or just smarter. To pass time, she decides to test the radio's accuracy by taking an informal tally of her friends who have threatened suicide. It is either this or grade freshman essays.

For each friend who has openly offered to kill herself but would never really do it, Barcelona places a fried zucchini on the lip of her plate. Four zucchinis are stacked upright like crusty vertebrae. For each friend who had threatened and might someday try it, she rips a hunk of lettuce the size of a rose petal from her hamburger and places it in a separate pile. Two. For those who have dabbled at it and failed, she stacks pickle slices. Two. For those who have done it—slashed, gassed, or pilled themselves into oblivion—she uses maraschino cherries. Actually, there has been only one woman she knows personally who has succeeded. Darlene. Darlene hanged herself with an extension cord in the guest bathroom on August 16th, the anniversary of Elvis Presley's death.

Barcelona plucks the neon-red cherry floating in her

Diet Coke and twirls it by the stem, deciding where best to place it.

Suddenly ashamed of her own morbidness, she pops the cherry into her mouth and sucks out the delicious sweetness. For once she doesn't worry about what the Red Dye No. 45 is doing to her insides.

'Did you order yet?' Trina asks, appearing suddenly and sliding into the booth opposite Barcelona. The wobbly table jiggles and the stack of fried zucchinis tumbles over. Trina exists in a perpetual state of being harried. Her clothes are elegant Liz Claiborne and Anne Klein II suits, but she always looks rumpled, like a hastily made bed. Her makeup is uneven, as if applied with a putty knife while running up steep stairs. Even her hair looks anxious, frizzled black curls yanked and tugged grudgingly into submission. Yet she has a lusty, sensual look that men always seem to notice. Trina eyes Barcelona's half-eaten hamburger and frowns. 'Yeech. How late am I?'

'Twenty minutes.'

'Shit, that's not even late for me.'

'It is for me. I still have to go back to work.' First lie.

'You can always fake it. Not me. The Candidate wants me to dig up something on Councilwoman Bennington.'

'Dirt?'

'What else? Dirt is what fuels the machinery of modern politics. I just made that up. Profound, huh? Hey, waitress.' Trina wiggles her chipped fingernails at a slender young woman in a short skirt which flares over her hips but doesn't quite cover the matching maroon panties underneath. 'Soup and salad. Ranch dressing. Glass of white wine.' She hands the waitress the menu and waves her away. Trina watches her walk away and makes a face. 'Christ, I hate staring into some eighteen-year-old's twat when I'm ordering food. Who designs their outfits anyway, lifers at San Quentin?'

'So how's The Candidate doing?' Barcelona asks. Trina is a publicity flak for Cory Meyers, Kennedyesque candidate for Los Angeles City Council, one of the most powerful political offices in the state. Trina alternately refers to him as either The Candidate or The Great Pretender, never by his name.

'He's up in the polls. Another half a percentage point.'

'That's terrific.'

Trina shrugs. 'Not good enough to win.'

'Well, if he doesn't, it won't be your fault.'

'Doesn't matter who's at fault, kiddo, just who gets blamed.'

Barcelona raises her left arm to look at her watch, remembers she'd taken it off back at her office because it ticked too loudly during the faculty meeting. She reads Trina's watch upside down. 'Where's Diva? She's never this late.'

'Oh, I forgot to tell you.' Trina snatches the pile of pickle slices on Barcelona's plate and stuffs them into her wide mouth. She chews as she does everything in life, vigorously. Barcelona always has the feeling that Trina fears someone is after her seat, her car, her food, that everything in life must be consumed immediately before stolen. Trina swallows the half-chewed lump and says, 'Diva can't make it today. Rehearsal.'

'What is it this time? Some soft drink?'

'Ketchup, I think. Or mustard. Relish, maybe. I don't know, some condiment.'

'She'll be there tonight, won't she?'

'Natch. We'll all be there. Where else would we be?'

Barcelona shrugs. 'Dixie's still working Vice. They may have her on hooker patrol again.'

'Not anymore. I had breakfast with her this morning. She's now undercover in a high school busting students. Can you imagine? I mean, high school was awful enough

11

the first time around.' Trina reaches again into Barcelona's plate and grabs the fried zucchini slices. She sticks out her tongue, lays a breaded zucchini on the wet gummy membrane, and pulls it back into her mouth.

'Every time you do that I expect you to give change,' Barcelona says.

'The Candidate told me it reminded him of a bullfrog snagging a fly.'

'What were you eating when he said this?'

Trina grins and looks Barcelona in the eyes. 'Him.'

'Oh?' Barcelona doesn't permit herself to look surprised. 'I didn't know he'd issued a position paper in that regard.'

Trina folds a napkin and sticks it under the table leg to keep it from wobbling. 'It just happened. No big deal. We were in Burbank taping an interview show—"L.A. Morning," "Wake up, L.A.," "Pick the Sleep Crud from Your Eyes, L.A.," something like that. They had some problems with the video equipment. We went out for a snack and ended up in some motel doing it standing in the shower. We didn't plan it or anything.'

'How was it?'

'Okay, I guess. Thing was, the whole time we were bouncing away, I kept wondering if this position would give me varicose veins. Kinda distracted me, you know?'

'What about his wife?'

'She already has varicose veins.'

'Yuk, yuk.'

'Okay, so she doesn't really. She's truly gorgeous, like out of *Vogue* or something. They stand us next to each other. I'd be the "before" picture.'

'Then what's going on between you two? Love or sex or boredom?'

Trina laughs and starts choking herself with both hands. 'God, I'm the last one to ask about these things. Definitely not love. More like curiosity, I guess. We've worked so hard together for the past year, maybe it was just inevitable. Besides, they're getting a divorce. Keep that to yourself, Barcy.'

'The sex part or the divorce?'

'The divorce.'

'Who would I tell?'

'She's staying with him until after the election, then they're splitting up. She doesn't want to hurt his political chances right now. They're both so adult and civilized about the whole thing it's nauseating.' Trina shakes her head and laughs. 'She's who I want to be when I grow up.'

Barcelona reads Trina's watch upside down again. 'I've got to get back. Students will be lining up outside my office in about twenty minutes.' That too is a lie, but she isn't quite ready yet to tell Trina the truth. Not until she knows the extent of the bad news. Maybe tonight, at dinner, when they are all together. She'll tell them then.

'Hey, I met someone who'd read one of your books,' Trina says.

'Which one?'

'A guy over at the mayor's office.'

'I mean which book?'

She shrugs. 'I don't know, the one about the planet where there were too many women so they had to undergo forced sex-change operations to balance the sexes out.'

'*Balancing Acts.*'

'Whatever. He got off on that idea. He was shocked as shit when I told him B. Evans Lee was a woman.'

'Was he at least cute?'

'Looks like that scruffy actor who never shaves. The one in *Barfly*.'

Barcelona rolls her eyes. 'Mickey Rourke.'

'Yeah, him.'

'All my fans look like Mickey Rourke.' Barcelona stands up.

'Hang on,' Trina says, sliding quickly out of the booth as if she's just discovered it was on fire. 'I'll walk you out.'

'What about your food?'

'I gave them fifteen minutes. They can't bring a lousy soup and salad in fifteen minutes, fuck 'em. I'll pick something up at the deli.'

This makes Barcelona very uncomfortable. Guilty. A coconspirator. Certainly there must be some kind of law about ordering food and leaving before you are served. But she knows there is no way she will change Trina's mind. To make up for it, she leaves double the tip she'd planned to leave.

Trina sees what she is up to, shakes her head, grabs one of the dollar bills from the table, and stuffs it back in Barcelona's purse. 'Don't encourage incompetence.'

All the way back to the car, Barcelona feels badly. Despite Trina's chattering about The Candidate's newest TV commercials, Barcelona keeps thinking of all the possibilities of why the waitress had been slow to serve Trina's meal. The cook, perhaps a recent emigrant from Baja, had misread the order slip. Maybe the waitress saw the soup was not steaming and had handed it back to the cook with a firm scolding, 'I can't serve cold soup to my customers.' Maybe she'd started her period today and had run to the bathroom to change her tampon. Maybe . . .

'You want me to run by and pick you up tonight?' Trina offers.

'I'll drive.' She hesitates before telling her why, but knows she'll have to tell her eventually. Besides, one secret a day is all she can handle. 'I promised Eric I'd stop by tonight before dinner. Just for a minute.'

'Christ, Barcy!' Trina gives her a disgusted look. 'I didn't realize tonight was your night for self-torture. Why not slam your head into your refrigerator and save the mileage?'

'Give me a break, okay?'

'Will *Luna* be there?' She says the name as if it were a venereal disease.

'I don't know. It doesn't matter.'

'Yeah, right. It doesn't matter.'

Barcelona unlocks the door of her blue 1977 Chrysler, an oversize car that she'd inherited last year from her deceased grandmother. The Geezemobile, the others called it. She slides behind the wheel. No bucket seats, just a benchlike seat as long and hard as a Catholic pew. She could seat the cast of *Twelve Angry Men* in here, give them something to really be pissed about.

'Don't be late again, okay?' she tells Trina. 'We only do this every two weeks. Coming late makes everybody feel you don't care.'

'I care, I care. Honestly, I'd rather be with you guys tonight than on a date with a disease-free rich man who loves children and is not afraid of commitment.'

'Really?'

'Almost.' She winks, squeezes Barcelona's arm, closes the car door. 'Tonight, kid. It'll be wild. I promise.'

She watches Trina march purposefully across the sidewalk, heels clacking cement as if sparks should fly with each step. Trina is one of the fried zucchinis, a threatened suicide six months ago. She'd called Barcelona at home, a little after one in the morning, catching her watching TV while grading student papers. David Letterman was still on, cackling at Stupid Dog Tricks. Barcelona had hit the remote switch that shut the TV off. 'Life sucks,' Trina had said, not waiting for a hello. 'Life sucks but I don't.' She'd laughed sadly. 'Get this, this will kill you. The miniseries of my life. I just come home from a date with this guy, an assistant d.a. I met last week at that dinner for the governor. Anyway, this is our first date, we've had dinner at some swank French place out in the Valley. He brings me

15

home in his new Mercedes, still has that new-car smell. Did I mention that he was wearing a goddamn tuxedo? Looked gorgeous, like Harrison Ford getting an Oscar. Anyway, we're back at my place. We're sipping this modest white wine I've been saving, nibbling some brie. We kiss. Kiss a little more. A little light tongue action. Okay, so far so good. What do you think would follow? Huh?' Barcelona had started to say something but Trina cut her off. 'You figure a little grab and stroke, some tender buildup, hands running along thighs, some ass-squeezing, ear-nibbling, buttons suddenly falling open, music swells, so does he, and eventually some serious humping. No, sir. This guy kisses me twice. Two fucking times. Half-assed kisses at that. Next thing you know, he asks me to go down on him. Not later. Right now. Pulls his fly open and whips out the hairy beast. Doesn't even want to get undressed, for God's sake.' A long weary sigh followed. 'I mean it, Barcy, if this is what it all comes to after thirty and divorce, I'd rather check out now. I fucking mean it.' And she'd hung up. Barcelona had called her back immediately. They'd chatted a few minutes. Trina seemed to calm down. Barcelona had offered to go over, spend the night. Trina had laughed, said she was too old for a pajama party. She'd be fine, she'd go to bed now, had a million things to do in the morning.

Unable to sleep, Barcelona had turned David Letterman back on but couldn't concentrate. She'd call Trina back but the line was busy. Next day she found out from Diva that Trina had called Dixie and told her the same story. Dixie had rushed over and stayed with Trina that night. 'I would have gone over,' Barcelona had explained to Diva. 'She told me not to come.'

'Told Dixie the same thing,' Diva had said. 'Dixie went anyway.'

Ever since, Barcelona feels a little guilty when seeing

Trina. Perhaps she should have rushed over too, ignoring Trina's protests. Isn't that what a true friend does? But Barcelona isn't that pushy. She takes people at their word. Dixie, on the other hand, is a cop. She's used to taking charge. She thrives in emergencies.

Barcelona turns on the radio. Janis Joplin is singing 'Get It While You Can.' Afterward the news comes on and repeats the story about suicides. Barcelona thinks of Darlene, the successful suicide. Not a friend really, a vague neighbor about the same age. Occasionally Barcelona would be pulling into her garage just as Darlene was out walking her dog, a tan Lhasa apso named Foxy. They never looked at each other when they exchanged greetings, chatting about the homeowners association or such. Instead they would speak to each other while staring at the dog as he raised a leg and peed or squatted to defecate, which Darlene would immediately scoop up with neatly cut squares of newspaper and stuff into a brown lunch bag. Barcelona smiles at the memory of Darlene standing there with a lunch bag full of shit discussing the parking problem. She realizes now that if asked, she could better describe the dog's features than Darlene's.

Every once in a while Barcelona runs into Darlene's husband, Dave, and they have almost identical conversations to the ones she and Darlene used to have, each still watching the dog, the dog still squatting and grimacing on the greenbelt, Dave holding a lunch bag of shit.

Barcelona pulls into the heavy Westwood traffic, concentrating on maneuvering the aircraft carrier Geezemobile so she won't think about Eric. But every store she passes is one she and Eric had been in at some time or other in their frequent visits here. There is the Nike store where they'd bought matching running shoes. He'd worn his out in six months. Hers were still practically new in the back of her closet. With the new tennis racquet

17

and the skis and handball gloves. He'd wanted her to become more competitive, like him. Enter mixed-doubles tournaments. But she'd never enjoyed that aspect of herself. Didn't like how it made her feel squirmy and edgy.

Now that they were split up, she went to the health club every day and took a jazzercise class. She'd lost her six pounds she'd put on after the split, plus another eight she'd been meaning to lose for the six years they'd lived together. Dixie has been trying to talk her into lifting weights with her. Dixie is in remarkable shape. She once demonstrated the benefits of weight lifting by picking up a quarter from the floor between her buttock cheeks. Barcelona doesn't think she is quite up to that yet. Her stomach is flat, her butt firm. What more could she expect from life?

She follows Wilshire Boulevard past the San Diego Freeway entrance that would take her back to her home in Orange County. No need to tell Trina that there is another reason she is in L.A. today, other than to have lunch together. Not until Barcelona finds out what this mystery is all about.

Yesterday afternoon the strange phone call had surprised her. 'Can you buzz in tomorrow?' her agent had asked.

'I teach in the morning.'

'After lunch then?'

Barcelona rarely spoke to her agent and even more rarely actually saw her. This was very unusual. 'Why? What's up?'

'We'll talk about it tomorrow. Two o'clock, okay? It's important.'

So here she is, carefully piloting the Geezemobile through Beverly Hills among the Porsches, Mercedes, and Jaguars until she finds the parking lot behind the Banana Republic. She parks, walks the two blocks to her agent's building, where they have underground parking, which she purposely avoided. She doesn't like the hollow echo of her heels down in those places. The sound of emptiness amplified.

She walks past the sleepy security guard who waves his soggy sandwich at her. She smiles at him, catches a strong whiff of tuna salad, and hurries to the elevators. She waits for the next car with two tidy young men in business suits. They are in their late twenties, about five years younger than she. Their suits are drab but expensive, indicating some important corporate position. She still isn't used to seeing so many people younger than she in responsible positions.

When the elevator door hisses open, one man enters first, the other holds the door open for her. She nods, walks in, feels his eyes behind her starting at her ankles and finger-walking up the backs of her thighs, curving over her buttocks, lingering there a moment, wondering, then moving up, jumping off midway up her back. When the door closes and the three of them are alone, sliding up the shaft, the two men return to their discussion of some investment property over in Riverside County, completely ignoring her. This is a recent phenomenon, something that has happened more and more often in the four years since she'd turned thirty. Young salesmen in their twenties who used to vault over three older customers to wait on her, now let her wait her turn with the other adults. She is still attractive, still a big hit with men her own age and older, but she misses that special attention she'd always gotten from the young. When had she stopped being one of Us and become one of Them?

Barcelona gets out on the eighteenth floor. She looks around a moment, disoriented. It has been so long since she's been here, she isn't sure this is the right floor after all. She starts walking the halls, reading nameplates. Nothing looks or sounds familiar. J. G. HEIM, PRODUCER.

19

LAURA LISTER, DDS. HAROLD K. BARRETT, AT-
TORNEY. Some of the office doors are open and she can
see massive color-coordinated suites with several young
secretaries, all of whom are dressed better than she is. The
whole floor smells of new carpeting.

Her armpits are dripping now, cool drops of sweat
skating down her ribs. Her stomach rumbles. She must be
getting closer. This anxiety is the reason she never meets
with her agent. Barcelona considers herself lucky to have
an agent. Though she has written six published science
fiction novels, none has been much of a success. Modest
advances and modest sales keep her living slightly better
than her assistant professor's salary would afford, but not
enough to help support an office in a building like this.

When she finishes a novel, she sends it to Grief, her
agent. Within a few months to a year, she receives a letter,
some contracts in the mail which she signs without reading,
and a year later the book appears in the paperback section
of bookstores. Like magic. Barcelona prefers to think of
it that way. Not muck around with the voodoo of publishing. She never expresses disappointment than the advances
aren't higher, or that her books don't sell more copies.
She is pleased to be published at all, enjoys the minor
celebrity status it gives her among her students, the occasional fan letter from Kansas City or Jacksonville usually
addressed to *Mr*. B. Evans Lee, the look of respect from
someone new when they find out she is a writer.

She sees the corner office down the hall and knows
without reading the gold plate that this is Grief's office.
She hesitates, knowing full well why Grief has asked her
down here today. To dump her. Toss her out of the agency.
Take your stupid science fiction books and peddle them
yourself. They don't even pay for my stamps. Barcelona
leans against the wall, rummages through her purse until
she finds some spearmint Breathsavers, scratches the lint

off the top one, pops it, and bites down hard. A rush of bittersweetness stings her mouth.

She continues down the hallway. The office door is closed, the lettering on the gold plate in lavish medieval script: *Grief Fenton-Happs, Literary Agent.* Barcelona pushes open the door and enters.

Grief's young secretary, who looks a lot like the waitress at Hamburger Hamlet, is on the phone telling the caller that Ms. Fenton-Happs was out of the office for the afternoon but would call back first thing in the morning. Barcelona feels a cold shiver as she wonders if she's gotten the day wrong.

But suddenly there she is. Grief doing an exaggerated tiptoe past the secretary who is still on the phone denying her boss's presence. She waves for Barcelona to follow her into her inner office. Barcelona does, noticing that Grief is in her stocking feet. Also noticing a knobby bunion bulging on the side of her left foot like a toadstool. As soon as she gets close to Grief, the taller woman grabs her in a firm shoulder hug and says, 'It's so good to see you, Barcy.'

'You too.'

'That yutz on the phone thinks I'm going to sell him this hot new author I just started handling for popcorn and a fingerfuck. Forget it.' She collapses into her chair behind her huge and unbearably messy desk. She looks at Barcelona for a long minute as if wondering what this meeting was about. Finally she leans forward and smiles. 'So, Barcy, what do you want first, the good news or the bad news?'

2

Trina storms into The Candidate's office without knocking. She waves the memo from him she just found on her desk. 'What the hell does this mean?'

He looks up from behind his desk and smiles. 'Hello to you too.'

'This says you want me to fire someone.'

'Right. I don't care who. Your choice.' His perfect smile widens to reveal even more perfect teeth as square and white as Chicklets. Trina realizes it is his teeth that make him a successful politician. Someone with teeth like that is very cautious, practices preventive hygiene. People admire that in a leader.

'What are you talking about?' Trina asks. 'Why fire anybody?'

'Because we can't afford five full-time people on staff anymore.'

'Donations are way up,' she reminds him.

'Yes, and I know I have you to thank for that.' Impossibly, his smile widens even more and she sees yet another group of perfect teeth. She wonders if his teeth continue down his throat, line his stomach, intestines large and small, all the way through his body. If she pulled his pants down and bent him over would his asshole snap at her like those chattering teeth you buy at novelty stores?

'Then what's all this crap about firing somebody?'

22

'You sound like Jack Lemmon in *Mr. Roberts*. Remember at the end when he bursts into James Cagney's office and says, "What's this crap about no movie?" God, I loved that.'

'Save the charm for the voters, slick. We're not exactly broke around here. I mean, it's not like you're spending all your money on my salary.'

He laughs. 'We both know you're underpaid and overworked. Don't think I'm not appreciative of everything you've done.'

She thinks maybe that 'appreciative' crack and this smug smile refer to their shower sex the other day, but she's not sure. Suddenly she realizes that she's not really sure they even went to a motel or had sex or if she just dreamed it. She thinks about asking him, but decides not to.

The Candidate yawns long and loudly. He is the only man she's ever met who looks startlingly handsome even while yawning. He leans way back in his chair, tilting it off balance, webbing his fingers together and stretching them over his head. Several fingers crack. The sound seems to surprise him and he looks closely at his knuckles as he laces the fingers and slowly cracks them again, his eyes so intent as if looking for the exact moment the knuckle swells up out of the socket under the tight skin. Two knuckles pop and he leans back with a sigh, his scientific curiosity satisfied.

Trina sits down on the leather sofa away from his desk. Her head hurts. She doesn't even remember driving here. The last moment she can clearly picture was walking away from Barcelona at the Hamburger Hamlet in Westwood. She must have gotten into her car and driven here, but she can't recall sticking her key in the ignition, fastening the shoulder harness, driving here, parking. She looks down and sees the red cardboard parking stub from the lot down the street wrinkled and twisted in her hand. Her thumb is red from rubbing it. That is where she must have parked her car, though she doesn't remember.

'You okay, Trina?' the Candidate asks, getting up from behind his desk and walking toward her.

She stares at his desk, one of those ultramodern jobs, smoked glass top and black wire baskets for drawers. She can look straight into each drawer and see what's in it. Part of his open, nothing-to-hide image.

'Trina, you okay?' he repeats. He sounds honestly concerned.

She notices he is not wearing socks with his Topsiders. She has warned him against this habit. 'Where are your socks?' she asks suddenly. It is the same tone she uses with Karyn, her twelve-year-old daughter. The Candidate is forty-two.

'You look a little pale,' he says, bending over her.

'You could get away looking like that when you were campaigning for Jerry Brown. But we don't want to happen to you what happened to him. The Flake Factor. Makes people think you're laughing at them. People won't stand for that. You can lie to them and steal from them, but you can't laugh at them.'

He walks over to the Sparklettes tank and draws a paper cup of water. He carries it back to her. 'Drink this.'

She sips from it. 'Let's learn from his mistakes, okay?'

'Sure. Wear socks, don't date rock queens.' He sits beside her on the sofa. He smells faintly piney. 'You feel better?'

'I'm fine. Just a little light-headed. I skipped lunch.' She finishes the water. He takes the paper cup, crushes it into a ball and shoots it across the room at the Plexiglas wastecan. The paper wad bounces off the rim and rolls under his desk.

'Plexiglas isn't as forgiving as metal,' he says.

'You mind if we put your jump shot on hold and discuss

24

this stupid memo? With the campaign in its final months, we need more people, not fewer.'

'And we'll get them. Later. Right now we need to do two things. One' —he holds up his thumb—'we need to reduce the staff so we can afford to send this newest mailer. Hopefully the mailer will get us more money to hire more people. And two'—he jackknifes another finger—'we need to remind our employees that that is exactly what they are, *employees*. Sometimes they act as if they were crusaders.'

'What's wrong with that?'

'We haven't been rising in the polls as fast as we'd all hoped. They're depressed, slowing down. They need a shot of inspiration.'

'This is more like a shot through the head.'

'Damn right. Remind them that we pay them a salary, and if they want to keep getting that salary, they'd better start working for it. From now on around here, it's blow job or no job.'

Trina laughs. 'Can I quote you?'

'I already sent it to Bartlett's.'

Trina sips her water again, dabs some on her eyelids with her fingertips. It helps. She likes the staff, knows they all need the money. She can't bear having to fire any of them. 'Can't you just talk to them? Give them one of your famous pep talks?'

'I'm not famous for my pep talks. I'm famous for my . . .' He pauses, then laughs. 'Actually, I'm not famous for anything. That's why I'm losing this election.'

Trina kicks off her shoes, rubs her toes against the carpet. 'Give them a talk anyway.'

'Actions, as any voter can tell you, speak louder than words.'

'Even shitty actions?'

'Especially shitty actions.'

Trina sighs. A sudden picture of herself getting into her

car in the Hamburger Hamlet parking lot flashes into her mind. Her hand reaching for the ignition. Turning on the radio. The image vanishes.

'You having a drug flashback or something?' he asks. 'You look zonked.'

She glances over at him and shakes her head. 'The Great Pretender to the throne of L.A. sees all.'

'I like to think of myself as The Great Contender. Thanks to you.'

Suddenly Trina has another flash: she sees herself pulling into the parking lot down the street, getting the stub from the young Mexican kid with the porcupine moustache who stares openly at her breasts. The image fades and she concentrates on The Candidate. 'So, who should I fire? Do you have a sexual or ethnic preference?'

'You pick,' he says. 'It doesn't matter. Except Trudy. She's the only one who gets the lunch orders straight.'

'You can be a real bastard sometimes,' Trina says.

'Yes, but a bastard for the right side. Isn't that why you're working for me?'

'I'm a hired gun. In it strictly for the money.'

'You'd like to be. But I know you better.'

'You do, huh?' She stares directly into his eyes.

He gives her a long thoughtful look. 'Maybe I don't.'

His smile snaps away like a rubber band and she can see he doesn't like this firing business any more than she. She also can see that he is right. The staff has been slacking off as they get closer to the elections and their man doesn't look like a sure winner. Firing is a cheap incentive program.

He picks up a pencil and begins drumming on the edge of his coffee mug. 'So, factoring in the latest polls, the media editorials, and what you've overheard in the various women's rest rooms, what are my chances of actually winning this damned election?'

26

'You want the truth or a pep talk?'

'I'm hoping they're the same thing.' He is smiling again, but she can glimpse the flicker of fear in his eyes. She has seen it at some time or other in the eyes of every candidate she's ever worked for, even the ones way ahead in the polls. It is as if they glimpse a picture of themselves losing everything, humbled, stripped naked and shivering in front of millions of laughing people. Trina admires men and women who run for office, even the ones whose policies she doesn't agree with. What tremendous courage it takes to put yourself through all that. She doesn't have that kind of courage, never had. The only courageous thing she ever did was have Karyn.

'Well?' he asks. 'Just how thick is the soup?'

'You want charts and tables or just the bottom line?'

'Depends whose bottom is on the line.'

'You've got a pretty decent chance. With some luck.'

He thinks about this for a minute, nodding to himself as if he were carrying on a lively interior debate, still clacking his pencil on the mug rim. When he looks up at her his face shines with resolve and determination. 'Then we'll just have to make some luck, won't we?' he says. 'Work harder.'

'Meaning dig up more dirt.'

'The harder you work, the luckier you get.' He changes the tempo of his drumming and sings, 'Work all night till de morning come.'

'You're nuts,' Trina says, laughing.

He reaches over and plucks a piece of lettuce from her lapel. 'This is so much more practical than a carnation.' He tosses the lettuce into his mouth and chews loudly.

Trina laughs again. She admits that he is fun to be around, not only handsome, but good-natured, witty, caring. The kind of man you'd remember having sex with. Yet, still she isn't sure. She seems to recall the hot water sluicing down her spine, trickling between her buttocks. Her hands pressed flat against the wet tile, her feet spread slightly, squatting a little as he entered her. But she can't remember what he felt like inside of her. Did she come? Did he? Maybe she had dreamed it.

He reaches over again and she thinks he will find yet more food on her. That is not uncommon. She always returns from meals wearing a sampling of whatever she ate. But his hand rests on her shoulder in a friendly, concerned manner. He squeezes his fingers and she can feel their strength even through her shoulder pads. 'Maybe you need a couple days off, Trina.'

'Yeah, right. Perfect time to take a vacation. The peak of the goddamn campaign.'

'A day or two won't make a difference to the great city of Los Angeles. Me neither. Drive down to Palm Springs for the weekend. Dayna can take over.'

Dayna is his wife, officially his campaign manager. But despite her good wishes for her husband's success in the election, lately she has abdicated more and more of the daily responsibilities to Trina. No one has even seen Dayna at the headquarters for weeks.

'I think you've been working too hard,' he says.

'First you think the others aren't working hard enough, then you think I'm working too hard. Make up your mind.'

'They're employees, Trina, you're a friend.'

We must have done it then, she thinks. 'I'm fine. Really.'

'You look like you just got out of bed. Like you dressed last night, went to bed, and just got up, fully dressed and came to work.'

'Hey, that's my look. I work hard for it. That decadent, anyone-can-have-me look.'

He gets up, returns to his desk, scratches the bare ankle above his Topsiders. He looks at the papers on his desk. 'Whoever you fire, you can hire them back again in about a week. But don't tell them that. Blows the whole purpose.'

He opens the top basket drawer of his desk, reaches under some papers, and takes out a pair of argyle socks. Even the glass desk has secrets, she thinks. He kicks off his shoes and starts putting on the socks. 'Look, Ma, socks.'

Trina gets up and goes to the door. She is closing it behind her when she impulsively pokes her head back in and says, 'Just for the record, did you and I screw in the shower the other day?'

3

'Make up your mind, Barcy,' Grief says. 'I need to tell him something.'

'I don't know what to tell him,' Barcelona says.

'Think of something, dear. He'll be here any minute.'

Barcelona tries to concentrate, but she can't take her eyes off Grief's feet. The plump bunion that bulges from the ball of her left foot fascinates her. It strains against the stocking like a robber's face. She imagines it may be the petrified fetus of the twin sister Grief has always longed for but never known. She glances up and sees Grief staring at her, expectant. Barcelona shrugs. 'What am I expected to do?'

'Do? Do whatever you want, dear. It's your life, your career. It's all up to you.' Grief looks amused. Her tone is always condescending. Maybe this comes from being so tall, Barcelona thinks, forty-plus years of looming over others. She is over six feet, though all of it built solidly as a marble column. Her skin, by contrast, is pale and delicate, taut as Saran Wrap. She wears pleated black slacks and a white pirate's blouse and Barcelona realizes that this is the same color combination Grief wore the other times they met. Black slacks, white blouse, or white slacks and black blouse. Sometimes pearls. She has fine silky hair so blond that it is almost white, and white-blond eyebrows that are invisible from more than two feet away. The

30

invisible eyebrows and tight skin give her face a slightly scalded look.

'You look different,' Barcelona says.

'Yes?' Grief says encouragingly.

'I don't know how, just different. Maybe not. I just haven't seen you in a couple years.'

'No, no, you're right. There is something different. You're the first to notice. I should have known you would.'

Barcelona feels some pressure how to guess what is different, scans Grief's face for some sign, finds nothing. She shrugs. 'I don't know.'

'The eyes,' Grief prompts, delighted. She leans forward so Barcelona can take a closer look.

'New makeup?'

'Eyeliner. It's not makeup. It's a tattoo.'

'You had your eyes tattooed?'

'Do you like?'

Barcelona leans closer. Her own eyes water and burn at the thought. 'It looks like makeup, maybe a little thicker than before.'

'It's great. I never have to put eyeliner on. And it never washes off. I go swimming, I come out of the shower, it's still there.'

'But the needle, so close to your eyes. I don't think I could do that.'

'Nonsense. Nothing to it. The only thing I miss is when I cry, there's no more smearing and smudging that makes me look like a harlequin. Used to drive my husband into instant apology and an expensive gift. I noticed I cry a lot less now. What's the point?' She laughs as if to show that she's just joking.

The phone on her desk buzzes and Grief picks it up. 'Yes, Bette? Okay, give us a minute, then send him in.' She hangs up the phone and smiles at Barcelona. 'He's here. Anything you want to ask me first?'

Barcelona thinks hard. There are a thousand questions colliding in her head like carnival bumper cars, but none stays in focus long enough for her to snag it. The good news, Grief had told her fifteen minutes ago, was that they were about to meet with a film producer who is interested in optioning one of her novels for a feature film. Barcelona had broken out into a huge smile. 'That's great! What's the bad news?'

'I don't know yet,' Grief had said. 'But with these guys, there's always bad news. Sooner or later.'

Barcelona looks toward the door. She feels like a matador awaiting the release of the bull.

'Are you ready?' Grief asks.

Barcelona nods. 'Olé.'

The door opens and Bette leads a man into the room. Barcelona is startled. Though she has never met a real producer before, her mental image of one is of a fat, double-chinned man puffing a thick wet cigar and smiling too easily. What stuns Barcelona is that that's exactly what this man looks like. Rotund, thick lips, little hands, he walks in with a big smile and grabs Barcelona's hand as she rises from her chair.

'So this is the young lady who's going to make us all rich,' he says. He releases her hand and puffs the cigar again. 'Pardon the cigar, but my doctor's got me on this strict diet and it gives me bad breath. Ketosis. This kills the taste.'

'Roger,' Grief says, pecking him on the cheek, 'this is Barcelona Lee. Better known as B. Evans Lee. Barcy, this is the infamous Roger Carlyle.'

Roger Carlyle chuckles as if he likes the roguish image Grief's introduction implies. He points a plump finger at Barcelona and grins. 'Read your book, Ms. Lee. Read the whole thing in one sitting. Grief here sent it over to me two years ago, I stuck it up on some shelf, never read it.

I'll be honest with you, I don't even like to read. I especially don't like to read science fiction. Space ships, warp speed, crazy stuff. Christ.' He makes a dismissing gesture with his hands. 'But last week I get a call from a friend of mine, a source really, a spy. If you're going to be successful in this business you need to have spies. It's like a fuckin' war. You think I'm kidding. I'm not.' He laughs a gravelly laugh that is part chuckle, part gargle. 'Anyway, my source tips me that Lynda Kramer is coming to town to look over possible film ideas.'

'Lynda Kramer,' Barcelona repeats, impressed. Lynda Kramer is the classiest young actress around. In her mid-thirties, she has already starred with every major actor in a variety of films, most of which called for her to look mysterious and vulnerable and use an exotic accent. Academy Award nominations are automatic.

'Lynda took a year off to have her daughter and stayed pretty holed up in her husband's London apartment. Wouldn't even look at any scripts. Now she's on her way back and has let it slip, at least to my source, who is part of her entourage, that she'd love to do some kind of futuristic film, something classy, with a message. Like *On the Beach* or *Clockwork Orange*, something along those lines. Not just the usual cowboy rip-off, and no *Star Wars* flicks where special effects dominate. Something simple, but with heart.'

Roger Carlyle has said all this still standing in front of Grief's desk. Barcelona is standing less than two feet in front of him, reeling a little from the combination of cigar and ketosis. Like having her face ground into an ashtray.

'Sit, Roger, sit,' Grief says, waving him toward the chair opposite Barcelona. She looks at Barcelona, 'You, too.' Barcelona is already in her seat as Roger lowers his bulk into the chair and the bones in his pudgy knees crackle. Barcelona notices he is wearing stiff dry-cleaned black jeans with razor creases and a black polo shirt, perhaps in an effort to hide his girth. There is a sprinkling of dandruff on his shoulders and Barcelona imagines him getting dressed that morning, naked, looking at himself in the mirror, trying to decide whether to go with the white shirt to hide the dandruff, or the black shirt to hide the gut. How long had he stood there staring at his naked flab and snowy scalp, weighing the pros and cons?

'Anyway, I call Grief here, remembering at the back of my head some sci-fi stuff she'd tried to peddle a few years ago. She tells me about an even better book you wrote—'

'*Live Wires*,' Grief says.

'Yes. *Live Wires*. Great title. So I read it, one sitting like I said. Love it. Every page. My wife wakes up in the middle of the night, can't believe I'm reading. And worse, not even a script. She thinks it must be pornography, rips it out of my hand, reads a few lines, nods, gives it back, goes to sleep. It was hysterical.' He laughs again and Barcelona smiles to show she appreciates the compliment.

'So what did Lynda have to say?' Grief asks.

'I went over there two days ago, pitched it to her, left her a copy of the book. She called me yesterday, wanted to talk more. I went right over.' He stops suddenly to return to his cigar. A move, Barcelona realizes, designed to add suspense. It works. She wants to scream at him to tell her what Lynda Kramer said.

'Anyhow,' he continues, 'Lynda wants to see a script.'

'Ah,' Grief says and leans back in her chair smiling.

'Yes.' Roger Carlyle nods.

Barcelona waits for him to continue, but he too leans back with a satisfied smirk. She looks over at Grief, who is nodding to herself. They both look like two people who have just finished having sex.

'What happens next?' Barcelona asks.

'Well, that depends.' Roger Carlyle stubs his cigar out

in an ashtray shaped like a sleeping cat. He takes out a pack of Velamints, removes two, and thumbs them into his mouth. 'It could go a lot of ways from here. We give her a script, she doesn't like it, we either get a rewrite, or we drop the project. Or she likes it and wants a rewrite. Or the studio doesn't like it. Or everyone likes it but before it gets made the studio changes heads and we get put in turnaround by the new studio head. But'—he crosses his pudgy fingers and smiles—'if God is smiling on us, we go into production and the three of us sitting here are suddenly hot properties in this town.'

Barcelona likes the idea of being a hot property. When she'd first walked into this office this afternoon, Grief had made some offhand comment about a hot young writer and Barcelona had felt a jealous gnawing in her stomach. Her own writing had started as a lark, a break from the academic tedium of graduate work. Her speciality in school was Middle English Literature, the medieval writings in England from 1150 to 1500. The late hours she had labored, poring over Old English, reading the small print dissertations of obscure scholars on the homosexual rhythms in the London dialect of Chaucer. The toenail motif of Malory. Studying the dusty texts of Lowland Scots, the ballads, folk lyrics, and miracle plays that were passed down for centuries orally before they were eventually written down, often incompletely. Then at the end of the fifteenth century William Caxton set up his printing press at Westminster. This is what Barcelona had gladly spent her life reading and writing about.

But during her last year of graduate school, when her dissertation on John of Trevisa's translation of Higdon's *Polychronicon* was finished, she found herself scribbling short stories, poems, character sketches, anything to amuse herself, remembering what it was like to just love the story, before she began toe-tagging and autopsying each work.

One short story she started just wouldn't end. She had never read science fiction, except for a few of the classics her friends had pushed on her with fanatic fervor. She had remained lukewarn to their charms. Yet her story, merely an updating of an anonymous thirteenth-century ballad, began in California and soon drifted off the planet into another galaxy. Suddenly she was a science fiction writer.

'Our plan, then,' Roger Carlyle is saying, 'is to present Lynda with the best possible script and go from there.'

'Who are you getting to write it?' Barcelona asks.

'You,' Roger Carlyle says with a wink.

Barcelona looks at Grief. Grief smiles, nods. Barcelona uncrosses her legs, bangs her ankle on the edge of Grief's desk. Pain corkscrews through her leg then shoots into her stomach, splashing hot acid around. She shows no outward sign of discomfort.

'I've never written a film script before, Mr. Carlyle. Actually, I've never even read one.'

'Easily fixed. I'll have a dozen scripts sent over to you from my office. Jerks with a lot less talent than you are making a fortune writing movies. Imagine what you could do with all your talent.'

Barcelona isn't worried about the script. She has faith in her ability to conquer any form. She's not even thinking about that. She is thinking about Lynda Kramer, gorgeous, intelligent, talented. She imagines herself on the set, chatting with Lynda, maybe going on a shopping trip, holding her child on the set while Lynda goes off to perform another scene. She would never admit this to anyone, but she thinks of Lynda Kramer as a woman with secrets to share about being a woman. Whenever men see her photo they sigh the sigh that translates, 'If only . . .'

She asks, 'Do you think Lynda Kramer might actually do it? Make this movie.'

'She's interested,' he says. 'That's the first step.'

Grief goes to work then. She stands quickly, guides Roger Carlyle to the door, promises to get in touch with him tomorrow about the deal memo. He winks again at Barcelona, not in a sexual way, in a way that suggests he has everything under control.

When she is alone with Grief, Barcelona asks, 'What do you think?'

'The money's shit and he's an asshole.'

Barcelona is surprised. 'He was lying?'

'Lying is relative.' Grief sits in the chair that Carlyle was in. She shifts uncomfortably as if he had somehow done something awful to it. 'He was telling the truth in that Lynda Kramer probably is interested. But there's no studio involvement, no development money yet. That means Roger's putting up the money. That's one of the reasons he's willing to hire you. He can pay you off in pennies.'

'How many pennies?'

'Ten thousand dollars.'

'That's more than I got to write the damn novel.'

'Half of that goes to your publisher, dear. They retained fifty percent of the film rights. You get five grand, minus my ten percent.'

Barcelona thinks of her $163 in her checking account. 'I'm not complaining. At least it's a chance to make more, isn't it?'

'Sure. If the film actually gets picked up, you'll get another hundred thousand. Split with the publisher, of course.'

'And minus your ten percent.'

'Minus my ten percent.'

'So are you saying I shouldn't do this?'

Grief laughs. 'Your naïveté is charming, Barcy.'

'What does that mean?'

'Of course you should do this. Carlyle is scummy, but he's willing to plunk down some of his own money to bring

37

this off. That means he really does have a shot. If, by some miracle, the movie gets made, you will be the next golden child of Hollywood for about forty-eight hours. Plus your novels will fetch more money. But until we see the green of his money, it's just what is known in Hollywood as "good air."'

Barcelona finds 'good air' is heady stuff. She is excited by the prospect of making more money. She hadn't ever really considered it much because it never really seemed a possibility. Now that it is, she is surprised at how feverish she feels. She wants to go right home and start the script.

'Goodness,' Grief says, pointing at Barcelona's leg. 'You're bleeding.'

Barcelona looks down, discovers the scab on her ankle where she'd nicked herself shaving yesterday is bleeding. It is where she had earlier banged herself on Grief's desk. The blood sieves through the panty hose like a Rorschach ink blot. The pattern reminds Barcelona of a sea urchin. She wonders what that means. Nothing good probably.

Grief offers her Band-aids and peroxide, but Barcelona refuses. She returns to her car, looks around to make sure no one is coming, then rolls off her panty hose. In the first aid kit in the glove compartment she finds gauze and adhesive tape which she applies to the scab, though it has already stopped bleeding. She keeps her skirt bunched up across the tops of her thighs and feels wicked as she drives down the freeway without underpants or pantyhose, the car vent blowing cool air between her thighs. She feels her pubic hairs rustle and she begins to sing 'Get It While You Can,' imitating Janis Joplin's crushed-larynx style.

After two verses, Barcelona's throat begins to sting at the back. She can only do Janis Joplin for short periods before she becomes hoarse and unable to speak. She digs a Breathsaver out of the ashtray where she also stores loose coins, individually wrapped toothpicks, and a plastic box of mint-flavored dental floss. She begins to plan how to turn her novel into a screenplay. Lots of ideas come to her. She realizes how much of the book she will have to change, whole characters will have to be axed, entire subplots ignored. She doesn't care. She is thrilled by the challenge. She imagines Lynda Kramer shaking her hand and saying, 'This is the script I've been waiting my whole career to play.' She makes a mental list of the people she will thank on Academy Awards night.

She turns on the radio and switches the channels around. She flies past Jackson Browne, Willie Nelson, Stray Cats, Bon Jovi. None of them are right for this special moment. She thinks this is what it is like orchestrating a movie, matching music to mood. She jabs the Seek button which plays five seconds of a station before automatically moving on. It slips past Phoebe Snow, Iggy Pop, Tom Waits, The Bangles, jazz, commercials. Suddenly Janis Joplin comes on singing 'Down On Me.' This is not one of the songs she likes, but the coincidence is such that she feels it would be bad luck to skip past it. Barcelona presses a button to keep the station.

For some reason she begins to think of Darlene and her dog, Foxy. She pictures Darlene and herself watching the dog squat and shit. The dog looking over his shoulder, his face contorting with effort. She laughs at the image until a couple of tears drip down her cheek. Barcelona suddenly feels depressed. This dark mood catches her by surprise, makes the air thick and stuffy. She turns the air conditioner on.

To shake the mood, she focuses back on her screenplay, Lynda Kramer, The Ideal Woman. But mostly she concentrates on how she imagines Eric's face will look when she tells him the news this evening. More than anything else,

39

this breaks the sad mood and makes her smile. She begins to sing 'Get It While You Can' again, though using her own voice now.

4

Trina sits on the cracked wooden toilet seat and pees. When she is done she spreads her knees and looks down into the toilet bowl. Her urine is bright yellow, like lemon meringue. She smiles because that means her vitamins are working. Dixie has had her taking Joe Weider vitamins for six months, ever since that night she mentioned suicide. Not that she would ever, ever, ever have gone through with something so asinine; she just liked saying it. Hearing it aloud made it a real option.

She explained all that to Dixie, but all she got in response was that skeptical cop's nod and four giant jars of vitamins. Dixie is convinced there are no problems that vitamins and hard exercise can't fix. Each morning Trina gags down six rat turd pellets with a can of Diet Cherry Coke. Trina admits that now that her urine looks so bright and cheerful, it makes her more cheerful too. Visible proof of self-improvement. Trina also knows that she is bullshitting herself, but since bullshitting is what she does for a living, she admires her own technique rather than questions the results.

Trina pulls off a huge fistful of toilet paper, much more than is necessary, and dabs herself dry. Rob, her ex-husband, always complained that she used too much toilet paper. 'Half a roll,' he'd say, grinning, standing over her while she sat on the toilet. 'Half a roll to blot your pussy

41

and another three-quarters of a roll to wipe your ass. It's getting so we can't afford your bowel movements anymore.' Then he'd laugh, thumbs hooked in his back pockets. Thing was, even though he was laughing, Trina knew he was serious. 'It's not the goddamn paper,' he said. 'I make over a hundred grand a year. We can afford toilet paper.' Somehow Rob always managed to work the magic number 'hundred grand a year' into most of their arguments. A hundred thousand dollars a year was exactly twice what his father had earned the best year of his life before dying of prostrate cancer three years ago. 'It's not the paper, it's what it reveals. A wasteful attitude. Like leaving the lights on all day when you go to work. Or leaving the iron on. Which is not just wasteful, it's danger-ous. What if the iron didn't shut itself off?' 'But it does shut itself off,' she'd reply. 'What if?' he's say meaningfully.

Trina stands up carefully, her panty hose bunched around her calves, and hops from the bathroom to the bed. She feels like a bound liquor store hostage who's worked her gag free and is making a break for the back door. It's uncomfortable stripping on the toilet. The oak seat has a crack the same shape as the one in the Liberty Bell and if you turn a certain way, it pinches your left butt cheek. She plops down on the edge of the bed and rolls her panty hose off her feet. The skin on her calves feels prickly from the sudden rush of fresh air. Her dress is already off and hanging from one of the posts of the four-poster bed. Each post is decorated with an assortment of her clothing. Her entire wardrobe from the previous week can be traced day by day by walking clockwise around the bed.

Trina lies back on the bed wearing only a bra. When she is alone she likes to be naked except for her bra. Her breasts are large and pendulous with white stretch marks like cartoon lightning bolts zigzagging back from the nipples. The bra offers her support and hides the fault marks. Someday she plans to get them surgically reduced.

She looks at the clock radio. Five-thirty. Two hours before she meets Barcelona, Dixie, and Diva. She's relieved that she won't have to tell Barcy that she'd been mistaken about The Candidate.

Three hours ago she hadn't been so certain:

'*What*?' he'd squawked when she'd asked if they'd had sex. 'What did you say?'

'I have this memory. You and me in a steaming shower. Thing is, is it real or is it Memorex?'

'Are you kidding me?'

'No.'

He didn't even smile, he just raised one cashmere eyebrow. 'You realize how amazingly unflattering this question is? I mean especially if we'd had sex.'

'Right now, I don't really care. I'm more interested in where I parked my mind than in flattering you.'

He smiled. 'Seems to me the most prudent answer would be no, we did not shower together.'

'Don't screw around here, Cory. I'm serious.'

His face looked suddenly concerned. 'You really are serious.' He sat up, crossed his hands in a formal pose behind his desk. 'Yes, Trina, we made love in the shower of the Travel Lodge. We were going to do it again in the bed, but we had to get back to the studio.'

Trina had sighed a long relieved gust of air. She wasn't losing her mind, just small memory lapses. Fifteen minutes later, as she'd left his office, she'd been able to picture the whole event for the first time. Everything came to her at once. She could feel him inside her, his penis wide and insistent, trying to go deeper than physically possible, a gold-crazed miner searching for the Mother Lode. That's what she'd thought at the time and had started to laugh, the laughter squeezing him out.

43

Suddenly Trina realizes why she had been so forgetful. What is causing it. Of course, it's so obvious. She is pregnant! Her period is not due for another week but she knows without any doubt that she is pregnant. She just knows. And she knows who the father is.

'Hi,' a familiar voice says and Trina looks around the bedroom and sees no one. Then she realizes her eyes are closed. She opens them, looks at the clock. Six-fifteen. She has been sleeping for forty-five minutes. She sits up quickly and holds her head as blood rushes to her brain and makes her dizzy. She pulls the bedspread over her naked body. 'What are you doing here?' she asks without looking at him.

'Dropping Karyn off,' Rob says.

'Thanks. See you in two weeks.'

'You look good. How's it going?'

'I use too much toilet paper.'

'I should've bought stock in Charmin.' He laughs at his lame joke and she peeps an eye at him.

'See you in two weeks,' she repeats. She finds an earring on the bed that must have come out while she napped. She works it back into her lobe.

'I get the feeling you're trying to get rid of me,' he says with a smirk.

'For a guy who only makes a hundred grand a year, you catch on quick.'

His smirk disappears. Trina makes $125,000 a year now and he knows it. 'Fuck you, Trina,' he says and walks out. His new leather jacket makes crinkly sounds as his sleeves brush against his side. She hears Karyn saying good-bye to him at the front door, the door closing.

'Karyn!' Trina calls.

Karyn comes running. She jumps on the bed next to Trina. 'You made him mad again.'

'Sue me.'

Karyn looks at her mother's nakedness, the forest of clothes surrounding the bed. 'This is gross, Mom. It's like a bear cave.'

'I need you to keep me in order.'

'You need a maid.'

'Maybe I'll hire you for the job.'

Karyn tilts her nose in the air in a snooty pose. 'Speak to my agent.'

They both laugh. Trina hugs Karyn to her. Karyn resists hugging at first, part of the game she plays. Then she gives in and hugs back, her body collapsing against Trina, her head falling just so in the same place on Trina's shoulder it has for twelve years. Trina imagines the shoulder bone to be slightly curved in that spot, a permanent sway to cradle Karyn's head. Karyn's left ear is next to Trina's nose and Trina can smell Karyn's special scent, a scent so light yet earthy it reminds her of some exotic Chinese tea. Blindfolded and bound, Trina could sniff Karyn out of a crowd of a thousand little girls.

'You'll be late,' Karyn says, breaking away.

The hug is over too soon but Trina knows better than to try to recapture her. If she does, Karyn will be stiff and impatient and that feels worse than anything else in the world to Trina.

'What'd you do in school today?' Trina asks.

'Stuff.'

'What kind of stuff?'

'You know, school stuff.'

'Oh, you mean useless cramming of information that can't possibly have any relevance to anyone in the whole world?'

Karyn nods. 'That's what I said. School stuff.'

Trina makes a parental face and Karyn giggles victoriously. Neither ever grows tired of this game.

Trina stands up, aware that Karyn is studying her body.

Sometimes she catches Karyn staring at her boobs with something like fear, as if they were an affliction, giant tumors Karyn prays would never curse her. The rest of Trina's body is relatively normal. Her ass isn't as trim as Dixie's or Barcy's, but not as jiggly as Diva's. Her legs are legs. Not thin, but not fat either. Her waist isn't exactly skinny, but it curves in appropriately. She has what men call the voluptuous look. She thinks of herself as overripe.

'Mom?'

Trina walks into the bathroom and starts the tub water running. 'Hmmm.'

'What's affectation mean?'

'How was it used?' She asks this because Karyn often asks the meaning of words but sometimes mispronounces them. She might mean affection, affliction, asphyxiation.

'Someone at school said my name was an affectation.'

'Why?'

'Because it had a "y" where there should be an ".'''

'What'd you tell them?'

Karyn hesitates and Trina knows she is trying to think of a lie. 'Come on, the truth. What'd you tell them?'

'To eat shit and die.'

Trina laughs. 'Did you tell your father that?'

'No.'

'Good.' Instantly Trina feels a little pain in her side that quickly vanishes. Nothing more than an invisible poke really. It is the feeling of loss she gets when she wants to share something funny with Rob but remembers she can't. The pain is always in the same place as if there is a physical scar there where they'd been surgically separated when divorced. 'Karyn with a "y" is an old and revered name with a long and honorable tradition. You were named after a princess from Austria who had three blue dogs and twelve red cats. All the people of Austria loved her madly.

46

One day this handsome knight rides into the village—'

Karyn isn't listening. 'I told them that Lynda Kramer had a "y" where she should have an "i" so I could have one too. Did you name me after Lynda Kramer?' She says this hopefully.

Even though, according to *People* magazine, Lynda Kramer was an unknown theater major at Yale when Karyn was born, Trina nods yes because that will make more sense to the kids at school than an Austrian princess with blue dogs and red cats.

Actually, Karyn's 'y' *is* an affectation. Rob's idea to make her special. He is in advertising and decided on his daughter's name the same way he would a product. 'Research shows people prefer products that begin with K. You know Keds, the sneakers? What's that word mean? Nothing. They were originally going to be called Peds, you know, like peds for feet. But market research found out the public prefers "Ks".' Trina hadn't argued much because of the difficulty she'd had with her own name, Trina Bedford, Jr. That had been her mother's idea, the junior, because her mother thought that would help Trina be taken more seriously in business. Her mother was, still is, a vice-president at Prudential Insurance. Trina had kept her maiden name of Bedford even after marrying Rob Barre, so she could keep the junior. Her mother had been right. People did take her more seriously.

Trina walks into the bathroom, and turns on the water. After the tub is filled, she shrugs off her bra, and climbs in.

The ledge around the tub looks like an explosion in a chemistry lab. Spilled puddles of cream rinse and different colored shampoos polka dot the white surface. Three soap slivers thin as credit cards are glued to the tub. A brown plastic scalp massager clogged with clumps of gnarled black hair sits like a furry mutant, perched on the hot water

47

knob. Once again she is reminded that she needs to hire a new cleaning person.

'Can I wash your hair?' Karyn asks, kneeling beside the tub.

'I'm not washing it right now. I'm already running late.'

'Boy, that should shock them.'

'Smart ass punk,' she says, flicking water from her fingertips into Karyn's face.

Karyn giggles, a sound so sweet and moving, Trina feels tears in her eyes. She dunks her hair under the water and hands Karyn the aloe vera shampoo. 'Wash away, kid. Go crazy.'

Karyn's fingers dig into Trina's hair like hungry worms nibbling at her scalp. Occasionally Karyn scrubs too hard and yanks a hair or two out at the root. Trina helps. 'Hey, you want me to be bald.'

'Yeah. Daddy's getting bald, you can be bald together.'

There was a time Trina wouldn't have minded even baldness if it meant they'd be together. That was the old her. The pre-vitamin her. Before her urine became cheerful. Now she closes her eyes and leans her head back against the tub. Karyn's fingers dig and claw with such intensity that she wonders if she might be bleeding. She opens her eyes and a drop of shampoo leaks in and stings her. She doesn't rinse it, she doesn't move. She doesn't want to disturb Karyn's concentration.

Her scalp tingles and a shiver works it way down her spine and legs to the tips of her feet. The shiver is icy despite the steaming bathwater. The feel of Karyn's fingers washing her hair is the best definition of happiness she can think of. She thinks about telling Karyn that she is pregnant. Sharing her own delight. Maybe she should wait until she's had the medical tests. Maybe she should test the waters on Barcy, Dixie, and Diva tonight at dinner. She tries to imagine their reactions, the expressions on their faces. Diva and Dixie will be enthusiastic, offer up toasts. Barcy will ask probing questions, reveal no emotion.

'We'll see,' she says aloud.

'You're mumbling again, Mom,' Karyn says and digs her fingers deeper into Trina's hair.

'The miniseries of my life, kiddo,' Trina says, closing her eyes.

5

As Barcelona approaches Eric's street, three military helicopters appear ahead rising up over the horizon. Framed
by the setting sun, to her they seem frozen in the sky like
fat preening flies. Sunset flickers off their blades. She is
reminded of *Apocalypse Now* and Martin Sheen lying in
bed drunk, listening to The Doors sing 'This Is the End.'
She begins to hum the song, thinking this is appropriate
music for her visit to Eric's house.

The helicopters are from the nearby El Toro marine
base where the young pilots are being trained. Every day
these drab green helicopters circle over Orange County,
usually in loud packs like growling dogs. There have been
several crashes lately and yesterday Barcelona read in the
newspaper that there will be a federal probe of the
company manufacturing the helicopters. The manufac-
turer in question is also in Orange County and residents
are afraid that the investigation will force the plant, which
employs thousands of people, to be closed down. Residents
are also afraid that a defective helicopter will crash through
their roof and drop into their living rooms. Residents aren't
sure which to fear most.

Barcelona is not so much afraid of the helicopters as she
is of how crazy people around here have been acting over
them lately. Ever since the *Twilight Zone* crash that killed
Vic Morrow and those children, everyone has been

nervous about helicopters. Last month 'Sixty Minutes' did a story about the frighteningly high crash rate of emergency medical helicopters. The pilots interviewed blamed their long shifts, and described how they would fall asleep while flying. On the news there have been numerous reports of mysterious bullet holes in the police helicopters from random snipers, kids they think. Last week two police helicopters chasing a teenage car thief accidentally crashed into each other and both pilots were killed. They've charged the teenager with murder. Fear of the sky has made people vindictive.

Right now Barcelona is pleased to see the three helicopters because they add drama to the moment. Good production values. 'Production values' is a phrase she picked up that afternoon from a book about writing scripts she bought at the mall. She's not sure exactly what the phrase means, but she knows these helicopters escorting her to Eric's house have something to do with it.

She is on Eric's street now and sees the security gate to the parking lot of his apartment complex. The black iron gate is wide open. Barcelona carefully guides the Geezemobile in and drives around the perimeter of the buildings looking for a parking space large enough for her car. The huge car rolls over each speed bump with a mysterious rattle and Barcelona hopes this means the car is finally dying. She wants to get rid of this albatross and buy a sleek new car, preferably Japanese, but this is the only thing she has of her grandmother's and feels compelled to keep it until, like her grandmother, it dies too. The only change she's made on the car was to put in a new stereo, and she feels guilty about that.

Barcelona eventually finds a parking space not just for compact cars. Even so it is a tight squeeze, her car sucking up all the room between the cars on either side. The driver's door opens just wide enough for her to struggle out, banging her ankle on the edge of the door. It is the same ankle she'd cut shaving, the one she'd banged in Grief's office. She stoops over, peels down her lime green sock. A tiny pinpoint of bright blood peeks through the crusty scab. She pulls the sock back up.

She hurries through the apartment complex, past the giant palm trees and spreading ferns, the loud streams and brooks that wander throughout the place. Over a thick bush she sees a lean young man in a tight Speedo bathing suit dipping his toe in the Jacuzzi. A girl laughs, but Barcelona can't see her because of the foliage. The laugh sounds teasing, definitely sexual. Even from here she can see the outline of the head of his semi-erect penis through his skimpy bathing suit. She thinks of Eric's penis. 'Eight inches of tempered blue steel,' he used to say in a mock-Bogart voice, standing naked in front of her, aiming it like a gun. 'Die, Commie bastard,' he'd say. 'Rat-a-tat-tat.' And she'd grab it hard and yank and they'd both fall to the bed laughing.

Barcelona thinks this is a bad time to be thinking about Eric's penis. Someone else is yanking his tempered blue steel now. Luna.

She decides it is a good thing that she has purposely timed her arrival so that she has only twenty minutes to spare before she must leave to meet Trina, Dixie, and Diva. She forces herself not to picture him standing there, holding it, pointing it at her. Rat-a-tat-tat. She notices her hand has curled involuntarily as if it were holding him now. She brushes her palm against her jeans.

Up the stairs, second floor. She knocks. The door opens almost immediately.

'Hey,' he says. There is an awkward space after 'Hey' because he used to always say, 'Hey, baby' or 'Hey, honey' or 'Hey, sweetheart.' Now it's just 'Hey' and those two empty syllables are choked off like a smothered baby.

'Hey yourself,' she says and enters.

They hug clumsily, though she thinks it is she who is clumsy because she is unsure where her hands should go. He seems perfectly comfortable holding her close, then releasing her with a peck on the cheek. He used to hold her, squeeze her ass, then release her. His hands now, however, remain politely above waist level.

'Where's Luna?' She had promised herself she would not be the first to mention the name, but somehow it slipped out.

'She'll be here any minute. She has a late class tonight.'

'Oh? What class?'

'The Women Followers of Freud. An unfortunate title, but the course is pretty solid. Ruth Mack Brunswick, Anna Freud, of course, Helen Deutsch—'

'Melanie Klein, I would imagine.'

'Sure, the English School.'

Barcelona nods. She is comfortable with academic subjects. She is knowledgeable, widely read, remembers almost everything she's ever learned. Discussing psychology is much easier than thinking about eight inches of tempered blue steel.

'Drink?' he asks.

'Alcohol?'

'White wine. A buck-a-gallon brand. Luna drinks it.'

'Pass.' She looks around the living room. Though she has never been here before, everything looks familiar. It is small, dimly lighted with one table lamp and one floor lamp. The furniture is old and beaten, longing for retirement. Against the wall is a cinder-block-and-particle-board bookcase jammed with scholarly textbooks on psychology, anthropology, language. Barthes's and Lévi-Strauss's names are prominent on many of the book spines. The room looks just like the one they used to live in at graduate school. It is a student's apartment. She supposes that is appropriate since Eric is technically still a student, though he is thirty-five. Barcelona owns a town house in Irvine, a planned community eight miles south of here. In Irvine, people pick up their dog's shit immediately or pay a fine to the Homeowner's Association. People in Irvine have overhead track lights so the rooms are always bright. Barcelona is not embarrassed that she likes bright rooms and no dog shit.

'So what was so important?' she asks.

'Boy, you get right to it, don't you. Enough with the pleasantries.'

'I'm meeting Trina and the others for dinner in a few minutes.'

'Ah, the bimonthly meeting of the Gourmet Mafia.'

He is smiling, but she recognizes the disapproving tone. He doesn't think her friends are smart enough for her. He wants her to join Mensa as he did. She taps her watch and says, 'I don't want to be late.'

'I just thought you should know,' he says, not finishing the sentence, walking over to the Formica counter that separates the tiny kitchenette from the living room. He picks up a bound typewritten manuscript, hefts it lovingly, and hands it to her. 'It's done. Finally.'

'Oh, Eric,' she says, truly pleased. She smiles, kisses his cheek. 'That's wonderful. My God, you must feel so good!'

He laughs. 'Well, I've been working on this bastard for five years. At first I used to imagine how good it would feel to have written a brilliant scholarly text lauded by experts. After a couple years I imagined how good it would feel to have written a text mildly appreciated by an adoring few. These last few months, though, I just imagined what it would feel like to be finished. Just done.'

'Well? How does it feel?'

He grins. 'Good. Very fucking good.'

'Is this my copy to keep?'

'It's the least I can do. You did a lot of the research for me. If it wasn't for you, I'm not sure I'd have finished it.'

Barcelona is embarrassed by his honest expression of gratitude. It makes her feel shoddy and mean after her earlier thoughts. She looks away from him and studies his manuscript. The title is *Toward a Semiotics of Battered Women*. This is his doctoral dissertation, five years in the making. The typing looks very professional. Good production values.

Eric's field of study is somewhat complex: the use of language in violent households. He believes that from studying the patterns of speech, violence can be predicted. It doesn't matter what the educational backgrounds are of the household members, or the extent of the vocabulary, simply by the juxtapositioning of certain words, images, phrases, the potential for violence can be uncovered. He makes a very convincing case and for that reason has always been the darling of his professors. He is also extremely handsome, black hair and lean rodeo cowboy's body, which has always made him the darling of women. But Eric doesn't exploit his good looks, Barcelona admits, he doesn't even seem conscious of them.

'Can you believe it?' he asks. 'Finished.'

'Hard to believe.'

'I still have to defend the damned thing in front of my committee, but Dr. Goulart says it's only a formality. I'm in. Dr. Eric Jasper Fontaine.'

'I'd lose the Jasper,' she says, then kisses his cheek again. 'That's great, Eric. It really is.'

Eric will now get his Ph.D. in psychology. He finished all his course work five years ago and has been struggling with the dissertation ever since. To support himself, he works full time at a refuge home for battered women. He counsels, comforts, helps them find jobs. He has also been instrumental in establishing day-care centers within several local companies. Over his left eye is a thin white scar that cleaves his black eyebrow. He received the scar when an angry husband tried to drag his wife out of the refuge home. Eric wouldn't let him take her and the man clubbed Eric with a stapler from the desk. In return, Eric smacked the man in the face with a heavy tape dispenser, breaking the man's nose and slicing open his lip with the serrated edge that cuts the tape. The woman stayed, the man left. Eric gives them books to read, suggests composers, rents foreign videotapes for them. The women there love Eric.

Barcelona hates to admit it, but Eric is a better feminist than she is. They espouse the same principles, but he does something about them.

She turns the page and sees her name. This is the dedication page. It says: 'To Barcelona, without whom this would not be possible. And to Luna, without whom this would not be valuable.' She is both flattered and insulted. Better not to be named at all than to share billing with Luna. In her book on screenwriting, she read a passage about screenwriters who have unwillingly shared billing and have had to go to arbitration to settle who actually wrote the produced script. Perhaps she could do that here. Who deserves most of the credit for helping Eric finish this manuscript, Barcelona, who encouraged, flattered, critiqued, and researched for four of the five years? Or Luna-come-lately, who has only been in his life for the last year, and at twenty years old, is still too young to have been much help on the actual manuscript?

'Well?' Eric says, grinning happily as Barcelona stares at the dedication page.

She looks up at him, his boyish smile beaming, and realizes he has no idea that she is hurt. He thinks only of the compliment he has given her. For all his work with women, all his empathy and support, he is finally insensitive to what goes on deep inside. He doesn't see that their

56

six years of living together has some priority. Although they'd separated out of mutual agreement, Barcelona feels that his meeting and marrying Luna within three months of their split-up, trivializes their former relationship. Especially since during those six years he'd been as adamant as she about the faults of the institution of marriage.

Barcelona has seen Luna only once, at a distance, in the shopping mall. Eric and Luna were eating at Forty Carrots, splitting frozen yogurt and fruit, both reading and discussing a magazine spread out on the table in front of them. It was the same thing she and Eric had often done. From where she stood, she could see only that Luna was young and pretty, with long black frizzy hair and thick pouty lips. Bee-stung lips. She had been tempted to walk over and join them, but was able to control such high school instincts. Barely.

'It's lovely, Eric,' Barcelona says, closing the cover. 'I'll read it later.'

'Let me know what you think. Your opinion means a lot to me.'

'I will.' She makes a show of looking at her watch again. 'Better be heading out. The gang's waiting.'

'You can spare a couple of minutes.' He sits on the sofa and gestures to the nearby chair. 'What have you been up to? How's the balancing art of writing and teaching?'

Barcelona knows she should walk out the door now, but her feet move over to the chair and her butt sinks down into the too-soft cushion. The chair smells greasy, like a combination of the last five hundred meals cooked in the kitchen. Kitchenette. 'I'm still teaching, of course. Can't give that up.'

'Still power-crazed, huh?' He laughs.

She smiles, loads her bomb, sights, fires: 'And the writing is going well. In fact, I was just hired to do a screenplay of *Live Wires* for Lynda Kramer.'

He nods, but not in an impressed way. More like a professor whose prize student has given an answer that is close, but not exactly what he wants. 'Just be careful of priorities.'

'What's that supposed to mean?'

'You're still a teacher first. You have a responsibility to those kids.'

'Don't tell me my responsibilities, Eric. I know what I am. I am a teacher and a writer. Not one over the other. A combination. Teacher, slash, writer. Like being both a woman and an American.'

'Relax, Barcy, I didn't mean anything. I'm just talking about balance, that's all. You don't always have to control everything.' His gaze is calm, benign, that of a therapist. 'Will you be using your own name?'

'I always use my own name.'

'You know what I mean. Your full name. So readers will know you're a woman.'

This is an old argument between them, but she falls into the trap anyway. 'What the hell difference does it make, Eric, as long as they like my work?'

'Who are you fooling, Barcy?'

'It's a business decision, nothing more. Don't try to turn it into a moral issue.'

'Don't you think forcing yourself to conceal your sex, hide your true self, is a moral issue?'

She ignores his question. 'Have you even read *Live Wires*?'

He looks away toward the kitchen, then looks back, eyes fixed directly on hers. 'You know I don't have the time for that kind of stuff. I have serious reading to do.'

'Ah, so my stuff isn't serious.'

'That's not what I said.'

'That's exactly what you said.'

He shakes his head. 'You're trying to turn this around,

Barcy. I meant that I don't have much time for recreational reading anymore. Just because you feel some guilt at having wasted your talents on genre writing—'

'Die, Commie bastard,' she says, holding her hand out the way he used to when playfully aiming his dick. 'Rat-a-tat-tat.'

'What's that supposed to mean?' He is angry, flushed.

'Figure it out, Eric. You're the psychobabblist.'

'Don't play games, Barcy.'

'Then don't use your education like your dick. It's a tool, not a weapon.'

He stands up, walks slowly to the kitchen, jerks open the refrigerator, and leans his head inside. He returns with a can of V-8 juice. 'Maybe we should drop it.'

'Maybe.'

The front door opens and a young girl with long frizzy hair and bee-stung lips stands in the doorway taking her backpack off. She is younger-looking and more beautiful than Barcelona remembered.

'Ah, honey,' Eric says. 'Barcy, you've never met my wife.' The way he emphasizes 'my wife' shows he wants to get one last dig in. 'Honey, this is Barcelona. Barcy, Luna.'

'Hello,' Barcelona says.

'Hi.' Luna smiles with what appears to be genuine pleasure. She tosses her backpack on the floor and rushes over to shake Barcelona's hand. 'I've read all your books, you know.'

'Oh?' Barcelona is surprised. She looks over at Eric, but he is looking at something in the distance, pretending he hasn't heard.

'God, yes. I started reading you when I was in high school. Way before I met Eric. I used to read them in the cafeteria during lunch. I just love them. I don't mean to gush, it's just that I've asked Eric a dozen times if he would introduce me to you, but he never gets around to it.'

Barcelona doesn't know what to say. She says, 'Ah.'

'I don't want you think I'm one of those sci-fi nuts, like a Trekkie or something. God, that must sound awfully smug. Forget it. Let me start over.' She plops down on the sofa next to Eric. Eric reaches for her as if to kiss her, but she slides away as if she didn't see him. Barcelona realizes Luna has done this so as not to embarrass their guest. It is a compassionate gesture and Barcelona appreciates it. Eric leans back with an annoyed expression.

'Isn't it shitty,' Luna says, 'the way they brainwash you about art? What is and isn't art. Speaking of which, I'd talk to somebody about the cover art on your books. God.'

'I know.' Barcelona nods.

'When my girlfriend first gave me one of your books to read, I took one look at the cover with this naked nympho with a sword straddling some dragon's tail—'

'*The Beauty Circuit.*'

'Yes! And I told her no way will I read this sexist shit. But she made me promise to give it a try. I read it that night, cover to cover. Great stuff.'

'You wrote that your first year teaching, didn't you, Barcy?' Eric asks. 'When we had that apartment over on Hudson Street.'

'Yes. You thought the book was too long. Too much plot.'

'That's not what I'd said at all. Writers have such selective memories. I said the characters did too much running around without thinking about what their actions meant.'

Luna laughs. 'That's the point, Eric. Not everyone analyzes everything they do first. Then they have to suffer the consequences. Like life.'

'Like some people's lives,' he says.

She laughs again, the sound deep and throaty like a lawn mower. 'God, Barcy, was he this bad a snob when you lived with him?'

'I think he's gotten worse,' Barcelona says.

Eric seems to enjoy the attention now. 'Sure, pick on poor Eric. Easy target.'

'Deserving target,' Luna says, patting his knee affectionately.

Outside the front door, someone screams in terror. The voice is so high and crazy that Barcelona can't tell whether the screamer is a man or woman, young or old. 'Help! My God, please help!' the screamer cries. 'Help me!'

'That's Mrs. Finney,' Luna says, running to the front door. Eric is right behind her as they rush outside. 'Mrs. Finney, what's wrong?' Luna calls down the stairs.

'Please, oh please. Please . . .' she sobs. 'Please help.'

Luna and Eric run down the wooden steps. Barcelona can feel the apartment shake with each step. She goes outside, sees Luna and Eric following a plump woman in her sixties. The woman is wearing a pink quilted bathrobe and no slippers. Barcelona also runs down the stairs and follows after them, not certain why she is tagging along but knowing whatever they will find will not be pleasant. No one says 'please help' the way that woman did until it's too late to help.

The three of them round a corner ahead and Barcelona loses them in the lush foliage. When she rounds the same corner they have disappeared. She looks around. She can see the Jacuzzi now, but the young man with the tight trunks is gone; so is the giggling girl. The Jacuzzi is empty, but she can see the steam rising.

'Please! Please help him!'

Barcelona turns and sees the open door under the stairway. She hurries toward it and enters the apartment. She smells cat urine and something sweet and sour, like baked ham with pineapple rings.

Somewhere down the hall the old woman is wailing, her words incomprehensible again. Barcelona takes a deep

61

breath and plunges into the hallway. The smell is beginning to bother her. She enters the bedroom. The bed is neatly made, with a handmade quilt covering it. A fluffy calico cat sits on the bed licking her tail. She takes long deliberate licks, as if it were an ice cream cone. The sobbing and wailing don't disturb her.

'What's happened?' Barcelona asks. She sees Eric holding the old woman by the shoulders, comforting her, murmuring soothingly to her. Their backs block the doorway to the bathroom, but she can see Luna on the floor, bent over something. Barcelona walks toward the bathroom. She looks over the old woman's pink-quilted shoulder and gasps.

An old man with cottony tufts of white hair lies sprawled facedown on the floor. He is naked and wet. One leg is bent against the tub sticking straight up into the air. One hand flops into the kitty litter box next to the toilet. Green pellets stick to his arm like candy sprinkles.

'Get her out of here,' Luna says.

Barcelona backs up a step, thinking Luna means her. But Eric guides the old sobbing woman into the bedroom and sits her down on the bed. The cat looks up, then jumps off the bed and runs down the hall.

'We were getting ready to go out for dinner,' Mrs. Finney says. Her speech is slow and awkward, her eyes unfocused. 'Henry likes the Malibu Chicken at The Sizzler. I usually get the soup and salad bar.'

Barcelona looks over at the straight-back chair by the closet. Slacks, a shirt, underpants, socks, belt, and shoes are neatly laid out awaiting Henry.

'It's my fault,' Mrs. Finney says, sobbing again. She burrows her face into Eric's chest. He pats her gray head.

'It's nobody's fault, an accident,' he says.

'No, no, no,' she says, shaking her head, though her face is still pressed against Eric's shirt. She looks up into his eyes. 'My fault. I took my bath first. I always took mine first, then left the water in for Henry. I always take so long with my hair.' She looks away, embarrassed, then stares at Barcelona. Until that moment, Barcelona had felt invisible. Now the old woman speaks directly to Barcelona, ignoring Eric. 'I took two towels to dry off. I always take two towels. One for my body, one for my hair. Always two.'

Barcelona nods, glances into the bathroom, sees Luna flipping the pale bloated body over. There are feces and urine on the floor, running down the side of the tub, down the man's legs. Luna arcs the man's neck, pinches his nostrils closed, then places her pouty bee-stung lips over his. She breathes into his mouth.

'Two towels,' Mrs. Finney says again, her voice trailing off as if she'd lost her train of thought. But her eyes stay on Barcelona, bright and glittery from the tears. 'After I dried my hair off, I laid the towel on the counter next to the sink. I always do that. Right next to the sink. I came out here to pick out Henry's clothes. He's color-blind, you know. Can't match anything. If it weren't for me, he'd dress like a circus clown.'

Luna is still breathing into the man's mouth. She looks up at Eric. 'Call the goddamn ambulance, Eric!'

Eric looks around the bedroom. 'Where's your phone, Mrs. Finney?' He sounds calm, but Barcelona is surprised to see that he is so shaken.

'In the kitchen. We can only afford one phone.'

Eric nods to Barcelona, who takes his place on the bed, looping her arm around the old woman. Luna is still breathing into the man's mouth, counting, breathing again. There is a string of spittle hanging from Luna's lower lip and Barcelona wonders if it is hers or the old man's.

Mrs. Finney doesn't pay any attention to what Luna is doing. She has already accepted Henry's death. Now she must tell her story, that is all that she has left. Her story. 'Usually there are three towels in the bathroom. Two for me, one for Henry. He only needs one. He never towels his hair because he says it damages the follicles. Maybe he's right, I don't know. But today there were only two towels. The third one was in the wash. Henry always wipes his mouth on it after he brushes his teeth. I tell him to rinse off first, but he just goes over and wipes all that white foam on the towel. Then it dries and gets hard. I don't know about you, but I don't want to put a towel like that to my face, would you?'

Barcelona thinks this is a rhetorical question, but when Mrs. Finney continues to stare at her with a questioning look, she finally says, 'No, I wouldn't.'

'Me neither. So there are only two towels. One lying on the counter, and one wrapped around me out here in the bedroom. Henry is ready to get out of the bath, he doesn't see a towel, he starts hollering at me for a towel. I tell him to wait a minute and I'll bring him a fresh one from the linen closet. Not that we're poor people with only three towels in the house. But you know Henry, so impatient. He must have taken one step out of the tub, gotten a hold of the towel by the sink and yanked it toward him.' She does a yanking motion, banging her elbow into Barcelona's rib. She doesn't apologize. 'Underneath the towel was my curling iron, which I was waiting for to heat up. The towel must have snagged the iron and pulled it into the tub.'

Eric returns to the bedroom. He is holding the calico cat in his arms, petting and comforting it the way he had Mrs. Finney. 'The ambulance is on its way.'

Luna stands up, shakes her head. 'Sorry, Mrs. Finney.'

Mrs. Finney looks at her, then down at Henry. She starts to sob again and Barcelona hugs her close. She can feel the woman's tears soaking through her blouse, stinging her skin. Mrs. Finney stops crying. 'I'm sorry,' she says, wiping ineffectually at the damp spot on Barcelona's blouse.

'No, don't be,' Barcelona says.

The cat jumps out of Eric's arms and runs into the bathroom, walking across Henry Finney's wet chest to hop into the litter box. She squats, pees, scratches the box, hops back out, scattering green pellets from her paws like BBs.

'Nature calls,' Mrs. Finney says. Barcelona isn't sure whether she's referring to Henry or the cat.

'You were very good in there,' Barcelona tells Luna as they walk back toward the apartment. Police and paramedics are in Mrs. Finney's apartment. Luna has called Mrs. Finney's niece who is on her way over now. 'I was very impressed.'

'Luna is pre-med,' Eric says.

'Oh, a doctor.'

Luna shrugs. 'I don't know. Maybe. Right now I'm not feeling too keen on medicine.'

Eric slips his arm around her and kisses her cheek. She leans wearily into him. 'You handled yourself very well, sweetheart. I have to admit, even I was a little frazzled by the sight of Henry lying there like that. Christ.'

'Would you like to stay for dinner, Barcy?' Luna asks.

'Thanks, no. I'm supposed to be meeting some friends. I'm already late.'

'Another time,' Luna says.

'Sure.' Barcelona hurries away. As she rounds a rather lush and fierce-looking bush, she glances over her shoulder and sees Eric kissing Luna. He is squeezing her ass.

6

Barcelona hurries through the dimly lighted restaurant drawing stares from several of the startled diners. There is less light in here than in Eric's gloomy apartment and she has to grope her way among the tables, diners, and waiters. In her hurry, she knocks her sore ankle against the edge of a booth. Sudden pain blooms through her leg. She can feel the crusty scab fold back under the sock. But she hates being late worse than pain and rushes ahead, determined to at least shave a few seconds off her tardiness.

'Sorry I'm late,' she says, still ten feet from the table. Trina and Diva and Dixie are already sipping red wine, their menus open in front of them. A half-empty carafe sits in the middle of the table. Her place setting is undisturbed, the pink linen napkin folded like a tulip still nested in the clean wineglass. Barcelona pulls her chair out and sits, grabbing the napkin and spreading it across her lap. 'A guy next door to Eric electrocuted himself in the bathtub.'

'Jesus,' Diva says.

'Never mind that,' Trina says. 'Let's stick with the important matters first. Sign this.' Trina hands Barcelona a pink linen napkin. There is writing on the napkin in bold black letters from a eyeliner pencil: WE THE UNDERSIGNED ATTEST TO THE FACT THAT ON THIS DAY, THURSDAY, APRIL 23, BARCELONA EVANS LEE WAS NOT ONLY LATE, BUT LATER THAN

TRINA BEDFORD, JR., BY MORE THAN FIFTEEN
MINUTES. The three of them had each signed it with
elaborate flourishes. It looks like the Constitution.

Barcelona takes the offered mascara waud from Trina
and quickly signs her name. 'Okay,' she says, handing the
napkin back to Trina, 'but I'm not paying for the napkin.'

'Neither am I.' Trina winks, stuffing it quickly into her
purse.

'Unh uh, Trina,' Dixie says. 'Don't force me to make
an off-duty arrest. You wouldn't like prison life. No henna
to cover the gray hairs.'

'Whoa, look who's talking.' Trina reaches over and lifts
a lock of Dixie's sandy-blond hair. 'These roots were made
for walking.'

They all laugh, including Dixie.

Diva laughs too but then says, 'I don't get it.'

'The song,' Dixie explains. 'Remember? "These Boots
Are Made for Walking."'

'Yeah, Nancy Sinatra. But what's that got to do with
roots?'

'Jesus, Diva,' Trina says and shakes her head.

'She means I bleach my hair so often that the roots are
so brittle they could walk.'

'I didn't know you bleached your hair.'

'I don't,' Dixie says.

Diva frowns. 'Then I still don't get it.'

Barcelona pours the red wine into her glass. 'Ridicule
and humiliation. It's a male bonding technique.'

Trina nods. 'Yeah, it's like in the movies when two
guys beat the shit out of each other over nothing, then
afterwards start laughing their asses off and are instantly
best buddies.'

'Yeah, their faces all swollen and bloody and they toast
each other with beer.'

'A beer sounds good,' Diva says.

'I heard this joke today over at City Hall,' Trina says. 'Why does a woman have a cunt?'

'I heard this one,' Dixie says.

'I haven't,' Diva says. 'Why?'

'So men will talk to them.'

'I heard it a little differently,' Dixie says. 'I heard it was so men wouldn't put a bounty on women.'

'My version is dumb,' Trina says. 'Yours is ugly.'

'Yeah,' Dixie agrees, 'I heard it at the station. Either a cop or a felon, I can't remember.'

Barcelona laughs and realizes how happy and comfortable she is right now. Her anxiety about Eric and Luna is practically gone. Her depression over the old man's bizarre electrocution is waning. Her nervousness over the screenplay job is melting away.

'You notice how most of the jokes you hear lately are about AIDS?' Trina asks.

'That's sick,' Diva says. 'I never hear any jokes about AIDS.'

'People don't tell you jokes because you never get them.'

Diva nods. 'That's true. Makes me feel stupid.'

'You're not stupid,' Dixie says. 'The jokes are.'

Barcelona looks at Dixie, impressed by how supportive she is at all times. It's almost eerie.

'But it's weird how jokes go in these cycles,' Trina says. 'Remember all the dead baby jokes when we were kids? What's the difference between a truckload of babies and a truckload of bowling balls? You can't pitchfork bowling balls. Jokes like that.'

'I remember all the Polish jokes a few years ago,' Diva says.

'And now the AIDS jokes. And condom jokes. I heard a bunch of condom jokes the other day from Senator Grodin's press secretary, Herman Fordham. Why did the guy put condoms over his ears?'

68

'Over his ears?' Diva repeats, confused.

'Because he didn't want to get hearing AIDS.'

Barcelona blows a raspberry, Dixie laughs. Diva says, 'I get that one. It's not funny, but I get it.'

'I heard a combination Polish and condom joke,' Dixie says. 'A Polish cop I worked with on Vice told it to me. Why did the Pollack put ice in his condom?' Pause. 'He wanted to make the swelling go down.'

They all laugh.

'Fine,' Barcelona says, still giggling, 'now we're bigots.'

Barcelona pours wine in everyone's glass, finishing the carafe. She thinks of Eric squeezing Luna's ass the way he used to squeeze hers. She wonders if he also draws cartoon characters on Luna's breasts the way he did with her. Somehow he always managed to work the nipple in as the focal point of the drawing. Bugs Bunny chewing a carrot, the tip of which was her nipple. Elmer Fudd chasing Daffy Duck, Daffy's tail with a target painted on, the bull's-eye Barcelona's erect nipple. If it wasn't already erect, he'd lick it erect, 'for that 3-D effect.'

'Are you ready to order, ladies?' the waiter asks. He is young, mid-twenties, with blond hair moussed into a curly pile on top of his head like a plate of thin noodles. He smiles with confidence, like a gigolo. He knows he is handsome and he also thinks he is charming. He is obviously anxious to practice this charm on the older, more mature women at his table. They run into this often. Boys who act as if they are doing these elderly women a favor by lavishing attention, flooding them with sexual vibrations. He smiles at Barcelona and she smiles back because she knows Trina will not let this boy's smugness pass.

'I think we're ready, aren't we, *ladies*,' Trina says. She lingers on the word ladies.

'What will you have?' the waiter asks, slowly removing

his pen from his jacket, as if writing it down were a mere formality required by the management. A man like himself would never forget a word spoken by such women as these. His smile roves around the table like a sniffing dog, his eyes finally resting on Trina, eyes flicking off her chest to her eyes, not wanting to seem obvious. Poor baby, Barcelona thinks, everyone looks at Trina's chest first, even women. Especially women. It is the perfect chest, the size and shape that every magazine, movie, novel, and dreamy-eyed man ever described as perfect from the moment they knew what breasts were.

'We'd like more wine,' Trina says.

'Of course,' he agrees, writing. 'And an appetizer perhaps? May I suggest some Calamari Marinati or the Lumache Borgogno? The former is, of course, marinated calamari on a bed of lettuce. The latter is our own escargots with garlic butter and white wine. Delicious, ladies.' He smiles broadly now, really rolling, thoroughly enjoying his part.

Trina looks up at him, her smile lovely and patient. 'You're a very good-looking young man,' she says.

The waiter's smile widens, but his face reddens a little. He is clearly embarrassed. This is not how the game is played, not so overtly.

'High school sports, right?' Trina continues.

The waiter is confused. His smiles winches down a few turns. 'Baseball, some football.'

'And you plan to go to college when you graduate?'

'I am in college,' he says stiffly. 'Part time at Sand Coast College.'

Barcelona, feeling embarrassed for him, pretends to wipe her mouth with her napkin to hide her face. Diva, too, pretends to drink, though Barcelona can see her lips are closed tight against the tilted glass to keep from laughing. Only Trina and Dixie stare directly at the waiter, both with pleasant but steady expressions.

'You know, young man.' Trina continues. 'I'd hate to see a boy like you, his life ahead of him, making any mistake that might jeopardize his whole life.'

'What are you talking about?'

'About serving liquor, young man. You do know that you must be eighteen to serve alcoholic beverages?'

'Of course.' His voice is a ragged blend of annoyance and fear. Trina's voice is authoritarian, hinting at secrets she knows. 'I'm twenty-four,' he blurts out.

'You can prove that to Officer Cooper here, can't you?' Trina nods at Dixie, who flashes her badge from her purse.

'Hell, yes.' The waiter reaches for his wallet, drops his pen into the basket of garlic bread sticks on the table, fishes the pen out, drops his order pad, picks that up. Finally he has his wallet out and flashes the driver's license at Dixie and Trina. They study it, look at the photo then up at him, back and forth like that a few times.

'Okay, Bobby,' Trina says.

'Robert,' he says.

'We're ready to order now.'

'So the old guy fries himself with his wife's curling iron?' Trina asks.

'Yes,' Barcelona says. She is cutting her *petti di pollo alla Marsala* into small bite-size pieces. She spears a piece of chicken and two mushrooms and slips it into her mouth. She presses the food with her tongue before chewing, enjoying the hint of Marsala wine.

'Maybe it was suicide,' Diva says. She is picking at an *insalata di spinachi Caldo*, a spinach salad. She is the youngest and pudgiest of the group and always eats salads. She hasn't lost a pound in the three years Barcelona has known her.

71

Dixie shakes her head. 'People seldom choose electrocution as a form of suicide.'

'I wish it had been suicide,' Trina says. 'Once the papers and TV get ahold of this story, there'll be all kind of snide comments and clever jump lines at the end. The whole implication will be that women and all their beauty crap are dangerous to men. Women's vanity is hazardous to men's health, something like that. Wait and see.'

'You're overreacting,' Dixie says.

'Dixie, publicity is my business. I know what will play and what won't with the public. I know this is a perfect little ironic device they love. You'll see.'

Dixie shrugs. She concentrates on her *bistecca al Pepe*, pepper steak with cognac and cream, which Bobby the waiter prepared sulkily at the table. She slices the beef, stares at it on the fork a moment before putting it in her mouth. To Barcelona, she looks as if she's examining evidence. Because Trina owes her a dinner, she told Robby/Robert to give her the most expensive dish on the menu. Dixie is the shortest of them. Five three. She also has the best body. Under her baggy blue sweater and white slacks, her arms and legs literally ripple with muscle. She lifts weights daily after her shift and even on her days off. The only time she misses her workout is twice a month when they all get together like this. Barcelona has seen her naked many times in the locker room after they've taken a jazzercize class together. She can't help but stare in admiration at the bumps and ridges, the rocky sinew of Dixie's body. She wishes she had Dixie's discipline.

'Was his hair all frizzed?' Diva asks.

'Frizzed?'

'Like in cartoons. When someone gets electrocuted, their hair frizzes out.'

Barcelona can only think of Luna's frizzy hair. 'He was bald,' she lies.

72

'That doesn't happen too often,' Dixie says, chewing. Most everyone else is done eating, but she has hardly touched her food. She pokes listlessly at it while she talks. 'I've seen a couple electrocution deaths, and the hair wasn't spiked either time. Although I did see this cat once that had jumped on one of those tranformers. His hair stood straight on end, like he'd just come out of a clothes dryer or something.'

Trina laughs. 'Maybe we can come up with a new home perm. Put a little metal thimble on your finger, stick it in the socket. Voilà. Which twin has the Toni?'

'The what?' Diva says.

'That old television commercial. Which twin has the Toni?'

'I didn't watch much TV as a child. My parents were very strict. Dinner, dishes, homework, the Bible, then bed.'

'You've been culturally deprived, child,' Trina says.

'Dessert, ladies?' the waiter says. He smiles, but there's no confidence now. He is merely polite.

Barcelona feels bad about what they did to him. She feels like a bully. She wants to make it up to him. 'What would you recommend?'

He gives her a careful look as if suspecting some trap. His voice is flat and tentative. He recites now rather than charms. 'Perhaps some sherbert to clear the palate.'

'Fine.'

'Sherbert all around,' Trina says.

'Except me,' Diva says. 'Just coffee.'

When the waiter leaves, Diva says, 'I've decided to become a vegetarian. No more meat.'

'Starting when?' Trina asks skeptically.

'Starting yesterday. I haven't had any meat since the day before yesterday.'

'Sure you did,' Trina says. 'Just now.'

73

'No I didn't. I had a spinach salad.'

'There's bacon in the salad.'

'Not real bacon,' Diva says, looking down at the place where her salad used to be. 'Nobody uses real bacon anymore.'

Barcelona kicks Trina under the table. Trina says, 'That's true. Most of them use a soybean imitation. I forgot.'

Diva finds a stray bacon bit and nudges it with her thumbnail. 'I can't tell.'

Dixie reaches over, presses her finger over the bacon bit. It sticks to her finger and she flicks it off onto the tablecloth in front of her. She picks up a spoon, crushes the bacon bit into a brown powder. She examines it closely, sniffs it as if it were a possible illegal drug, tastes it with a loud smacking sound. 'Soybean,' she pronounces.

Diva relaxes with a smile. 'That's a relief. I just can't stand the idea of eating other animals anymore. I keep seeing their faces. I know it's childish and that this will only confirm your already low opinion of me, the only living species that feels guilt about what we eat. Can you imagine any other species worrying so much? The anteater saying, "Gee, I keep picturing those poor little ant faces in my mind every time I slurp them up."'

'That's an easy answer, Trina,' Diva says.

'No it's not. It's a sane answer.' Trina finishes her wine. 'We're all part of some gigantic cycle. We all feed off each other, die, turn to fertilizer, then the whole process starts again. Like a big house of cards. Sometimes the queen of hearts is on the bottom, but eventually the house collapses and when it's rebuilt, she may be on top. It doesn't matter, because no matter how often it's built, how much prettier or complex the structure is, it always falls and is always rebuilt. That's the great chain of life. We're all pissing into the same pot.'

74

'No more wine for you, Trina,' Diva says.

'Barcy knows what I mean, don't you?'

Barcelona shrugs. She doesn't want to get into this now. She often feels the way Diva does but so far has managed to push it out of her mind when the steaks are served.

'What about vegetables,' Trina says. 'They were alive, had offspring.'

'That's different. They don't think.'

'How do you know? It's been proven they like classical music and being talked to, just like humans. Maybe they're thinking up a storm.'

'Come on, guys,' Barcelona says. 'What's the difference? If Diva wants to eat vegetables, let her. Diva, enjoy.'

Dixie, who's remained curiously quiet during the exchange, dabs her napkin in her water glass and scrubs her lips. 'I don't like eating anything anymore.' She say it so matter-of-factly that everyone thinks she's kidding.

Diva laughs. 'It's not like you have a choice.'

'You don't like eating?' Trina says. 'What's not to like?'

'I don't know,' Dixie says. 'Food doesn't appeal to me. I'm never hungry.'

'You order a twenty-buck entrée I have to pay for and you weren't even hungry?' Trina pretends to be mad.

'That was revenge.' Dixie smiles. 'You bet no guy would offer more than fifty dollars when I worked Vice. First john out of the chute is ready to pop for a hundred.' She leans back in her chair, pushes the sleeves of her sweater up over her forearms. Barcelona looks at the muscles of her arms. The skin is tight over them, the veins protrude slightly. 'I have to eat, I know that. I'm not starving myself or anything. It's just that I don't get any pleasure from it.'

'Try chocolate,' Diva suggests. 'Chocolate cures everything.'

'Maybe you should see a doctor,' Barcelona suggests. She is uncomfortable with Dixie's confession. She feels

helpless, the way she felt when Trina threatened suicide,
'There's nothing wrong with me. Food is just boring.'

'Maybe you're overtraining at the gym,' Trina says. 'Pumping too much iron and not enough men.'

'You're not taking steroids, for God's sake,' Diva says.

Dixie laughs. 'No, I'm not taking steroids. I want strength, not a moustache.'

'Could be an allergy,' Barcelona says.

Diva agrees. 'I read an article somewhere about certain reactions to food allergies.' Diva is famous for her tidbits of information from obscure articles in even more obscure magazines. Because singing in commercials requires a lot of sitting around during technical adjustments, she always has a magazine in her purse. 'You may be having a reaction to white flour or something.'

'You think?' Dixie asks, intrigued. 'Like white bread or something?'

'Could be. They have to run some tests on you to be sure.'

'I'll check into that,' Dixie says and Barcelona knows she will because Dixie always does whatever she says she will do. Of the four of them, she is the one most capable, most in control of her fate. Barcelona admires that in her. They met three years ago when Dixie took a medieval poetry class from Barcelona at the college. For contrast, Barcelona had brought in a dozen contemporary poems with similar themes. Dixie had liked the poetry, though had no particular feel for its complexities. She didn't like the contemporary poems that didn't rhyme, that weren't strictly metered. In class, she'd made a joke about herself as a Meter Maid of Poetry and everyone had laughed. Barcelona had admired her self-awareness. Analyzing poems bored Dixie, an intellectual crossword puzzle, she called it.

Once they'd been discussing a poem by W.D. Snodgrass,

'Mementos I.' The poem was a sometimes bitter account of the narrator's divorce, but ended with a longing for his estranged wife. Dixie raised her hand immediately after the poem had been read aloud by another student. Barcelona expected her to comment on the poem's clever use of rhyme and rhythm. Instead, Dixie said: 'The problem with this poem is the guy is pissed at his ex-wife because he blames her.'

'For what?' Barcelona had asked in her teacher's voice.

'For not making him happy. Men blame us because nothing in their lives make them truly happy. Even if they achieve success in their careers and whatnot. They know something's missing. They think women are the answer. They expect us to make them happy and we don't. Not in the way they expect.'

Another girl raised her hand. 'Are you saying we deserve their contempt?'

'I'm just making an observation. They think of women as mind-altering drugs. We'll change reality, make it all better for them. Ain't gonna happen. You have to learn to live with that, treat men as suspects in a drug bust. Perpetrators.'

They got a laugh. After class, Barcelona invited Dixie to join the group.

'What kind of group?' Dixie had asked.

'Just some women friends.'

'Not a support group or anything like that. I'm not into bitching. That wasn't bitching back in class, that was just an observation. I don't hate men.'

Barcelona had laughed. 'None of us hates men, Dixie. Men have nothing to do with this. We're just friends who get together twice a month and have a fabulous meal at an expensive restaurant. Nothing more to it.'

Diva had not been a part of the group then. Glenda Carson had been the fourth member. But she had moved to Tucson when her husband's parents were killed in a burglary and he inherited the family children's clothing store. Trina brought Diva in after they met during a local charity telethon Trina was publicizing. Diva had been a singer on the show. Diva was a nickname given her by Trina. Her real name was Dianne Klosterman.

Diva pulls a cigarette from her purse. It is gnarled and black and looks like a freshly dug up tree root. She roasts the tip with her Bic. Lighting it seems to take a long time.

'I can't believe you're still smoking those things,' Trina says, waving the smoke away from her face. 'Healthwise, you'd be better off eating a dozen cows. Probably even cow dung.'

'They help make my voice throatier.' Diva lowers her voice and sings a few bars of 'Girls Just Want to Have Fun,' only she sings it slow and sultry, in Marlene Dietrich's accented voice; 'Girls juz vant to hahv fun.'

'That's pretty good,' Dixie says.

'I'm pretty good,' Diva says. 'I'm especially good as peanut butter. That's what I'm doing now.'

'The radio commercial,' Barcelona says. 'Trina told me.'

'Yeah, I'm doing backup with three other white girls while some black chick gets the lead. They wanted a soul sound to capture the black market or something. Shit, man, I can do goddamn soul.' She puts her brown cigarette in the ashtray and sings the melody of Aretha Franklin's 'Respect': 'P-E-A-N-U-T, show your little nuts to me. B-U-T-T-E-R, eat you while we're in the car.'

Everyone laughs but it's true that she doesn't sound very soullike. She sounds like Petula Clark.

'Well, can I do soul or what?' It is not a question but a statement so no one replies. Diva puffs frantically on her cigarette.

'I've been asked to write a screenplay,' Barcelona announces. She says it quickly because she doesn't know how

78

to share the news without making it sound pretentious.

'Jesus,' Trina says, grinning. 'That's great.'

'You're kidding,' Diva says. There is a hard edge of envy under the smile.

'When did this happen?' Dixie asks.

Barcelona tells them the whole story. She resists embellishing it to make it sound like more than it is. She finishes with, 'It's a long shot.'

'A long shot at Lynda Kramer is better than a sure shot with most others,' Diva says with authority. Because she is a professional singer, she has always been their resident expert on show business.

'Oh God, I just thought of something,' Trina says with a melodramatic gasp.

'What?' Barcelona asks.

'That scene in *Live Wires*, the one where the woman has sex with the alien ambassador in the space shuttle. That was me and Rob on the shuttle from L.A. to San Francisco. I should never have told you about that. Now everyone will see it.'

'That was you?' Diva says, surprised.

'Rob's idea. The only good one he ever had. I think that's when Karyn was conceived.'

The sherbert and coffee arrive. Diva sips her coffee and lights another twisted black root. Barcelona and Trina eat their sherbert. Dixie digs her spoon into hers carving a face, but never eating any.

Trina is already finished with her sherbert and takes Dixie's away and starts eating it. 'Shit, if you're going to make snowmen from it, I'll eat it.' She spoons some into her mouth and talks, her tongue and lips orange. 'I kinda like the idea of being immortalized. Having Lynda Kramer play out something that happened to me. Maybe they'll hire me as a consultant, you think?'

Barcelona smiles. 'I wouldn't count on it.'

'Fuck them then.' She spoons the rest of the sherbert into her mouth.

'Any new perps in your life?' Dixie asks no one in particular.

Barcelona looks at Trina. Trina winks but doesn't say anything. Barcelona realizes now that The Great Pretender is to remain a secret between the two of them.

'Same-o-same-o,' Diva says, lighting yet another black root. Diva has a live-in boyfriend named Calypso. He claims to be half-Jamaican, but Diva has expressed some doubts about that. Calypso is a drummer with a local band, Fast Lane. 'Calypso wants me to marry him, have kids.'

'Jesus,' Trina says. 'There's a frightening thought.'

'He's not so bad,' Diva says halfheartedly. Then she sighs. 'He has the names of the kids picked out already. Sport if it's a boy, Spring if it's a girl.'

'Sound like dog names,' Dixie says.

'Doesn't it? That's what I said. He laughed, said maybe we should get dogs then. I think he just wants something to hang those names on.'

Trina yawns. 'No men talk tonight. Too boring.'

'Be right back,' Barcelona says, rising. She grabs her purse and heads for the rest room. The wine is expanding by the second in her bladder. She takes a couple of wrong turns before she finally finds the hidden corridor that leads past the telephones to the rest rooms. A silhouette cutout figure is on each door, but they look so similar, she isn't sure which is a man and which is a woman. An old short woman with elastic wraps around her swollen ankles pushes past her and enters one of the doors. Barcelona follows.

She sits in the stall and is surprised that there is no graffiti. She is also surprised that there is no toilet paper. She makes both discoveries after she is already in the process of peeing. She is thankful that is all she has to do. Under the gap between the two stalls, she can see the older woman's left foot. The wraps around her ankle look tight, the skin above the wrap puffing out over it. She is making a noise that sounds like crying, but suddenly the noise stops, the toilet flushes, and the woman leaves without washing her hands. Barcelona doubts that the woman even had time to go. When she finishes, she searches through her purse for a tissue, finds one crumpled up with lipstick on it, refolds it for a clean surface, and wipes herself dry.

She leans over the sink and washes her hands. She presses her palm against the soap dispenser. A few drops of pink lotion fizz out, but not enough to really lather up. She pumps the plunger a few more times but it too is empty. The door behind her opens, she looks up into the mirror. It's Dixie.

'What's all this crap about not eating?' Barcelona says.

'I didn't say I didn't eat, I said I was never hungry.'

'You should see a doctor. Really.'

'Maybe it's just psychological. I mean, sometimes I feel hungry, then by the time I cook something up, I've lost my appetite.'

'Go to restaurants.'

'That's even worse. I pay money and still don't want to eat it. Besides, it's not just the food. It's the process of eating that bothers me. The biting, chewing, swallowing. It'd kinda sickening if you think about it.' She steps up to the mirror and pulls down the collar of her blue sweater. There's a small bruise on her neck.

'What happened to you?'

'Just what it looks like. A hickey.'

Barcelona laughs. 'You? A hickey?'

'Part of my undercover assignment at that high school. I'm supposed to be infiltrating this group of kids they think sells drugs.'

'Do they sell drugs?'

Dixie looks at Barcelona in the mirror. 'The head kid, name's Joseph Little, does about two hundred thousand dollars' worth of business a year.' She points at her hickey. 'He likes me.'

'Sounds dangerous, Dixie.'

Dixie shrugs. 'Not really. I'm not going to bust him, just gather some evidence for a week or so, then disappear.' She pulls a folded toothbrush out of her purse, opens it, squeezes a dab of toothpaste on and brushes her teeth. She talks around the toothbrush. 'Your mom still getting those obscene calls?'

'I don't know. I haven't talked to her in a while.'

'She contact the local cops like I suggested?'

'I told her to, but who knows what she actually did. She has a mind of her own. Besides, they're just small-town cops. They wouldn't do anything except tell her to change her number and make sure it's unlisted. I've already suggested that.'

'But she won't, right?' Dixie rinses off the toothbrush, folds it, zips it back into her small black purse. She examines her teeth in the mirror.

'Right. I think she's worried some long-lost friend she hasn't seen in twenty years will suddenly get the urge to call and not be able to reach her.'

Dixie leans toward the mirror, examining the hickey more closely. 'Jesus, that little nipper has a bite doesn't he?'

'I've seen worse.'

'I've given worse.' She laughs. Her laugh is lovely, like unexpectedly overhearing a few notes of a favorite song. 'That was a long time ago, of course. I'm not that kind of girl anymore.'

Barcelona smiles. 'Of course. Me neither.'

'Of course.' She laughs again and they return to the table together.

'Diva met this guy,' Trina tells them as they sit down. 'You gotta hear this. Tell them, Diva.'

'No big deal, just a guy,' she says, but she is smiling wickedly.

'Yeah,' Trina says. 'Just a guy with a verifiable ten-inch tongue.'

'What do you mean "verifiable"?' Dixie asks.

'He measured it for me,' Diva explains.

'Start at the beginning,' Trina says. 'When he approached you.'

'Okay. This was last week when I was doing that loan company ad, you know, where I sing like Bette Midler?' She taps the ashes from her black cigarette. 'We were on break, some technical shit with the ad copy. Anyway, this sound guy who works at the recording studio comes up to me and asks me out on a date. He's not very cute, looks a little like that guy does the camera commercials on TV.'

'John Newcombe?' Barcelona asks.

'No.'

'Ben Cross?' Trina asks.

'No.'

'Laurence Olivier?' Dixie asks.

'God, no. He's too old. This guy was young, my age. Anyway, I tell him no, tell him I've got a boyfriend, I live with a guy. He tells me he doesn't care and neither will I. Then he sticks out the tip of his tongue. "Ten inches," he says. "Bigger than most men's dicks." I started to laugh, but he sticks it out again, only this time he sticks it out all the way and the thing just keeps coming at me, I swear I must've backed up a couple steps. Then he whips out this tape measure he has clipped to his belt and measures it. Sure enough, ten inches, just like he said.'

They are all laughing.

'I could make him president,' Trina says.

'He sure has the brass,' Dixie says.

'More important, he has the tongue.' Trina reaches her spoon across the table and scrapes up the last bite of Barcelona's leftover sherbert. 'Is it my imagination, or is it getting weirder out there?'

'We're just getting older,' Barcelona says.

'Bullshit,' Trina says. 'It's fucked up in Romanceville, kiddo.'

'Trina's right,' Diva says. 'I run into the strangest guys lately. I'm just lucky I've got Calypso.'

'Yeah,' Trina says. 'He's heaven-sent.'

'You don't like him because he's half black.'

'No,' Trina says. 'I don't like him because he's completely stupid. Barcy doesn't like him because he's half black.'

'I don't care that he's half black,' Barcelona says. 'I don't like him because he's a leech. Dixie's the one who doesn't like him because he's half black.'

Dixie shakes her head. 'That's the only thing about him I do like.'

Diva laughs. 'Well, to tell you the truth, I don't think he's really half-Jamaican like he says. You know those dreadlocks of his? He gets them permed. I promised not to tell, but I think that's so *strange*.'

They all laughed.

Diva sighs, puffs her black cigarette. Her fingernails are painted a metallic pink with tiny green palm trees growing out of the cuticles. 'I don't know. It's easy for you guys. You're all gorgeous. I'm too fat to get the really good men.'

'That's bullshit,' says Trina. 'You know why?'

'Because a good man won't care that I'm fat?'

'No. Because there aren't any good men.' Trina laughs loudly and draws stares from nearby tables.

84

'I thought we weren't going to talk about men tonight,' Dixie says. 'Your suggestion, Trina.'

'I was overruled.'

Diva points at Dixie's left hand, the ring finger. Dixie wears a simple gold band. 'I can't believe you wear that ring on that finger.'

'Why not? It was my mom's.'

'Why not? Because guys will all think you're married and stay away.'

'Not today they won't,' Trina says. 'I think it may even encourage them. They figure you're horny for some variety with no strings attached.'

'I wear it to keep the creeps off at work,' Dixie says.

'The cops or the criminals?' Trina asks.

'The creeps,' Dixie repeats.

Trina chuckles. 'I'm still hungry. Hey, Bobby.' She waves at the waiter as he passes. 'Let me see the dessert menu again.' He nods stiffly and hurries off.

'Are you drunk?' Diva asks.

'Why, am I too loud?'

'No more than usual,' Dixie says.

'That's too bad. This has not been a usual day.' Trina stops, looks at them in a funny way. Barcelona thinks she is about to say something important, but the moment passes and Trina smiles. She is not drunk.

The waiter returns and hands Trina the menu. He scuttles off again.

Trina licks her lips as she reads the menu. 'God, this stuff sounds good.'

'It's all fattening,' Diva says, lighting her third black cigarette.

'You ever notice how it always sounds better than it actually tastes?' Dixie says.

'I have,' Barcelona agrees. 'I mean, even if it tastes good, it never tastes quite as good as you've expected.'

Trina nods. 'That doesn't keep us from ordering, does it? Thing is, what we need is a menu of men that we could order from. That would make things so much easier.'

'Absolutely,' Dixie says. 'With guys listed according to their appeal. Like some guys are merely appetizers, some are desserts.'

'And some,' Diva says, grinning lewdly, 'are full-course meals.'

'How about something like this,' Trina says. 'Beef Ribs à la Jack. Huge slabs of meaty ribs that take all night to finish.'

Barcelona laughs. 'With juicy, buttery corn on a stiff cob. On the side.'

'That's the way I like it best,' Diva says.

They play with the idea for a while, each topping the others in their descriptions. They laugh loudly. When the waiter returns for Trina's order, she says she's changed her mind about dessert and asks for the check. They continue playing the Man Menu game while they divide the bill.

Diva lays a twenty in the middle of the table. 'Let's do it for real.'

'Do what?' Barcelona asks.

'Make this menu. With men on it.'

'That's crazy.'

'No, it's not,' Diva says. 'We all know and meet lots of men. Some of them you're interested in, but some of them you're not. Maybe one of us would be.'

'This sounds a little like high school,' Barcelona says.

'Not today's high school,' Dixie says.

'It doesn't sound like high school,' Trina says. 'It sounds like business. Diva's talking about networking.'

'Yeah, networking,' Diva says tentatively, as if uncertain what the word means.

'Exactly,' Trina says. 'We're all professional women. If

86

we were in the same profession, we'd be helping each other in business, giving leads to jobs or clients, that sort of thing. Why shouldn't we try to do the same thing in our personal lives?'

'Are you serious, Trina?' Barcelona asks.

'She's serious,' Diva says.

Dixie makes change for everyone and figures out a tip. She hands two dollar bills back to Diva. 'I don't know what you're so hot about, Diva. You're living with a guy.'

Diva stuffs the bills in her purse. 'We're living together but not really *involved*.'

'You were just talking about having kids. Remember Sport and Spring?'

'Yeah, that's a good point.' Diva lowers her head, stares into her purse a minute. Then she lifts her head and smiles. 'I can still look though. I don't have to date any of these guys, right? Besides, the only kind of sex Calypso is interested in lately is anal. I'm starting to think he may be secretly gay.'

'Jesus, Diva,' Trina says, 'we just ate.'

Barcelona says, 'Boy, living together ain't the thrill it used to be.'

Dixie hands Barcelona a five. 'What are we talking about? A physical menu with guys' names on it?'

'Yes,' Trina says. 'Their names and a description, in food terms only, of who they are. We can use the price column to describe their income. Expensive means they're raking it in. Moderate means they're able to pay their bills in Yuppieland. Inexpensive means they're artists and get ready to spend some of your own dough. I'll type the whole thing on my computer.'

'Count me out,' Barcelona says. 'This is too weird.'

'Come on, Barcy,' Trina says. 'It's just for fun.'

'Yeah, you could share some of those professors you know.'

'I can give you the rundown on them right now. "Chicken fried steak à la Tweed. Chewy and dry. Beverage and dessert not included."'

'That's pretty good,' Dixie laughs.

Barcelona looks at Dixie. 'You're not taking part in this lunacy, are you?'

'Why not? I know a couple cops might be of some interest. And, of course, there's always my new friends at the high school. You can come to the next sock hop.'

'Come on, Barcy,' Diva says.

Barcelona shakes her head, but then sighs. 'Okay, I'll contribute to the menu, but I'm not ordering anything from it.'

'Probably none of us will,' Trina says. 'But it's fun dreaming.'

'What about married men?' Diva asks. 'Should we include them if they're real hunks?'

'No,' Barcelona says.

'Fair game,' Trina says. 'If they have a steady income and a dick, good enough.'

'No,' Dixie says. 'I agree with Barcelona. No married men.'

'Unless physically separated from their wives,' Trina compromises.

Dixie shrugs.

Barcelona listens to them discuss it for a few more minutes as they walk through the restaurant toward the exit. They're having fun and she doesn't think it will ever get past the talking stage. Occasionally, Trina or Diva will give funny descriptions of a man as an entrée and they will all laugh.

In the parking lot, they hear the rotors of helicopters overhead. They look up but can't see the crafts, only their blinking red lights. There are three of them.

'The CH53-E Super Stallions,' Dixie says, looking up.

'That the one they're trying to ground?' Trina asks.

Dixie nods. 'Twenty marines dead so far in crashes.'

They stare up into the darkness a few more seconds before splitting up. Dixie and Diva head for their cars. Trina lingers to walk with Barcelona. 'It'll be fun,' she says. 'You're taking it too seriously.'

'People often refer to me as a saint,' Barcelona grins.

'Yeah, but they usually follow it with Bernard.'

They laugh, lean against each other.

'Shit, look at that asshole,' Trina says suddenly, breaking away. A red Porsche is parked at a diagonal across two parking spaces. 'I had to park in Cambodia because the lot's so full and this jerk takes two spaces.'

'He doesn't want his car scratched.'

'Fuck him,' Trina walks over to the car, stoops by the rear tire, uncaps the inflation valve. 'Find me a small pebble,' she says.

'What are you doing?' Barcelona asks.

'Here's one.' Trina plucks a tiny stone from the ground, stuffs it into the cap, and screws it back on the valve. Barcelona can hear the air hissing slowly from the tire. Trina stands and slaps her hands clean. 'Asshole.'

Barcelona sees a couple coming out of the restaurant and she pulls Trina away. 'Why'd you do that?'

'Trust, Justice, the American Way.' She smiles. 'And because it felt good.'

PART TWO

Networking

**In Which the Friends Determine
How to Put the Men
Back in Menu**

7

Diva wakes up because she feels her hand being lifted from her chest. She is too confused to open her eyes. Her hand is held by the wrist and is being moved upward until her knuckles scrape the sheet, then it moves horizontally, like those marine helicopters that are always crashing. Finally it is slowly lowered onto a very serious erection. She feels her hands being shaped around a large pole, her fingers being curled around it one by one. Both the hand shaping hers and the erection are very warm.

She sits up and looks over at Calypso. 'What the hell are you doing?'

He is grinning. 'I've got a hard-on.'

'How nice for you.' She pulls her hand away and gets out of bed. She is naked but not embarrassed by it even though she is only 5′4″ and 160 pounds. Six inches shorter and ten pounds heavier than Calypso. The weight certainly isn't her breasts, which are small but pudgy. Her stomach sags a little, as do her arms, her butt, her thighs. She has been dieting for three years and has yet to lose any weight. She has gone to many doctors, hoping for some glandular excuse that medication would adjust. The last doctor just shrugged and said, 'Hey, you're just one of Nature's fatties. Live with it.'

Diva walks across the room to the battered old stereo. Officially, the stereo is in the living room. But since only

93

a folding rice paper screen separates the bedroom from the living room, it is a meaningless distinction. She flips the stereo switch. One of the speakers has a low buzz which she has been ignoring for the past two years. She lets the record already on the turntable play, though she doesn't remember which album is on. When she hears Laura Nyro, she is pleased and sings along as she heads for the kitchen. *'Surry down to a stone soul picnic/There'll be lots of time and wine . . .'*

The refrigerator is nearly empty. Half a carton of nonfat milk two days past the expiration date, three nonfat yogurts, a jar of crunchy peanut butter they gave her from the commercial she did yesterday, and a couple of bulbous yellow squash. She'd left twenty dollars with Calypso yesterday to buy a few groceries but, as usual, he forgot. If she went to his jeans right now she'd find the two tens balled up at the bottom of the pocket with some guitar picks, loose change, maybe half a joint. He's not evil, not into booze or serious dope or any of that shit. He just forgets.

The chilled air from the refrigerator teases her naked skin and her nipples harden. For some reason she puts one hand protectively between her legs as she bends into the refrigerator. She finds an open can of Diet Rite Cola. She drinks. It is flat and syrupy. She finishes it anyway. Afterward she rinses the can in the sink before tossing it into the trash. They have to be very careful with the trash now. This is ant season.

The only window in the apartment is in the living room. The place is so small that this window is visible from anywhere in the apartment. It looks out onto the complex's east parking lot. The other side of the building looks out onto the street, a row of beach houses, and finally a little scrap of the beach and ocean. Those apartments cost $45 more a month for the view. Diva can't afford the view. It's enough for her knowing the ocean is over there, this close.

The whole complex is pretty run-down. The hallway smells rancid, as if people have been storing dead fish and rotting vegetables under the already mildewed carpeting. The smell of dope is heavy. The laundry room is dangerous, not just to the tenants, two of whom have been raped in the past year, but also dangerous to the clothing. The washing machines are more like blenders, the dryers like flame throwers. The parking lot is like a swap meet of stolen goods and drug deals. But Diva, for the sake of her soul, must live by the beach and this is the cheapest she could find, even though it still takes most of what she earns every month. There's so much going on down here all the time. The energy is tremendous. Even now, glancing out the window on a weekday morning, instead of seeing a lot of people driving to work, she sees three boys in wet suit jackets with surf boards under their arms heading for the beach.

She returns to the bedroom area but Calypso is not in bed. There is a small passageway to the bathroom, about five feet wide. This is the closet. She walks through the closet to the bathroom. Calypso is sitting on the toilet, naked, jerking off. He is grinning at her while he does it.

'This turn you on?' he asks, stroking himself.

'Yeah. I'm all wet.' She leans over the sink, turns on the faucet, and splashes water on her bangs. They are too long and she's been meaning to cut them for a couple of days. Later this morning she has an audition for a car dealer commercial, singing the freeway directions to the guy's lot. She wants to look good. She opens her drawer but can't find the scissors. 'Where are the scissors?' she asks Calypso.

His eyes are closed as he slowly but steadily continues to thump up and down. 'I don't know.'

Diva roots through the drawer some more but comes up

95

empty. Finally she settles on a pair of manicure scissors. She curls several strands of wet hair around her fingers, pulls straight out, and whatever is leftover, she snips off. The sink fills with spikes of brown hair.

'Oh, man, Diva,' Calypso moans. 'This feels good.'

She continues snipping. She thinks of Barcelona, the movie deal with Lynda Kramer. She feels very jealous. Not that Barcelona doesn't deserve her success, but so does she. She thinks of all the years of singing, the endless auditions, the record companies she's been haunting the past few years. She deserves some success too. She doesn't want to be singing radio commercials all her life. She wants to rock 'n' roll. Have her own album. Walk into Tower Records and see her own CD up front with the Picks of the Week.

'Oooh,' Calypso says. His breathing is getting shallower, his hand is moving up and down his shaft faster. She glances over. His eyes are still closed. There are a few drops of creamy semen on the tip of his penis. His hand is jerking up and down in a blur. His mouth is tight with devotion. Goddamn, it *is* sexy after all. 'Oh, for Christ's sake,' Diva finally says, slapping away his jumping hand and replacing it with her own. She kneels down next to him, starts tugging up and down. He pumps his pelvis up and down into her fists, his skinny butt bouncing on the toilet seat. It takes only a few more strokes and he arches his back and shouts, 'Ihreeeeee,' which is Jamaican slang for 'Everything's cool.' His thick gummy come starts to shoot crazily, splatting Diva on her left breast. The rest dribbles over her knuckles, down between her fingers.

He leans back against the toilet lid, wiping himself with yellow toilet paper. Diva washes her hands. 'There,' she says. 'Happy?'

'Actually, yes.'

She laughs. It is not her nature to be angry about

anything for long. 'You should have seen your face when you were pounding away. You looked like a little boy doing it for the first time.'

'Every time is like the first time. Just as good.'

'Is that true? Really? It's always good when you masturbate?'

'Yeah, it is. It's like scoring a hundred percent on a test every time you take one.' He stands up and goes to the bedroom. He finds yesterday's underpants and puts them on. They are black Calvin Klein's. They are the only pair he owns, along with three pairs of jeans, four shirts, two pairs of shoes, three pairs of socks, and a white tuxedo jacket he found lying around after a bar mitzvah party he once played at. 'Isn't it always good for you?' he asks. 'Jerking off.'

'Not always. Sometimes it's hard to come. I have to concentrate real hard. It's difficult to concentrate and rub at the same time.'

'Hmmm, I see your point.' He pulls on his jeans. He is so thin that no matter how small the size of jeans he wears, they always sag at the butt. He comes back into the bathroom while she is rinsing off her toothbrush. He stabs his fingers at his dreadlocks, puffing them out. Against his pale skin and freckles, they look silly, like a Shirley Temple wig.

'How do you like it?' he asks.

She puts the toothbrush away and returns to the bedroom. She starts to make the bed.

'Seriously, mom.' He is starting to speak in his Jamaican accent now. 'How do you like de hair?'

'Your dreadlocks look more like dead lox.'

He studies them in the mirror for a minute, tilting his head this way then that way. He shrugs and laughs. 'I'll show you a dead lox.' He runs back into the bedroom and leaps onto the bed. He grabs Diva around the waist and pulls her on top of him. His tongue is licking her every-where: hips, legs, nipples, eyelids. She is giggling as he rolls her over and over, tongue lapping her skin.

'Stop,' she says, hoping and knowing that he won't.

'Dead lox patrol,' he says, licking, licking, licking.

She feels his rough tongue on her ass, then in the crack, then right up against her hole. She recoils at first, embarrassed. But he pulls her back and continues licking her there. When she realizes it is too soon for his dick to get hard enough to use on her there, she relaxes and enjoys what he is doing. He works his way even farther down and has somehow turned her onto her back without ever stopping his burrowing and licking. His head is between her legs now, the tongue drilling inside her, then playfully tapping at her clitoris. His tongue beats a pattern against her as skillfully as if he were playing the steel drums. He whips his head from side to side now, the tongue tripping over her clitoris repeatedly.

She is vibrating with pleasure. She is having trouble catching her breath. 'You skinny son of a bitch,' she yells, pulling his head tight against her, squashing his nose into her pubic bone.

He lifts his head and shouts, 'You pudgy pigorama!'

'Bony bastard!'

'Fat fuck!'

Her thighs tense against his head, her signal that she is ready to come. He picks up the pace, slips his thumb deep into her vagina and stutters his tongue on her clitoris. She moans, stiffens, her legs suddenly shoot straight out, her toes pointing downward toward China.

Afterward, she showers and when she comes out, Ca-lypso is gone. The two tens she gave him yesterday are on the kitchen counter. A note lies under it. It says: *Pizza tonight*?

She sits on the sofa, still naked except for the towel

98

wrapped around her hair. She begins thumbing through an old issue of *Rolling Stone*. In the classifieds are ads for songwriters. None for singers. Wait a minute, she thinks. That's it! Every major decision in Diva's life has come in on a flash of inspiration, an epiphany of revelation so great she shudders on the sofa with almost the same intensity she had earlier with Calypso's tongue inside her.

A songwriter. That's what she'll become. She would still keep humping at singing, but now she would add songwriting to her talents, which would make her much more commercial to the record companies. She'd be like Joni Mitchell, Laura Nyro, Phoebe Snow.

She jumps up and begins cleaning the apartment. A new life decision always requires cleaning house. Starting fresh. As she changes the sheets on the bed, she smiles at how good sex with Calypso had been that morning. She'd had one of the deepest orgasms she'd ever had in her life. For a moment there she'd felt as if she'd vacuumed Calypso right up through her vagina and into her womb, and if she didn't fight her way back to consciousness, she would suck up the apartment building next, then the beach, the ocean, and more. Like a black hole of the universe. God, it had been terrific.

After she changes the sheets on the bed, she gathers Calypso's clothing and stuffs them into a plastic trash bag. The white tuxedo doesn't fit so she folds that neatly and lays it on top. She pins a note to the lapel: *Dear Calypso, Sorry no pizza tonight. And please move out. I'm changing my life. Diva.*

8

Dixie is eating lunch in the school courtyard with her new friend from algebra class, Melody Krauss. Melody is drunk from spraying the contents of an Opium perfume bottle from her purse into her mouth. The Opium bottle is filled with Southern Comfort. She has offered to spray Dixie's mouth a couple of times and Dixie let her once right after gym class.

'God, this is good stuff,' Melody says, spraying her mouth again after eating a Twinkie.

'I wish I could say the same about this,' Dixie says, listlessly stabbing her mashed potatoes with her fork. She had taken a bite of the corn and an even smaller bite of the roast beef. She pushes the tray away. 'We should've gone to Burger King.'

'Just needs some seasoning.' Melody giggles. She sprays Dixie's roast beef with her Opium atomizer. Southern Comfort mists the table. Some lands on Dixie's arm and she licks it.

'Yum. My compliments to the chef.'

Melody laughs but stops suddenly when she sees a teacher approaching their table. Dixie spots Mrs. Filborne's loud plaid skirt and clashing striped blouse and feels a tingle of rabbit fear. Once again she is surprised at how quickly she has fallen into the undercover cop's typical Us versus Them Syndrome. She identifies with the kids, shares their resentment of the teachers, even the ones they like. The same thing happened when she went under as a hooker. She could feel her fear of cops budding. It's not unusual; they warn you against it before each assignment. Still, she is surprised how easily it happens.

Mrs. Filborne, the history teacher, stops at their table. She is black with a two-inch Afro and a slight gap between her front teeth. 'Mr. Peterson wants to see you,' she says to Dixie.

'What about?' Dixie asks.

Mrs. Filborne narrows her sharp eyes. 'He didn't say. I'll write you out a hall pass.'

While Mrs. Filborne scribbles on the pink hall pass, Dixie shrugs at Melody to show she doesn't know what this is all about. Melody is busy stuffing her Opium atomizer back in her purse. She looks scared. Finally Mrs. Filborne finishes, tears the pink hall pass from her pad and hands it to Dixie. 'Right away, Dixie.'

'Yes, ma'am,' Dixie says.

Mrs. Filborne looks Dixie over with an openly appraising eye. She has seen Dixie only twice in class, and Dixie was careful not to volunteer any answers. But Dixie can feel the woman's opinion hardening like cement already. New girl, hangs around with Melody, a known lush, seen with Joseph Little the drug pusher. Short skirt and too much makeup. Tramp, dummy, druggie. Dixie feels Mrs. Filborne's eyes drawing a careful line through her name, crossing her out of the list of good students. Dixie even feels like a loser now, hopeless. Her anger toward this woman is suddenly fierce, made worse by the frustration of her position.

'Jesus, Dixie, what'd you do?' Melody asks when Mrs. Filborne has walked away.

'Nothing. I didn't do anything.' Dixie smiles nervously. 'Well, I'd better go see.'

'Good luck.'

'Yeah, thanks. See ya.' Dixie walks off toward the principal's office. Her anger lessens as she walks. She understands Mrs. Filborne's own frustration. Too many students, many of whom are drugged or drunk or just don't care. This isn't some urban school with forced bussing or welfare children. This is Newport Beach and the children are dressed in colorful but expensive clothing from the mall. Their parents are educated. The student parking lot contains over a million dollars' worth of spotless automobiles. The faculty lot is exclusively Japanese compacts.

'Come in, Dixie,' Mr. Peterson, the principal, says. He gestures at the chair across from his desk as he circles around her and closes the door. He is a good-looking man in his early forties, slightly balding at the sides. He is the only one in the school who knows who she really is.

Dixie sits. 'Yes, Mr. Peterson?'

He lowers his voice to almost a whisper. Civilians often do this when talking to cops who they know are undercover. 'What have you found out so far?'

'Not much that you didn't already know. You've got a lot of drugs and booze flowing through this school.'

'Damn.' He looks miserable.

'I'm not telling you anything new. You knew all this going in. That's why I'm here.'

'Yes, yes, I know. I just thought, hoped . . .' He sighs, leans back in his chair. 'I don't know.'

'You hoped it was some kind of mistake, maybe an isolated incident confined to one or two students.'

He smiles. 'You've been through this before.'

'Several times.'

They met only once before, briefly, at the police station. He had been very nervous:

'I'm just not so sure this is necessary,' he'd told Captain Janeway that day.

'Well, Peterson,' Captain Janeway had said, 'your school board members disagree. They called us in.'

'It's a tricky situation,' Mr. Peterson said. 'What with student rights. God, it's just so damn sneaky. I know, I know, things have gotten out of hand. I tried drug programs, teen AA meetings. They seem to be helping.'

'Not fast enough for the school board, I'm afraid,' Dixie said.

'Yes, the school board.' He nodded thoughtfully.

Captain Janeway explained the setup, how Dixie would go undercover, identify only the student pushers, possession with intent to sell, establish patterns when they would be carrying, and then let the uniforms come in and bust them. Hopefully that would be enough to scare some of the fringe users from continuing to buy. 'Probably not,' Captain Janeway said, 'but let's give it a try anyway. We're not out to bust the whole student body.'

Mr. Peterson stood up. 'I appreciate that.' Then he looked at Dixie, as if for the first time. He frowned. 'I know you know your business, Captain Janeway . . .'

'But?' Captain Janeway said.

'But I've been around high school students for the past twenty years. No offense, Ms. Cooper, but you don't look like a high school student.'

'You mean I'm too old?'

He stammered, embarrassed. 'You're not *old* old. I mean, you're very attractive. What are you, twenty-seven, eight?'

'Thirty-three.'

'Oh. Well, see, you look much younger. But seventeen, eighteen, that's a big leap even from twenty-seven. Certainly you have younger cops, kids just out of the academy.'

'You've been watching television, Mr. Peterson. Cop shows, right?' Captain Janeway asked.

Mr. Peterson grinned.

'I thought all you academic types watch PBS, those British imports.'

'Sometimes,' Mr. Peterson said. 'If the Lakers aren't playing and I've already seen "Murder, She Wrote".'

'Believe me,' Captain Janeway said, shaking his hand. 'You won't recognize Sergeant Cooper once she goes under.'

Now sitting in Mr. Peterson's office, Dixie could tell that he was replaying that scene too.

'It's remarkable,' he says, squinting at her. 'You look eighteen.'

'A lot of eye makeup, comb my bangs straight over my forehead to hide any wrinkles. Wear these long earrings to keep them from looking too closely at my skin. And the short skirt distracts them from my face a bit.'

Mr. Peterson glances down at her smooth stockingless legs. 'Works for me.'

Dixie stands. 'Anything else, Mr. Peterson?'

'Kevin. Please.'

'Better keep it Mr. Peterson for now. Helps me keep in character.'

'I understand. Perhaps I should give you an hour of detention, just to make it look good.'

She smiles. 'That's making it look too good.' Dixie starts for the door. 'It's probably best if you don't call me again, Mr. Peterson. Captain Janeway will keep you informed of our progress.'

'Okay, sure. Good luck.'

Dixie leaves his office. Good luck. It's what Melody had said to her too.

Dixie detours into the girl's lavatory. Two tenth-graders are sharing a cigarette. They are both a little plump. One has a sprinkle of acne across her forehead, the other has thick braces.

'He's pissed because I won't lend him my U2 album,'

the one with acne says. 'He wants to tape it and I told him to go buy his own.'

'What'd he say?'

The one with acne looks over at Dixie, takes a long drag on the cigarette, and blows the smoke out the side of her mouth. She returns the butt to her friend. 'He said, "Fuck me in the ass, cunt," and gave me the finger.'

The girl with braces giggles.

Dixie is applying more mascara to her eyes.

Another girl comes in, a senior with hair dyed so black it is almost blue. Other than that she dresses in very expensive sports clothes. The collar of her polo shirt is worn fashionably up. A white sweater is tied around her waist.

'Quit smoking in here,' she tells the two younger girls. 'You're stinking the place up.' She waves her hand in front of her face.

The girl with braces tosses the cigarette into the nearest toilet. It sizzles loudly. The two girls leave.

The senior leans over the sink, cups one hand under her right eye, and pops out her contact lens into her hand. She removes a plastic bottle from her purse, squirts the lens, replaces it in her eye, blinks rapidly, then leaves.

Dixie is alone for a moment, staring into the mirror, carefully applying mascara to erase fifteen years of aging. She realizes how rare and precious this moment of being alone is here. It is the way she felt when she had guard duty at the jail. Never alone. The thought isn't even completed when the door opens and three more girls come in chattering. Two go to different stalls, the third removes her earrings, replaces them with a different pair, shrugs, adds yet another pair, shrugs, then adds the original pair. Each ear has three earrings now. During the whole process of peeing and earring changing, the three girls have not stopped talking.

Dixie watches her eyes in the mirror as she circles them with eyeliner pencil. She is lucky and knows it. Her mother is Iowan, but her father is Chinese. His Chinese genes have given her the smooth skin and slightly tilted eyes that keep her looking younger than her years. This is one of the reasons Captain Janeway finds her so valuable working undercover. She has a range of ages from eighteen to forty. She could show Lynda Kramer, famous actress, a thing or two out here, where if you screw up your performance the critics don't kill you, the audience does.

Most people miss the Oriental heritage in her face because of the sandy hair. Her mother's contribution. That and eight years of piano lessons before she died of a malignant melanoma hidden in her pubic hairs. What was surprising about that was that Dixie's father was a doctor, an internist who had never noticed that his wife had a mole on her pussy that was turning black and ugly. Dixie had always sensed things were strained between them, but only after her mother died did she realize to what extent.

Dixie's father, despite his forty years in this country, still speaks with a heavy Chinese accent almost indecipherable to Dixie's friends. His practice is in Santa Monica. After his wife's death, Dr. Lo had abandoned his internist practice to devote himself to acupuncture. At the time, Dixie thought it might be some attempt of his to return to his Asian roots, as if he had somehow defiled his ancestors by marrying the blond piano teacher from Iowa. His practice became an enormous success. He was flown all over the world to stick needles in celebrities. He treated Teddy Kennedy's bad back, George Wallace's dead legs, Kareem Abdul Jabaar's migraine headaches. Once—and this Dixie read about in one of her father's medical journals—he had been flown to Mexico to see this wealthy man's wife who had been in a coma for two weeks. According to the article, because her father never talked about it, he had entered her hospital room, examined her for fifteen minutes, stuck a needle in her left foot, and she had immediately awakened from the coma. Her father had made several trips back to China now, bringing back photographs of women watching, smiling happily, while doctors performed a Caesarian birth on them. Even patients with eyes open, smiling, a thorny crown of needles haloing their shaved heads while surgeons poked through their open skulls at the exposed brain.

In high school, Dixie had typed her father's medical articles about Chinese herbal medicine for him. Occasionally, she tried making sense of them, but too much of it was steeped in the ancient philosophies. The world divided into five symbolic elements: Wood, Water, Metal, Earth, Fire. Each element generates another element while at the same time subjugating another element. Wood generates Fire, but Wood subjugates Earth. Dixie thought of it as the old hammer, scissors, paper game. Paper covers hammer, but hammer smashes scissors.

The only paper of his she can clearly remember anymore is the one she typed for him on *malva verticillata*, or *dong kui zi*. Also called farmer's tobacco. The seeds were said to help people having trouble urinating, but also facilitate secretion in breast-feeding mothers. Dixie had always thought that an odd combination. Surely piss and mother's milk weren't related. One was poison, the other nourishment.

As his business increased, her father's English worsened. They had never been close, but now visiting him was like seeing a complete foreigner. Except for an occasional phone call for his birthday and at Christmas, Dixie had no contact with him.

The name Dixie had been her mother's idea. A name

so utterly American, she couldn't be mistaken for anything but a homegrown native. Cooper was Dixie's husband's name. After the divorce, she kept it.

'You work out or what,' the girl with all the earrings asks, looking at Dixie's muscular legs.

'Yeah,' Dixie says. 'I go to the gym with my mom.'

One of the girls comes out of the stall zipping the back of her skirt.

'Aren't you afraid?' the earring girl asks.

'Of what?'

'I don't know, scaring the guys away. Getting too buffed.'

The girl zipping her skirt agrees. 'Tim says girls with muscles are too much.'

The other girl comes out of the stall. 'I think it looks cool. I'd love to have muscles.'

They have cut Dixie completely out of the conversation and they leave the rest room still discussing the matter. Dixie hears the word 'dikeoid' just as the door closes behind them.

She walks down the hall, stops at her locker for her history book, and continues toward her next class. She passes the cafeteria and wrinkles her nose at the medicinal smell of the institutional food. She thinks back on the meal last night at the restaurant and wishes now she'd eaten more of it. Then she remembers Trina's idea for the Men Menu and smiles. Perhaps she should put Kevin Peterson on the menu. He is nice looking, although he combs his hair straight back and the bald spots on the sides make him look a little like an eagle. He's intelligent, has a sense of humor, isn't a felon . . .

'Yo, Dixie Cup.' Joseph Little, purveyor of fine narcotics, is suddenly walking next to her. He is California handsome, sun-blond hair, colorful shirt with a silk tie carelessly knotted just so, royal blue suspenders, a shapeless linen sports jacket, an expensive trigold watchband to hold a campy Gumby watch. 'Where to?'

'History.'

'The World According to Filborne, huh?' His hand was on the small of her back.

'I don't think she likes me.'

'She doesn't like anybody who isn't dead or quotable.' His hand slips down to the top of her ass. His fingers scratch at the fabric of her skirt.

She twists away from him. 'I'm already on Peterson's shit list. I don't need anymore trouble.'

'You're still mad about that little hickey, aren't you?' He places his fingertip against her neck, looking for it. He rubs the spot and she winces slightly. 'There it is. You covered it with makeup. How modest of you.'

'I haven't been here that long, Joe. I don't need a reputation.'

'Reputation?' He laughs. 'How quaint. You sound like a Fifties movie.'

Dixie is worried she may be blowing it. 'Fuck you, man,' she says and walks quickly away.

'Hey, I'm sorry.' He catches up and walks with her. 'I can be a jerk sometimes. I don't mean anything. I just like you, that's all. No big deal.'

Dixie looks at him. He is truly gorgeous. He is also a straight-A student. His parents appear to be happily married, both working professionals. His older sister graduated three years ago and is studying architecture at San Luis Obispo. But if Dixie threw him up against the wall right now and patted him down, she'd undoubtedly find cocaine, marijuana, pills, and maybe even heroin on him. So far she had found no evidence that he took the stuff himself, only that he sold it. The question now was, who did he buy it from?

'I like you too, Joe,' Dixie says. 'But you are a jerk sometimes.'

He smiles. 'I'm working on it. I expect to be jerk-free by the summer.'

Dixie laughs, kisses him on the cheek, then ducks into the classroom. Mrs. Filborne is writing on the blackboard, 1873 in large letters. She takes her eyes off the blackboard to watch Dixie walk to her desk. Finally she faces the rest of the students and says, 'Now, class, what's so special about 1873?'

9

Trina sits behind two guys in rags. They smell like lemon-scented furniture polish. They are unshaven and scratch their necks a lot with dirty ragged fingernails. Watching them scratch makes her feel itchy and she finds herself scratching her own neck. She doesn't move, however, because she is nicely hidden by these two. She is spying.

At forty minutes after ten o'clock the city clerk once again calls roll. The Los Angeles City Council is supposed to begin its meetings at ten, but these meetings never begin on time. A quorum of ten of the fifteen council members is required to start. Only eight are here now, including the object of Trina's spying, Carla Bennington.

Councilwoman Bennington is sitting at her desk talking on the telephone. While talking, she peers down her nose through bifocals at the pink phone message slips her female aide is handing her one at a time. She laughs into the phone, her head thrown back with glee. Her laughter bounces off the polished marble surroundings. One of the other council members looks up from his newspaper, smiles, then returns to the paper. It is that kind of laugh. Trina finds herself smiling too.

Carla Bennington hangs up the telephone, hands two of the pink slips back to her aide, and begins to pore over some papers in front of her. Even from here, Trina can sense the woman's energy. She is forty-six, with long black hair that drapes neatly over her shoulders. A gray streak two inches wide starts at her widow's peak and continues back, curves around to the left, and tapers off as it mingles with the rest of her hair. She parts it in the middle like early Joan Baez and wears unflattering suits that hang shapeless on her trim body. She wears no rings, a simple Timex watch, and earrings completely inappropriate to her face, hair, and clothing. She dresses like a mother completely outfitted in Mother's Day gifts from her small children.

Trina writes all this down in her notebook.

The clerk calls roll again and finally there is a quorum. A few more scruffy men and women shuffle in and take seats in the audience. Today is a discussion about the homeless. Several well-dressed businessmen from China-town are disturbed that the city is housing the homeless in hotels there. Both sides will plead their cases. The five-minute speaking limit rule will be strictly enforced.

Trina gets up and leaves. Now that Carla Bennington is occupied for the next few hours, Trina can get to work.

She climbs the stairs and walks down the hallway, stopping at a public phone to call her gynecologist. She makes an appointment for tomorrow afternoon. She already knows for certain that she is pregnant, but she wants to make it official. After she hangs up the phone, she searches for the office where she has her secret meeting.

'You're late,' Howdy says as Trina enters his office.

'How late?'

Howdy looks at his watch. 'An hour.'

'Hell, that's not late for me.'

'That's true.' He nods.

Trina goes around his desk, leans over, kisses him on the forehead, wipes the lipstick off his skin with her finger-tips. She licks her lips as if tasting something. 'You using moisturizing cream now, Howdy?'

'Count the wrinkles, sweetheart. One for each birthday plus two for every year we dated.'

'We dated for two months, kiddo. Two month over summer because we were in summer school and most of the rest of the kids in summer school were gorps.'

'Skags.' He laughs, stands up. 'Let's talk somewhere else, okay? Somewhere private.'

'Sure.'

She lets him lead her down the hall. He is making this more cloak-and-daggerish than necessary, but she plays along. Howdy White works for Councilman Nicastro, so it isn't exactly out of line for him to be talking to a representative from The Great Pretender, Cory Meyers. The twist, though, is that Howdy is engaged to Lila Steinmann, the shapely aide who'd been handing Carla Bennington her pink phone messages.

Howdy leads Trina down several dark corridors, the glossy marble floors reflecting the dim overhead lighting like lily pads in a scummy pond. They pass several council members' offices, with their little shingles hanging out announcing name and district. They don't speak. Hardly anyone does in the hallways. Voices carry.

Finally Howdy stops in front of a door with no shingle. He knocks. When there is no answer, he opens the door. Several desks are stacked on top of one another. Chairs and boxes are also stacked along the wall.

'We'd better hurry,' Howdy says. 'Councilman Shea likes to come in here and smoke a joint during break.'

'You're kidding?'

'No.' Howdy looks very serious. 'He has kidney cancer. The chemotherapy is wiping him out. The dope seems to help.'

Trina knows about the cancer. His seat is not yet up for re-election, but she's already been approached by two hopeful candidates who are planning to run as soon as he dies or steps down.

Howdy gestures around the room. 'They're going to make this either a day-care room for building employees with small children, or another conference room, depending.'

'Depending on what?'

'The outcome of this election. All plans are on hold until we see who's in and who's out.'

'You're sitting pretty. Nicastro hardly has to campaign.'

'You want me to feel guilty?'

'A little, yes. He's such a schmuck.'

'Yes, but he's a Hispanic schmuck. And I'm the token Jewboy on his staff. He's running against two other Hispanic candidates, a black woman and two white businessmen this time. Any one of them would be better than Nicastro, but he's been in the office so long they'll have to catch him with his hand in the till before they can shake him out of office.'

'From what I hear, that's not impossible.'

Howdy smiles. 'That would put me out of a job.'

Now they were getting down to it. Trina unstacks one of the chairs and sits down. 'There are other people you could work for.'

'Oh?' He tries to look innocent, but the god of that had left him long ago. He merely looks more devious.

'I take it there's no room on Carla Bennington's staff,' Trina says. 'After all, you do have connections there.'

'She's happy with her current aides.'

'There will be new members of the council after this election.'

'Sure, but they already have a loyal staff.'

'There's always room for a smart, knowledgeable man.'

'Your word?'

Trina hesitates. She hasn't discussed this with The

114

Candidate yet. But she is sure he will go along with her suggestion. 'If what you have is helpful.'

'Ah, the big If.'

'What'd you expect? Unconditional surrender?'

Howdy hops up onto one of the desks. 'Your word is gold with me, sweetheart.'

Trina looks at him with curiosity. Yesterday she couldn't remember if she'd had sex a few days earlier with The Candidate. But today she remembers with unnatural clarity the only time she'd slept with Howdy White. In his dorm room at the University of Redlands. She'd fumbled with the foam contraceptive. He'd watched her inject it and made a kind of sour face. During the actual intercourse, her legs sticking straight up in the air, his roommate had stumbled in drunk, a six-pack of Coors in each hand. She'd looked up over Howdy's sweaty back, between her stiff legs upright as goal posts, and stared at the reeling roommate. She tried to tell Howdy, calling him, punching his arm, but he didn't seem to notice or thought her punches were signs of urgent passion and quickened his pumping. The roommate grinned at Trina, winked, then quietly left, locking the door behind him.

One of the reasons they'd split up was because they couldn't find anyplace to have sex again. Trina's dorm room was out because her roommate was a hypochondriac who never left the room except for class, and immediately rushed back for her medication and a nap. Motels were out because both were broke. Howdy's room was out because she couldn't stand the thought of seeing the roommate again. It all worked out okay. Howdy started dating Gretchen Fowler, whose roommate had dropped out midway through the semester with hepatitis and had a dorm room to herself. Trina had married Howdy's roommate, Rob Barre.

Now looking at Howdy, though, Trina finds him a

perfect candidate for the Menu. Lanky, dressed for success, a thick moustache, intelligent. Yes, he was engaged, but that only meant intentions to be married. Until a better offer came along.

'So when's the wedding?' Trina asks.

'We haven't set an actual date yet. Lila's waiting for the election to be over.'

'And you?'

'I'm just waiting.'

Perfect for Barcy, Trina decides. Smart but not brainy, manipulative but not a martyr. Not like Eric.

'I don't have much time, Trina,' Howdy says.

'Then tell me what you know.'

'Agreed that if Cory wins, I get a staff position commensurate with my current position?'

'Agreed.'

'With a ten percent raise.'

'Five percent.'

'Shit, Trina, we're old school chums.'

'Not quite. I went to the school of hard knocks, Howdy.'

'Hard knockers is more like it.' He frowns.

She grins. 'Five percent.'

He sighs. 'Okay, Lila isn't exactly a gossip about Carla. In fact, she's about as dedicated to the woman as you can be. Lila's still a little naive that way. If she'd been around when Eugene McCarthy was running, he'd probably been president. She even worked on Gary Hart's campaign before the big sexposé, boffing in Bimini.' He grins and shakes his head. 'She'll learn.'

'I thought you didn't have much time?' Trina says flatly.

'This is all I know: Carla gets up about five in the morning every fucking morning, weekends included, and jogs about eight miles. Her ex-husband Phil sometimes joins her, isn't that cute? They've been divorced for four years but that hasn't hurt her any. If anything, it probably increased her popularity. Attractive, sexy woman on the loose.'

'I know all this, Howdy.'

'Let me do it my way, okay?' There is an edge in his voice, but he quickly smiles to show no hard feelings. Howdy does not like to be bossed, a condition common among those who know they are smarter and more capable than the person they work for. But Howdy is also smart enough to recognize he does not have the kind of personality that will win elections for himself. He is too direct and intellectual. This scares voters. 'She has two daughters. Erin is at UCLA, Alice is waiting tables in Venice Beach living with a performance artist.'

'Ah, an artist,' Trina says. 'Drugs?'

'Probably. I can't verify.'

'What's Carla doing about it?'

'What can she do? Lila says it's eating her up. Alice is twenty-two, quit college after one year, has lived with a variety of men, all artists of some sort.'

'Arrests?'

'She was stopped once for a broken taillight. Cops found a half-smoked joint on the car floor. Looked like she'd just dumped it. They took her in but as soon as they found out who she was they let her go with a warning.'

'Carla lean on the cops?'

'No. She didn't even know about it until Alice was out. Tell you the truth, even if she'd known I don't think she would've leaned on the cops.'

'Come on, Howdy. She has a say in overtime pay for cops. That's a lot of muscle.'

'And that may be why the cops let Alice go. I'm just saying Carla didn't ask and probably wouldn't have asked.'

Trina sighs. 'So far you're talking yourself into unemployment, pal. No one's that clean. She's good looking, sexy, bright, powerful. Who's she fucking?'

'She dates occasionally. Always very public places, always someone safe. One of three guys: David Kraft, the electronics millionaire; Stephen Pomadeer, the millionaire TV producer; Evan Frankel, the millionaire plastic surgeon.'

'I see a common denominator. Anything there? Private campaign loans.'

'None that Lila knows about.'

'What about the plastic surgeon? Some after-hours nip and tucking, a secret face-lift?'

'Not that Lila knows about.'

'What the fuck *does* Lila know?' Trina asks in frustration.

Howdy smiles and Trina knows he's been saving something. 'Carla does take off for weekends.'

'Gosh, wow. Stop the presses.'

Howdy laughs. 'No, I mean, she goes off on weekends, sometimes even during the week. She never gives a place or phone number. Instead she calls in her office twice a day in case something comes up.'

'How often does she do this?'

'Every month at least.'

Trina thinks about this. 'Could be she just needs to get away. City Council is a demanding job, she works hard at it.'

'Sounds like you like her,' Howdy teases.

'She's good. That doesn't mean someone else wouldn't be better.'

'Hey, no need to convince me. As far as I'm concerned, whoever pays my salary is better.'

'Where do you think she goes? Does Lila ever speculate?'

'Yeah, sometimes when we're naked in bed we make up scenarios. Secret Colombian drug connections to finance her campaigns, teenage surfers she picks up and takes to Hawaii, two men in black socks with leather hoods and her alone in some basement in Pasadena. Afterwards, Lila and I make love.'

'Thanks for sharing that special moment.' Trina stands up and paces. 'This is very unusual. I wonder where she goes, what she does.'

The door suddenly opens and Councilwoman Carla Bennington is standing in the doorway. She looks first at Howdy, then at Trina. There is no expression on her face. She tucks her hair, including the gray steak behind her ear.

'Howdy, Howdy,' she says.

'Hello, Councilwoman Bennington.' Howdy is on his feet, standing straight and looking guilty. 'Do you know Trina Bedford, the Bedford Agency?'

'Nice to meet you,' Councilwoman Bennington says, looking at Trina.

Without hesitation, Trina walks over and shakes her hand. She is taller and bustier than Carla and uses her height and chest to overcome any awkwardness caused by the situation. 'Nice meeting you too, Councilwoman.'

Councilwoman Bennington glances at Howdy. 'I was looking for Councilman Shea. Have you see him?'

Howdy shakes his head. 'Not this morning.'

'Thanks.' She looks back at Trina but does not smile. 'Good luck,' she says. She leaves, closing the door behind her.

Trina is wondering what she means by that. Good luck with the campaign. Or good luck trying to dig something up on me.

'I'm in big trouble,' Howdy says, frowning. 'Lila is going to slice, dice, and julienne my nuts.'

'Tell her the truth, you were spying for me.'

'I'm better off if she thinks we were in here screwing. That's understandable. Betraying Carla is worse.'

'From what I can tell about the woman, she probably won't even say anything to Lila.'

Howdy considers that for a moment. 'You're right. I'm safe.' He opens the door, turns around, wags a finger at Trina. 'You're the one in trouble. Carla knows you're sniffing around.' He smiles at her. 'You are still sniffing around, aren't you?'

Trina playfully pushes him out the door. 'Every time I'm alone in a room with you, someone walks in. Explain that.'

'Because every time you're alone in a room with me, you're doing something nasty.'

Trina walks silently beside Howdy as they stroll down the corridor. 'Yeah,' she finally says, 'I'm still sniffing around.'

10

'I really don't understand, any of this,' Ben says. 'Maybe I'm too dumb.'

Barcelona says, 'Just be patient.'

Ben Leopold nods uncertainly. He is sixty-two years old, three years from mandatory retirement. He repairs photocopiers for Xerox. His fingernails are remarkably clean but slightly grooved, as if scrubbed regularly but with bristles that are too hard. He is in Barcelona's Early British Poetry course where they are currently studying John Milton's *Samson Agonistes*.

Barcelona sits behind the brown metal desk in her office in the Literature and Language Building. Ben sits miserably next to her desk holding his term paper about John Milton's imagery. His clean fingers have worried the erasable bond into permanent wrinkles. She recognizes the accountant-fine red pen marks on the front page of his paper, her scribbled notes in the margins telling him what's wrong. The grade is hidden on the last page, but she can see it plainly through the top five pages as if she had X-ray vision. C minus.

'Well,' he says, 'if I'm not too dumb, then I must be too old.'

'Come on, Ben, let's not play this game.'

He looks over his shoulder through the narrow strip of glass next to the office door. The glass runs floor to ceiling and is maybe a foot wide. It is embedded with heavy wire mesh. Ben points at the Literature and Language secretary's office through the glass. 'I was fixing your department's machine last semester. You guys jam that thing up maybe once a month, don't ask me how. I overheard you talking about poetry to some kids and figured, what the hell, I'm gonna retire in a couple years and I don't really know much about anything except photocopiers, so I signed up for your course.' He runs his pale hand through his short grey hair. 'Dumb.'

'Is this where you say, "Can't teach an old dog new tricks"?'

Ben smiles. 'Would it help?'

'John Milton was sixty-three years old when he finished *Samson Agonistes*. And he was blind.'

'You're just like my son, won't let me get away with anything.'

Barcelona takes the paper from his hand and goes over the flaws in it point by point. Ben Leopold hunches over the desk and listens. He nods, asks questions, argues occasionally, laughs good-naturedly at some of his own statements. Outside the office, through the strip of wire-meshed glass, Barcelona can see another of her students standing, peering in. She holds up four fingers and waves him away, telling him four more minutes. Ben looks over his shoulder, sees the other student walking away.

'I should go now,' he says.

'No rush. You understand my comments any better?'

'Sure,' he says. 'I'm not blind.'

She laughs. 'Rewrite the paper and I'll change your grade.'

'What if the paper is worse?'

'Then I'll change your grade to a lower one.'

'You be nice to me, young lady. I'm a widower and there aren't that many eligible bachelors around anymore.

I read last week that after thirty there are eight women for every man. Couple more years, I'm gonna start looking pretty good to you.'

'See you in class, Ben.'

'Did I mention my substantial pension?'

'How substantial?' she says.

He laughs and leaves. The other student, Grant Treemond, enters. He is eighteen, gangly, very serious. He carries a battered skateboard under one arm. His hair is cut so short he looks almost bald, except for the eight-inch lock of hair that sticks out of the back of his head and is braided and tied with a lime green shoestring. 'I wanted to talk about my paper,' he says as he plops down in the chair. He sets his skateboard under his feet and rocks it back and forth on the blue carpet.

'You got an A on your paper, Grant,' Barcelona tells him.

'A minus,' he corrects her. 'I don't agree with some of your comments.' He takes his paper out of his backpack. It is folded into a little square the size of a baseball card. He unfolds it and lays it out on her desk. There are hardly any red marks on it. This was the best paper in the class. 'On page two,' he says, 'where I compare Homer's blindness and the blinding of the Cyclops with Milton's blindness and the blinding of Samson. You didn't like that.'

'I like the idea, but you never do anything with it. You mention it as being perhaps significant, but you never explain how or why. It's basically an aside that detracts from the main thesis of your paper. Either develop it or kick it loose.'

Grant thinks about that a moment then nods. He flips the page. 'What about this?'

Barcelona reads her note. 'Okay, here you compared Delilah in the poem with her biblical counterpart. You

123

mention that in the poem Milton made her Samson's wife, though in the Bible they aren't married. But you fail to comment on why he did that. Why make such a drastic change?'

'Maybe he was having marital problems and wanted to say something about marriage, you know, a dig at his wife. The old goat was married three times.'

'Maybe.'

'Or maybe he thought the illicit nature of their affair in the Bible undermined the impact of the betrayal.'

Barcelona smiles. 'Maybe.'

Grant stares at her a minute, then smiles too. 'Maybe? That's like saying, "Look it up," right? Look It Up. The teachers' national anthem.'

'In the Peace Corps they have a saying: "Give a hungry man a fish and he eats one meal; teach a hungry man how to fish and he eats forever."'

'You in the Peace Corps?'

'Almost.'

He shakes his head. 'I should've figured you for an ex-hippie.'

The office door opens and Harley Buss, the English Department chairman, sticks his head in. 'I hear you're about to become rich and famous.'

'Hi, Harley.'

He steps in with one blue-jeaned leg. He is holding a steaming mug of coffee. He has sleepy blue eyes, perfectly coiffed gray-black hair, a low friendly voice. Barcelona and Harley have been dating casually for a few months, since Christmas break. Over Christmas vacation Harley's young girlfriend left him to become an actress. He is forty-five, the young actress is twenty-two, a former student from his Shakespeare class which he taught before he became department chairman. After she moved to L.A. he was so depressed that everyone in the department was

124

worried about him. One day after class, Barcelona had stopped by his office to try to cheer him up. They ended up going out to dinner. He is extremely bright and charming, handsome in a boyish way. They slept together after a couple of weeks, not that Barcelona wouldn't have sooner, but he'd never made the move. Finally when they did go to bed, the lovemaking had been somewhat lethargic on his part. Workmanlike, she kept thinking while he crawled around her body. As if he had a standard repertoire of techniques, a sexual Things To Do list that he completed and checked off. Afterward they lay in bed watching TV and he made funny jokes about the shows. She laughed until she ached, enjoyed that part of the evening much more than the sex.

'So you're on the brink of celebrity,' Harley says from the office doorway.

'Oh?'

'The screenplay. For Lynda Kramer.'

'Ah,' she says.

'You doing a script for Lynda Kramer?' Grant asks.

'Trying to.'

Harley sips his steaming coffee. 'Lunch later?'

'Maybe.' She isn't being coy, she just doesn't like it when faculty pop into her office during a conference and then talk around the student as if he isn't there.

'We're proud of you,' Harley says. He sips his coffee, winks, and is gone.

'You're going to make a fucking fortune,' Grant says, snatching up his paper. 'No more of these dumb Milton papers for you. Go for it, man.' Then he too is gone.

Word is out. Barcelona has mentioned it only to her office mate, Susan Mesa, as they had exchanged news that morning before class the same as they had every morning for the past six years. Now everyone knows. Barcelona doesn't mind; already she's been congratulated by half

125

a dozen faculty members. This surprises her more than anything, because these are the same people who have never read any of her novels because they weren't 'serious' literature. When Barcelona had sold her first novel, she had been so excited that she threw a little party for her friends in the department. She had rented the recreation room at her apartment complex. Eric had placed a wooden door over the pool table and they used it to serve the cold cuts and dips and extremely cheap champagne. Everyone showed up, congratulated her. She thought that during the weeks to come they would mention the book, how they liked or didn't like it. Finally, after asking around she discovered that no one had actually read it or even bought it. 'I don't read science fiction,' a few had said. Others, 'Over summer vacation, I promise.'

And so it had continued ever since. The rest of the faculty thought she was wealthy because of her book sales, having no idea how small the advances are. When she joined the other teachers in an after-school drink, they always expected her to pick up the check. She stopped joining them.

She wrote, she taught. A full-time teaching load consisted of four courses. Everyone taught two sections of Freshman Composition, which was why they were so proprietary over the one or two courses they got to pick for themselves. Three years ago Barcelona had petitioned to teach an introductory creative writing course, but the faculty committee had turned her down, as they have every year since then. 'While we applaud your ambition,' Foster Malone, the novel writing teacher had explained, 'we don't think the publication of two genre works qualifies you to teach the complexities of the creative process. We are, after all, a college and should be focusing on relevant literature.'

Foster Malone is Irish with a rolling brogue and a gray-flecked beard and mussed long hair that shouts Writer! ten feet in every direction around him. He has had eight poems published in Ireland and six in this country in the twenty-two years he's been teaching at Sand Coast College. The other creative writing teacher, Hester Hoffman, had a published novel sixteen years ago, but hasn't sold anything since. Instead she opened her own literary agency and has sold five of her student's novels during those years. She agreed with Foster. 'It's not enough to have published,' she'd said. 'One must be able to teach the delicate craft of writing.'

So Barcelona has been delegated to the ghetto of pre-eighteenth-century British literature. The twentieth century was already staked out by Gary Lehman. Nineteenth-century poetry belonged to Barbara Foley; nineteenth-century novels was Arnold Dickey's domain. Shakespeare, which was within her allotted time frame, was the exclusive property of Marvin Endright.

Finally, Barcelona stopped her petitions. She continued teaching Milton, Chaucer, Malory, Marlowe, Donne, and the others as she had done since graduate school. No one else wanted them, they required too much preparation and weren't as popular with the students. Unpopular courses risked being canceled unless they had a minimum of twenty-two students sitting in their desks on the first day of class. If your class got canceled, you were assigned yet another section of Freshman Composition.

Now, however, Barcelona is thinking of quitting. The idea has come upon her suddenly and takes her by surprise. Never before has she even considered such a move. Such a drastic change. She is not fond of changes anyway, especially drastic ones. Still, she is thrilled at the daring of such a thought. Though she doesn't make as much money as the others imagine, she makes enough to support herself without her teaching income. And now that she is writing a screenplay, opportunities seem to be everywhere around her. She gathers her papers into her briefcase and decides she could live without Grant's battered skateboard and Ben's grooved fingernails.

Barcelona is eating onion rings. They are called onion fritters by the fancy restaurant, but that is because they are very thin. In no way do they resemble any kind of fritters. Harley Buss is sitting across from her eating the wheat fettuccine.

'Why did you quit teaching, Harley?' she asks him. She figures it is okay to ask him this now because they spent the first thirty minutes of lunch talking about Debbie, his former actress-girlfriend. She came by last night to pick up a few clothes she'd left behind. She cried, said she missed him, that she wished they were back together again. When he suggested she move back in, she started screaming at him that he was doing it again, trying to 'kill her ambition.'

'Can you figure her out?' he'd asked Barcelona after they'd ordered. She realized now that they started every date with a discussion of Debbie or how well Harley was coping without Debbie. He always asked Barcelona's assessment of the progress of his split-up.

'Were you killing her ambition?' Barcelona asked him.

'What ambition? She wanted to be an actress.'

Barcelona didn't know what else to say. 'Shouldn't she be in Los Angeles then, or New York?'

'I wanted children. So did she. We both did.'

'Did she have an agent? She needs an agent if she wants to be a professional actress.'

'She has a portfolio. Photographs of her in different outfits and moods. She drove up to L.A. a couple of times for auditions but she told me she hated it. Too humiliating. I was trying to protect her.'

'Catcher in the rye, huh?'

'Maybe Holden had something there.'

The meal had come then and Barcelona said nothing. She ate the blackened Cajun chicken sandwich.

'You know,' he said. 'I saw her act a couple of times. Local plays. Chekhov's *Three Sisters*. Something else, uh, *Luv* by Murray Schisgal. To tell you the truth, she wasn't very good.'

'I don't think that's the point, Harley.'

He sucked in a stray fettuccine and nodded. 'I know. The point is I'm too old for her. I know some people talked about our age difference, God knows I sure would have. What was the talk around the department? That I was afraid of women my own age, doubted my own masculinity, wanted to play Big Daddy? What? You can tell me.'

'All of the above.'

'People don't understand. I mean, I've been married twice before, both times to women my own age, one had a goddamn Ph.D., the other made more money than I did, working in a loan company. So I'm not afraid of strong, smart women. I just wanted a fucking family. Wife, kids, house, the whole deal. Now all I've got is the fucking house.' The house, Barcelona thought, that really is the sad part. Harley had sold his old house and bought a large five-bedroom home in Laguna Hills with a large yard and plenty of room for children. He and Debbie had picked it out after a year of house-hunting. Escrow closed last month and now he was on the hook for the house payments. He'd moved in by himself last weekend. 'The house just makes things worse,' he said. 'Makes me think about the kids we were going to have.'

He mentions kids on every date. Barcelona always finds that topic uncomfortable. She feels he is somehow interviewing her, trying to get her opinion about having children. She doesn't have an opinion, which is why she feels uncomfortable. Some days she is certain she wants to have a baby, the next day she is relieved not to have one.

Barcelona repeats her question, 'Why did you quit teaching?'

'I didn't quit, I'm chairman of the department. The Big Enchilada.'

'But you don't teach anymore, you're an administrator.'

'You're not going to start in on me, are you? Teachers versus administrators crap.'

'No. I'm just curious. You were an excellent teacher. I constantly heard students praising your courses. They loved you and from what I could tell, learned a hell of a lot.'

He looks wistful. 'I was good. But the lure of money, power, sex, the awe of my fellow teachers, human sacrifices in my name. It was too much!' He cackles like a mad pirate then laughs. 'Why? You thinking about taking the money and running? Going Hollywood on us?'

'Fuck you.'

'Ah, a raw nerve.'

Barcelona shakes her head. 'The same bunch of faculty members who've always been so contemptuous are now congratulating me on writing a screenplay. A screenplay, for God's sake, the most mundane of forms.'

'They're impressed by the glamour, the bucks.'

'Swell. You don't see any hypocrisy here.'

'Sure, but you make it sound like a conspiracy. Let me remind you, I've only read one of your novels myself.'

'You don't try to hide your shallowness,' she says.

'Please, your flattery embarrasses me.' He laughs and pays the bill. She lets him.

Outside they sit by the fountain and enjoy the sun.

'I have to get home,' she says. 'Fame and fortune and Lynda Kramer are calling to me.'

'Just a few minutes,' he says, tilting his head back and

130

looking straight into the bright sun. When he looks back at her, he is squinting. They sit quietly for a few minutes and Barcelona thinks how pleasant this is. Not sexy, not heart-thumping panties-wet passion, just pleasant. Nice. For some reason she thinks of Trina's menu and wonders if she should include Harley. She imagines Trina or Dixie going out with him, Diva and he would never do. She feels absolutely no jealousy. She sees them in bed, Trina's large breasts swaying over his open mouth. Nothing. Dixie's oak-hard thigh muscles flexing as she lifts her hips to his. *Nada.* Still, there's no way she's going to get involved in such a ridiculous idea. Men-u. Christ.

She watches Harley as he watches the women walk by. The restaurant is nestled between two towering glass office buildings. The clouds are mirrored in the buildings, making them seem somehow reverent, modest about their own existence. Totems in awe of Nature. Barcelona smiles at such thoughts. Don't put any crap like that in the screenplay, she thinks.

Well-dressed women from the buildings walk by in groups of three or more on their way to or from lunch. Their high heels clack out a military cadence. Harley is grinning as he watches them.

'So this is girl-watching, huh?' Barcelona says.

'Yup. The real thing. Up close and personal.'

'That's all there is to it? Just sit and stare?'

'Well, some guys may shout things, make rude noises, but that's a rarity among the true aficionados. Mostly we just stare.'

'What do you think about? Screwing them?'

Harley looks at her with amusement. 'I can't tell you. That's guy stuff. Telling you would be breaking the code. It'd be like a magician telling how he made the rabbit disappear.'

'Consider it research.'

Harley sighs. 'I'm probably making a big mistake here, but okay. I will share my uncensored thoughts with you as I girl-watch. However, you must promise not to hold anything I say against me. Remember, everything I say comes directly from the id, unfiltered by super ego.'

'Christ,' she says.

Three women in their twenties walk by. Harley puts on his sunglasses and looks in the opposite direction.

'See,' he says, 'this is how you can stare at them without seeming like a lech. You have the sunglasses on so they can't see your eyes.'

'Obviously.'

'But the trick here is to look away from them, toward where they are walking. That way, when they walk into your sight, they are walking away from you and you can stare at their legs and asses but you don't look like you've been staring at them. They just happened to wander into your line of vision.'

'Ingenious.'

'Fucking A, kid.'

'Okay, but what do you think about when you stare at their legs and asses?'

He tilts his head at the three women as they walk away. 'They all have fat asses. The one on the left in the red has nice ankles. The one in the middle has too much hair spray, I'd have to be drunk to go to bed with her. The one on the end looks like she likes to give head, but she looks dumb too, giggles too much. Probably watches "Three's Company" reruns, Harvey Korman is her favorite comedian.'

Barcelona laughs. 'You're a pig.'

'Hey, hey, we made a deal.'

'I'm sorry.' Barcelona is not really offended, she thinks it's funny. More, she finds it oddly erotic to be listening to Harley's commentary on the women passing by.

Four more women come out of the same restaurant they just ate at.

'Uh oh,' Harley says. 'Here comes The Mild Bunch.'

Barcelona notices that, like the other women they've seen, these four all have extraordinarily complex hairdos. Lots of curls and swirls and puffing up. A blow dryer would not be enough for any of them. Electric curlers, a curling iron . . . She thinks of the curling iron that killed Eric's neighbor. The old man, naked, bloated, lying with his one foot propped up against the tub. Luna bent over him huffing air into his dead lungs. She is ashamed at how useless she was in an emergency. Luna, the young keeper of Eric's eight inches of tempered blue steel, knew just what to do. So did Barcelona. The difference, Luna acted.

'Look at that one,' Harley says, chuckling.

'Which one?'

'The blonde in slacks, the one with the panty line.'

'Oh.'

'She'd be my pick of the litter. The two on either end can barely fit into their panty hose. Those babies are on so tight they need an exorcist to get out of them.'

Barcelona laughs and the blonde turns and looks at her. Harley turns his head and pretends to be looking at the restaurant. When she looks away again, he returns his gaze. 'You're gonna queer the whole gig, baby.'

'Does this kind of activity make you talk like that?'

'It puts me in the mood, I pretend to be a poor, ignorant, happy relative. Distant relatives. Stop in for a beer every night at the same bar, talks about the girls walking by outside. I feel less guilty.' He points to the blonde again. 'She's the only one I'd actually want to get naked with. The others should be sent to the glue factory.'

'You're so arrogant. You assume all these women want to sleep with you.'

'Sure.' He stares silently at the women as they enter

133

the office building. 'It would never work out between us though.'

Barcelona is startled, she thinks he is talking about her and Harley.

'She's the kind of woman who has hobbies. Backpacking up steep hills. Bicycling with those dumb helmets with the little mirrors on them, wearing those tight pants that show the bulge in your crotch. Or worse, horseback riding. Yeah, that's probably what she does. Every Sunday we'd be out at some stinking barn fighting the flies, digging horseshit from their hooves. I'd look up and she'd be smiling, talking baby talk to a horse, kissing his snout. Is that what they're called? Snouts?'

'Muzzle, I think.'

'Whatever.' He shakes his head and Barcelona is surprised at how angry he seems. He is not joking now. 'Instead of lying around reading the Sunday paper, going to brunch, maybe taking in a matinee, I'm fucking shoveling straw or hay and busting my nuts on a horse. I love Sunday brunch and the Sunday paper and a Sunday matinee.'

'I didn't know girl-watching could be so complex,' Barcelona says.

He glances over at her and a smile slowly returns to his face. 'It's not as easy as it looks.'

And not very rewarding, she thinks. Harley doesn't daydream about sexual conquests when he ogles these women. He looks into the future, as if all of these panty hose-encased rumps formed some giant fleshy crystal ball. He looks into the future and sees conflict, compromise, and finally failure.

'Maybe she is married,' Barcelona says, trying to cheer him up. 'I think I saw a ring.'

'Maybe,' he says. 'But she's still single. Haven't you heard? Everybody's single, or expecting to be.'

Barcelona is tired of this and starts to get up. He grabs

134

her arm and gestures at the two women walking toward the restaurant.

'Oh, God, look at those two,' he says. 'That hair. My God, she must have washed it in a flushing toilet. She thinks she's real sexy, the way she walks. Those six-inch heels, the black stockings.' He looks at her a while longer. 'Hmmm, she is kind of sexy after all. The one with her though, nice butt and legs, but that face has so much makeup you know she's trying too hard. Too hungry.'

Barcelona looks at her. She is talking animatedly to her sexy friend, but she manages to catch a peek at Harley. Her eyes linger a moment, then flick over to Barcelona. She looks away as quickly as a camera blink. Barcelona tells him, 'She likes you.'

'Gosh, maybe you can call her brother and tell him Harley likes his sister. Then we can meet at the malt shop for a float.'

She ignores his joking. 'What do you mean "too hungry"?'

Harley stands up, takes off his sunglasses. 'Let's go. I've seen enough.'

Barcelona drives home thinking about the screenplay. A black Porsche convertible cuts her off as she tries to change lanes on the freeway. She honks her horn at him and he turns around, smiles, and waves at her. 'The asshole thinks I'm making a pass at him,' she says aloud. Probably all men who drive black Porsche convertibles think all women are making passes at them. She thinks about ramming his rear bumper, see what he thinks of that, but she knows she won't. Still, she drives close enough to him to give him a scare, she hopes. He has a red and black bumper sticker that says: GAS, GRASS, OR ASS. NOBODY RIDES FOR FREE. He waves at her in his morror, pulls out of the lane, and roars away.

Barcelona returns to her screenplay. She already has some ideas on what to keep, what to cut, and which characters need to be consolidated. She is very excited by this project. And not just the challenges of it, but the potential for her future. Her life has followed such a predictable routine over the past decade that she welcomes this new aspect. She has decided to postpone any decision about teaching until she finishes the screenplay. By then it will be summer vacation and she can think more clearly. By then, too, she'll know whether or not she can even write a screenplay.

When she arrives home, there is a UPS package on her doorstep from Roger Carlyle. She tears open the thick mailing envelope while standing on the doorstep. Inside are three scripts. Two are from movies she has seen, the other is a teen sex comedy she avoided. She unlocks her front door and hurries inside with her booty, anxious to get started. She wonders what Lynda Kramer is doing right now, right this second. Is she wondering how the script is coming? Is she having a quiet moment with her husband? Feeding her baby daughter? It seems to Barcelona that Lynda Kramer lives in a world where there are no bad decisions. No fear and trembling. Whatever she decides is the right decision.

Barcelona grabs a Diet Apple Slice and takes it upstairs to her study. On her way up the stairs she flips through one of the scripts to get an idea of proper format. Just as she is about to enter the study, her doorbell rings.

'Damn,' she says but doesn't move. She hasn't decided whether or not to answer it. She knows it is probably some school kid wanting to sell her a subscription to the *Register* or someone from the Fireman's Fund with thirty-three-gallon plastic trash bags for sale. The doorbell rings again and she turns around and skip-hops back down the stairs.

She peeks through the door viewer and sees a distorted pumpkin face. Immediately she opens the door.

'Eric?'

'Hey.' He comes in. They stare at each other a second.

'What's up? I haven't read your thesis yet.'

He shrugs as if his thesis was the least important thing in the world. He sighs sadly and reaches out toward her in a friendly way for a hug. She hesitates, then steps into his arms, gives him an awkward hug, and starts to back away. He doesn't let her. He hugs her tighter. His hand slips down and squeezes her ass.

11

Trina is driving to the house of the father of her baby. She hasn't seen him in three weeks, since the time he impregnated her. She hadn't really expected to see him ever again, unless by accident but she feels she owes it to him to tell him about the baby. Trina can't think of anything worse than one day discovering you have a grown child, realizing you missed out on its growing years. She remembers a few years ago reading about Hugh Hefner being told he had a teenage son. There were photographs in the newspapers of their reunion at the Playboy mission. Hugh Hefner had a pipe in one hand, his arm around the boy. They were both smiling. Hugh Hefner looked genuinely pleased. Months later she read that the blood test on the boy didn't check out and he wasn't really Hugh Hefner's. She wonders whether they still see each other.

Trina has no expectations from this man she is driving to see. Certainly she doesn't want his money, nor does she want to further any relationship between them. This is just a courtesy call.

Their sexual encounter had been totally unexpected. They had both been at the California Women's Press Associates' monthly meeting. Trina has been a member since her days as a reporter for the *Los Angeles Times*. He was one of a panel of three guest speakers, the only man in a roomful of professional women. Each member of the panel was a foreign correspondent returning from some distant hot spot. One of the women, an old news horse with leathery skin and a cigarette constantly hanging from her dry lips, had just returned from Lebanon. The other woman, a young Japanese-American beauty, was a former weather girl, now a local anchorwoman. She had recently gone to Nicaragua with her camera crew. She had heard shooting down the street. They showed film of her reporting the sounds of gunfire, holding her microphone toward the window, then crawling under a bed in her hotel, whispering breathlessly while gunshots continued to crack down the street. The camera stayed on her throughout the brief battle. Afterward, they showed her crawling out from under the bed, looking very serious, declaring that she now knew what these people must be going through. Most of the women in the audience managed to keep a straight face, but a few chuckled. The anchorwoman didn't seem to notice.

Then Jamison spoke. Jamison Levy had just returned from El Salvador. He had slides, black and white, that he took himself. The film had to be smuggled out. Though he didn't say how he did it, he did imply that revealing the hiding place would be personally embarrassing. Some of the slides were humorous, some domestically touching, as if they could have been taken in anyone's home anywhere in the world. But others, the ones he had to smuggle out, they were heartbreaking. Most of them were bloody, small children wandering among piles of mangled dead bodies looking for their lost mothers. A woman arranging the pieces from several corpses, trying to puzzle together the remains of her ten-year-old son. When Jamison spoke of these things, there was the deep power of his convictions in his tone, but there was also the tremor of compassion. He had impressed them all.

Trina couldn't remember who spoke to whom first, or

if they'd even been introduced. Somehow they just wound up chatting together near the open bar. He was drinking ginger ale.

'Too early for you?' she'd asked him, sipping her own scotch and soda.

'It's always too early for me.' He'd smiled. 'I'm an alcoholic.'

'You and about half the people in this room.'

He'd looked around with an appraising eye. 'More like seventy percent. Fifty percent know it, the other twenty don't yet. What's your vice?'

'Toilet paper.'

'Pardon?'

'I use too much.'

He laughed so heartily that she had to laugh too. 'That's the first time a woman has ever admitted anything like that so soon.'

'Hey, get with it. This is the nineties.'

'I know I've been gone awhile, but I thought we were still in the eighties.'

'Technically,' Trina said. 'But I read in *Esquire* magazine that decades never start when they should. Some start early, others late. I've decided that the eighties is too boring and we should start thinking of this as the nineties decade. Maybe it'll be more interesting then.'

He'd given her a funny look and Trina knew right then that they would end up in bed together. They'd gone back to his house in Laguna, made love, and played Scrabble afterward, naked in bed. She won by three points. He had called her a couple of days later and they had talked for forty minutes on the phone about nothing really. Both had laughed a great deal. She had expected him to ask her out, but was relieved when he didn't. That had surprised her. He was a terrific man, witty and charming and pretty damn good in bed. But there was something about him that made

140

her nervous. Maybe his intensity. Maybe she felt a little intimidated by his dedication to his work. Here was a guy who walked among people whose lives were a daily tragedy. He was trying to make the world better. What was she doing? Trying to get a man with perfect teeth elected to the City Council.

She was being unfair to The Candidate. She wasn't just working on his campaign because she'd been hired to. She believed in him, found him to be strong, decisive, humble, intelligent, and informed. He cared about people but wasn't a naive idealist. Trina also knew that if he didn't win this election he would win the next. And after that he would slowly work his way up, perhaps to mayor, then governor, then senator. He had the stuff.

She is driving high up into the hills of Laguna. Some of the hillsides are spotted with the jumbled debris of crushed homes that slid down with the mud after last year's rainy season. She sees one new home being constructed on the ruins of an old home site. She can't decide whether she admires the owner's optimism or condemns his idiocy.

She remembers his street, but can't remember the exact address. All the houses look different, but in a way they all also look the same. The same manic attempt to look individual blurs any substantive distinction. It is like driving around in a huge art gallery filled with giant abstract sculptures. Finally she thinks she recognizes his car, a battered old Datsun with huge rust spots on the rear left fender.

As she walks towards the front door, three marine helicopters buzz overhead. She shades her eyes and looks up at them. They seem to be moving slowly, like green blimps. The little red lights flashing on their bellies seem to be some code meant just for her. She smiles at the notion. What would their message be? Stop where you are! Do not proceed! Go home, bitch.

141

She continues up the walkway and rings the doorbell.

She hears footsteps, then a pause at the door and she knows he is checking her out through the door viewer. She turns her face away and pretends to look at the birds of paradise bushes on either side of the door. She doesn't like the way those door viewers distort your face into something grotesque. Imagine what he would think if he saw her boobs through one of those things.

The door opens and she swings back around to face him. He is wearing a bath towel around his waist and is rubbing his wet hair with another smaller towel. Both towels are black with a single yellow strip running the length of each. They look thick and luxurious.

'Trina?' he says. There is surprise in the way he says her name, but not really in his tone.

'Hi,' Trina replies. 'Got a few minutes?'

He hesitates and makes a slight gesture with his left wrist as if he wishes to check his watch, but stops himself. Maybe because he remembers he isn't wearing one. 'Sure, come on in. I'm running a little late though.'

'Won't take long.'

Once inside, she realizes she has no idea how to tell him. Just announcing that she is pregnant sounds very spiteful or accusatory. If she acts too pleased, he might think she's trying to hook him. Trina now knows she hasn't thought this thing through nearly enough. What if he too is delighted and decides he wants to get married? She hardly even knows him and definitely isn't in love with him. Or he may want to share custody the way Rob shares custody of Karyn. Every time Rob comes for Karyn, Trina's heart contracts into a tight fist and stays that way until he brings her back home. Now that pain will be doubled.

She needs a couple of minutes to compose herself, figure things out. 'Got anything to drink?' she asks. 'Soda water

142

or something. Plain water's fine.' No more booze, she reminds herself, not even beer or wine. Bad for the baby.

'Sure.' He walks out of the room. She watches his toweled behind, the firm tapering thighs, the bulge of calf muscles. No doubt about it, he's still great looking. Whichever one the kid looks like, he or she will be a looker.

Trina looks around the living room trying to get some fix on who this guy is. Last time she was here it had been dark and they had rushed right upstairs to the bedroom. She is impressed with the decor. The walls have salmon-colored textured wallpaper, the carpet is that thick nubbed cotton and still looks new though she remembers he said he'd lived here seven years. The artwork on the walls are original oil paintings, mostly giant brightly colored abstract forms merging with other darker, sharper-edged abstract forms. At the point of merger is a bright white line that looks like a tear in space, a flaming new sun trying to emerge. She recognizes the artist's name from some magazine article she's read someplace.

He returns with a glass of sparkling water and ice. 'You look a little dehydrated.'

'Thanks for noticing. You're looking good too.'

'So, it's like that, huh?' He grins. 'Should I slip into something comfortable, like a catcher's cup?'

Trina laughs. She can't decide what to say. Tell him or not? Yes, he's a goddamn charm machine, a juggernaut of suave. But if she didn't tell him, she'd have the baby all to herself, not have to share it with anyone. She smiles broadly at that idea. Jamison misinterprets the smile, thinking she meant it for him and he smiles back.

'I don't mean to be an ungracious host, Trina,' he says, 'but I really am running late.'

What to do? she wonders. She really doesn't know him

at all. Beneath the charm . . . what? Maybe nothing. There is no way to reason this out, no applicable logic. She can't leave and think it over because she knows if she leaves now she won't ever tell him, her own selfishness will take over. She needs to figure him out, now.

'I was in the neighborhood,' she says. 'Just wanted to say hi. I should have called.' She puts the glass down and gets up from the sofa. She starts for the door.

'No, I don't mean you have to rush out right now.' He follows close behind her. 'We still have some time to chat.'

As Trina turns back to face him, she lets her hand swing out a little and brush the front of his towel. 'Oh, sorry. You okay?'

It wasn't a hard hit and she knows it. He shakes his head. 'I'm fine.'

'You sure?' She reaches out, puts her hand on his waist, her fingers lightly touching his warm flesh. She drags her fingertips down a couple of inches and he shivers.

'Yeah, fine.'

'Well, okay.' She leans over and stands on her toes as if to give him a little good-bye peck on the cheek. He leans his face toward her and suddenly she steps into him, her hip nuzzling against his crotch. She kisses him on the cheek, but lets her lips linger while her hip rubs his lap. He turns, kisses her full on the mouth. His teeth nip at her lower lip and he reels her into his arms and hugs her. His hand is cupping her butt. He hikes her skirt up with one hand, rubs his palm across her panty-hosed behind. A callus on his palm scratches the material. His hand lifts her buttocks and forces his tongue deeper into her mouth. She can feel his penis stabbing against her hip and grinds a little against it.

'Let's go upstairs,' he says.

He takes her hand and leads her. His towel is poking

144

straight out in front of him as they climb the stairs. As they near the bedroom, she hears the television. She recognizes David Letterman's voice.

'He isn't on now,' Trina says, looking at her watch.

'Tape,' he says. 'I can't stay up that late anymore. I've lived in too many places with sporadic electricity. If you can't read at night or watch TV, you have to drink or screw or sleep. One is expensive, the others dangerous. That leaves sleep.'

'Which is expensive and which is dangerous?' Trina asks, unzipping her skirt and hanging it on the doorknob.

He whips off his towel and neatly peels back the white down comforter, folding and refolding it across the bottom of the bed. His neatness is mathematical, his concentration intense. Trina unbuttons her blouse and takes that off too. She looks around the room and notices it is as gorgeous as the downstairs. This is one of the best parts of sleeping with someone new, exploring their bedrooms. As she sits on the edge of the bed rolling off her panty hose, she feels like an archaeologist at a fresh dig. What mysteries can be learned about the inhabitants by examining these artifacts. The textured wallpaper, the earth tones of brown and white broken only by the bright explosions of color on the walls, the cracks of light behind the merging geometrical figures. Trina decides that not only is the room beautifully decorated, like a model home, but it is also the cleanest home she's ever been in. Even the baseboards are dust free.

David Letterman turns on the fountain in front of his desk and then they cut to a commercial.

'He interviewed this guy earlier,' Jamison says, climbing under the sheet, waiting for Trina. He has removed the towel but his penis is still poking up the sheet in front of him as he talks. 'This guy, they call him the wild man or something. He goes through Central Park eating the

145

plants. First they arrested him, now they've got him giving tours.'

'I read about him,' Trina says. She is naked now except for her bra. She unfastens the front, but turns her back to him as she opens it. She doesn't want him to see how her huge breasts pop out and flop against her chest. She tosses the bra on the floor and slides into bed next to him.

'The guy was showing Letterman some of the plants from the park. There was this one called gout weed. Used to be called goat weed, but over the years the name degenerated to gout weed. Thing is, people then thought it was called that because it had a medicinal effect on gout. So ever since they've been eating this weed just because they misunderstood the word. All these people eating this weed because they got the name wrong. Imagine that.'

'A rose by any other name,' Trina says, snuggling closer.

Jamison reaches over to the bedside table, glistening darkly with furniture oil, grabs the remote unit, and shuts the TV off. The tape machine continues to whirr faintly beneath the dark screen.

Compared with the last time, this sex is more urgent. Last time he had been inventive, resting between various maneuvers, chatting and joking. There had been a lot of stroking and patient fondling. Like a tub slowly being filled with water. This time it is more like a damn bursting and a flash flood. She likes this just as much.

He is inside of her within minutes, but she wants him to be, asks him to enter. She can feel the sheets beneath her buttocks soaking wet and cool against her skin, all the moisture leaking from her. When he enters her, he does so slowly, almost politely. Trina can't wait. She arches up with a quick hip thrust, swallowing all of him in a gulp. He moves in and out until she is panting, on the brink, then he stops a few seconds, starts in again. Her eyes are closed and she sees herself swimming toward shore. Her

146

friends are picnicking in the sand. Barcy is there cooking something on a small hibachi. Trina can see the smoke, almost smell the barbecue sauce. Dixie and Diva are playing smash ball, whacking the little ball back and forth with their wooden paddles. Each hit is like the crack of a gunshot. Diva is wearing a bikini and looks like she's lost weight. Jamison is sitting on a towel, naked, his dark skin glistening from suntan oil he is rubbing into his thighs. He waves at Trina to join them. Trina is swimming harder and harder. Kicking her legs, thrashing in the water. The shore doesn't seem to be getting any closer. Then Jamison begins to rotate his hips in a circular stirring motion. The shore changes colors, has a yellowish hue. Jamison begins to thrust harder and deeper, his breathing tight bursts of air. Trina swims harder, her arms and legs exhausted. Suddenly a large wave swells under her, lifts her high above the water. It is an impossible wave, twenty, thirty feet above the ocean. The height makes her dizzy. It sweeps her toward the shore in a blur. She is certain she will be killed when the wave crashes against the sand, but she doesn't care. The speed is intoxicating, worth whatever happens.

Jamison comes in one long spasm followed by four shorter ones. His body jerks against hers. His spasms bring her the rest of the way and she comes with a loud holler that startles him. He lifts his head. Through half-opened eyes she can see his confusion at her noise. He looks embarrassed, as if she's farted.

'Don't look so surprised,' she says.

'You didn't scream last time.'

'First date. Nice girls don't scream on the first date.'

He laughs. 'You're incredible.'

She wonders if she's so incredible, why is he looking at the clock and getting out of bed. That is an unfair thought, she realizes. He'd warned her he was running late. She had seduced him. If he had to dress for another date now, she had known that going in.

She remains in bed and watches him as he hurries about the adjoining bathroom. He moves very efficiently, turning on the shower, then going back to the sink, setting out his toothbrush, deodorant, cologne like a police lineup. Trina knows that they are arranged in the order that he will use them. She thinks that his neatness is amazing for someone who spends so much time in war-torn countries. Perhaps that's why he is so neat back home, from chaos to order. His obsessiveness would be too much for her, but he might be perfect for Barcy. It's hard for Barcy to meet people her own intellectual equal, though she would never admit that Jamison, though, is very smart.

Trina decides to tell him about the baby. He deserves to know. Besides, as a foreign correspondent, he will probably be out of the country most of the time anyway and not want to share custody. 'Jamison,' she says.

'Speak, wench.' He tears open a new box of Tone soap and sticks it in the shower. He tests the water temperature, adjusts the knob.

'I came over here today . . .' She doesn't like that opening. 'I wanted to talk . . .' That's even worse.

'Uh oh,' Jamison says, looking down at his penis. He turns toward her holding it in his hand and she can see its bunched skin and bald head crusted in red. He touches it and a pink flake snows to the floor.

Trina looks between her legs, sees the blood on her thighs. The yellow sheet is also pink with blood. She has started her period. She is not pregnant.

'Why don't you hop in the shower?' he urges. Meanwhile, he is getting a washcloth.

Trina climbs out of bed and walks toward the shower. She feels tremendous heat in her stomach, as if she has just lost a child. She knows that is silly, there was no child. Still, she grieves.

She washes quickly, soaking off the blood. When she emerges, Jamison holds the damp washcloth he's scrubbed the sheet with in one hand. In the other hand he holds a blow dryer and is methodically blow-drying the sheet. Obviously he is expecting to be sharing the bed again this evening and doesn't have time to change all the sheets and pillowcases so they match.

'I'll do that,' Trina says. 'Go shower.'

He hands her the blow dryer and she finishes drying the sheet. She remakes the bed. She finds an emergency tampon in her purse and inserts it. She is standing in a half-squat, pushing the tampon inside when he emerges from the shower and watches her.

'God, that's sexy,' he says. His penis starts to swell a little in confirmation.

'You're running late,' she says. She balls up her panty hose and shoves it in her purse. She dresses quickly. They exchange a few clever lines that she forgets as soon as she is out the front door. She is in a hurry to get home.

As she walks toward the car, the tampon feels huge and uncomfortable inside her. She starts to walk a little bow-legged, even though she knows she is exaggerating the size and discomfort in her mind.

12

Dixie sits in a cold concrete room with twenty-three teen-age girls in their underwear. Gym class. Last period of the day. The sport of the week is basketball. They are all changing into their gym clothes: a pair of maroon shorts with the school's name in yellow lettering on the right leg, and a yellow T-shirt with the school's name in maroon letters across the chest. Maroon and yellow are the school colors. The T-shirts also have a cartoon aardvark wearing sunglasses and riding a surfboard. The aardvark is the school mascot, a bit of whimsy from the school's first graduating class nine years ago. Recently parents have been trying to have the mascot changed because it isn't dignified. Some parents have actually shouted at school board members over this issue.

The girls are all crowded together on the wooden benches that separate the banks of red metal lockers. Dixie is amazed at the variety of underwear. When she attended high school, underwear was white, blue, or pink. To her right, a girl is taking her contact lenses out and storing them in a little white case. She is wearing a dark red lacy bra that shows the nipples. They are small breasts and small nipples, but in that bra they look provocative. The girl to Dixie's left is standing, reaching into her locker for her yellow T-shirt. Her buttocks are eight inches from Dixie's face. Her panties are cobalt blue, consisting of a small patch of fabric to cover her crotch and narrow blue elastic strings that ride high over her hip bones, meet at the small of her back, then disappear in the crack of her buttocks only to emerge again between her legs and connect with the patch of fabric. Dixie winces a little to think how uncomfortable it must feel to walk and sit all day in that.

Dixie realizes now she has made a serious mistake. When Captain Janeway gave her department money to buy clothes for her undercover assignment, she neglected to buy special underwear. She figured she could just use her own. Underwear is underwear, she thought. She was wrong.

She is still sitting in her short skirt and blouse, reluctant to get undressed. She fumbles with her combination lock, stalling. She can feel the mucky dampness in the air from the last class's showers. Fat drops of condensation dribble down the sweaty red lockers. Around her, girls chat, gossip, giggle. She sees one frighteningly skinny girl with sleepy eyes pop a Benzedrine into her mouth and swallow dry. The girl's ribs protrude against her pale skin like fingers poking against a plastic balloon. The bones seem to be the only thing keeping her body from completely collapsing in on itself.

The girl in the red bra tucks her contact lens case in her purse and removes a pair of glasses from her locker. She attaches an adjustable length of elastic to each endpiece and puts her glasses on, shaking her head to make sure the glasses won't fall off during any movement. She looks over at Dixie. 'What's the matter? You getting turned on?'

Dixie smiles. 'I'm just trying to think of some way to ditch.'

'Forget it,' the other girl says, the one with the panty strings in her crack. 'You can ditch any class in this school but gym class.'

151

'We always could ditch gym where I come from,' Dixie says.

'Where's that?' the red bra asks.

'Oregon.'

'Well, shit, this is California. Nobody ditches gym.'

Dixie quickly strips out of her clothing. Her own panties are women's Jockeys, pink. Her bra matches. She is the only one in the locker room whose bra and panties match. She might as well be wearing her badge.

Red bra stares at Dixie's body. 'God, what did you do in Oregon, move pianos?'

A few of the other girls look down at Dixie's underwear-clad body. Even relaxed, not pumped up from lifting, the muscles in Dixie's arms and legs twist and bulge like braided bread. Her stomach is as flat and hard as the tiles in the shower. She looks at the other girls' bodies, some thin, some shapely, some hefty, but all somehow un-formed, doughy. Like the half-formed pods in *Invasion of the Body Snatchers*. Dixie's body, however, is the result of many years of training, daily discipline. Only her face is as flat and unlined as theirs. Her character shows in her body; a California version of Dorian Gray.

'Fuck, man,' the girl with the string between her butt says. 'Look at those veins. Fuck.'

Dixie glances down at the ropy blue veins worming just under the skin of her forearms. 'I was on the dive team back home at school,' Dixie explains. 'High dive. Took a bad dive during competition and hit the diving board coming down. I was unconscious when I hit the water.' She parts her hair at the back of her head as if to show them the scar. But no one looks. 'I was in a hospital bed for three months. They thought I might not walk again.'

'God, that's horrible,' red bra says.

'They put me in physical therapy after that, you know, lifting weights and stuff, and after a while I started to get better. Took me two years before I could get out of that damned wheelchair. My mom still makes me keep it up though. I think she's scared that if I stop, I might not be able to walk anymore. She's kinda superstitious and all. I graduate in a couple months and then I'll be going to UC Santa Barbara. Then I can stop.'

'UCSB,' red bra says. 'I hear that's a real party school.'

'Hope so,' Dixie says. 'After being crippled for two years, I'm ready for some partying.'

The girls turn away from Dixie, not wanting such bad luck to rub off on their own young and charmed lives. There is a general lacing up of Reeboks and L.A. Gears and Etonics. Dixie's matching underwear is forgotten.

Back at the station, Dixie leans over the drinking fountain. On the back of her tongue sits a white tablet, 500 mg of vitamin C. She sips some water, tucks down her chin, and swallows. Most people think you should throw back your head to swallow pills, but in fact that constricts the throat. Serious vitamin takers know to tuck the chin to the chest. Dixie has been telling people that for years, but still she sees cops tossing back their morning aspirins, head tilted toward the sky, grimacing as they swallow. People never learn.

Next is the green tablet, her favorite. It contains calcium, magnesium, zinc, iron, copper, kelp, and manganese in a base of trace minerals from montmorillonite and horsetail herbs. She places the tablet on her tongue, leans over the fountain, sips water, tucks chin, swallows.

'Dixie,' Captain Janeway says.

'Sir?'

He is carrying an armful of file folders. 'You wanted to see me?'

'Yes, Captain. Just for a few minutes.'

153

He hands her half of the file folders. 'Make yourself useful.' He starts off down the corridor.

She still has one vitamin left, a red-speckled table containing vitamins A, D, and E. She pops it in her mouth, steals a quick sip of water, swallows, and hurries after Captain Janeway.

'How's that Mustang of yours holding up?' he asks her as they near his office. He's been wanting to buy it from her for years. He would like to start restoring cars as a hobby. He has never restored a car, in fact knows little about cars. He told her he would like to learn on her '70 Mustang. When she sells it to him he will begin his new hobby, that way he'll have something to do when he retires in ten years. Dixie senses that, despite his many offers to buy the car, he would be more grateful if she never sells it to him and wouldn't have to start learning how to restore it. Of course, now she is stuck with the car. She can't sell it to anyone else or he would feel slighted. But if she sells it to him, he would start to resent her for forcing him to live up to his proclamations of restoring the damn thing. That's why Dixie never locks her car. Her only hope now is that someone will steal it.

'The car's fine,' she tells Captain Janeway.

'How's the carburetor?' he asks.

Dixie would be surprised if he even knew where the carburetor was. 'Fine, sir.'

'I'd probably start with the carburetor. Work on that first. Get the engine perfect before starting on the body.'

'Good idea.'

They are in his office now. He plops the file folders on his desk, takes her bunch and plops them on the desk also. He sits behind the desk, loosens the laces on his left shoe, and leans back with a sigh. 'How's the blackboard jungle going?'

'I need some more clothes allowance. About fifty bucks.'

'You really are starting to sound like a teenage girl.'

'Underwear, Captain. I need to buy certain underwear.'

He looks at her funny. 'They wear special underwear?'

'This school's a little more affluent than some of the others. Just take my word for it, you don't want to know.'

He laughs. 'Thanks for protecting my boyish fantasies.'

Dixie smiles at him. He has a daughter who just turned fourteen. Her photograph sits in a silver frame on his desk. So does one of his wife and a third of the three of them together at Disneyland on the Mad Hatter's Tea Party ride. Captain Janeway is spinning the saucer while his wife and daughter hold on to each other screaming and laughing. He smiles gamely, though he looks a little nauseated. Several times Dixie has been in here for meetings and caught him accidentally looking at the photograph and smiling contentedly.

Captain Janeway is the most decent man Dixie had ever known. Everyone in the department respects his honesty and integrity. He has been decorated twice for bravery. He served in Vietnam, was wounded twice, once losing three toes on his left foot. He returned to the States and joined the LAPD. He married and divorced twice, no kids. Both wives wanted him to be more ambitious, but Captain Janeway just wanted children. He began dating again. Though plain looking, slightly overweight, with sad eyes and a large nose that made him look older than his mid-forties, he was kind and caring and managed to meet a lot of women. None seemed right. Finally, frustrated with dating, he began corresponding through one of those Asian mail-order bride services with a Vietnamese girl living in Hong Kong. He wrote to her in Vietnamese, she wrote back in English. One day, without telling her, he took his vacation and went to Hong Kong. Embarrassed by his surprise visit, Trang confessed the truth she had kept from him: she could not have children. He brought her back anyway and they married. Two years later they adopted a four-year-old girl, half black and half Mexican. The little girl's right leg was permanently crippled from a beating with a broom handle she received from her drunken father. Captain Janeway had taken her to many doctors, had arranged several operations on her leg, sitting beside her hospital bed teaching her chess while she recovered from each one. To Dixie they were like some kind of miracle family, the kind they make TV movies about. Dixie had been over to their home many times for old-fashioned backyard barbecues. He actually wore one of those silly aprons with an American flag on it with the caption: RED, WHITE & BLUE. THESE COLORS DON'T RUN. Underneath he wore the last pair of madras shorts in the country and white socks and sandals. Captain Janeway and Trang seemed very happy together. Their daughter, Shawna, still limped slightly, but otherwise laughed a lot and hugged a lot and worried about her grades and dating like all the other girls her age. She called Dixie 'Aunt Dixie.'

Some of the women cops were offended by the mail-order bride aspect of the relationship. They speculated that Captain Janeway had been looking for an Oriental slave, an unliberated women he could boss around. But from what Dixie had observed, that wasn't the case. Trang raised Shawna, but also took classes at Sand Coast College several evenings a week. Her English now was much better than most native Americans, and she was on the verge of getting her real estate license. Orange County had hundreds of thousands of Vietnamese residents, which could make her a valuable asset to any real estate agency. Captain Janeway had encouraged her to pursue whatever interest she had.

'Anything shaking out there?' he asks.

'I've made contact with the main dealer.'

He points to the faint hickey on her neck. He doesn't miss much. 'I'd say you made more than contact.'

'He's a little rambunctious. Nothing I can't handle.'

'Don't let the fancy cars and clothes fool you. The kid's dealing, that means he has to buy it from someone. Somewhere down the line there are some very bad men with their hands on the bucks. They give hickeys with .44 magnums.'

'Thanks, Dad.'

Captain Janeway chuckles. 'Okay, okay, end lecture. What have you got?'

'Joseph Little is really the only one to worry about. There are plenty of drugs floating around the place. These kids can afford them. Some minor sales, just among friends, a few joints, some poppers here and there. But the big action goes through this Little kid.'

'Who's his ratboy?' Meaning who's his supplier, the one who checks the quality of the dope, the one they were really after. Street slang always sounded funny coming from Captain Janeway.

'I don't know yet. I've hung around him a few days now on and off, not enough to make it seem like I'm looking for him. He likes me.'

'Yeah, well don't get your prom dress out of moth balls just yet. I want this rapped up within the month. Find his connection and let's take them both down. I'm getting some pressure from the federal shines.' Shines are the bureaucrats, recognizable from the shine on the bottom of their pants from sitting all day. 'The new federal law means any sale within a thousand yards of a school is automatically one to forty years in prison. That makes the stakes a little higher, China Doll.' Captain Janeway rubs his left foot through his shoe, massaging the missing toes. He closes his eyes. 'How's Principal Peterson holding up?'

'Thinks this is "I Spy." Another week he'll be wanting to use passwords and decoder rings.'

'He's all right. I like him. Reminds me of me.' He opens his eyes and smiles.

'How about that fifty dollars?'

Captain Janeway scribbles on a form and slides it across his desk to her. 'Fifty bucks for underwear. Jesus.' He plops his hand down on the form as she reaches for it. 'Kidding aside, Dixie. Be careful. High school or not, when there's this much money involved, there's always somebody around who likes to play rough.'

'I'll be careful, Captain.' She takes the voucher and leaves. She can feel his worried eyes on her back and is grateful.

In the policewomen's locker room Dixie sees more women in their underwear. These bodies are nothing like the ones she saw earlier. These are more like their lockers: battered, rusted, and chipped. Most of these women have bruises on their arms or legs, fist-sized on the arms where they've been grabbed by men unwilling to be arrested by a woman, and foot-sized bruises on their legs where they've been kicked by kids, women, and weak men unwilling to be arrested by a woman.

Dixie mostly notices how much bigger these women seem than the girls from the high school, even though they aren't really. There is just something about the way they walk, sit, stand, an attitude that seems to take up more room. Whatever you've got to show me, I've seen, they seemed to be saying, so get the hell out of my face. Dixie wonders if that is just a cop attitude or an adult woman attitude.

Lena Walker comes from the shower with a towel wrapped around her waist. Both eyes are purple and she has a shiny metal cast taped over her nose. Her breasts are bare and the right one has a nasty bruise that extends from her collarbone down to the nipple. It looks as if someone has spilled tea on her skin and stained it. Dixie went to the Academy with Lena.

'Jesus, Lena,' Dixie says. 'What happened?'

'You want the truth or something interesting?'

'Is your nose broken?'

'Fucking right it's broken. You think I'm playing Liberty Valance or something?'

'I thought maybe it was a new fashion look.'

Lena laughs. 'The Bruised Broad Look. Maybe we can get Cybill Shepherd to do the *Cosmo* cover. I could do her makeup with this.' She makes a fist. For some reason no one understands, Lena hates Cybill Shepherd and never misses an opportunity to bad-mouth her.

'So what happened?' Dixie asks.

'Dumb. Goddamned dumb.' She reaches into her locker and pulls out her panties, slipping them on as she speaks. 'I stop this car, a blue Impala with Texas plates. Cracked windshield. No big deal, a quick fix-it ticket and I'm on my way to lunch at the Mexican restaurant over on PCH.' She steps into her jeans, which are at least a size too small. She struggles into them. 'I call it in, nothing on the computer. I go over to write him up and the bastard jumps out of the car like a madman. Slams the car door into me.' Her pants are stuck at the knees and Dixie can see the bruises on her thighs from the car door. 'I drop to my knees and the son of a bitch slams the car door into my face. Busts my nose and cracks my cheek. Drives off like some crazy guy.'

'Jesus.'

'He looked a little like Jesus. Long brown hair, beard. Ten-gallon hat.'

'I don't recall anyplace in the Bible where Jesus wore a ten-gallon hat.'

'If he had worn one of those babies, no way they'd have crammed some crown of thorns on his head.'

Dixie flips expertly through the combination on her lock and pops open her locker. 'What does Barry say about all this?' Barry is Lena's husband, a CHP motorcycle cop.

'He wants me to quit, as usual. Hell, someone cusses at me and he wants me to quit. That boy needs to get a thicker skin.' She lifts out her bra but doesn't put it on. She rolls it up and sticks it in her gym bag. Dixie notices the bra matches the panties. 'The damn things rub my bruise and stings like hell.' She pulls her sweatshirt over her head. 'Things work out the way we plan, me and Barry'll be buying a house in a year.'

'Really? That's terrific.' Lena has wanted a house for as long as Dixie has known her. But money has been tight and they haven't been able to save enough for even a small down payment. Dixie doesn't want to pry, but assumes they came into some kind of inheritance.

As she undresses she has a sudden rush of camaraderie with the other women in the locker room. She is happy to be naked among her own kind. The bruises, the lumpy butts, the sagging flesh. Despite her own chiseled body, she feels that this is where she belongs, among women whose bodies are broken in.

'Here's the deal,' Lena says abruptly, in a confessional rush. 'I'm going to have a baby . . .'

'Hey, congratulations,' Dixie says. She knows Lena and Barry have wanted children, but had decided to wait until they bought a house first.

'It's not what you think,' Lena says. 'I'm not pregnant. I'm going to get pregnant. But not with Barry's baby.'

Dixie doesn't want to know anymore. She is too tired for moral complexities. She just wants to change into her sweats and go upstairs and lift weights. Today she works her chest, back, and legs. She is looking forward to the exhaustion she knows she will feel when it's over.

Lena looks directly at her. The nose brace glints the overhead fluorescent light back in Dixie's face. 'It's going to be one of those in vitro deals. In vitro fertilization. Won't be Barry's sperm and it won't even be my egg. I'm just the incubator.'

Dixie opens her mouth to say something, but doesn't know what to say. She closes her mouth and thinks about doing lat pull downs.

'I've already had the blood tests, hormone injections, sonograms. They changed my oil and spark plugs while they were in there. I'm ready to race, baby.' She laughs as she ties her shoes. 'You should see this couple, the expectant parents. Nerds from Hell. Guy actually carries one of those plastic pocket protectors stuffed with pencils and pens. He's some kind of engineer. His wife looks like the one who always did the decorations for the high school dances but never had a date to one.'

'Why are you doing this, Lena?' Dixie finally asks.

'Yeah, yeah, I know it sounds crazy. But we're doing it for the same reason most of the people we arrest do what they do. For the money. We want a house, we want kids, we can't afford either. We've been saving for a down payment for five years, we've got about two fucking grand. Good luck trying to buy anything in Orange County for two thou down. The Nerdlys are paying me ten thousand bucks plus my salary for maternity leave. With that we can buy a house and start our own family. Makes sense, doesn't it?'

Dixie has to admit it does make a certain amount of sense. But there is something about it she doesn't like. 'What does Barry think about all this?'

'He says as long as I don't have to fuck the guy, it's okay.' She leans toward Dixie and grins. 'Hell, for ten thousand bucks, I'd've even boffed the little squirrel.'

Dixie knows that's not true. Lena is a tough-talking cop, but she is also a practicing Catholic. 'Doesn't the Pope frown on this kind of thing?'

'Hey, the Pope can afford to frown. He already has a house.' But she looks down at the floor guiltily. 'I figure the kid's not any part mine, so it won't be as hard to give up. And God has provided a way for me to finally be able to build my own family. He gave me this body, this brain, my health, the smarts to figure this all out. This thing can't be a sin.'

Upstairs in the gym, Dixie does an extra set of each exercise. She lets out a strangled cry of exertion with each additional rep. Vaguely it occurs to her that she sounds as if she were giving birth.

Dixie sits in her evening law class barely able to hold the pen to take notes. The professor is lecturing on why those nasty little 'technicalities' that everyone is always screaming about aren't really so little. She has heard all this before in courtrooms during cases in which she has testified.

Dixie has a plan. Night school for another four years, then she will have her law degree. Passing the bar exam will be tough, but she will do that too. She has always accomplished everything she has set her mind to do.

She looks around the room. Randy is not here. Randy Vogel is her boyfriend, significant other, lover, whatever the hell you'd call it these days. Dixie prefers boyfriend, but Trina always makes fun of her when she uses that term. Trina says, 'We're adult women now, for Christ's sake, not on the pep squad.' Dixie agrees but still feels most comfortable with the word boyfriend. It's familiar, and somehow not too intimate. Significant Other sounds like a business partner. Lover is too personal, like he gives her gynecological examinations every night. Boyfriend means we date, occasionally have sex, share some meals, talk vaguely about a future together, but never get around to any specific timetable. Boyfriend.

The door at the back of the classroom opens and Randy enters, tiptoeing, looking embarrassed at disrupting the class. Naturally everyone's head swivels about to watch him creep to the closest desk. The professor's eyes lock on target, fire a quick blast of disapproval, reducing Randy to ashes, and he moves on, continuing his lecture.

Randy slumps down in his chair and winks at Dixie. She smiles back and returns to her note-taking. She can share them with him after class.

Dixie has been dating Randy for six months. They met last semester in Introduction to Criminal Law. Dixie wants to be a criminal law attorney; Randy wants to go into entertainment law. He was a child actor, having had a small but reoccuring role on the old 'Dennis the Menace' TV show. He played one of Dennis's Hillsdale neighborhood friends. Mr. Wilson, the put-upon neighbor, was originally played by Joseph Kearns. Randy says he was a real nice guy who used to joke with the kids all the time. But he died during the filming of the 1961-62 season and was replaced by Gale Gordon as his brother. The next season brought Gale Gordon back but not Randy Vogel.

Randy says he and Jay North, who played Dennis, used to get in a lot of trouble around the set. Jay was every bit as mischievous as Dennis. After Randy left the show, though, he never saw Jay again. Randy did a few cereal commercials, but he never really caught on again. As a red-haired freckled kid in a baseball cap he'd been cute. As a red-haired freckled adolescent he just looked gangly and homely. He went to USC, studied film editing, and got enough TV jobs to support his cocaine habit for six years. Now he was clean.

Dixie wonders why all the mothers on those old shows always seemed so old. Not the stars of the shows, of course, but all the neighbor mothers looked like they were fifty or sixty with ten-year-old children. At the rate Dixie was going, that's how old she'd be if she ever had a child. Trina says Dixie doesn't need to have a child, she just dates them.

Dixie looks up because she realizes she missed what the professor had just said. She glances over at the young man next to her and copies his last notation. He moves his arm so she can see it better and she whispers thank you.

Trina contends that Dixie finds the stray dogs, the losers, the weaklings, and nurtures them like some Sixties earth mother, then is disappointed when they can't stand on their feet. 'Why should they,' Trina says, 'when they can stand on yours?'

Dixie suspects there may be some truth in that. Not with Randy, of course, but with her past relationships, especially her ex, Karl. She remains friendly with Karl, though not as friendly as he wants. He calls often just to chat. Sometimes he casually suggests they give it another try. She ignores him when he says things like that, but he is determined.

Trina is not one to talk about relationships, Dixie concludes. Of the four friends, she is the most promiscuous. She remembers the evening she went over to Trina's. There was no real danger of suicide, Trina loves Karyn too much to do that to her, but Dixie had learned enough about people from this job never to take chances. They had talked, laughed, cried, eaten pizza and ice cream. The next day Dixie had to run an extra four miles just to work off the junk she'd eaten. She smiles at the memory. Trina is not just the most sexual of the group, she is the most passionate. Dixie envies that.

Diva is the dreamer of the group. Her eyes are always

164

focusing on the future, waiting for the Big Break. Record a hit record, make millions. She buys a lottery ticket every day just to hedge her career bets. To Diva, buying lottery tickets is the same as opening an IRA. Her relationships with men are chaotic, accidental. She meets someone, they move in together the next day, live together for a week, a month, a year, drift apart, she meets someone else a few days later, the guy serving her a hamburger at Coco's. Diva just knows things will work out, that she's heading for fame and fortune, even if there is no concrete indication of it in her life at a given time.

Barcy's the odd one. She is the smartest woman Dixie has ever known. Not just knowledgeable, but smart, quick-witted, intelligent. She is the conscience of the group, the one who weighs the cause and effect of every action. Dixie should have that role, considering her job, but she doesn't. Dixie realizes she isn't deep enough to grapple with some complex problems. Give her the rules, the laws, and she will enforce them. Ask her to write new laws and she is lost. She hopes these classes will change that.

Barcy's relationships are perplexing. She meets plenty of men, dates them, seems to like them. She has been proposed to several times. But something happens, she always says no. Dixie thinks Barcy analyzes everything too much.

The professor stops talking and people start to put their notebooks away. Several students hover around the professor with questions. The rest gather their books and leave. Randy is waiting by the door for her. As Dixie walks toward him her legs begin to feel leaden and slow and she wonders if that is just from the workout.

13

'The bar is closed,' Barcelona tells Trina.

'You're kidding.'

'Does this look like I'm kidding?' Barcelona holds up a glass of Diet Coke.

'Well, shit,' Trina says.

Trina is twenty minutes late, not bad for her. Barcelona, Dixie, and Diva are already seated at a booth in the festively decorated Hot Pepper Mexican restaurant. Life-size piñatas in the shape of donkeys and dancing women and banditos dangle from the high ceiling in bright tropical colors. Barcelona munches a couple of warm tortilla chips from the basket and gestures at the empty seat next to her. 'Sit, Trina. You can go on the wagon for one night.'

'The fucking bar's closed?' Trina says, sitting. 'I've never heard of a bar closing on a Friday night. No wonder the place is so dead.'

'It's not dead,' Diva says. 'We're here.' She is drinking Perrier, lazily poking her fingernail at the fetally hunched slice of lime adrift with the melting ice cubes. Her finger-nails are glossy water-melon red and have little white unicorns painted on each one. Some lime pulp sticks to one nail. In the ashtray beside her drink smolders a half-smoked black cigarette.

'No bar,' Trina repeats, shaking her head. 'They re-modeling or something?'

'Court order,' Barcelona says. She hands Trina a little placard that sits on the table. On it is a cartoon of a teddy bear in a sombrero. The caption reads: 'Please bear with us. The State Dept. of Alcoholic Beverage Control will not allow us to serve alcoholic beverages temporarily.'

'What gives? Were they caught serving minors?'

'Remember that discrimination suit some Chicanos brought last year?' Barcelona says.

'Yeah, they accused the place of turning minorities away from the bar at night. Mexicans, blacks, and Arabs.'

Dixie nods. 'This is a real pickup joint after work. Half the office buildings in Irvine empty out into here. There's so much cocaine snorted in the bathroom you can get a contact high just by taking a leak.'

Trina laughs. 'You take all the condoms from the guys' wallets on a weekend night here and you've got enough rubber for all the sneakers in the whole NBA.'

'So this is where you meet your dates,' Diva teases.

'Yeech. You sleep with any of these guys and in the morning you'd have to douche with a blowtorch.'

Diva frowns in disgust. 'God, Trina, where do you come up with that stuff?'

'When I was in uniform,' Dixie says. 'I came over a couple times to break up fights in the parking lot. Even three-piece suits like to go at it every once in a while.'

'Anyway,' Barcelona says, 'apparently they were turning away these ethnic guys—'

'Just the guys?' Diva asks.

'Of course,' Trina answers. 'These places don't care what a woman looks like as long as she has a pussy. Hi, do you know me? I cured cancer and did away with nuclear arms. But when I travel men don't recognize me. That's why I carry this.' Trina points at her crotch. 'My cunt. Welcome in more places than American Express.'

'Jesus.' Diva chuckles.

Barcelona grabs a few more tortilla chips. 'Turns out the whole chain of Hot Pepper restaurants was doing it. So the judge ordered their bars closed for one week as part of the punishment.'

Trina opens her menu, scans it quickly, and closes it. 'Well who picked this place then?'

'I did,' Diva says. 'I like Mexican food. I didn't know about all that other crap.'

'Don't you read the papers?'

Diva shrugs. 'If it's not in *Rolling Stone*, how important can it be?'

Trina playfully throws a tortilla chip at Diva and it gets caught in her hair. Diva untangles the chip from her hair and eats it. Everyone turns to their menus.

'Maybe we shouldn't eat here,' Dixie says. 'If this place discriminates, I don't think we should.'

Diva makes a face. 'We're already here, Dixie. I mean, we've already eaten two baskets of their chips. We can't just get up and walk out.'

'Sure we can,' Trina says. 'Want to?'

Barcelona recognizes the glint in Trina's eyes. The opportunity to walk out of a place, make the grand gesture, sizzles in her eyes. She lives for that kind of thing. Extravagant actions. Barcelona does not like grand gestures. She prefers quiet activism. Volunteer work, letter-writing campaigns, petitions. When she was in college during the Vietnam War, she was deeply involved in antiwar campaigns. She was in charge of the Coca-Cola boycott on campus. She hustled up over three thousand people to sign postcards to the Coca-Cola Company declaring that they would not drink Coke until the war ended. The theory was that they would force Coke to pressure Congress. Barcelona also worked in the student government spearheading a draft-resisters' advisory office on campus. Once she even drove two eighteen-year-old boys into Canada

168

over Christmas break. Their draft lottery numbers had been announced on television the week before, very much like the lottery shows on TV now. One of the boys, Jimmy Remo, had been in her French class. During the drive, he confessed to Barcelona that he had a crush on her and begged her to stay with him up in Canada. They'd get an apartment together, he'd find a job maybe in a bookstore. They could get married if she wanted. This revelation was news to Barcelona. When she mentioned that they had never even dated, he gave her a defeated look and nodded in disappointment. Already he'd become an expert in hopelessless.

She drove back from Canada in the middle of the night, her wipers brushing off a light eyelash snow from her windshield, her radio blaring, the heater working only intermittently. Sometimes the vents would pump too much hot air and she'd have to open the window, other times it stopped working altogether and she'd pull her scarf up over her nose and mouth. For some reason, as she got closer to home, she kept turning the radio up louder and louder, WOR from Chicago. Marvin Gaye sang 'Inner City Blues.' Slade sang 'Coz I Luv You.' The Chi-Lites sang 'Have You Seen Her?'

She never marched, never carried signs, never threw vegetables at buildings, never shouted obscenities at cops. No grand gestures.

'Whaddaya say, Barcy,' Trina encourages, 'should we blow this racist place?'

'They've changed their policy,' Barcelona says. 'And they've already been punished. Let's just eat, okay?'

Trina shrugs, returns to her menu. The others do too.

Barcelona is having difficulty reading the menu. The letters are furry. In her purse are a pair of cheap reading glasses she bought at Thrifty's drugstore a month ago. They are wire-rimmed and rectangular, like the granny glasses all the kids used to wear when she first went to college. Only those glasses were usually colored pink or blue or yellow to make the world look brighter and happier. These are just plain reading glasses. So she can read her own books as she writes them. She hasn't told anyone that she uses them. Except Eric.

The waitress comes over. She is wearing a short yellow skirt with a ruffled hem that stops at mid-thigh. The neckline plunges halfway down her breasts and pushes them together so they strain a little against the neckline. The blue veins beneath the pale skin of her breasts are so visible they look as if they've been traced with ink. The waitress is in her late forties and wears little makeup, just some eyeliner and lipstick. Her outfit seems to embarrass her, but she is very enthusiastic and helpful when they order. Diva still can't decide, so the waitress agrees to return in a few minutes. 'Meantime, let me get you a couple more baskets of chips, girls,' she says with a smile. 'The hot salsa should take your mind off the fact that you're drinking Cokes instead of margaritas.' She leaves, tugging down the back of her skirt as she walks.

'Well, let's get right to it then,' Trina says, snapping her fingers impatiently. 'Let's see what you've got.'

Diva taps the menu with her unicorn fingernails. 'You think I can get a decent vegetarian meal here?'

'You picked the place,' Dixie reminds her.

'Yeah, that's true.' Diva nods agreement as she scans the menu. 'This *chalupa* sounds good. Deep-fried corn meal cup, stuffed with beans, red beef chile . . . Shit, beef. Maybe I can get them to make it without the meat.'

Trina is incredulous. 'That's not the menu I'm talking about, kids. Let's see what gourmet delights await us out there in the real world. Who'd you select, Diva?'

Diva hesitates, flushes. 'I couldn't think of anyone.'

'No one?' Trina asks.

'No one I think any of you would be interested in. Except maybe Calypso. We split up a couple of weeks ago.'

'Really?' Dixie says. 'Why didn't you tell someone?'

'I told Barcy. But I made her promise not to tell you guys. Just until I was sure we really were finished.'

Trina looks at Barcelona. 'I hate the way you can keep a juicy secret.'

Barcelona sips her water so she doesn't have to say anything. To be honest, she is able to keep Diva's secret so well because she'd forgotten about it. Though she likes Diva, even has a fondness for her ditsy life-style, Barcelona does not feel close to her. Not secret-sharing close. Yet, for some unknown reason, Diva continues to confide in her, call her up to chat, ask for advice. Diva is flighty, unpredictable, undisciplined—the opposite of Barcelona. But still Diva treats her as if they were soul mates, as if Barcelona would understand her lunacies.

'So, are you two finished?' Dixie asks Diva. 'Calypso is gone for good?'

'Yeah. I haven't seen him in over a week now. Funny thing is, I never really missed him. I got myself all geared up for depression and an eating binge, maybe some heavy crying. Never came. You think it's delayed shock or something?'

'I think you're just glad to be rid of him,' Trina says. 'Now you can look for someone with an actual personality. Or at least a job.'

'You sound like my mother.'

Barcelona laughs. 'She sounds like everyone's mother.'

'I *am* everyone's mother. Earth mother. With tits like these I can afford to suckle the universe.' Trina turns to Dixie. 'How about you? Any decent perps?'

Dixie pulls out a slip of paper. 'Against my better

171

judgment.' She hands it to Trina. 'My only contribution, so don't bug me later.'

Trina sips her wine and begins to read aloud: '"*Kevin Peterson. 6'2", approximately 175 pounds, slightly balding, black on black . . .*"' She looks questioningly at Dixie.

'Black hair and black eyes,' Dixie explains.

'"*High school principal, drives a 1983 Volvo, rents an apartment in Tustin, plays tennis and skis. Divorced, one male child, eight. No scars or distinguishing marks. No arrests, no warrants.*"' She grins at Dixie. 'Very thorough, Officer Cooper. But is he cute?'

Dixie ponders the question a moment then nods. 'Yeah, he's cute. Reminds me of a young Jimmy Stewart.'

'I love Jimmy Stewart,' Diva says.

'Promising,' Trina says. 'What else have we got? Barcy?'

'I'm not involved in this lunatic idea,' Barcelona says.

'Come on, you made a deal.'

'It's just for fun, Barcy,' Diva says. 'We're not conspiring against them for God's sake.'

Dixie touches Barcelona's hand. 'Don't make me the only one who actually brought a name.'

Barcelona smiles as she reaches into her purse. 'Okay, but if Gloria Steinem plasters our faces on wanted posters, you'll know why.'

'This isn't sexist,' Trina says. 'This is a group of women using their skills and know-how to maximize their companion-searching efforts. Think of it as if one of us worked for a large corporation in need of a good CFO. Of course we'd advertise in the usual publications, but we'd also put out feelers amongst our friends in the business world so we could be sure to get a highly qualified candidate. Why should dating be any different? This is matchmaking at its most efficient, nonsexist manner.'

Barcelona hands Trina a folded piece of paper. 'Here. It's the least I can do for feminism everywhere.'

Trina looks at the name. 'Harley Buss? Aren't you dating him?'

'On and off. Nothing serious and I don't think it ever will be. Not from me anyway. Maybe one of you will have better luck.'

Trina reads the paper aloud. '*"Harley Buss, forty-five, blue eyes, premature gray hair."*' She grins. 'Every guy I know claims his gray hair is premature. When exactly is it mature gray hair?'

Dixie says, 'When they realize it won't go away on its own like a sunburn.'

Trina returns to the paper. '*"Ph.D. in English. Very handsome."* I've seen him and can agree. He's a looker. What else have you got on him? *Divorced*, naturally. *"Two daughters in junior high school. Income about $50,000. Owns 5-bedroom house in Laguna Niguel. Likes sailing, theater, books, restaurants."* Sounds good.'

'He's recently split with his girlfriend,' Barcelona warns. 'So expect some fallout.'

'How is he in bed?' Trina asks. 'A moaner or a screamer?'

Dixie laughs. 'Or a whimperer. I hate that the most.'

'Find out for yourself,' Barcelona says.

The waitress returns with another basket of tortilla chips and two bowls of hot salsa. She takes their orders and leaves, again tugging the back of her skirt as she walks away.

Trina sips a Diet Coke and spreads Dixie's paper next to Barcelona's paper. Then she removes a neatly typed sheet from her own purse. 'This guy's engaged, but I don't think it's a serious engagement.' She describes Howdy White.

'Sounds good,' Diva says. 'But how do you approach a guy who's engaged?'

'How do you approach any of these guys?' Dixie asks.

173

'I mean, you don't just walk up and say, "Hi, your name was on my take-out menu."'

Trina laughs. 'Why not? Just call one of these guys up, say you're a friend of whoever introduced him to our menu, and say you'd like to meet him for a drink after work. What's the problem?'

'We don't all have your balls,' Barcelona says.

'Most guys don't have your balls,' Diva agrees.

'We could have a dinner party,' Trina says. 'Invite four guys to Dixie's or Barcy's place, theirs are the cleanest, and we could mingle and choose then.'

Barcelona shakes her head. 'Count me out. I'd feel like I was back in high school. What if two of us go after the same guy, or two guys go after one of us. It makes the others feel shitty. I don't like it.'

'I agree,' Dixie says.

Trina thinks it over, shrugs. 'Well, then everyone's on their own. We just keep adding names to the menu and let each of us decide what to do with those names. Something or nothing. Okay?'

'Okay,' Barcelona says. She has no intention of using the stupid menu anyway.

Apparently, Eric had been waiting for her the afternoon she'd come home from lunch and lessons in girl-watching with Harley.

'I was watching from my car,' he said, still holding her. His hands cupped her buttocks in that familiar way. She thought she should say something, pull away, but it felt so good, so comfortable, that she didn't move, didn't say anything. His fingers kneaded her butt affectionately. When he spoke, his voice was a warm mist in her ear. 'I've been out there for hours.'

'Oh?'

'Okay, half an hour. But it felt longer.'

'You never liked cars.'

'I tried reading.' He broke away to pull a large paperback out of his jacket pocket, *Not in Our Genes*. 'About the invalidity of biological determinism. Really fascinating. You should read it.'

'Sure,' Barcelona said. 'Now?'

He laughed nervously. 'No, not now. When I'm done. I'll lend it to you.'

'Okay.' She looked up into his dark eyes. The crooked scar that cleaved his eyebrow caught the light from the window and gleamed a pure white. 'Anything else?' she asked.

'Huh? What do you mean?'

'You didn't wait in the car for all that time just to tell me about this book, did you?'

He looked confused, embarrassed. 'Yeah, well . . .'

Barcelona walked out to the kitchen, Roger's scripts still clutched in her arms. Eric followed. She set the scripts on the kitchen table and went to the refrigerator. 'Want something to drink?'

'What have you got?'

She tossed him a can of Diet Squirt. 'This or nothing.'

He popped the can and sucked up the foam. 'How can you still drink this stuff? Tastes like acid.'

Barcelona didn't know what to do or say. She felt like she was in a play she hadn't rehearsed and for which she didn't know her lines. The actor's nightmare, it was called, though she had only ever been on stage once, in her high school's production of *Oklahoma!* She was in the chorus. She moved around the kitchen straightening the toaster, wiping the counter, opening a can of cat food for Larry, her cat. She rarely saw Larry. Occasionally she would hear him enter the cat door and hear him eat. But he never hung around the house. He didn't like to sleep with her nor did he like to be picked up or petted. She wasn't even sure why she fed him; she really didn't have any feelings for him. A year ago she'd agreed to keep him for some friends while they moved to Utah. Later they'd called to say they weren't allowed to have pets in their new apartment. They asked Barcelona to have Larry put to sleep. They'd reimburse her the thirty dollars. But Barcelona couldn't do that. It was easier for her to open two cans of 9 Lives Sliced Beef in Gravy every day than to have him killed.

Eric sat at the kitchen table making interlocking wet rings with his can of soda on the glass top. Finally Barcelona had no more props to fuss with and she sat in the chair next to his.

'What's the matter?' she asked. 'You look glum.'

He looked in her eyes, a gaze so direct and unblinking she winced a little. 'I don't know what I'm doing here,' he said.

She had the feeling he was about to say something that would complicate both their lives, make things sticky and sneaky and uncomfortable. She tried to head him off. 'How's Luna?'

He blinked. 'Fine. Great. She's a terrific woman. Well, you saw.'

'Yes.'

'And she's very smart. She doesn't apply herself as she should, but she has great potential.'

'For what?' Barcelona asked.

He blinked again, shrugged. 'For whatever she wants. She gets straight A's in her classes, has a 4.0 GPA. She's also on the swim team at school. Does the butterfly stroke. It's very beautiful, very sensual to watch. I go to all her swim meets.'

'Cozy,' Barcelona said and immediately regretted the snideness in her tone. This was not how she wanted to act, not at her age.

'I won't talk about her if it makes you uncomfortable.'

'No, I'm sorry. I'm just preprogrammed for sarcasm. I liked Luna, I really did.'

Eric nodded. 'She's something special.'

What am I, Barcelona thought, *yellow waxy buildup*? She said, 'She certainly is.'

Eric reached across the table and laid his hands over hers. 'Thing is, Barcy, I miss you.'

Barcelona's heart squirmed uncomfortably in her chest. This is what a baby must feel like jockeying for position in the womb, she thought. She concentrated on breathing, deep soothing breaths.

'I know it sounds funny,' Eric said. 'But it's true.'

Barcelona decided to play it casual, not fall into any traps. She removed her hands from under his and patted his arm in a friendly manner. 'I miss you too, Eric,' she said with a sisterly smile. 'That's natural.'

'You know what I mean, Barcy.' His eyes were slicked with moisture. 'I'm already squirming, no need to kick me too.'

'I don't know what you want from me, Eric. I really don't.'

He leaned across the kitchen table, pushed the pile of scripts out of the way. One slid off the top of the pile and splatted onto the wood floor. Eric ignored it. There was something so theatrical about the script falling and Eric ignoring it that Barcelona almost laughed. But then Eric leaned closer toward her until he was kissing her and she wasn't stopping him, not only not stopping him, but opening her lips, her mouth, receiving his tongue, not wanting to laugh anymore, not wanting to do anything but this, keep kissing him. His left hand cupped the back of her head and pulled her mouth even tighter against his. His other hand cupped her breast and she pushed herself tighter against his hand. His fingers found her nipples through her bra and he pinched hard, which she liked. A sudden moan vibrated up from her throat and into his mouth.

Even as they dropped to the kitchen floor, she knew this was a big mistake. Did she really want Eric again, or did she just want to get back at Luna? Was he leaving Luna or was this a quick fuck for old times' sake? They should talk about it first. But there didn't seem to be a chance. They were busy struggling out of their clothes, piling them under Barcelona's back and buttocks as a cushion against the hardwood floor. She wasn't in the mood for much foreplay, she wanted him inside her now.

He was rocking on top of her, her legs clamped over his hips, her ankles hooked together. The scab on her right ankle kept rubbing against the other with each thrust, but the pain didn't bother her. He said I love you half a dozen times but that didn't bother her either. Behind her she heard the heavy rubber flap of the cat door open. She opened her eyes, saw that Eric's were still closed tight in concentration. She glanced upside down over her shoulder. Larry, fat and gray, was sniffing the fallen script. He batted it once with his paw, then turned away and went over to his bowl of food. He ate noisily. Never once had he even looked at Barcelona or Eric.

Barcelona closed her eyes again and tightened her grip on Eric's shoulders. She felt a button from her blouse grinding into her shoulder blade and shifted. But the button was stuck to her skin and moved with her.

She was on the verge of coming but Eric was stopping a lot, something he always did when he wanted to last a long time. But she didn't want him to last a long time. She wanted to come and she wanted him to come. She wanted to feel him exploding inside of her, feel his body sag against hers, collapsing into her arms. She reached around behind him, between his legs, gently cupped her hands around his balls, and squeezed just a little. His body arched with pleasure and he began pumping faster. She stroked his tight sack a few times and he thrust deeper and harder against her. She slammed her pelvis up against his and he moaned. Suddenly he was coming, his hips spasming, his elbows wobbly. Feeling him coming made her come too and she clutched against him the way she imagined locusts cling to corn husks. Odd image, she thought as she heard the rubber flap of the cat door again as Larry exited.

They silently stood up and walked up to the bedroom, got in bed, and held each other while both drifted in and out of sleep for the next hour. It was the most comfortable Barcelona had felt with a man in a long time. She didn't worry that she would drool or snore in her sleep. Eric had seen it all before. He just held her tight. She had to admit, he was the best cuddler she'd ever known. He never grew impatient with the closeness and rolled away. He could sleep for hours while holding her in his arms, an attribute she found more desirable than sexual agility. Which he sometimes also had.

Finally, when they were both awake and staring into each other's eyes, he wound his finger through her hair and said, 'What about Luna?'

Trina dips the tip of her napkin in her water glass and tries to scrub the enchilada sauce from her blouse. 'Damn, this blouse is practically new.'

'It had to be christened sooner or later,' Dixie says.

'Why couldn't it have been a cream sauce?' Trina says, scrubbing.

The waitress arrives to clear the dishes. As she stacks them efficiently in one arm, she asks if anyone wants dessert.

'Want to split something?' Trina asks Barcelona.

'Like what?'

'There is only one thing worth pigging out over. Death by Chocolate.'

Barcelona made a nauseated face. 'God, Trina.'

'We'll have one,' Trina tells the waitress. 'Two forks.'

The waitress nods. As she reaches for Dixie's almost full plate she asks, 'Do you want to take this home?'

Dixie shakes her head.

The waitress stares at the plate. 'Something wrong with it?'

'No. It was fine.'

The waitress balances the plate on top of three others and whisks away.

'You still not eating?' Barcelona asks Dixie.

'I eat,' Dixie says. She takes a package of vitamins out of her purse, tears it open, and begins swallowing them one at a time, washing each down with water.

'Vitamins are okay,' Trina says. 'But they don't compare with Death by Chocolate.'

'Have you been taking yours?' Dixie asks Trina.

'Want to check my urine? Bright as sunshine.' She picks up her water, sees the junk floating in it from when she scrubbed her blouse, picks up Diva's water instead, and drinks the whole glass. 'God, I wouldn't mind some wine right now.'

'Causes breast cancer,' Diva says. 'I saw that on the news the other night. Some study said so.'

Trina nods. 'I read about that. One glass a week of booze ups your chances by fifty percent. Is there anything left in this world that doesn't go straight for our breasts? It's all a woman can do these days to hold on to these things for a lifetime.'

'Alcohol causes cancer,' Dixie says. 'So does diet soda. So do those cigarettes.' She points at Diva's black root in the ashtray. 'And that chocolate monstrosity you ordered will clog those arteries like hair in your drain. Half the stuff we consumed right here at this table tonight is trying to kill us from the inside out.'

'Now what's the bad news?' Trina says and they all laugh.

Barcelona goes to the rest room. She doesn't wait to see if anyone wants to go with her. She wants to go alone. She's avoided Trina the past couple of weeks because she didn't want to tell her about Eric. She feels guilty enough, but Trina would also make her feel stupid.

Only the handicapped stall is available. Barcelona hates using it, though she has no reasonable explanation for feeling that way. She's not afraid of catching anything, being crippled isn't contagious. Mostly she's terrified that while she's in there someone in a wheelchair will come in who really has to go and can't use any of the other stalls. How would Barcelona feel stepping out of the stall seeing a woman wriggling frantically in a wheelchair waiting for her?

Barcelona pulls down her jeans and panties and sits. The urine starts to flow and it burns. Her vagina is sore, from membranes to muscles. During the past two weeks, she has made love with Eric at least a couple of dozen times. Baker's dozens. They have tried new positions and locations that they never did even when they lived together. Last night they had tried to make love but both were too sore. The head of Eric's penis looked inflamed and angry.

She washes her hands, and returns to the table. The Death by Chocolate has been served and Trina has eaten most of it. 'What a swine,' Barcelona says, pulling the plate away from Trina.

'I'm doing it for you,' Trina says. 'Every bite I eat is five hundred fewer calories on your hips.'

Barcelona eats a bite, makes a rapturous face at Trina.

'Go ahead, eat the rest. You're doing me a favor,' Trina

says. 'I took Karyn in to see the orthodontist last week to see if she needed braces. Son of a bitch says Karyn's teeth are fine but that *I* could use braces. Said I could look just like Kathleen Turner.'

Dixie laughs. 'What'd you tell him?'

'I asked him whether it bothered him having people look up his nose all day long. Did he worry about what they saw or did he pick his nose before each patient?'

Barcelona choked on her dessert, washed it down with water.

'Has anyone else noticed,' Trina asks matter-of-factly, 'that as guys get older, the hair in their noses gets bushier? Am I the only one who's noticed?'

'Maybe you've had more opportunity to make that observation than the rest of us,' Dixie says.

'Maybe. But it's true. Someone ought to tell them, though. Considering the position that women usually are in, we have to look up those things a lot.'

'Maybe that's why people close their eyes during sex,' Diva offers.

Barcelona leaves a few bites of chocolate and pushes the plate over to Trina. 'Here, you've grossed me out of the rest of it.'

'Good, it worked.' Trina gobbles the chocolate hungrily.

The check comes and everyone begins counting out cash. Diva throws her Visa card on the plate. 'I'll charge it, you guys can pay me the cash.' No one disagrees, but she hurries on with explanation. 'I'm getting my hair permed tomorrow and ever since I bounced a couple checks, they want cash from me.'

'I see on the news that The Candidate's up a couple points in the polls,' Dixie says.

Trina tosses a twenty on top of Diva's Visa card. 'Still not enough to win, but we're nipping at Carla Bennington's butt.'

'You able to turn up anything scandalous on her yet?' Barcelona asks.

'Not yet,' Trina says, but in a tone that Barcelona recognizes as meaning she is close. Trina is very good at her job; if there's something to find, she will find it. She turns to Barcelona, obviously anxious to change the subject. 'How's the screenplay coming?'

'It's coming,' Barcelona says. She turns away from Trina, a sign they all recognize as meaning she doesn't want to discuss it. Once Barcelona has started a project, she never talks about it with anyone.

In the parking lot, Trina tells them she will make copies of their menu and send each one a list. Three of them split up and hunt down their cars. Only Dixie has used the valet parking. Trina walks part of the way through the lot with Barcelona.

'What's with you lately?' Trina asks.

'What do you mean?'

'I haven't heard from you in a week. You can't be that buried in your work.'

Barcelona hesitates, wanting to confess everything, tell about Eric. She can't. Not yet. 'Screenplays aren't as easy as they look. I've had to do a lot of research.'

Trina looks into her eyes. Barcelona holds the gaze, not wanting to give anything away. 'Okay,' Trina finally says. 'Maybe we can have lunch this week.'

'Sure. Monday's good. I'll be in L.A. anyway. I'm driving my script up to Grief.'

'Fine. Stop by the office, we'll go from there. About eleven-thirty we can miss the lunch crowd.'

Barcelona agrees. She waves to Trina as she gets into her car. Trina waves back and squeezes between two parked cars on her way to the next row.

The drive home is unusual. She turns on the radio, presses every preset button but can't find a song she likes.

183

Several of the buttons are for oldies stations, but she doesn't recognize the songs because they are too recent. She considers that a bad sign. She tries using the Seek button, but nothing satisfies her. She gropes for a tape cassette from the glove compartment, slips it in. Smokey Robinson and the Miracles sing 'I Second That Emotion.' She immediately ejects the tape. Nothing seems right. Even dinner tonight seemed somehow off-kilter. Dixie still not eating, gobbling vitamins. Trina pushing that stupid menu idea on everyone. Diva depressed and jealous.

Barcelona takes a shortcut through an undeveloped section of Irvine. The wooden skeletons of clusters of new condos under construction hunker in the dark on either side of the road where eight months ago were strawberry fields. Deep gulches wide as a stream follow the contours of the narrow road like black rivers. This is where the sewage pipes will go. She can see the giant pipes stacked on the side of the road. In a year, these will all be homes for more young middle-class couples with little children. Barcelona does not begrudge the future owners their piece of the planned community of Irvine. She is happy for them. But as far as she knows, there are no plans to increase the number of supermarkets in the area. Lines are already intolerably long. Rather than shop for the week, Barcelona limits all her purchases to ten items or less and carries enough cash to go through the express lines. Lately, even those lines are long.

She is debating whether or not to stop by Von's right now to pick up some panty hose and Diet Squirt, when she feels something thud against her car. She is alone on the dark road and pulls over to the side, careful not to drive into the sewage gulch. Her heart is bouncing as she jumps out of the car. She knows it must be a small animal, a rabbit maybe or a gopher, but fears it may be someone's pet cat or dog. She looks down the road, sees a black blob of something on the road. It is screaming, leaping, heaving its mangled body off the ground, but each time it flops back to the ground with a tortured shriek.

Barcelona is running now, running down the middle of the road. In the distance, maybe a mile away, she can see headlights approach. She has only about a minute to do something. If it is someone's pet, she will have to take it to a vet, contact the owners. If not a pet, then what? Leave it?

She is within fifty feet and now she knows what it is. The scent hits her at first almost sweetly, then, halfway up her nostrils, it bites the membranes with a sour stench. Skunk. She stops running toward it. She watches the car in the distance approaching. The animal is not wrenching itself anymore, it is merely quivering. She can see the black liquid puddled around it. Barcelona doesn't know what to do. She thinks of Luna, how she had taken charge with Henry Finney's bloated body as he lay on the bathroom floor in his own waste. Barcelona had sat on the bed and watched, listened to Mrs. Finney eulogize her dead husband, his clothes all laid out less than five feet away for dinner at The Sizzler. Malibu Chicken.

The headlights flicker ahead, rounding a curb, then disappearing behind the bend next to one of the condo development sites. Barcelona inhales deeply several times, holds her breath, and runs the rest of the way toward the skunk. Even without breathing she can smell it, its scent seeping through her pores. She had read somewhere that skunk secretions are used as a perfume base. Perhaps the Tuxedo perfume she is wearing right now has skunk in it.

The skunk's eyes are open. She can't tell if it is alive, if it is breathing under all that blood-matted fur. It doesn't have a white stripe down its back like cartoon skunks. It has two stripes that curve back from the top of its head

185

down along the side of its body, across the hindquarters, and disappear into its tail.

Barcelona's lungs are burning. She needs air. What she has stored in her lungs is seeping out of her mouth.

The other car's headlights are full on her now, coming down this straight stretch of road. She looks around the side of the road. Some jagged chunks of plywood are discarded in the weeds. One is flat and wide enough that she could use it to scoop him up like a pizza and moved him to the side of the road. If he is still alive, she will drive him to a vet. The hell with her car. The hell with the smell. She is not afraid; she can take action like Luna. She exhales the rest of her air and takes a shallow, tentative breath. Not as bad as before. This isn't that bad. Quickly she climbs down into the gulch, reaches into the weeds for the plywood, and scrambles back up to the side of the road.

Too late.

The approaching car whooshes by, the left front and left rear tires bouncing over the skunk's body. If it had been alive before, it definitely is not now.

Barcelona tosses the plywood into the sewage gulch and slaps the dirt off her hands. She hurries back to her car and drives away.

When she arrives home, she immediately turns on all the lights and the TV. She flips the channels until she finds a 'M*A*S*H' rerun. The phone answering machine is next to the refrigerator. She pushes the playback button and pours wine into a coffee mug while listening. The first message is from her mother: 'Hi, sweetheart. Nothing new, just wanted to see how my Hollywood girl is. Talk to you soon.' The second message was from a student: 'Ms. Lee? This is Trudy Cornelius. Um, I was in your class last semester. Thing is, I got a D. They're talking about taking away my Social Security for school. Can I do some extra credit or something now and maybe you could change my grade? My number is 678-0998. Thanks a lot.'

Barcelona sits at the kitchen table. Alan Alda is sniffing a pair of socks, making a face. She can still smell the dead skunk's scent and thinks it a funny coincidence that Alan is sniffing his socks.

The third message: 'Hi, Barcy, it's Luna.'

Barcelona turns and looks at the answering machine as if it were Luna and she had just caught her in bed with Eric. She feels her pulse thumping as much as it had when she'd hit the skunk.

The machine continues: 'I'd like to talk sometime, if you've got some free time. Give me a call.'

The voice is friendly, not threatening, not hurt. Not accusing. The machine shuts itself off, but Barcelona continues to stare at it until the theme song to 'M*A*S*H' plays and she turns to see the closing credits roll by too fast to read any names.

14

Diva lies in bed singing.

'Cocktail waitress don't have a smile to spare/Gotta serve martinis then go fix her hair.'

She stops, scratches her pubic hairs, thinks about the lyrics. She's been working on this song daily for two weeks. So far she has only these two lines, but no definite melody. She's been lying in bed for the past hour singing variations on the same two lines.

She sings the words again with a different tune, going higher at the end of each line rather than lower. She shakes her head unhappily. Something's not right. She tries it folksy, then rockabilly, then with a country twang. Nothing is right. She likes the lines but the melody sucks. She looks around for some paper and a pen.

She tugs open the drawer of the bed stand, rummages through the magazines, three old *TV Guides*, *Self*, *Vegetarian Times*, *Spin*, *Rolling Stone*, some coupons for free frozen yogurt at a new store down the street. A stub of a yellow pencil lies on the bottom of the drawer, sticky from God knows what. The pencil's point is broken so she picks and peels at the wood until a nub of graphite peeks through. It reminds her of a dog's dick unsheathing and she laughs. She picks up *Rolling Stone* and leafs through it searching for a page with an ad that has lots of white space. Page 72 has the perfect ad, one for Infinity speakers.

She begins writing her lyrics above the simulated oak-finished speakers.

Immediately, she gets another idea and starts singing: *'Cocktail waitress ain't got an easy life/She gotta talk like the devil and soothe like a wife.'*

She writes that down, looks it over, crosses out 'soothe' and writes 'serve' above it. She sings it with the new word. She isn't happy with that. She crosses out 'serve.'

'Fuck,' she says and scratches herself with ferocity. The crevices of her pubic region itch badly where she shaved them last night. The skin is stubbly and raw with red irritated splotches. She hates shaving there but the new bathing suit she bought yesterday is worth a little discomfort. After trying suits on in fifteen stores, this was the only one that didn't make her look pregnant.

Diva stares at the last line she wrote, but her eyes drift down to the stereo speakers in the ad. RS-4000s with polypropylene drivers and an EMIT tweeter. She could use new speakers, ones that didn't hum and buzz all the time. Something she could listen to without . . .

Listen!

She scratches out 'serve' and writes 'listen.' She sings it in her Bette Midler voice. *'Cocktail waitress ain't got an easy life/Gotta talk like the devil and listen like a wife.'* She sings it again. And again. She likes it. Her soon-to-be hit song, 'Cocktail Waitress,' is finally coming alive. She draws a couple of dollar signs next to the lyrics. Since she was in high school she has tried to write songs but never finished one. The frustration of not finding the right words, or having them sound too much like other songs, always sabotaged her determination. This time will be different, she vows, this time she's serious. Before she was immature, not ready for success. Now she is.

She scoots over to the side of the bed and reaches for her guitar. She strums the D chord and A chord. Back and forth. Then the G chord and D chord back and forth. She tries to sing the lines she has so far using these chords. She doesn't like the way it sounds.

The laminated wood of the guitar is cold against her breasts, making her nipples pucker into hard rubbery tips. Actually, this whole songwriting thing has surprised her. She always imagined the words would be the hardest part and that the music would come easily. Maybe the lyrics had to be worked out very methodically, then the melody would come all at once in a sudden flash of inspiration. So far it hadn't. She tries a dozen different combinations of chords and melodies but doesn't really like any. She takes the guitar off her lap and leans it against the night table. Little red lines are cut into her thighs from the edge of the guitar. She rubs them with her fingertips and they fade a little but don't disappear.

Her song could be a big hit if she could only finish the lyrics and get the right melody. She already knows how it should be sung, with an exotic sensuality, the way Maria Muldar sang 'Midnight at the Oasis.'

Diva sits and daydreams about her song while continuing to scratch her pubic area. Absently her finger dips down and bumps against the clitoris. Diva shivers. She looks down, but her belly sags out just far enough to hide her own crotch from her. She sucks in her gut and watches the white unicorns on her red fingernails romp among the forest of curly brush. She thinks of Calypso sitting here a couple of weeks ago, whacking off with that moronic cross-eyed grin. Still, she doesn't stop rubbing herself.

Her middle finger is slicked with moisture, some of it urine, but most of it thicker and stickier juice. She plunges her finger deep inside herself, spreading her knees apart to accommodate. She probes and stirs, surprised at how good it feels. Feeling good always surprises her. She slides

190

another finger inside herself, not moving them around much, just enjoying the sensation of them inside her, filling her up. Calypso's penis felt this way, the few times he put it in this opening and not the other one.

Diva slides her fingers out and drags them slowly up the moist path to her clitoris. Lazily she massages around it, her fingers flat so her nails don't accidentally scratch her. The warmth in her lap is spreading up through her stomach and into her chest. Her neck feels flushed. She keeps rubbing but misses the full feeling of something deep inside her. She doesn't want to get up now to get her worn plastic vibrator with the dead batteries. Instead, she brings her left hand down and inserts two fingers as deep as they will go, until she can feel each knuckle inside her. With her right hand, she keeps rubbing, picking up speed, feeling the clitoris swell and throb. The heat down there is so great, each pubic hair feels like a live electrical wire shocking her with hot volts. Her head rolls back and she closes her eyes. She is rubbing so fast her hand is cramping up. But she can't stop. She pictures a door, big wooden doors, carved with grotesque creatures from the Middle Ages. The doors are locked but there is something on the other side, some powerful force. The doors bulge and stretch the way they do in cartoons as the force on the other side tries to break through. Diva rubs faster, her sharp fingernail nicking her sensitive membrane. She jerks from the shock but doesn't stop. The door is stretching thinner and thinner. She rubs, feels the heat in her chest spreading. Her right leg shoots out and grazes the guitar, the toes brushing the strings, strumming some strange chord. Her left hand burrows even deeper inside her. She continues, watching the door stretch, but it never bursts. She is getting sore now and stops rubbing, withdraws her fingers from inside her. She got close that time.

Diva sits there a minute catching her breath. Then she

stands up, walks into the bathroom, washes her hands in the sink, and brushes her teeth.

'Wanna beer?'

Diva shakes her head and drops her towel and bag next to his beach chair. 'Too early.'

'Early? Shit,' Coma says. He is leaning back in his chair, head tilted toward the sun, eyes closed. A white visor shades his eyes. His long legs are stretched out as far as they will go and his feet are buried up to the ankles in sand. A battered 18-panel Spalding beach volleyball sits in his lap. One hand spiders the ball with his fingers, the other holds a paper bag with a can of beer inside. It is only ten in the morning and Diva can smell the beer sweat on his body. She looks up and down his body. It is a magnificent body. Long and lean and tan and muscled. He is twenty-seven. His real name is Jarrod Reisner, but everyone calls him Coma because he seems to live in one. He is slow-moving, slow-talking. Except when he plays volleyball. Then he is the fastest, toughest, fiercest player out here.

'You off work today?' he asks her without opening his eyes.

'I have a couple hours free. Thought we might play a couple games.'

He opens his eyes and squints at her. 'That can be arranged.'

Only sex, drugs, or volleyball can rouse Coma from his beach chair. During their friendship, Diva has given him all three. The sex was only once and that was over a year ago. It was a cold overcast day and nobody had come down to the beach to play volleyball. Coma had been there for four hours, drinking and waiting. Finally Diva had shown up, just off a radio commercial in which she sang the radio station's call letters. Coma had been drunk and bored and horny. Diva had taken him across the street to her apartment to sober him up before he drove home. He made a pass at her over the instant coffee and she didn't resist. They'd screwed quickly and afterward napped for a couple of hours. When she awoke he was gone and neither had mentioned it since.

Coma's family had money. They owned several of the fanciest restaurants in Newport Beach. Last year his uncle had pulled out of his gated driveway, driven two blocks in his black Porsche with a cassette of Crosby, Stills, and Nash playing on the stereo system, stopped at a stop sign, and was shot five times in the head and neck by a passing car. Police reported it as a gangland-style slaying and the TV speculated on drug connections, but Coma never seemed to have any drugs of his own and was always bumming them off other people.

Apparently the family expected Coma to enter the family restaurant business once he grew out of this beach phase of his. Diva doubted that this was a phase. This was just who he was.

He sits up, tosses her the ball. 'New suit, huh?'

Diva beams. 'You like?'

'Cute.'

The suit is a one-piece, mostly white with some blue and white mountains at the abdomen and seven tiny blue kangaroos hopping across the stomach. Boxed in red across her breasts was the word Australia.

He stretches out, looks around the beach for some competition. The locals know not to challenge him unless they are at the top of their game. Coma doesn't have a beach rating because he never plays in tournaments, though several pros have asked him to partner with them. He turns them all down. In fact, he doesn't even bother playing at other beaches or even other nets. He plays exclusively at this net and everyone who plays serious

193

beach volleyball knows where to find him. Occasionally the unwary, the uninitiated wander by and, in a friendly way, not knowing who he is, ask him to play. He just shakes his head and naps in his beach chair until worthy opponents came by.

Diva is an excellent player too, though nowhere near his league. She grew up around here, has played beach volleyball since she was a little girl, even played on her high school indoor team. Coed volleyball is not really taken seriously down here, but is played as a kind of relaxing intermission. For the guys. The women have to hustle their butts off or forever be banned.

Diva stands on the court and practices setting the ball to herself while Coma slowly saunters onto the court. He tosses some sand up to check the wind direction. He scans the beach looking for someone to play.

'Let's just warm up,' Diva suggests. 'Someone will come along.'

They set the ball back and forth a few minutes, then do some hot pepper spiking and digging practice.

'You want to hit some?' she asks him.

He shakes his head. 'Too hot.'

Surfers wander back and forth, toting their fiberglass boards. Some look over in Diva and Coma's direction, but they don't challenge.

After twenty minutes a couple of guys walk up, watch Diva and Coma set for a few minutes. From their short square haircuts, Diva knows they are marines from the El Toro base. One of them is big and muscular, with a neck as thick as his thigh. The other is skinny, not as tall, but also well built. They are bare-chested and hairless, both have tan lines on their arms and necks from their uniform T-shirts.

'How about a game?' the big one asks.

Coma doesn't even look at them. He just watches the

194

ball soaring back and forth between him and Diva. 'Sure.' He lets one of her sets drop through his hands and he butts the ball with his head toward them. 'Warm up.'

The two marines hit it back and forth a few times, practice their spikes. Diva thinks they are pretty good.

When the game starts, the marines serve only to Coma, which is a courtesy because that allows him to pass the ball, Diva to set, then him to spike. The theory is this makes the teams more evenly matched since he had to play with a female. After Coma crushes their first serve down so hard the ball bounces back up over their heads, they stop this courtesy and serve to Diva. However, she is also a good hitter, dinking, cutting to the sides, and even spiking a few into the back court. The game is over at 11-1. They play two more games. 11-0. 11-1.

The marines leave without saying anything. As they walk away the bigger one punches the thinner one in the arm, knocking him sideways. The thinner one rubs his arm, shouts 'Fuck you!' at his friend and walks down to the ocean and dives in. The bigger guy sits on the sand and watches his buddy swim.

'Beer?' Coma offers Diva. He opens his cooler and there are half a dozen 16-ounce 7-Up bottles inside. It is Coma's clever habit to replace the soda with beer so he can drink it on the beach. The one in the paper bag he'd been drinking when she first arrived must've been the one he'd been drinking on the drive down.

'Sure,' Diva says. She takes one and drinks a large gulp. She doesn't have much time. She has to be at her other job soon, the one she keeps a secret, even from Barcy, Trina, and Dixie.

'Hey, dude,' Cliff says as he and Bart walk up.

'Hey,' Coma said, squinting up from his chair. 'It's the fag patrol.'

'You wish,' Bart says, reaching into the cooler. He tosses

a beer to Cliff and takes one for himself. They are both about twenty, tanned, well built. They might have been Coma's little brothers. But then Diva thinks most of the guys on this beach looked as if they could be related. Hairless bronzed bodies with large pecs and narrow waists. They'd have made attractive girls.

'Hey, Diva,' Bart says, 'how's the singing?'

'Same,' Diva says. 'How's your job?'

'I quit, man. Fuck that shit.' He'd been a valet at a fancy French restaurant owned by Coma's family. 'It was cool driving those red cars, man, but they all thought, you know, that they were better than me, just because they drove a Jag or a Rolls or something.'

'They are better than you, man,' Cliff says.

Coma laughs. 'Yeah.'

After a couple of minutes, Ed Dortmunder and his girlfriend, Diedre, stroll by eating ice cream cones. Ed is almost as good a player as Coma, so they naturally are pretty good friends. Diedre is a knockout blonde with large breasts and long legs. She wears a bikini so small that Diva is certain she'd had to shave all her pubic hairs to wear it. Ed's parents own a lot of real estate on Lido Isle. He and Diedre both attend USC together, but come down to Newport Beach on weekends.

They all converse about nothing in particular, but Diva feels herself slowly being edged out of the picture. Not on purpose, but by virtue of some jungle instinct in these guys. They all face Ed and Diedre, directing comments to her just so they would have an excuse to stare at her. When they think she isn't looking, their eyes flick down to her breasts, the outline of her nipples against the thin fabric, or down to her crotch where the material creased in along the crevice of her hairless cunt. Diva feels herself getting fatter by the second. Her thighs are ballooning, her stomach puffing out like a blowfish. Soon her new suit would simply burst apart and she'd have to run home naked.

'See you,' Diva says, gathering her stuff.

'Yeah,' Coma says. 'Thanks for the games. We showed them marines.'

'See ya,' the others say, including Diedre.

'You can leave your panties on for now,' she tells Diva.

Diva does so, stepping out of the bathroom wearing only her panties, the rest of her clothes folded neatly in a pile in her arms. She sets them down in the usual place, the antique wooden rocker by the bay window.

This is only Diva's second time here. She is still unsure of herself.

Toni Hammond is carefully unwrapping the plastic cover from the half-formed figure. 'This is a water-based clay,' she explains. 'If I don't keep it covered, the clay dries out.'

'Oh.' Diva nods. She stands self-consciously in the middle of the studio. She knows it's ridiculous, but she feels as if she should cover her breasts until they start.

Toni continues to study the figure, touching it here and there, running her fingers along the clay, following ridges of cheekbones, the hollow of the neck, the jut of the jawbone. She chews on the inside of her mouth as she circles around the figure. Diva decides the face looks nothing like her own and that maybe Toni is not very good at what she does. Still, the pay is good, and Diva needs all the money she can get if she's to make this songwriting thing work.

'Don't worry about the face,' Toni says. 'It's not supposed to look like you.'

'How'd you know I was thinking that?'

Toni smiles. 'I've been doing this a long time.' She strokes the brow over the figure's left eye. 'Needs some shaping here.' She takes out some instrument with a

197

wooden handle and a metal triangle on the end and starts shaving some of the brow away. Toni is about forty. She is dressed in jeans and an extra large tuxedo shirt that is smeared with dried clay. At first sight she appears attractive, but after a while there is something about her that is slightly disconcerting. Her limbs are too elongated, like someone standing in front of a distorting fun house mirror. Her arms and legs and fingers, even her neck and face seem stretched beyond healthy limits, as if she were some sort of elastic doll whose extremities had been tugged on by a nasty child. 'What do you do, Dianne?' Toni asks. 'I mean when you're not doing aerobics.' They met in aerobics class last week. Toni had walked up to Diva in the locker room while Diva was struggling to peel off her sweaty leotard. 'Your body is perfect,' she'd said and handed Diva a business card. Now here she was.

'I'm a singer,' Diva answers. 'And songwriter.'

'Yeah, I used to be an artist/secretary. Then I was an artist/salesclerk, then an artist/seamstress.'

'Now you're just an artist,' Diva says.

Toni laughs. 'How sweet.'

'What do you mean?'

'Not many would call making mannequins an art. They think of it as something like illustrating comic books or something.'

'Looks like art to me,' Diva says. 'Anyway, you seem to work hard enough at it that they should give you the benefit of the doubt.'

'I'm afraid how hard one works is not always the main criteria for what constitutes art.'

Diva is getting in over her head here. She is not well read nor very intellectual. Her philosophy is if you like it it must be art. 'I don't know much about the visual arts,' she says. 'I'm mostly into music.'

198

'You said you sing.'

Diva nods. 'And write songs. I'm working on a tough one now. I don't care what anyone else says, when I'm finally done with it, I'm calling it art.'

Toni laughs, puts down her tool. She walks over to Diva and starts staring at her face and body, studying it in a way that makes Diva uncomfortable. Toni stares too long at Diva's plump belly. 'Perfect,' she says, placing her hand on it, sizing it like a melon in the supermarket.

'This is weird,' Diva says. 'I still don't get it. Why would anyone want fat mannequins?'

Toni doesn't say anything. She'd explained the whole thing the other night and Diva knows enough about the woman to realize she does not like repeating herself. All Diva remembers is that Toni designs the prototype mannequins from which the rest are cast. She works for an L.A. mannequin company whose visual director told her that there was a new demand for chubby mannequins, not just for specialty stores catering to overweight women, but even for the major department stores. Nordstrom's wanted a couple of hundred. Apparently, there are millions of fatties out there who were tired of seeing waifish mannequins with hollow cheeks, flat stomachs, and no rumps.

Toni starts arranging Diva into a pose. It is not a very difficult pose, hips a little forward, back arched slightly. 'I want to get the chest right today.' She stares at Diva's breasts and frowns. 'What size are you?'

'Dress size?'

'Breast size. What's your chest measurement?'

'Uh, thirty-six.'

'Hmmm.' Toni goes over to the drawer of a desk and pulls out a red tape measure. 'Probably a lot of those inches are due to the size of your back.' She lays the tape measure across Diva's chest, from armpit to armpit. Then she shakes her head, thinks, and measures each breast, strapping the tape across each breast separately.

'I hope they're the same,' Diva says.

'Huh?' Toni looks up. 'Oh.' She smiles. 'Yes, they're fine. Breasts are very tricky in the mannequin business. Usually we make them different for each style of clothing. For example, with lingerie I want the breasts to look bigger, so I make the back smaller. It's different for sportswear, where they want the bodies to look smaller and younger, more active. Then I pull the rib cage out wider and flatten the chest. See?'

Diva nods. 'I didn't realize how complicated it is.'

'It's not really,' Toni says. She returns to her clay, starts forming the breasts with her hands, cupping and rubbing and building and smoothing, all with her fingers in muddy clay.

Diva finds it a little unnerving to have a woman staring at her breasts while fondling another pair, even if that other pair is clay. There's something weird about it. She doesn't say anything. She decides this is a perfect opportunity to work on her song. She quietly hums different melodies to the four lines she has written.

After twenty minutes Toni gives her a break. 'You're a good model,' Toni says, handing her a robe. 'Most models can't hold a pose longer than twenty minutes. You looked like you could just keep going.'

'I was thinking about my song.'

'Oh? Is it ready for public singing? I'd love to hear it.'

'God, no. Not yet.'

Toni nods, walks over to the mini refrigerator. On top of the refrigerator is a coffee maker with half a pot of coffee. 'Want something to drink? Juice or coffee?'

'Juice, please.'

'Apple, grape, tomato.'

'Apple.'

200

Toni hands Diva a can of apple juice. Diva pulls the tab and drinks. She looks around the studio at various mannequins standing against the walls. She wonders if maybe there's a song in all this. 'Now what?' Diva asks. 'I mean when you're done what happens?'

'The mold-makers come over here and pull a plaster waste mold.'

'Waste mold?'

'They call it that because it gets thrown away later, along with the clay model. See, they cast a fiberglass prototype that looks just like this thing. Then they cut it at the hip and leg so they can be more easily packed and dressed and undressed. You know. Then they use the fiberglass prototype to make the production mold.'

'Must be a kick to go shopping and see your mannequins in the stores. Like having a gallery showing of your work.'

'Not quite,' Toni says, sipping coffee. 'But it's rewarding.'

'What about men?'

Toni looked startled, her cup frozen halfway to her mouth. 'Pardon?'

Diva realizes Toni thinks the question is personal. That's why she looks as if one of her mannequins had just started speaking, like on that old 'Twilight Zone' episode. 'I meant male mannequins. Are there going to be any in this chub line?'

'Not yet. Frankly, I'm relieved. Male mannequins are the hardest. You can't do them in any type of motion or it's considered effeminate. Mostly you have them either leaning forward like bird dogs, or sitting down with their legs apart, looking tough. And with their hands in fists, always in fists.

Diva laughs. 'That seems so silly.'

'To us. But no guy wants to buy clothing from a mannequin that looks swishy.'

'Well, some guys do.'

Toni laughs. 'I'll create that line when they ask me.'

They go back to work. Diva is arranged in the same pose, Toni is back smoothing the breasts of her clay model. After a while she stares unhappily at the breasts, looks at Diva's breasts then back at her clay breasts. She shakes her head. 'The nipples aren't right. Each breast has a specific kind of nipple that is right for that particular shape.'

'And I don't?' Diva asks.

'Of course you do. I just haven't captured it yet.' Toni walks over to Diva, looks at her breasts, reaches out with both hands and pinches Diva's nipples. Hard.

'Hey!' Diva says. Her nipples swell out, erect.

'That's better.' Toni walks back to the model and re-shapes the nipples.

Diva doesn't know what to say. She never had a woman pinch her nipples before, not since elementary school anyway. She wasn't sure whether she should be angry or embarrassed or what. It was a strange thing to do, but Toni is an artist. She needs erect nipples. Maybe that's the difference between Diva and a real artist. A real artist thinks only of the work, concentrates only on completion, no matter what it takes. Even pinching some other woman's nipples.

Diva is flushed with new purpose. For two weeks she'd been dabbling at her song. What then? Would she jerk around looking for some way to record a demo? Then wait around record company lobbies hoping to get someone to listen? No, she would get more aggressive than that. Be more like Toni. Starting now.

Diva stands frozen in the pose working on her song. When her nipples flatten out, Toni comes over and pinches them again. Diva doesn't mind. This whole thing has been a valuable lesson.

15

'Hurry,' Dixie yells, 'they're getting away.'

'I'm hurrying, damn it.'

'Faster.'

Randy is stooped in front of the sink, rooting through the cupboard. He is wearing only a nubbled bath towel around his waist, which keeps coming undone and which he keeps reknotting. 'For God's sake,' he says in frustration.

'Hurry, hon.'

He snatches up a can of Pledge and tosses it to Dixie. 'Use this in the meantime.'

'Furniture wax?'

'All this shit's the same.'

Dixie tosses the can back to him. 'It's right behind the Brillo pads. Red can.'

Randy continues knocking cans and bottles over in his frantic search for the Raid Ant & Roach Spray. Meantime, Dixie stands guard over the ten thousand ants that have formed a black stripe that goes from the garbage disposal up out of the sink and across the kitchen wall until it disappears behind the built-in microwave oven. When Dixie wandered out from the bedroom this morning to fix some coffee, she thought the black stripe was some spray-painted vandalism, the work of neighborhood punks. Until she saw the stripe moving, flowing like a black river. The stripe bubbled and boiled and jitterbugged with activity as the tiny ants marched back and forth in neat and orderly lines.

When she called to Randy, he stumbled sleepily and naked to the kitchen, took one look at the crawling ants, and ran back into the bedroom to wrap a towel around his waist. Perhaps he thought the towel would protect his crotch from the deadly predators, Dixie mused. Men were paranoid about their crotches. Actually, she hadn't called him out here for help, she just wanted him to witness the amazing sight of all these ants strolling across her wall in an almost perfectly symmetrical stripe. It was almost an art form.

Dixie stands in front of the hordes and stares with admiration at their calmness in the face of imminent destruction. What must they think the blue-eyed chink hovering nearby will do to them? Such trust, or arrogance. She wonders if they are capable of feeling fear.

Dixie is wearing a long yellow T-shirt. There are no clever sayings on the T-shirt, no dancing animals, no icons from popular culture. To find such a blank shirt took her several days of shopping. Under the T-shirt, she is wearing very sexy red panties that she bought as part of her under-cover costume. She hopes she can keep them after the assignment is over. Randy especially likes them. She's noticed that he seems hornier when he sees her still in her high school clothes and makeup than when he sees her as she usually looks. This bothers her a little, though she's sure it's just a harmless fantasy. Most men her age had such a bad time in high school they relish an opportunity to relive those terrible times, only this time they actually get laid.

'Here!' Randy says finally. He stands, hands Dixie the can.

She shakes it, removes the cap, and starts spraying. The poison mist rains on the ants. They don't stop right away,

204

though they do slow down, stagger about, seem confused by the sudden change in weather.

'Like Agent Orange,' Randy says, stepping back a few feet and making a sour face. 'Years from now the survivors will sue you. As a law student, I can guarantee it.'

'What's your advice, counselor?'

'Take no prisoners.'

Dixie laughs. sprays them again. They are slowing down now, wading through the sticky spray. Some are stuck to the wall, a few dead bodies drop to the counter.

'Yeech,' Randy says. 'Ugly little bastards.'

Dixie sprays the garbage disposal, runs some water, turns it on, lets it rattle and grind a few seconds, turns it off.

'Come on, let's get out of here,' Randy says. 'This stuff is making me sick.'

They retreat into the bedroom. Randy shuts the door dramatically, as if they were being chased. Dixie laughs.

'Hell of a way to start the weekend,' he says.

Dixie goes into the bathroom and shuts the door. Floating in the toilet is a used condom from last night's lovemaking. No matter how often she tells him, he never flushes them. He's still on a water conservation kick started a few years ago during the California drought. He stacks bricks in his toilet tanks and bathes in six inches of water. The condom is all stretched out and sickly looking. It reminds her of the molted skin of a snake. Bits of semen are suspended around it like tiny marshmallows in Jell-O. She flushes the toilet before sitting down.

Just as she reaches for *Time* magazine, Randy knocks on the door.

'What's the big secret in there?' he says. This is an old argument. He doesn't like Dixie to close the bathroom door when she goes. He thinks it's a barrier between them, some such Sixties nonsense.

'I'm pissing,' Dixie says. 'I'll give you a full report later.'

'Why the closed door? It's not like I haven't seen every inch of you before. Or tasted every inch of you.'

'You want a taste? I'll save some in a jar.'

'I never close the door when I go.'

'I wish you would,' she says and is immediately sorry. He will take that wrong, she knows.

There is a hurt silence. 'I see,' he says.

'No you don't. I just want this much privacy. It's not shutting you out, it's keeping me in. A moment to myself.'

'Yeah, right.'

'If it'll make you feel more intimate, I'll come out there and fart. Just let me pee alone. Okay?'

He pauses. 'Okay.'

She hears the mattress spring creak as he flops onto the bed. Good. He's in no hurry to go out and play tennis or go to breakfast or go to a matinee. They can laze around for a few hours, read the paper, watch HBO, make love again.

On the wall in front of her is a framed cartoon that Randy bought for her. It is one of those red circles with a diagonal line they use to tell you not to do something: no smoking, no skateboarding, etc. Inside this circle is a caricature of an Oriental man with slanted eyes and buck teeth, grinning moronically behind a steering wheel. No Oriental Drivers. This is a joke exclusive to Orange County, where so many Vietnamese families have settled. There are also large communities of Japanese, Koreans, and Chinese. They all have a reputation for being terrible drivers. Racial loyalty aside, Dixie knows this to be true. Every time she gets behind a car going 30 in a 55 mph zone, or changing lanes suddenly without signaling, or crawling through intersections at 5 mph, she knows it will almost always be an Oriental driver. Before the influx of Vietnamese, everyone ragged on the elderly and their

206

driving habits. A few miles south was a planned community for the elderly called Leisure World. The locals called it Seizure World. The driving for a ten-mile radius around the place was always erratic. Lots of honking horns. Driving slowly is the only sin in Southern California.

When Dixie enters the bedroom again, Randy is lying on his back watching TV. He holds the remote control switcher in his hand and is flipping through the stations.

'Anything good on?' she asks.

He grins. 'Yeah, there's something good on. Take a look.' He points to the towel around his waist. His penis is pressing stiffly up under it.

'Subtle,' she says, smiling.

'There's no time for subtle. The Lakers play in half an hour.'

He is kidding her. Randy likes sports, but he is not addicted to them. They have gone to a couple of Lakers games together. They both like watching sports on TV. Dixie prefers boxing, Randy enjoys baseball. Both like basketball, neither likes football. Seems perfect. She looks at him lying there on the bed, his head propped up with pillows, the white towel around his waist. He is not very tall, about 5'7", but he is burly, thick chested. He is the hairiest man she has ever known, except on the top of his head. While the rest of his body is one thick waterproof pelt of buffalo hide, Randy's head is barely covered by a short cap of thinning hair.

Dixie kneels on the mattress and lays her hand on his chest. The hair cushions her hand so much that she can't feel his skin. She has gotten used to this and kind of likes it. She likes him. He is somewhat of a fugitive from the Sixties, still has his old Give a Damn button. The late Sixties was the last time he fully remembers being sober. Sometime after Lyndon Johnson, during Richard Nixon, he started into the drugs and booze, not just dabbling like before. Finally, he ended up with cocaine as the drug of his choice, stealing film editing equipment from USC to hock to buy more coke. But he kicked it on his own. Dixie admires his courage. She's never had any addictions, never smoked, never drank except for an occasional glass of wine to be sociable. She rarely drinks more than a sip or two. She has never done drugs. She doesn't crave junk food or grease. She enjoys sex, but has gone for long stretches without. The only things she does habitually are eat and go to the bathroom. And lately the eating has been sporadic. It isn't that she doesn't eat; she forces herself to eat to keep her weight and energy up. She doesn't feel any desire for food. No appetite.

Randy has overcome so much. All she had to worry about was a little appetite.

Randy changes the channels again. Snatches of dialogue flash by in a jumble of interrupted sentences and images. Finally he settles on an old movie. Glenn Ford is a cowboy in this one.

Dixie looks at Randy, but his eyes are fixed on the TV. He is a good man, caring, honest, supportive. She likes being with him, having him here. But she realizes that she doesn't mind it when he's not here. She is pleased when he shows up, but doesn't miss him when they're apart. There is something wrong with that, she decides. Perhaps she is holding back; perhaps he is. She wonders if she should read one of those self-help books about women and relationships. Or maybe see the police shrink.

She lies down next to Randy, presses her nose to his neck. There is a faint scent of last night's cologne, Calvin Klein. The sweetness of the cologne has been dulled by Randy's own body odor. She likes the smell and inhales deeply. She watches Glenn Ford throw a drink in a man's face. Randy puts his hand on her hip and pats her lovingly.

The phone rings.

The doorbell rings.

'Shit,' she says.

'What the fuck?' Randy says.

They sit up.

The phone rings again. It is not Dixie's regular phone, it is her undercover phone. The number is different from her regular number. This is the phone number she gives out to her high school 'friends' so they can call her. The phone is red and sits next to her regular white phone. The red phone makes her think of Moscow or Washington. Hello, Mr. President?

'Get the door, okay?' she tells Randy.

He grumbles, gets up, tightens the knot in his towel. He lumbers out the bedroom toward the apartment door. Dixie stands behind the bedroom door looking through the crack at the hinges. From here she can see who's at the front door. She reaches for the red phone.

'Hi,' she says.

'Dixie?' It's Melody Krauss, her high school friend with the Southern Comfort spray.

'Yeah. Hi. What's up?'

Melody sobs. 'Oh, Dixie.'

Immediately Dixie thinks the worst. Child abuse, incest, rape. She has seen it all, five-year-old girls raped so brutally by their fathers that they needed stitches. 'What's the matter, Melody?'

'T-T-Toby.' She is crying freely now. The sobs catch in her throat and she coughs. Dixie wonders: Assault? Drug overdose? Attempted suicide?

Dixie peers through the crack of the bedroom door to see who is at the front door. Jesus Christ! It's Karl, her ex-husband. Randy is standing in the doorway holding his towel in place. Both men look uncomfortable.

'That rat bastard!' Melody cries.

'What's Toby done?' Toby is the yearbook editor. He

is handsome, wealthy, and drives a Jeep with more accessories than most luxury cars. Melody has a crush on him and has talked about him nonstop since Dixie met her. Although they share a chemistry class, Melody is certain Toby doesn't know she is alive. 'What's he done?' Dixie repeats into the phone.

'He *fucked* me, for starters.'

Dixie isn't sure whether this is literal or figurative. 'He raped you?'

'He fucked me. Then he fucked me over.' She is sobbing again. Her speech is slightly slurred. She's been at the Southern Comfort again. 'Please come over, Dixie. Please, Dixie.'

'Have you been drinking?'

Melody laughs nastily. 'Of course. What else is there to do?'

'Have you taken any drugs?'

'What're you, my mother?'

'Melody, answer me,' Dixie snaps. Her voice is so strange and authoritative it often surprises people.

'N-no,' Melody says. 'Just some booze. But I can get some shit if you want.'

Dixie sighs. Melody thinks she asked the question as a prerequisite of coming over. Dixie looks through the crack again. Randy and Karl are both inside now. They are talking back and forth. Randy gestures with his right hand, the left still clamped on his towel. Karl just stands still, his arms at his sides. They don't seem to be arguing. Dixie wonders what they are saying.

'Please come over,' Melody says.

'I don't know, Mel,' Dixie hedges. 'My parents want me to go over to my grandparents with them. It's a big deal.'

There's a long silence. Dixie feels lousy about this, but she's off duty now. She has a real life here, a boyfriend and ex-husband in the living room.

'Can't you get out of it?' Melody asks.

'Not likely. It's my mom's folks. She's heavy into family and stuff. Can't you call somebody else? I mean, you've only known me a few weeks.'

Melody sobs loudly. 'I don't know. I guess I trust you more.'

Dixie watches Randy and Karl sit. Randy keeps glancing anxiously at the bedroom.

'Okay,' Dixie says. 'I'll be over as soon as I can.'

'Thanks, Dixie,' Melody says happily. 'I mean it. I'm your friend for life. I swear.'

'Bye.'

'Wait, Dixie! Wait!'

'What?'

'Let's meet at the mall, okay? I've gotta get out of this place or my mom's gonna see I've been crying and want to have a mother-daughter talk. I'll wait for you in Nordstrom's. The shoe department.'

'Okay.' Dixie hangs up. She opens the closet. The clothing she wears for this undercover assignment are all neatly hung in one section next to the wall. She pulls on a pair of jeans and rolls up the cuffs, slips into a red plaid cotton skirt which she leaves unbuttoned to show her yellow T-shirt. She doesn't bother with a bra. She slips into rubber flipflops. In the bathroom she hurriedly applies makeup to her eyes and face, mousses her hair and scrubs her fingers through it.

'Hi, Karl,' she says as she enters the living room, still tucking in her shirt.

Karl nods formally. 'Dixie.'

Randy makes a strained face at her. 'I think I'll go change.'

'I've got to be going,' Dixie tells him. 'Business.'

'Fuck.'

Karl smiles. 'Some things never change.'

Dixie does not like this. It's bad enough to disappoint Randy, but to have Karl also being judgmental annoys her. 'What do you want, Karl?'

'We were supposed to go to lunch today. Don't you remember?'

Karl is always doing this. Claiming they have set up an appointment to do something, then acting hurt and insulted that she forgot. It is difficult to get mad at Karl, he is so good-natured and harmless. They met during Dixie's first year on the force. The department wanted some new computers and Karl was a salesman for a local computer store. He came in, looked over the department's needs and suggested they buy a dozen Macintosh computers. But Captain Janeway thought they looked like toys and went with the IBM PCs. Karl was busy around the station for several weeks, installing the new computers and training the personnel, rushing over whenever there was a glitch in the software or someone accidentally dumped their data.

One afternoon as Karl was leaving, he discovered one of his tires was flat. Dixie was leaving at the same time and saw him staring at the tire perplexed.

'You have a spare?' she asked.

'Of course,' he said. 'I think.' He lifted the trunk lid of his Honda. 'Guess not.'

Dixie peeled back the cardboard bottom and showed him the spare underneath. 'Haven't you ever changed a tire before?'

'Not really. Not on a car. On a bicycle once. I was twelve.'

She looked at him and shook her head. She had to smile, he looked so lost and confused. He was a handsome man, a couple of years older than her twenty-six years. He had the reddest hair she'd ever seen that didn't come out of a bottle. A cluster of freckles spilled down the side of his nose across one cheek, forming a constellation very much like Orion. As he bent over the trunk trying to get the tire out, she saw a long piece of thread hanging from the inside of his pocket down across his butt. Very cute, she decided.

'Here,' she said, grabbing the spare and the jack. 'I'll show you how.'

They dated for two years after that, though they were engaged to marry after six months. Karl still lived at home, trying to save enough money for a down payment for a house. Dixie suggested they could live together and he could still save money, but Karl was a strict Roman Catholic and was determined they wouldn't have intercourse until they were married. At first, Dixie thought this was crazy and she was ready to split up. But soon she got used to the idea, kind of liked the discipline of it, the challenge. It was very much like weight lifting. Just when you want to quit most, when your body is shaking and burning for you to stop, that's when you have to pump out just one more rep.

For two years they masturbated each other, had oral sex, used objects from fruit to frankfurters on each other. But they never had intercourse. After two years, Karl had saved the money. They married, bought a small fixer-upper, had sex every day the first week. After that once a week, then once a month. Six months later she left him.

Now Dixie looks back on that time of her life as a foggy experiment, the way some of her generation went off to live in a commune or joined the Peace Corps.

She still likes Karl. He hasn't changed one bit. He would have made a good brother. The only problem is that Karl still wants to spend time with her, more time than she can spare. He still loves her in his own way. He was perfectly happy with the way things had been going in the marriage. He has more than once suggested they live together again, not romantically if she preferred. Just as friends. That is too complicated for Dixie.

'Karl,' she says patiently, 'we were not supposed to go to lunch today.'

Karl brushes a lock of fiery red hair from his forehead. 'Why can't you just admit when you've forgotten something?'

Randy takes a step toward Karl. 'She said there was no lunch date, friend. So why don't you just leave.' Randy's broad hairy body is menacing, but his voice is high, still sounds like the little boy he played on 'Dennis the Menace.' Still, Karl is impressed enough to back up a step.

'I'll call you next week,' Dixie says, taking Karl's arm and guiding him toward the door.

'Sure you will.'

'I will. Next week.'

'We'll have lunch?'

'I'll call you.' She nudges him out the door. As he turns and walks away, she looks at his behind to see if there's any thread strewn across it. Not this time. The seven years since they met have not changed him much. She feels as if she's changed so much it's a wonder he recognizes her.

Dixie closes the door and turns to Randy. 'Sorry about that. He's not really a bad guy.'

'He seemed okay.'

She smiles at him. 'What was with all that posturing. Were you going to deck him?'

'Me? I haven't hit anybody since high school. I was just trying to be firm, assertive. Women like that.'

Dixie kisses him on the cheek. 'Will you wait for me?'

'How long are you gonna be gone?'

'I don't know. A couple hours maybe. It's hard to say.'

'We're supposed to pick up Lonnie at two.' Lonnie is his son, who is living with his ex-wife in Huntington Beach. Today is Randy's day with Lonnie and he wants the three of them to play miniature golf.

'I should be back way before then.'

214

He scratches his heavy day-old beard. 'I'll wait.'

'Good,' she says, kisses him quickly on the lips and leaves. On the way to the car she tries to decide whether or not she's glad Randy will wait for her.

'That rat fuck bastard!' Melody says. She is sitting in a chair in the shoe department of Nordstrom's. Four shoe boxes are piled next to her. She had two different shoes on her feet. 'Which one do you like best?'

A man in his mid-twenties with too much mousse in his hair kneels in front of Melody. He holds the partner to each of the shoes she has on. He smiles at Dixie. 'I like the sandal, how about you?'

Dixie sits down next to Melody. Melody's eyes are red, probably from a combination of crying and Southern Comfort. Southern Comfort was a favorite of Janis Joplin, Dixie remembers. 'The sandal is nice,' she says. 'So's the pump.'

'Great! I was hoping you'd say that.' Melody kicks both shoes off. 'I'll take them both.'

The salesman hastily packs the shoes back into their boxes. 'Cash or charge?'

'Charge.' She hands him her Nordstrom charge card. He takes it and the boxes and walks over to the counter and begins ringing the sale up. Melody wriggles her feet into her Topsiders and stands up with a grin. 'Now all I need are a couple blouses, a few skirts, a sweater, slacks, and we'll be done.'

'Melody, I didn't come down here to go shopping with you.'

'Why not?'

'Because I had other plans. I came because you said you needed to talk.'

'We can talk and shop at the same time. Shopping makes me happy.'

Dixie shakes her head. 'I'm leaving.'

Melody suddenly grabs her arm with surprising strength. 'No, please, Dixie.' Her eyes widen pleadingly. 'I need you right now. That asshole cocksucker Toby.' She starts crying. Women circle around at a safe perimeter, pretending to examine the shoes on display, but looking out of the corners of their eyes, watching. The salesman is waiting at the counter with the shoes and the charge slip. Melody can't stop crying.

Dixie sits Melody down in a chair and goes over to the counter. She takes the charge slip and the brown Nordstrom's charge card. She tears up the slip and pockets the card. 'She's changed her mind. Sorry.' She hurries back to Melody and guides her out of the store into the parking lot.

They sit in Dixie's vintage Mustang, Melody sobbing silently, shoulders hunched and shaking, Dixie holding Melody's hands.

'It's stupid,' Melpdy says now. She stops crying just as suddenly as she began. Her face is streaked with tears, shiny and moist as snail trails. Her eyes are red and puffy. A thin bubble of mucus expands at her nostril as she breathes, then bursts. Melody wipes her nose with the back of her hand. 'No big deal I guess,' she says. 'You know I've been crazy for Toby since the tenth grade.'

'You told me.'

'I told everybody. Everybody except Toby.' She opens her purse, takes out a silver flask and drinks. 'Want some?'

Dixie shakes her head.

Melody swigs again. 'I was over at Licorice Pizza looking at some records, and he comes up behind me and hugs me. I mean, the guy practically lifts me off my feet and he's never even spoken more than five words to me in three years. I'm wearing just my Jimmy Z shorts and that bikini top, you know, the one with the pink and black

216

polka dots. I figure he's mistaken me for someone else.'

Dixie nods. She isn't really much interested in these details, but she knows from experience victims need to tell their stories in their own ways. The details are really for their own benefit, as if they thought that reconstructing the scene down to every detail would give them the power to change the outcome. Dixie has never seen the pink and black polka dot bikini top, or the Jimmy Z shorts, but she can imagine what Melody looked like in them. She is not a pretty girl, her face is a little too pinched, the nose, eyes, and mouth bunched together in the middle of the face rather than spread out proportionately. That leaves a lot of forehead, cheeks, and chin with nothing on them but an occasional cluster of acne. Not much, just enough to keep the cool boys away. But she has a shapely body, long slender legs, wrist-sized waist, and breasts a little too large for the rest of her. In that way she reminds Dixie a little of Trina.

'He's got me in this bear hug, right? I mean tight. I can practically feel his dick stabbing me in the butt. He puts me down, says, "Hi, Melody." You believe that? "Hi, Melody." Like we've been buddies for years. I say hi back and go back to looking through the records. I'm reading the jacket to Tom Petty and he's still standing there. He starts talking about the record, how cool Tom Petty is, and he starts in on other music stuff. The kind of stuff you talk about when you're hitting on someone. I'm standing there thinking, hey, he's got a girlfriend. So I ask him, I mean, I ask him straight out, "Where's Missy?" He looks at me kinda funny, like he's never heard the name before. I mean, he's been banging her for his whole senior year. Then he just shrugs, says, "I don't know. We're not married or anything." I don't know what that means. Is he telling me he's busted up with her or what? I can't figure.'

217

Dixie shifts in her seat. Sitting sideways in the bucket seats of a Mustang is very uncomfortable. She steals a glance at her watch and tries to calculate how soon she can be home again. Randy would be pissed if she didn't go with him and Lonnie to miniature golf.

'So he invites me over to his house, go for a swim. I ask him where his parents are and he says they're gone for the weekend. Santa Barbara or something, some golf tournament his dad's in. We go to his place. We're not even all the way in the house he starts scamming me. He's kissing me and all. I mean, just kissing, frenching of course, but he hasn't grabbed anything yet.' Melody swigs again from her flask. She smacks her lips. 'So we go out to the pool and swim. I'm in my panties and bikini top, he's got these cool Maui trunks come down to his knees. He comes on to me in the pool, hugging and all, kissing some. I guess I was feeling kinda horny too, 'cause I let him take my top off.' Melody looks over at Dixie, waiting for a reaction. Dixie gives none and Melody continues. 'Anyway, we end up in his bedroom fucking. He's got these colored condoms, red, blue, yellow. He lets me pick one. I didn't care, shit, I'd never actually seen a guy even put one on before, they always, you known, turn their backs or something. I thought it was complicated. So I pick the red one and he slips it on. Then we do it.' She twists the cap on the flask on and off, on and off. 'Afterwards we're lying there listening to his Peter Gabriel records and the phone rings. He answers, then takes the call in another room. When he comes back he tells me I've got to go, Missy's on her way over. My panties and top are still in the dryer downstairs. He runs down, brings them up, and tosses them on me. They're still fucking wet. I don't know, I guess I blew it, but I started screaming at him. Missy had to work this morning, that's the only reason he came on to me. He saw me, was horny, and wanted to fuck. I

218

wouldn't have minded so much if he'd just been up front. Shit, I'd probably have fucked him anyway, but I hate being lied to like that. Treated like a slut. You know?'

Dixie stares at Melody. It wasn't rape or incest or child abuse. No drug o.d. or teen suicide or assault. It was just the usual lesson in adolescent love. Not as dramatic as the crimes Dixie was used to, but just as heartbreaking to the inexperienced. Melody was in real pain, felt used and ugly. Her damp panties thrown at her while she was lying in the bed of the boy she'd wanted for three years. Dixie feels bad, not just for Melody, but because she had been impatient with the girl's pain because it was merely normal human suffering. Nothing criminal. Dixie starts the Mustang up and pulls out of the lot.

'Cool car,' Melody says. 'Where are we going?'

'I love nachos,' Melody says.

'Me too.' Dixie used a tortilla chip to scoop up some guacamole, sour cream, and spicy chicken. A long string of melted cheese hangs from the chips as she lifts it to her mouth. Melody reaches over and snaps the cheese string. 'Thanks,' Dixie says and eats the loaded chip. She is hungry for the first time in days.

They are sitting in the Atrium Court of Fashion Island. Fashion Island is like no other place in the country. It is an open-air shopping center that sits on a hill in Newport Beach overlooking the Pacific Ocean. As shoppers wander from Neiman-Marcus to Robinson's to Buffum's, they can actually see the ocean, the luxury boats sailing by. Many of the people who live near Fashion Island own large million-dollar homes. There are many stores here that cater to these people, but there are also a few that cater to the cheaper tastes of the upper middle class.

Dixie used to shop here only for special occasions. Back then the Atrium Court was J.C. Penney's, but most of the shoppers here couldn't imagine what J.C. Penney's might possibly have that they would want to own. The store closed down, was gutted, and a few years later remodeled to include three floors of small but expensive clothing stores, plus a fancy supermarket on the bottom floor that features a sushi bar and exotic fruits and vegetables. And in the middle of the supermarket is a circle of specialty fast-food restaurants. Diners sit in a cluster of tables that surround a water fountain and grand piano. Sometimes a man in a tuxedo sits at the piano and plays while shoppers dine. The man in the tuxedo is not here today and Dixie and Melody eat their nachos next to the fountain and listen to the water splash.

Two boys sit at the table next to them. They are eating Chinese food with chopsticks. One is wearing headphones attached to his cassette player. He bobs his head rhythmically as he eats. The other boy wears an earphone attached to his Sony Watchman. He is watching the Lakers game. His shoulders feint and weave along with the players' moves. When the boys are done eating, they both walk off together and disappear up the escalator, still bopping, still feigning. Dixie never saw them exchange one word.

'This was a good idea,' Melody says. She scrapes her finger along the bottom of the empty plate for what's left of the black beans. She licks it off her finger. 'I feel better.'

'I'm glad.'

'He's still a fucking rat bastard.'

Dixie finds it hard to be too critical of young Toby. She is old enough now to know that boys don't always mean to be cruel, they just aren't used to the demands of their dicks. As a woman matures, she knows better what to expect, not to judge too harshly. Not to take everything so personally.

'I guess I was asking for it,' Melody says. She grins. 'I was blinded by the glamour, red condoms and such.'

They both laugh. People are standing around the perimeter of the dining area with trays in their hands waiting for empty tables. The one flaw in this grand design is that there are never enough tables for the diners and they are forced to walk in circles with their trays loaded with steaming food searching out someone who is almost ready to abandon his table. Then everyone dashes for it. Dixie finds this practice a little humiliating for everyone. 'Let's go,' she says and they stand up.

Immediately several tray-carrying diners break for their little table, weaving around the other tables, soup and beverage slopping over onto their trays. A middle-aged woman and her lanky blond daughter cut off a couple of other women in tennis clothes and slide into the chairs.

As Dixie and Melody head for the escalator, Joseph Little steps in front of them. He smiles, strokes Dixie's arm. 'Jesus, am I lucky or what?'

'Hey, Joe,' Dixie says.

'Hi.' Melody nods glumly. She is a frequent customer of his, but she obviously doesn't want him around right now. She looks at Dixie.

'I thought you said you were going off to your granny's today?' he says.

'Something came up,' Dixie says.

'Christ, if we missed a planned trip to my grandparents, they'd stroke out.'

Dixie doesn't answer. This is getting complicated. For the past couple of weeks he's been chasing her around. She's avoided him, claiming to be angry about the hickey he gave her. Captain Janeway keeps calling her in for progress reports, wants to know if she's any closer to Little's source. She tells him to be patient. Cops think it's easier to get close to high school students than to pimps or hookers or adult criminals. Maybe it used to be, but not anymore. They've seen too much TV, they've learned not to trust anyone. The best way to get close to Joseph Little is to run away, let him get close to her.

'Look, you guys,' Joseph says. 'I'm trying to pick something nice out for my mom for Mother's Day. Maybe you guys could help?'

Melody gives Dixie another look to indicate she'd rather they were alone. Joseph picks up on the look.

'Hey, I'll make it worth your while.'

Melody is interested. 'Like how?'

'What do you want?' He touches his finger to the outside of his nostril, makes a little snorting sound, and grins.

'Whatever,' Melody says, smiling.

The three of them go from store to store searching through thousands of items. Dixie can tell by the way he keeps touching her that he's hot for her, not just as a conquest like before, but as something more. This is a perfect opportunity to get closer to him, gain a little more of his confidence. She wants to give Randy a call to cancel their plans, but when she feigns having to go to the bathroom, Melody insists on coming along. She's excited about getting free cocaine.

They are browsing through May Company, women's sportswear. They've been at it for almost two hours.

'What is it exactly you're looking for?' Dixie asks.

He shrugs. 'I'll know it when I find it.'

They keep searching.

'Hey, this is neat.' He holds up a blue silk dress.

'Nice,' Dixie says. 'What's her size?'

'I'm not sure. She's about your height, a little bigger all around though.'

Melody comes over holding a sweater in front of her. 'This is nice.'

Joseph shakes his head. 'She's got more sweaters than teeth. I like this dress.'

'Yeah, that's good too,' Melody says.

222

He studies it on the hanger, holds it up at different angles to the light, puts it in front of Dixie, frowns. 'I don't know. It's hard to tell on the hanger. Would you try it on for me so I can get a better idea how it'll look on her?'

Dixie hesitates, then shrugs. 'Sure.'

She takes the dress into the dressing room, closes the door behind her. She hangs the dress on the door and checks the price tag: $258.00. She's never owned a dress that costs that much. Dixie strips down to her panties and is about to remove the silk dress from the hanger when her dressing room door opens and Joseph steps in. He is smiling wickedly.

'Hi,' he says and steps toward her. He is staring at her small breasts, down her stomach to her panties. Her skin tingles as if his eyes were a wet tongue.

'Are you nuts?' she whispers.

'Find out for yourself.' He is right against her now, holding her, kissing her ear, her cheek, her mouth.

Dixie stands rigid. She doesn't push him away, but she doesn't respond. Timing is everything in this kind of work. You can only push the man away so long; after that you wound his pride to where he doesn't want you around anymore to remind him. Dixie senses this is that turning point. He risked sneaking in here to prove his sincerity; if she kicked him out now, she might blow any chance of him showing her his drug supplies. Officially and legally, any sexual contact taints the case, though that is not always how things actually work out. Still, she has no intention of fucking him here, now, ever, anywhere. But she must encourage him, give him hope.

'I'm sorry about the hickey before,' he whispers. 'I was just showing off. I didn't mean anything.' He kisses her lightly on the lips, tentatively, as if he's not certain whether or not she will suddenly bite his lip off.

Dixie returns his kiss. Surprised, he kisses her harder,

223

plunging his tongue into her mouth. She sucks it in. He presses tightly against her until they are up against the wall, crushing the blue silk dress. His right hand comes up and holds her breast, squeezes it briefly and immediately moves to her crotch. He cups his hand outside her panties, his fingers nudging at the fabric over her vagina. Dixie is embarrassed to feel her own panties getting wet. She can even smell her own earthy scent.

Karl was an inept and indifferent lover. Randy is more experienced and satisfying. But Dixie is not used to this kind of urgency, the jungle swamp passion, the four-wheel drive need. She feels her own body responding though she concentrates on keeping her mind detached and objective. He is grinding his hips against her. He is kissing her breasts, sucking on the nipples, tugging them with his teeth. He sticks his hand down the back of her panties, holds her butt, slides his hand around to the front and rams a finger deep inside her, practically lifting her off the floor. Dixie feels the sweat dripping down her forehead as she straddles his hand, her clitoris pressing against his palm.

He unzips his pants, pulls out his penis and guides her hand to it. His penis is hard as a hammer head, warm. He thrusts it against her hand and she squeezes it.

Joseph is trying to get her panties down. He has them over her hips to her thighs. He pushes his penis toward her, against her stomach. He lifts her a little, trying to get her in position so he can enter her. Dixie knows she cannot let this happen, that that would be crossing the imaginary line. She quickly begins to stroke him, rapidly tugging on his penis, her palm building up friction. She looks at his closed eyes and feels something for him, not passion, but an almost maternal compassion, as if she were putting a hurting child out of misery. Maybe that's the greatest part of sex anyway for women. It doesn't seem to be for Trina. *Hell, what do I know*, Dixie thinks as she keeps stroking.

224

Joseph moans and his warm come shoots across her hand and wrist. He collapses against her and the rest of it pumps onto her stomach. 'Jesus,' he sighs, sagging. 'God.'

Dixie looks around, finds some tissue paper used to package shirts and sweaters. She wipes her hand and stomach, then wipes the tip of Joseph's penis. He seems embarrassed by this, like a little boy whose hair has been combed. He backs away, tucks himself back into his pants. He looks as if he'd like to say something important. Finally he speaks. 'I'll meet you outside.'

'Gross,' Melody says.

'Jesus, they're ugly,' Joseph says.

They are standing in Fashion Island's only pet store. Melody wanted to see the puppies. Joseph has one arm around Dixie, the other holding the bag with the blue silk dress gift-wrapped for his mother. The three of them are standing in front of a dry aquarium filled with the yellow frogs. The frogs' skin is rubbery and their eyes are red. They don't blink or move. There is a hand-lettered sign taped to the aquarium that says, ALBINO FROGS. YES, THEY ARE *REAL*.

'Well, they don't look real,' Joseph says.

There is another sign taped to the glass. FEED THEM FOR A QUARTER. Next to the sign is a coin plunger.

'Give me a quarter,' Melody says. Her face is practically pressed against the glass. She holds her hand out to the two of them. Joseph digs into his pocket and slaps a quarter into her palm. She slides the coin into the slot and pushes the plunger. A live grasshopper drops into the aquarium on to the back of one of the frogs. The frog doesn't move, his red eyes staring blindly ahead. The grasshopper sits on his back a moment, then hops off onto a rock. None of the dozen frogs move.

'Shit, they're not real,' Joseph says. 'They're plastic or

225

rubber or something. This is just some gimmick to get quarters.'

Dixie watches Melody's rapt face. Melody seems mesmerized.

'They're alive,' Melody says.

'How can you tell?' Joseph asks.

'I can see them breathe.'

'Batteries,' Joseph says. 'My sister has a doll that does the same thing.'

The grasshopper jumps around the tank undisturbed for a minute.

'Look!' Melody shouts. People in the store turn to see what she's shouting about.

Several of the frogs slowly stir, like dinosaurs suddenly thawed. They shift around on their rocks bumping into each other. Their eyes beam that unnerving red. They don't seem to know where they're going, just that they should move. One frog turns, knocks into the grasshopper, but doesn't make a move for it. Another steps forward and unknowingly steps on the grasshopper, pinning it beneath its webbed foot. The grasshopper wriggles and struggles, squirming to get free. The frog ignores him for more than a minute, then shifts his head toward it, stares for almost another minute. Then he swallows the grasshopper.

'Some hunters,' Joseph laughs, squeezing Dixie closer.

'Gimmie another quarter,' Melody says.

'No way,' Joseph says. 'We can't count on one of them stepping on it this time. It could take days for them to figure out the bug's even in there. It's a wonder they don't all starve to death.'

Melody snaps her fingers. 'Come on, I'll pay you back.'

'Shit.' Joseph digs out another quarter for her. After she plunges it into the machine another grasshopper drops into the tank, he leads Dixie out of the store. 'We'll wait outside,' he calls back to Melody.

Outside the sun is bright. Dixie shades her eyes and stares out over the ocean. Two enormous sailboats glide by. She wishes she were on one of those sailboats right now instead of giving handjobs to high school drug dealers and watching her "best friend" drop bugs into a frog tank. Christ, how did she get to this place in her life? Will she ever be able to shop at the May Company again? Of course, the activity in the dressing room won't appear in her report, that's part of the unofficial training you get in undercover work. Any infraction where it's your word against one other person, don't report. Maybe the public would be shocked to know that, maybe they'd rather not know, as long as the drug dealers are cleaned out. Still, Dixie feels awful. Moving among these kids, affecting their lives as she has already makes her feel so sneaky, a parent abusing a child's trust. Yeah, it's for their own good, she knows all that. Dixie takes a deep breath, smells the moist salt from the ocean mixed with the tangy soap scent from the May Company rest room where she washed herself off after Joseph exploded on to her. She looks at him, wants to shake him and give him a lecture. He's a bright, good-looking kid from a nice family. There's no good reason to be doing what he's doing. But lectures aren't her job. She must keep her perspective. In L.A., one woman cop doing this same thing got thrown off the force for having sex with one of the students. Another male cop quit the force to marry one of the high school girls he'd started dating as a cover. Perspective is everything in this job.

'I really like you,' Joseph says to her tenderly.

'I like you too.'

He nods, looks out to the ocean. 'Kinda strange back there, huh?'

'The frogs? Yeah.'

'Not the frogs. Back there.' He hooks a thumb over his shoulder toward the May Company. 'What we did.'

227

'It was nice.'

'I just didn't want you to get the wrong idea.'

Dixie doesn't say anything. They are standing side by side, both shielding their eyes with their hands as they stare out over the ocean.

'It wasn't just sex,' he says.

'No, I didn't think so.'

'Good. I really like you. I mean, I like sex, don't get me wrong. But I like you too. For who you are.'

Three helicopters appear out over the ocean. They are too far away to hear, but they move together in a precise pattern. A flock of sea gulls follows behind them.

'I just thought we might spend some time together. Outside school.'

'We are, Joseph. Right now.'

He looks at her. 'You know what I mean.'

She watches the helicopters turn and head back in the same direction they just came from. The sea gulls turn too and chase after them. She glances over at Joseph. 'I know what you mean. I'm just not sure. You're kind of a mysterious guy. I'm not crazy about that.'

He looks uncomfortable, like he'd like to tell her more but can't. 'No big mystery.'

'You deal drugs.'

'You've bought some off me, remember? That's how we met.'

'Buying a few poppers and some coke for recreation isn't the same as dealing. I'm not sure I want to get involved with someone who's got such a dangerous job.'

'Hey, you let me worry about that.' He tries to sound tough, but it comes out melodramatically, just the way Randy sounded this morning when he was trying to be tough with Karl.

'It's not you that frightens me, Joseph,' she says. 'It's the people you deal with.'

228

He thinks that over. 'I can handle myself.'

Melody comes out of the store. 'Gimme another quarter. It's so cool the way they finally figure out there's food in there. The thing has to practically hop into their mouths. Jeez. Come on, gimme another quarter.'

'This is getting old,' Dixie says.

'Yeah? So's this,' Melody says, nodding at Joseph's hand around Dixie's waist. 'I thought you and I came here to spend some time together.'

'We did.'

'Yeah, right.'

Dixie doesn't know what to say. She doesn't want to hurt Melody's feelings, but her job is to stick with Joseph. Now she's closer than ever. With a little pressure, she should be able to get enough info out of him over the next week to figure out when he makes his routine buy. Maybe even follow him.

'Omigod, Dixie!' a voice cries out. 'What the hell are you doing in that outfit?'

Dixie feels her stomach clench as she spins around and sees Diva and Barcelona walking toward her. Jesus Christ, no!

'Your hair!' Diva laughs. 'What is this, a masquerade?'

Dixie turns to Joseph and sees the smile on his face harden.

16

That morning, before running into Dixie:

Barcelona rolls over in bed and is surprised to bump into Eric.

'Ow,' he says sleepily. 'My shoulder.'

'When did you get here?' she asks.

'An hour ago. You were asleep.'

'Oh.' She is pleased that he is here. He has his own key now. But it bothers her a little that she didn't hear him or feel him enter her home. A naked man climbed into bed next to her and she didn't notice. This makes her nervous about break-ins and she thinks about having a burglar alarm installed.

'Rub my shoulder?' he asks.

His shoulder is sore from softball. He plays on a coed team from Austin House, his home for abused women. They are last in the Social Services league. Drug Rehab is number one. Eric tries to joke about this, but she can see that being last really upsets him. He is an exceptional athlete, one of the most competitive persons she has ever known. He takes being last personally and often discusses the faults of his teammates with her. Sometimes he cuts out articles from sports magazines about how better to field a ball, or he draws stick figures showing the proper way to swing a bat. He photocopies and hands them out to his teammates at work. Barcelona has seen his team play; drawings won't help. Eric doesn't agree. He believes practice and dedication and sheer willpower will bring their batting average up. In this way, he is a lot like Dixie.

Barcelona massages his right shoulder and he hums with pleasure under her touch. He scoots his bare butt backward until it touches her leg. His clothes are arranged neatly on the wicker clothes hamper against the wall: nylon shorts, white socks, mesh T-shirt, Tiger running shoes with gel in the soles. An ankle brace crowns the pile. Barcelona wonders why it is that every guy she's dated over thirty has a chronic sports injury of some kind. Ankle, knee, elbow, finger. With very little prompting, each will recall in detail the exact moment the injury occurred, during what specific play of the basketball/football/racquetball/softball game.

'What did you tell Luna?' Barcelona asks.

'That I'm out running.'

'Anything else?'

'Like what?'

She stops rubbing. 'She called me last night. Left a message on my machine.'

Eric sits up. He tries to look casual, but she can see the panic in his eyes. 'What did she say?'

'Nothing really. She wants me to call her. Have a talk.'

Eric thinks this over, absently twisting his lips with his fingers. Barcelona remembers this habit from graduate school. There she found it cute, endearing. Here she's not so sure. 'Maybe she just wants to get together. She likes you.'

'She told you that?'

'God, yes. After that first night you met. She thought you were so smart and beautiful and sophisticated. And she loves your writing. Really.'

Barcelona feels awful. She and Eric have not really discussed their new relationship, nor have they talked much about Luna, except in informational ways. Luna is at school. Luna went to visit her sister for the night. Bulletins of Luna's whereabouts so they could better arrange their lovemaking. Barcelona feels as though she knows Luna very well, merely through her schedule of activities.

She had not really felt guilty about her rekindled relationship with Eric until this moment. She always considered Luna the interloper here, the one who took Eric from her, not the other way around. This affair is merely rebalancing nature. Except that Luna is Eric's wife. But that's not what makes her feel bad. It's that Luna likes and respects her writing. She feels as if she were betraying a fan, as if she were writing something bad, sloppy with plotting, careless with prose.

'What now?' Barcelona asks Eric.

'What now?' he repeats. 'Now I get up and take a leak, then I come back to bed and we make love. That's what now.'

Barcelona nods. 'Sounds reasonable.'

He smiles at her and they kiss. He gets out of bed and she stares at his naked body walking toward the bathroom. She is again surprised at how the sight of his bare bottom cause her heart to literally vibrate. His lean body is bumpy with long sinewy muscles. He stands over the toilet bowl and aims.

'Jesus fucking Christ!' Eric hollers and leaps back from the toilet, startled. Some of his urine squirts onto the carpet before he controls his bladder. 'Holy shit!' he shouts.

'What's the matter?' Barcelona asks, jumping out of bed. Maybe he found blood in his urine?

'That!' He points behind the toilet bowl. There behind the toilet, between the plumber's helper and the bathtub, are two dead mice. One is brownish and big as a French roll. His back is torn open and his internal organs are exposed in a red meaty soup. He looks like an anatomy exhibit for a high school biology class. The other mouse is small and gray. It has been decapitated, its head bitten off and spit out a few inches from the rest of the body.

'Goddamn it, Larry,' Barcelona says. She recognizes his style. She glances over her shoulder into the bedroom hoping to see him, but of course he is not there. She nudges Eric out of the way. 'He does this about once a week. Don't worry.'

'I'm not worried,' Eric says, a little offended. 'I was just startled. Surprised. I wasn't expecting to see a rat head first thing in the morning.'

'They're mice.'

'Mice, rats, shit. Why don't you get rid of that cat?'

Barcelona looks at him for a moment. 'I don't know. I really don't. I should, I guess.'

Eric softens. 'I don't mean have him put to sleep. I mean give him away to someone. Maybe someone on a farm who needs rats caught.'

'Mice,' she corrects, stooping over. She looks up at Eric. 'Go ahead and use the other bathroom.' He hesitates a moment, but finally he trots off down the hallway. Squatting, Barcelona tears a handful of toilet paper from the roll and uses it to pick up the big brown mouse first. The body is stiff so Larry must have done it sometime last night. Once again she has an uneasy feeling as she realizes that Larry was killing and dismembering these animals ten feet from her bed and she hadn't even known. First rodent mutilation and then a full-grown man climbs into her bed. She sleeps through all of it. Something must be wrong with her instincts.

Barcelona drops the mouse and toilet paper into the toilet. It makes a loud plop and a couple of drops of the urine water inside splashes on her arm. She tears off more toilet paper, wipes her arm, then uses it to grab the small gray mouse. The body is warm and limp, a fresh kill. It is also too small to get a good grip without crushing it. She repositions the toilet paper and picks the mouse up by the tail. She lifts it a couple of inches off the carpet when the tail detaches and the little headless body drops back to the carpet, blotting it with blood.

She sighs and makes a sour face. 'Sorry,' she says to the mouse. She tosses the toilet paper and tail into the toilet, unfurls more paper, and scoops up the body. Then the head, so small and delicate, she feels like a surgeon just picking it up. She dumps it in the toilet and flushes without looking.

She walks over to the sink and scrubs her hands and fingers and arms all the way to the elbow.

'Are we having fun yet?' Eric says upon his return to the bedroom.

They decide to make love. At first Eric is angry because he can't find his condom, though he's sure he brought one with him. Usually he leaves a box here, but he'd remembered they'd used the last one a couple of days ago. He couldn't run out of the house carrying a box of condoms, not without Luna asking questions. So he'd tucked one into the tiny pocket inside his running shorts. He stands next to the bed rifling through his clothes, even checking his ankle brace and socks. Barcelona lies in bed, head propped up on one hand. Watching him search frantically makes her think about this whole condom issue between them. All the years they were dating and then living together, they'd never used them. Now that he is married to Luna though, he always uses them. He knows she is on the Pill, so she tries to understand the ramifications of the condom. Sure, everyone is afraid of AIDS and all the other diseases, but there are subtler statements being made. Barcelona feels as if she were under suspicion for some terrible crime. As if her vagina were a secret depository for biological warfare. Slipping on a condom implies you are a slut, pumped regularly by slobering degenerates with oozing pustules. Was Eric protecting himself for himself? Because he wanted to protect Luna? Because he didn't want to get caught? Were these the adulterer's equivalent of the burglar's rubber gloves? No fingerprints, no pecker tracks?

Barcelona flops back on the pillow. God, it is complicated now. Everyone is a potential killer. How could people fall in love today under these suspicions?

'Eureka,' Eric says finally, holding up the foil packet. 'It fell out of the pocket and slipped behind the laundry hamper.'

They return to their lovemaking, though some of Barcelona's enthusiasm has waned. She scolds herself for being so silly and forces herself to become more energetic.

Afterward, she patters downstairs to make them some breakfast. She cinches her bathrobe as she walks into the kitchen and sees Larry sitting on top of the TV cleaning himself. He pauses, looks at her, returns to cleaning.

'Men,' she says to him and laughs suddenly. The sound startles him and he jumps down to the floor and runs out the cat door.

Barcelona opens the refrigerator, takes out the orange juice, the Weight Watchers margarine, and four eggs. She puts the iron skillet on the stove and turns the flame on. Then she reaches for the telephone. No point in putting it off any longer. This way, at least, she can talk and cook at the same time and once the eggs are done, she'll have an excuse to hang up.

She dials.

'Hello?' the deep, German-accented voice says.

'Hi, Mom.'

'Barcy! How are you, sweetheart?'

'Fine. How are you?'

235

'Great. Terrific.' The voice is cheerful, peppy, energetic. Her mother's trademarks. Her mother is not a complainer. Any illnesses or injuries her mother suffers, Barcelona usually only hears about once her mother has healed. Her father is just the opposite. Most of his ills and injuries are imaginary, though described with great attention to physical detail, no matter how personal.

'How's Dad?'

'You know. He's been dying for forty years. Cancer's been killing him for the last twenty, though the doctors can't find any.'

'Things never change.'

'The more things change, the more they stay the same, right? How's the weather?'

'Hot.' Barcelona doesn't really know what the weather is like outside. All her blinds are down and it has been a little overcast and cool the past couple of days. But her mother doesn't want to hear that. She wants to hear that California is just as she remembers it from their trips out here: hot, sunny, bright.

'What's it like in Pennsylvania?'

Her mother sighs, begins to speak in German. 'Rain and more rain. The basement leaked water again and we had to have some guy come and pump it out for two days. Cost us an arm and a leg. Or as your father puts it, we have to sell two hundred dozen bagels to pay for it.'

'He always knows how to put things in perspective.'

'He's your father all right.'

Barcelona wonders what that means. She doesn't ask. 'How's business?'

'Booming!' she says in English. 'Hold on a second, sweetheart.' Her mother puts down the phone and she can hear her walking away on the linoleum floor. Barcelona pictures the green and red tiles in her mind. The store is so small you can hear every sound in it. 'This all you have,'

236

her mother is saying to a customer. 'A fifty-dollar bill for a cup of coffee and a toasted sweet roll?'

'It's all I have, Milan,' the man says. 'Unless you want me to owe you.'

'Owe me? Forget it. The way you tip I should just keep the change and you'd still owe me.'

Barcelona hears the man laugh, the ancient cash register ring, the drawer splat open, change being made.

'Bye, Tom,' her mother says.

'Bye, Milan.'

The door opens and closes.

Milan. She was named by her mother after one of the Italian cities she and her husband had visited on their honeymoon; Milan's sisters were named Florence and Roma. The tradition was continued by Milan, who honeymooned in Spain. Barcelona wondered if she too would follow the same tradition. But what would she call the kid if she did? Barstow? San Pedro? Anaheim?

'Hi, sweetheart, you still there?'

'Was that Tom Lipton?'

'Who else? Coffee and toasted sweet roll for lunch. And those damn fifties.'

'What's Dad doing?'

'Baking, natch? We have onion bagels on order, three coffee cakes, meat platters. And my waitress broke up with her stupid boyfriend so she moves around here like a zombie.'

Barcelona slices an English muffin and sticks it in the toaster. One slice doesn't quite fit so she takes it out and flattens it between her palms. Now it fits.

'So how's the writing going? What are you working on now?'

Milan Lee is sincere when she asks about Barcelona's writing. She proudly reads her daughter's books and tells all her customers to buy them. On the wall of their little restaurant where the Hebrew National kosher meats poster used to be, is a display of framed covers from all of Barcelona's novels.

'I'm writing a screenplay now.'

'A screenplay!'

'Relax, Mom, it's nothing. Just a possibility.' She explains the situation.

'Lynda Kramer! My God. Will you meet her?'

'Maybe. I don't know.'

'Hold on, honey, let me get your father.' The phone clunks down and her mother runs down the wooden stairs to where Max Lee, formerly Lebowitz, bakes onion bagels, sweet rolls, coffee cakes, and the rest of the goodies they sell upstairs. The actual restaurant itself is tiny, no larger than most people's living rooms. It is built as an addition onto an old Victorian-style house constructed at the turn of the century. Her parents own the house too, which they rent out as single furnished rooms to students attending the local Methodist college. The basement of the house serves as the kitchen for the restaurant. It also is where they store their dry goods and freeze the baked goods and meats. They have four large freezers down there. Barcelona's father keeps several T-shirts in one of the freezers. When he is finished baking for the day, he dries the heavy sweat from his body and slips into one of the frozen T-shirts. She remembers watching him do that, how he always braced himself against the cold but smiled in relief as he pulled it on. Once when she was fourteen, he offered to put her bra in there for her, but she called him disgusting and stomped away. His laughter made her laugh even though she felt embarrassed.

'Barcy?' her father says into the phone. His voice too is heavily accented with the harsh German inflection, tongue beating each word into submission.

'Hi, Dad.'

'What's this about some screenplay?'

'It's a long shot. You know Hollywood.'

'You're not quitting teaching? You still have your college job, right?'

'Sure.' This is not the time to discuss her plans to quit. That would involve a long lecture. She changes subjects. 'How's your health?'

'Oh, the same. You know.'

Barcelona cracks two eggs into the frying pan and they sizzle as soon as they hit. Steam rises to her face, the sour smell of frying eggs and burned margarine. She winces and backs away. 'How's your throat?'

'Sore. Always sore.' She can see him stroking his throat now, even as they talk. 'Like sandpaper inside.'

'Quit smoking.'

'You always say that.'

'You always have a sore throat.'

'Quitting smoking is not so easy. You don't know, you never smoked. You know how long I've smoked?'

'More than fifty years?'

'Yes, that's right. More than fifty years,' he repeats, sounding proud. 'It's hard to quit something, anything, after fifty years. Try quitting to breathe for five minutes. That's what it is like.'

Barcy looks at the clock on the stove. She flips two of the eggs, Eric's. She spreads plum butter on half the English muffin, hers. 'How's business?'

'You know. Sometimes good, sometimes bad. I have lots of orders today. Onion bagels, meat platters, coffee cakes.'

'Look, Dad, I'll let you know what happens with the screenplay. You take care.'

'Okay. I've got to check the ovens now. The coffee cakes should be done. Here's your mother.'

'Sweetheart?' Milan's voice says.

'Hi, Mom.'

'I went into B. Dalton's last week at the mall. They were all out of your books. I made them order some.'

'Thanks, now I can make that house payment next month.'

Milan Lee laughs. 'What are mothers for?'

'You still getting those obscene calls? Dixie asked me.'

'She's the singer?'

'The cop, Mom. That's why she asked.'

'Oh, the skinny one, right. No calls for almost a month.' The first calls started about six months ago, a muffled voice, not clearly male or female. Just a low whisper. 'Funny, but the guy's changed his dialogue. At first it was all sex stuff, things he wanted to do to me, and who could blame him with my gorgeous bod at fifty-nine. Now, though, it's mostly just foul language, calling me names.' In German, she mentions a couple of the tamer words.

'Does it bother you?'

'No, why should it?' Her mother pauses. 'Sometimes.'

'I've got to go now, Mom.'

'I won't ask.'

'Good, don't.'

'Is he at least good looking?'

'Very.'

'Has a good job?'

'Mom.'

'Single?'

'You weren't going to ask, remember?'

Her mother sighs. 'I ask because you expect me to.'

'That doesn't mean I want you to.'

'Doesn't it? Don't you see me as some comic Jewish mother out of some television show, nags about career and marriage? Isn't that how you prefer to see me? Keep me in my pigeon hole?'

Barcelona's heart thumps wildly in her chest. She is

surprised by her mother's outburst. 'Mom, why do you say that?'

'Never mind. I didn't mean anything. We've been busy, that's all. I'm tired. Customers, sweetheart, I have to go now.'

'Bye, Mom.'

'Good-bye, Barcy.'

The eggs are overcooked when she scrapes them out of the frying pan. The toast is cold, the juice warm. She still can't get over her mother's statement. Not like her at all. Barcelona is unsettled and anxious; the chat did not go well. She doesn't know why it didn't. They are her parents, she loves them. She sees them now, her mother joking with the regular customers as she bags doughnuts and rings up the sale. Her mother, who was born Catholic but converted after marrying Max, now sounds more Jewish than Mel Brooks. She sees her father, seventy, downstairs in the hot kitchen, bent over the baking bench, rolling bagels, wrapping the dough around his hand, a dozen centerfolds from *Playboy* tacked up in front of him by his wife. He probably hasn't even noticed them for at least ten years. They are covered with a mist of flour. Barcelona remembers helping her father with the baking as a child, staring at the young naked girls who were always smiling, their skin as tight as water balloons. Standing or lying, showing breasts, legs, buttocks. Not shyly, not embarrassed. Smiling. That's what Barcelona thought growing up to be a woman would be like: always smiling, always happy.

Now she realizes the girls were only children themselves, most of them barely out of their teens.

Barcelona carries her breakfast upstairs and hands a plate to Eric. He is reading her *New York Review of Books*.

'Fascinating article in here on the new bio of Sartre.'

Barcelona puts down her own plate, throws open her robe, and strikes a centerfold pose. She smiles so widely her jaw aches.

Eric stares at her.

'Well?' she says through smiling teeth.

'Well what?'

'Do I look happy?'

The phone rings. It is Diva.

'Have some spare time today?' Diva asks.

Barcelona looks over at Eric. He is dressed, stretching out on the floor for his run home. It is ten miles, but since he took the bus here, he should be able to make it. She doesn't know what he will tell Luna about why he was gone so long. She doesn't ask.

'Sure,' Barcelona says. 'Why?'

'Can we meet for lunch?'

'Okay. Where?'

'How about the Atrium?' Diva's voice sounds funny.

'Fine. You okay?'

'Yeah, I'm fine. I just want to talk to you about something.'

'Okay. Noon?'

'See you there.' Barcelona hangs up and watches Eric lean against the wall, stretching his hamstrings.

'We saw that Japanese film down at the Balboa the other night,' he says. 'You should see it. It's very witty, very satirical.'

He has been recommending books, articles, movies, art shows, and records since they've been seeing each other again. He gives her books and records as gifts, buys her tickets to showings (two tickets, he's so open-minded). His taste is very good and she has enjoyed most of what he's recommended. Nevertheless, she resents his suggestions. She's not sure why yet. Maybe because he assumes she

242

wouldn't read, see, or hear these things without him first recommending them.

When will I see you again? lies stillborn inside her.

'I'll call you tomorrow morning,' he says. 'Luna is in a racquetball league.'

She doesn't want to know these details, though he always insists on sharing them. As if they are spies together, he wants her to know what he risks for her sake. 'I may be out in the morning,' she says. She doesn't know why she's said this. She has no plans. Maybe so he would ask her where she might be.

He doesn't. He gives her a look, then shrugs. 'Tomorrow night then. I can probably sneak out of the house for a few minutes.'

'What do you mean "sneak"?'

'Huh?'

'Are you going to creep out of the house, crouched over like this?' She crouches and walks like a cat burglar.

'No.'

'Then you're not going to sneak out of the house. You're going to walk out under false pretenses.'

He frowns. 'I didn't realize you were heavily into semiotics and philology.'

'I am.'

He steps toward her, his voice soft, caring. 'What's the matter, hon?' He takes her into his arms and holds her. She likes the feeling and hugs him back. Her nose is against his ear and she sniffs his special smell.

'Nothing,' she says. 'Nothing's wrong.'

Diva comes running out of the Atrium Court and waves to Barcelona from the edge of the sidewalk. 'Don't park,' she shouts through cupped hands.

Barcelona sees her just as she is pulling into a tight parking space and brakes halfway in. Capturing a space so

243

close to the main building on a weekend is such a rare break, she hates to give it up. Nevertheless, she throws the gear shift on the steering column into reverse. Nothing happens. She shifts into drive then quickly back into reverse. Something metallic clunks under the hood and the Geezemobile starts to sluggishly back up.

Backing this tugboat out of the narrow space requires the concentration of a Zen archer. Slowly she coaxes the car out, aware of the danger of chrome and fiberglass and expensive paint jobs on either side. A shiny vanilla BMW waiting behind her for the parking space honks twice—long and irate blasts. In the rearview mirror, Barcelona sees the darkly tanned woman behind the wheel scowling. The BMW has two yellow BABY ON BOARD signs, one suctioned to the front windshield, another to the rear windshield. Barcelona sees no baby in the car. The woman blares the horn again for almost five loud seconds.

Barcelona shifts back into drive and chugs off down the long row of parked cars. In the mirror she sees the woman neatly tuck her BMW into the vacant space. At the end of the row, Barcelona swings around into the next aisle and pilots the car past dozens of shoppers hurrying to and from the stores. It doesn't seem to matter if they are coming or going; all scamper with intent expressions as if late for the lab results on their tumor biopsy.

Barcelona pulls up next to the sidewalk and Diva climbs in.

'I forgot to stop at my bank for cash,' Diva says. 'It's just a few blocks away.'

'I can buy lunch.'

'Fine with me. But I still need some cash.'

'Then you buy lunch.' Barcelona looks over her shoulder, waiting for a chance to ease back into the flow of traffic.

'What was that woman honking about?' Diva asks.

'I don't know. I guess I wasn't moving fast enough.'

They see the BMW woman walking across the parking lot. She is wearing a short blue tennis skirt that wraps snugly around her narrow hips. Each stride exposes her matching ruffled blue tennis panties. She is very tan. She walks briskly and carries a large Robinson's bag. Her back is stiff, her gaze purposeful. The look of someone returning faulty merchandise.

'Bitch,' Barcelona mutters softly.

'Asshole,' Diva says a little louder.

Barcelona grins. 'Shithead,' she says, even louder. A couple of teenage boys passing by smirk.

'*Cuuunt!*' Diva hollers at the top of her voice. Several nearby shoppers as well as the BMW woman stop to look at them. Diva flips her the finger. Barcelona laughs and quickly nudges the car into the traffic and drives away.

'That felt good,' Diva says.

'I hope she didn't get my license number,' Barcelona says. 'She looks like the type to hunt you down.'

Diva laughs and shrugs. 'Fuck her if she can't take a joke.'

Barcelona is surprised at Diva. This is not at all the type of behavior Diva has ever demonstrated before. This is something Trina might have done.

Diva suddenly looks very serious. 'You're right, though. It's best not to say anything to people like that. I read something scary the other day, really shook me up.'

Barcelona follows the unicorn on Diva's pointing finger around a corner.

'This kid,' Diva says, 'just seventeen. He's riding along the freeway in the passenger seat of his girlfriend's new Jetta. She just got the car for graduation. I think her dad was some kind of tax lawyer or something. Anyway, these two kids are heading north on the San Diego Freeway, in the fast lane, driving toward Magic Mountain to meet some friends from school. She swears they were traveling at sixty-five miles per hour. Suddenly this yellow Toyota or Datsun, I can't remember which, comes roaring up behind them, practically smacking their bumper. He starts honking and flashing his lights, trying to get them to pull out of the fast lane so he could pass them. Turn here.'

Barcelona steers the Geezemobile around another corner. She waits for Diva to continue her story, but Diva doesn't. She is staring straight ahead. 'So the yellow car wants to pass them . . .' Barcelona prompts.

'So he wants to pass them, but the girl gets so pissed at the guy's obnoxious behavior, she deliberately slows down to fifty-five. The Toyota or whatever swerves out into the right lane, pulls up alongside them, rolls down his window, and shoots the boyfriend twice in the neck. Kid dies immediately.'

'Jesus.'

Diva points to the building she wants. 'There. Pull up there.' She starts rummaging through her purse for her wallet. 'Later the girl tells the police that when the guy rolled his window down she could hear the Beach Boys' "Surfin' USA" on his stereo. How can you murder someone while listening to the Beach Boys?'

Barcelona pulls up in front of the Wells Fargo Bank. Three other people are standing in line in front of the automated teller. They look hot and irritable in the sun. One woman is uselessly fanning herself with her bank card. Barcelona looks at Diva. 'Is that true? Where'd you read that?'

'Some magazine.'

'You always say that. Can't you ever remember the names of the magazines you read all this stuff in?'

'What difference does it make?'

Barcelona loses interest in the discussion and leans back against the hard seat.

Diva opens her wallet and flips through the plastic windows past photographs, credit cards, a blood donor card, driver's license, to her list of phone numbers. 'My accounts have been closed at so many different banks for bouncing checks, I can never remember what my current ATM number is.'

'You shouldn't write it down. Someone steals your wallet, they can clean out your account.'

'I write it down as part of a phony telephone number under a bogus name. Here, see? Otto Teller.'

'Clever.'

Diva gets out of the car and looks down at Barcelona with a serious expression. 'I'm not dumb.'

'Of course not,' Barcelona says, but Diva's already walking away. What is wrong with everyone today? First her mother acts wacky on the phone, now Diva flips the bird at some strange woman then announces she's not dumb. Christ. Is there a full moon? Are they both having some new virulent form of super period?

Barcelona keeps the motor running. She doesn't want to take any chances that the engine won't start. The Geezemobile legacy includes an electrical system that occasionally dies for no reason. No one has been able to figure out what the problem is, let alone fix it.

Lately, Barcelona has taken to visiting new car lots. She wanders among the new models, sits in them, plays with the air conditioner, sometimes just smells the interiors. The Geezemobile smells too much of lilacs, her grandmother's perfume. It's even in the vents and comes blasting into her face whenever she turns the fan on. She can't bring herself to sell the car, though. Not just yet.

'All set,' Diva says, stuffing two twenties into her purse as she slides into the car. 'Let's eat. I'm starving.'

They drive back to the Atrium Court and park a few acres away. Inside, they try to decide what kind of food to eat. Neither is very hungry. Barcelona stops at the baked potato stand and gets one filled with broccoli and cheese. Diva order a burrito from the Mexican food stand. Rather than stand around like vultures waiting for a table to open up, they take their food outside, sitting on the steps of the courtyard, where there are sometimes noon concerts. Not today, though. Today there is just a little boy chasing a sea gull.

'What's the matter?' Diva asks.

'What?' The question catches Barcelona by surprise. They are here to discuss Diva, not her.

'You seem distracted. You okay?'

Barcelona is tempted to tell her about Eric. She hates keeping secrets, even her own. She hasn't yet been able to sort out her feelings from her thoughts, to think things through. She doesn't want to fall into the same traps as before, make the same mistakes. Sometimes at night, when Eric isn't there, she thinks of this whole thing as one of those cheesy in-love-with-a-married-man TV movies. But most of the time she doesn't really think of Eric as married. Maybe that's just convenient thinking, but it makes sense at the time. Still, she doesn't think Diva is who she would like to share her doubts with. She likes Diva, but sharing confidences has never been a part of their relationship. There is a pecking order of shared intimacies among the four of them. Diva shares with Barcelona. Dixie shares with Trina and Barcelona. Trina shares with all of them. Barcelona shares with Trina, sometimes. Now that she thinks about it, though, she doesn't really tell very much, mostly she keeps things to herself. Why then did she always have the feeling that she told Trina everything?

'I thought we came to talk about you,' Barcelona says.

Diva takes a big bite of her burrito. Some rust-colored juice runs down her chin and she wipes it with a napkin. She sips her Diet Coke. 'Just beans and salsa in here. And

248

some sour cream and guacamole. No meat. I'm still a vegetarian.'

'Great. I admire your dedication.'

'I don't really miss it much. I actually think not eating meat has made my voice better. People say my singing's improved.'

They both sit in silence while Diva eats her burrito and Barcelona picks disinterestedly at her baked potato. Barcelona watches the little boy chase the sea gull across the courtyard. When the gull finally flies away, the little boy tries to jump in the air after him. He jumps several times, perplexed that he is unable to fly with the bird. Finally in frustration he jumps so hard that he falls down and bangs his knee. He starts crying. Barcelona and Diva watch him cry for almost a minute before a woman younger than both of them runs up to the boy, picks him up, and kisses him on the cheek. She carries him away.

Barcelona waits for Diva to speak. She senses that Diva is uncomfortable about something.

'I was reading this article,' Diva says. 'About Borneo. They've got this bug there that bites you on the face, sucks out your blood, then when it's full, takes a dump next to the puncture. When you scratch the itch, you end up rubbing the bug shit into the wound. It takes anywheres from one to twenty years, but eventually you start to die from it. At first the symptoms are like malaria, but later on they're like AIDS. Can you imagine, dying twenty years later from a little bug bite?'

Barcelona mashes some stray broccoli chunks into her potato.

Diva continues. 'There's another one, another bug mentioned in the same article. This human botfly, whose larvae bore into your skin and eat little bits of you for forty days. After that they pop out as inch-long maggots. Like in *Aliens* or something.'

Barcelona pushes her potato away. 'Why are you telling me this?'

'I know, I know. It grossed me out too. But here's the one that really got me. In the Amazon, if a man walks into the river naked and takes a piss, they have this tiny fish, a candiru, that smells the urine and thinks you're a big fish. It swims right up the stream of piss, right up into the guy's urethra, burrows in, holding itself in place with some spiny barbs. They say the pain gets so bad he has to be rushed immediately to the hospital before his bladder bursts. Once there, he has to ask the doctor to cut his penis off.'

'Where do you read this stuff?'

'Magazines. I read lots of magazines. Wild, huh?'

Barcelona watches Diva finish the burrito. She eats mechanically, chewing, wiping her mouth whether or not it needs it, sipping her drink through a straw, then starting the routine over again. Bite, chew, wipe, sip. Her sandals scrape nervously against the steps.

'What's the matter?' Barcelona asks. 'You sounded desperate on the phone.'

Diva puts the stump of the burrito down. She looks straight at Barcelona. 'I need to borrow money.'

'How much?'

'I'm changing the whole focus of my career, Barcy. I've decided that it's not enough anymore to sing. I've got to have the right material. My own trademark.'

'You want to buy some songs?'

'I want to *write* some songs. My own songs. Then record them, make a demo. I need the money to make a demo.'

'How much?'

'About two thousand dollars.'

Barcelona stabs her plastic fork into the baked potato. She keeps stabbing it, thinking. Every few months someone comes to her to borrow money. Usually it's a teacher from school. They all think she has thousands stashed away

250

from her novels. They don't realize she lives from month to month just like they do. But for some reason she has always managed to lend them the couple of hundred they've asked for, even it it meant living lean for the rest of the month herself. But two thousand dollars! She doesn't have that kind of money. She still hadn't been paid the script money from that producer, Roger Carlyle. Apparently there were some legal details to the contract he and Grief were arguing over. To get the two grand, she would have to borrow from the teachers' credit union.

'Okay,' she says. 'Take me a couple days to get it.'

'Really?' Diva says. She smiles, tears surround her eyes. 'God, I didn't think you'd do it. I mean, I thought you'd think this was just another fucked up idea of mine, another dumb way to blow money.'

That's exactly what Barcelona thinks. But she wouldn't say that. She knows the record business is enough like the publishing business to put the odds of Diva ever selling her demo to a record company as very remote. According to statistics, she is more likely to be killed by terrorists, or marry happily.

'I'm taking every bit of cash I have,' Diva continues, 'and then I'm charging up my credit cards to their limits. I'm going to take all that, plus your loan, and make the best demo around. I've got lots of friends in the business who'll play for me cheap.'

'Have you written your song yet?'

'I'm working on it. It's kinda country, kinda rock. I haven't decided which angle to emphasize yet. But I feel good about it, I really do.'

Barcelona forces a smile. Diva is setting herself up for a long, hard fall. When that happens how will she react? Shrug it off as another valuable life experience? Go back to singing directions to car lots? Barcelona sighs. Diva is a fried zucchini waiting to happen. Or even a maraschino cherry. 'Let's walk,' Barcelona suggests, feeling the need to move.

They throw their paper plates and plastic silverware into the garbage. A couple of gray sea gulls perch on the nearby lamp, watching. As soon as the women walk away, they swoop down to inspect.

'Let's stop by the music store,' Diva says. 'I need a new capo for my guitar.'

On the way to the store, they chat about nothing special. The day is sunny and clear and they can see Catalina Island from Buffum's. Suddenly Diva swerves away toward a pack of high school kids.

'Omigod, Dixie!' Diva cries out. 'What the hell are you doing in that outfit?'

The three kids turn around. One of them is indeed Dixie, her hair combed straight down, her eyes heavily lined with mascara, her whole posture uncharacteristically slouched.

'Your hair!' Diva laughs. 'What is this, a masquerade?'

Barcelona sees the panic in Dixie's eyes and realizes that Dixie is working. The girl next to her is wobbly, bleary-eyed, maybe a little drunk or doped. The boy is clear-eyed and handsome. He is staring at Dixie with uncertainty.

'Dixie,' Barcelona says, quickly walking up to them. 'I can't imagine your mother knows you're out here dressed like that.'

A shimmer of gratitude flickers in Dixie's eyes. 'No, Mrs. Lee, she doesn't.'

'And your hair, young lady.' Barcelona shakes her head. 'You have such beautiful hair. Why not use it to your advantage?'

Diva stars at Barcelona a moment, then catches on. 'Yes, Dixie, we know she's bought you nicer clothing than that.'

252

'Come on, Mrs. Klosterman, it's the weekend.'

'People still see you, even on a weekend.' Barcelona says.

'Je-sus,' the girl with Dixie says and starts walking away.

'I think you ladies are absolutely right,' the handsome boy says. 'I try to get her to take more pride in her appearance, but what can you do? Every teen's a rebel these days. Until you take their credit cards away.' He laughs charmingly. 'Joseph Little,' he says, extending his hand toward Barcelona. 'Dixie's friend.'

Barcelona looks at Dixie but gets no response. She shakes Joseph Little's hand. 'Barcelona Lee. Friend of Dixie's mother.' She turns to Diva. 'We'd better hurry or we'll be late.'

'Yes,' Diva says. 'Yes, we'd better hurry.'

'Nice meeting you,' Joseph Little says with a big smile.

'Bye,' Barcelona says. 'Bye, Dixie.'

Barcelona locks arms with Diva and they hurry away. They don't stop trotting until they are in the parking lot.

'God, Barcy, what have I done?'

'It's okay. I don't think they noticed anything.'

Diva is trembling. 'I didn't know. I didn't expect to see her here on a Saturday being undercover. I mean, it's the goddamn weekend.'

Barcelona pats Diva's arm. 'Don't worry. We covered up pretty well. If anything, we may even have helped. Now they've had her identity confirmed by a couple outsiders.'

'You think?'

Barcelona nods, though she is not at all sure. The boy seemed nice enough, but there is no way to tell for sure. 'Where are you parked?'

Diva points. 'Other side of the building. I guess I shouldn't have walked over here, huh?'

'I'll give you a lift.'

They walk across the lot, weaving between parked cars.

'Feels funny to be leaving this place without carrying a couple packages,' Barcelona says.

'Speak for yourself. I'm leaving with two thousand dollars.' She laughs. 'Don't worry, when I make it big you'll have front row tickets to all my concerts.'

'What about backstage passes?'

'I'm saving those for my groupies.'

Barcelona walks between two cars and discovers a cement garden of some green spiny plant like mistletoe. These little patches are all over the lot. She tries to squeeze by, but she accidentally brushes against one of the overhanging leaves and it cuts her scabbed ankle.

'Damn it!' she says. 'This ankle's never going to heal.'

Diva wends her way over, looks at the ankle. 'Nasty. The plant do all that?'

'I had a scab from before.'

Diva toes the plant. 'Prickly pear. They plant a lot of this down on Balboa. Keeps the dogs from urinating wherever they're planted. Apparently they can cut their little dicks on the leaves.'

Barcelona laughs. 'I don't even want to know where you got that.'

Diva grins. 'Some magazine.'

A gray Volvo stops next to them. The driver is a heavy man with a thin mustache and bad skin. The woman next to him is young and thin and exceptionally attractive. 'You leaving?' he asks Barcelona.

'Yes,' she says. 'But we're parked two more aisles over.'

He looks around at the fender-to-fender parking lot. 'I'll follow you,' he says.

Barcelona and Diva continue to squeeze by the cars until they reach the Geezemobile. They can see the gray Volvo rolling down their aisle. He brakes ten yards away and waits for them to back out.

Once inside the car, Diva touches Barcelona's arm. She

254

has a very serious expression on her face. 'I know you think I'm a flake,' Diva says. 'That you won't ever see your money again. That I'm going to fall on my face.'

'Diva—'

'But I'm not stupid. I know the odds and still think I can beat them. I believe in myself, even if no one else does.'

'We believe in you, Diva. We all do.'

'I'm not stupid,' she says.

The gray Volvo honks loudly and Barcelona starts to back up. Silently, she kisses two thousand dollars good-bye.

17

'So when do I get my free coke?' Melody asks Joseph outside the Fashion Island pet store. 'Either that or give me some more quarters to feed those albino frogs. They look hungry.'

Joseph doesn't answer. Dixie can feel his sharp eyes on the back of her head as she watches Barcelona and Diva hurry away in a panicky trot. 'They're in my mom's aerobics class,' she explains casually. 'Major yuppies.'

'The fat one needs a few more classes,' Joseph says. 'But I wouldn't mind doing a few leg-lifts with the other one. Barcelona.' He lays his hand on Dixie's shoulder.

Dixie pretends to be jealous, shrugs his hand off. 'They're kinda old, for God's sake.'

'Experienced.'

'Fuck you.'

He laughs, walks up behind her and wraps his arms around her. 'Hey, I'm just kidding, Dixie. Just teasing.'

'This is so fucking lame,' Melody says, making a disgusted face at the two of them. 'Dixie and I are supposed to be shopping together, Joey. Then you come along and worm your way in. Okay, man, we helped you buy your mother a fucking dress, now give me my coke and split.' Her eyes are fierce and wet, her voice is loud enough that nearby shoppers glance at them.

Joseph grabs her by the elbow and jerks her quickly

256

along the sidewalk. 'Keep you goddamn voice down.'

'Ow, man, that hurts.'

Dixie runs after them. She still hopes to get home within the hour so she can have dinner with Randy and his son. She missed miniature golf, but she'd make it up with dinner and a movie, her treat. All would be forgiven. Eventually.

Joseph drags Melody around the corner behind the Brooks Brothers store and shakes her by the shoulders. 'You'd better learn when to shut up, Melody.'

'Eat shit, homo,' Melody says, pulling free.

'Hey, guys, cool it,' Dixie says. 'You wanna get us busted?'

Melody rubs her arm where Joseph had grabbed her. 'Fuck you too. You're on his side. You were supposed to be spending the day with me, remember?'

'I was supposed to be spending it with my family. I don't know why I let you talk me into coming here. I'm outta here.' Dixie swings her purse over her shoulder and marches away.

'Come on, Dix,' Joseph pleads.

Dixie keeps walking, her rubber flipflops slapping an angry rhythm.

'Hey, I'm sorry, okay?' Melody calls. 'I'm serious, Dixie. Jesus, just wait up.'

Dixie slows enough to allow them to catch up, but she keeps walking toward the parking lot. They run up on either side of her. Melody takes out her silver flask and swigs some Southern Comfort. She offers it to Dixie. Dixie pretends to drink then offers it to Joseph.

'I'm not into that shit,' he says.

'Speaking of shit,' Melody says. She lowers her voice to a hoarse whisper. 'How's about our free sample you promised.'

'I didn't say today.'

'When?'

'Maybe tomorrow.'

'Fuck, Joey, that's so fucked.' Melody stumbles over a crack in the sidewalk and Dixie catches her. 'I need something today, man.'

'Hey, I'm out. Running on empty. I've got to meet my source first. Restock the shelves.'

'When's that?' Dixie asks.

'What?'

'When you meet your source.'

He looks into her eyes. 'Why? You want to make a buy on your own? Be my competition?'

'Just curious when your shelves will be full so I can do some shopping.'

He doesn't answer. He buries his hands deep into his pockets and does a little soft shoe dance as he walks beside Dixie. He whistles 'Singin' in the Rain.'

'Oh, man, I saw that movie,' Melody says.

'Yeah,' Dixie says. 'With Gene Kelly. He was so cool.'

Melody laughs. 'Not that movie, the one with Malcolm McDowell. Remember the part where he's singing that song and kicking that old guy?'

'*A Clockwork Orange*,' Joseph says.

'I guess. Something like that.' Melody mimics Joseph's dance steps, singing the song: 'I'm singin' in the rain . . .' When she sings 'rain' she lets go with a vicious kick at the air. 'He did it like that. In the guy's gut.' She stops a moment, a little wobbly. 'That part was funny, but I was kinda mad at myself for laughing. Those guys were so *mean*.'

'Let's take her home,' Joseph says to Dixie. 'Before she passes out.'

'Let's find Toby and beat the shit out of him, the rat fuck,' Melody says. She stops, leans against the glass window of a fancy shoe store. The elderly clerk inside glares at them but Melody is rooting through her purse with

258

an intense expression. The purse is as big as a saddlebag so there is a lot of rustling, clanging, and jingling. 'You guys gotta try this shit . . .'

Dixie is afraid she will pull out a bottle of pills or crack, but when Melody's hand finally reappears it is clutching a can of soft drink called Jolt. The logo on the can reads: 'All the sugar and twice the caffeine.'

Melody pops the can and sips. 'This stuff really sobers you up.' She offers the can to Dixie.

Dixie refuses. 'I drink diet soda.'

'I read somewhere that Nutra Sweet kills brain cells immediately upon contact. Saccharin used to cause cancer in rats, but you had to drink gallons of the stuff every day over twenty years. But this Nutra Sweet shit works right away. Goes right in and kills them.'

'All that junk is bad for you,' Joseph says. 'We did an experiment in science class once where we dropped these human teeth and nails into a glass of Coke. A couple weeks later the teeth and the nails were gone, dissolved.'

'Come on, Melody,' Dixie says. She guides her to the Mustang and helps her into the passenger seat, buckling her seat belt for her.

Melody giggles. She drinks out of the can. Some brown liquid dribbles down her chin onto her blouse. She doesn't notice.

Joseph leans against the fender and shakes his head. 'This is so low-budget.' As Dixie walks by him to get into the driver's side, he grabs her wrist. 'I'll follow you, then we can go for a drive.' His other hand cups her butt and pulls her close so she's straddling his thigh. He nudges his leg up against her crotch. 'You want to go, don't you?'

Dixie hesitates. Randy is probably already fuming that she missed miniature golf; to miss dinner too would mean he wouldn't speak to her for days. It's happened before. Divorced men are especially sensitive about time you're supposed to spend with their kids. It's some kind of test they put you through.

'Come on,' Joseph coaxes. 'You said you were worried because of what I do. I'll show you what I do and you'll see there's nothing to it. It's just a big giggle.'

Bingo. Her way in. He said he was meeting with his supplier tonight; maybe she could be there to make an ID. Then they'd have both of them, which meant tonight would be her last day in high school. Randy would just have to understand.

'Yeah, okay,' she says. 'I'll go.'

Dixie parks the vintage Mustang behind Joseph's shiny black Suzuki Samurai Jeep. He steps out and strikes a model's pose next to his car, one hand on hip, the other placed on the roll bar of the Jeep. Cool California Dude Scamming Chicks on Sunday Afternoon at Beach. She's seen guys do variations of this pose all her life and it always makes her want to laugh. Instead, Dixie smiles coyly at Joseph and he abandons his pose to open her car door.

'Thanks,' Dixie says, hopping out.

'You keep up pretty well out there.' He'd driven the twisty stretch of Pacific Coast Highway at ninety miles per hour.

'No trick to driving fast,' she says. 'Just step on the gas and it goes.'

'The trick is getting there alive.'

She smiles. 'I'm here, aren't I?'

He puts his arms around her and kisses her. His body leans into hers, his weight pinning her against the Mustang. A few cars drive by, inches from their bodies, honking horns and shouting encouragement. One girl sitting on a guy's lap squeals, 'Go for it!'

Joseph's tongue is in her mouth and she almost giggles at the feel of it. Knowing that this case is now almost over has started her withdrawal process. This is what Cinderella must have felt like when she saw the gilded coach transform back into a pumpkin, the horses to mice. What was once big is now small. Joseph Little has reverted from drug lord suitor back to high school boy. His tongue in her mouth is comically intense, his hands on her ass and on her breasts seem like a little boy's urgent gropings. She feels a twinge of sadness, though, when she realizes that after tonight, these are the last breasts he'll touch for a while. Female breasts, anyway.

She gently pushes him off her. 'You trying to get us killed?'

'Not a bad way to go.'

'Yeah, sideswiped in Laguna Beach.' She brushes dirt from the car off the back of her jeans. 'So what're we doing here?'

'Let's go down to the boardwalk.'

She shrugs. She has been unable to get any information out of him about who his connection is or when they're meeting. If she brings the subject up he makes a joke or grabs her ass. Considering the close call back at Fashion Island, she decides not to press him too much.

Dixie does not get down to Laguna Beach much, though she was twice offered a job on their police force. Both times she turned down the job, despite the promotion that would have gone with it. Laguna Beach is too fashionable, the people too good looking. It is a hybrid community made up of wealthy professionals, surfer drones, gays, artists, revisionist hippies, beach yuppies and variations combining these groups. They are smug in their good fortune, self-congratulatory. They see themselves as the children of the sun and Dixie could never get committed to risking her life for these people.

The main beach stretches out along Pacific Coast Highway in the middle of town. During the spring and summer the beach is crowded every day of the week. The three volleyball nets are in constant use by serious players. The basketball courts next to the beach attract tough players from all over the county. It is a fascinating place to be, but living here would be the same as staying undercover in high school forever.

Joseph looks a little too dressy in his pleated white pants, powder blue Italian loafers, and yellow shirt with a giant colorful cockatoo emblazoned from shoulder to waist. He holds Dixie's hand very tight as they stroll amid the crowd along the boardwalk. She wiggles her fingers to get him to loosen his grip, but he doesn't.

'Hey,' she says, 'relax. I can't feel anything in my fingers.'

He looks surprised and immediately releases her hand. 'Sorry. I didn't want to lose you in this crowd.'

Dixie kisses him on the cheek and smiles. 'You won't lose me that easy.'

He smiles and takes her hand again, this time more gently. Dixie walks beside him, staying close to keep from getting jostled by the crowd. The scent of sun screen and coconut oil sweetens the air. Most people walking by are in swimming suits or shorts. The smell of their greased flesh and the kaleidoscope of bright colors makes Dixie a little dizzy.

'I'm thirsty,' she says. 'Let's get a Coke.'

'In a minute,' he says. Joseph seems nervous and distracted, not at all his usual cool and assured self. The closer they get to the beach, the more sullen and nervous he becomes.

'You okay, Joe?' Dixie asks.

'Let's sit here.'

'Joseph?'

'I'm fine.' He looks at her and flashes a big smile. 'God, you're gorgeous.'

They sit on the edge of the boardwalk, feet dangling near the sand. Joseph watches the teenage volleyball players in front of him, but his eyes keep darting off around the beach, down the boardwalk, across the street. He's looking for someone, Dixie realizes. Her own adrenaline starts pumping and she can feel her muscles tense across her stomach. The buy is going to go down right here, right now.

'I've gotta go to the bathroom,' she says. She needs to find a phone, get some backup down here.

'Sure. Over there.' He points down the boardwalk.

Dixie is about to get up when suddenly a shirtless teen on a skateboard rockets down the boardwalk right toward her. People jump out of his way. The plastic wheels rumble against the warped wood boards like a stampeding buffalo. Dixie thinks she will be hit by the shirtless kid on the skateboard and leaps off the boardwalk into the sand four feet below. She lands in the sand on her hands and knees.

The kid leans back on his rolling skateboard, swivels his hips, and brings the skateboard to a stop inches from where Dixie had been sitting. He steps off, stomps the curled lip of the board. It flips up in the air and he catches it.

'Hey, Brandon, knock it off,' Joseph tells him.

Brandon laughs. 'Learn to live with it, dude.'

'You okay, Dixie?' Joseph climbs off the boardwalk to help Dixie to her feet. He brushes sand from the knees of her jeans.

Dixie looks at Brandon, who is staring at her with a smirk. He is maybe sixteen. His bare chest and arms are well muscled for his age. His shaggy hair is brown but highlighted with blond streaks from the sun. People walking by seem to instinctively avoid him. He drops his skateboard into the sand and stands on the edge of the boardwalk with his back to Dixie. He springs into the air

263

and does a perfect back flip, landing in the sand next to her. 'Ta da,' he says. 'Applause is welcome.'

Joseph is obviously angry, senses that Brandon is some- how making a fool of him. But he is just as obviously a little afraid of him too. 'Dixie, this is Brandon.'

'Hi,' Dixie says.

'Yeah, hi.' Brandon's eyes are large and gray. Looking into them is trying to peer through a thick fog.

The teenage volleyball players at the net shout crude greetings to Brandon.

'Hey, Gary,' Brandon replies to one of them, 'you play like a fag.'

'You should know,' Gary says.

'You're a fudge-packing fool,' Brandon replies and they all crack up.

Joseph glances impatiently at his watch.

Brandon turns his attention on Dixie. 'What are you anyway? Nip or gook?'

'Chink,' Dixie says.

'My dad was in the Nam.'

'Which side?' she says.

He laughs. 'You're funny.' He looks her over more carefully now, his gaze so intense she feels as if she is being strip-searched. 'What school you go to?'

'My school,' Joseph says.

Brandon nods absently, his gaze now distracted by a couple of shapely women in bikinis strolling by on the boardwalk. One of them has large breasts hanging out of the too-small top. 'Jesus fuck,' Brandon says aloud enough for them to hear. 'I'd eat a mile of her shit just to lick the hole it came from.'

The women hurry away.

Joseph makes a face. 'I didn't come down here for this crap, Brandon.'

Brandon's smile is cunning. 'Then why did you come

down here, dude?' He touches Joseph's parrot with his finger. 'Not to get tan.'

'Don't screw around with me. You know what I'm here for, same as always. You want to do business or what?'

Brandon's smile stiffens on his face, an imitation of a smile. 'Since when do you have a business partner, dude?'

Joseph puts his arm around Dixie and pulls her next to him. 'Whenever I want one.'

'One thing I learned long ago. Never mix business with pleasure.'

Dixie has a bad feeling. Things aren't going down well. Brandon is suspicious. Maybe she's just spooked, maybe he's always that way. But she doesn't want to take any chances. She doesn't have enough for an arrest, not without witnessing the transaction, but at least she's been able to identify Brandon. Let the local police chase him down. She'll bust Joseph, which will take care of most of the drug traffic at Principal Peterson's school for a while.

'Look,' she says. 'Why don't you guys just do whatever it is you want to do. I'll drive home.'

'No,' Joseph says. 'Wait.'

'I'll meet you later,' she says. 'It's okay.'

Joseph fidgets with his watch. Dixie knows what is going through his mind: He doesn't want her to know that he is intimidated by Brandon, a kid two years younger. In high school two years' difference is a whole generation. He looks at Brandon when he speaks to her. 'No. I want you to stay. This won't take long.'

Brandon grins. 'Hey, stay. No biggie. You're a lot better looking than Joseph here anyway.'

Joseph's hand tightens around Dixie's waist, a secret squeeze of triumph. She climbs back onto the boardwalk and shakes the sand off each flipflop. Joseph and Brandon climb up beside her.

'Let's go to my place,' Brandon says.

Joseph nods and takes Dixie's hand.

'I've got to go to the bathroom,' Dixie says, still hoping to get a phone call off.

'Got one at my place,' Brandon says. 'Just a few blocks.'

Dixie feels their eyes on her and she shrugs. Things are tense enough between them that she doesn't want to push it. 'Let's hurry, okay?'

Brandon laughs. 'Girls just can't hold it like guys.' He waves to the volleyball players. 'See you faggots later.'

'Eat me,' one of them yells back.

'Tastes great but less filling,' Brandon says.

They all laugh, their faces sweaty and cunning.

Joseph winks at Dixie and squeezes her hand. He thinks this is a romantic adventure the two of them are sharing. She feels sorry for Joseph, smart and basically nice, about to go down for dealing drugs. She'll be at the trial to hear the testimony of psychologists who will explain why a smart boy like him with such wonderful parents and all the opportunity in the world does such terrible things. The psychologists' explanations will sound reasonable; they will probably be true. But Joseph will still do time, because that's the way the moral pendulum has swung lately. When she is sitting on the stand describing how she bought drugs from him and witnessed him buying drugs, she will be forced to look at him. That is standard testifying procedure, to look the criminal in the eyes while testifying, to show the jury that you are in the right. She will do that, but she will feel rotten afterward.

With Brandon, however, she will sit on the stand and stare at him, point her finger in identification, and describe in detail his crimes.

'This stuff I got is great,' Brandon says as they head down the street together. He has one foot on the skateboard and pushes himself along with the other. Sometimes he glides ahead and stops to wait for them to catch up. 'You're gonna love it, dude. The crack now comes in these pills, man, like aspirin. Only they got their own brand mark. This shit's got an R stamped on it, stands for Rocket.'

'An R,' Joseph says. 'Why bother?'

'Customer loyalty, man. See, you sell some crack to this dude, he gets off on it like never before. Next time he wants to make sure he gets the same quality, but how can he be sure? Easy, he looks for the one with an R stamped on it. Like Bayer aspirin. Ask for us by name. Satisfaction guaranteed.'

Joseph nods. 'Good idea.'

'Fuck yeah. That's why this first batch is so good, they want to build brand identification. Get it? Like a promotion gimmick.'

They have walked down several streets, back away from the business section up into the foothills where the residences are. They come to a large house hidden behind lush tropical foliage. Palm trees fan out overhead, slicing the sky into wedges of light that fall at crazy angles across the lawn.

'You live here?' Dixie asks.

'Nah, out back.' He skateboards down the driveway to the white two-car garage. He unlocks the side door and enters. Dixie and Joseph follow.

The inside surprises Dixie. The room is decorated and arranged with surprising taste. The double garage door is painted a bright red with the Coca-Cola logo in white in foot-high letters. The lettering is precise so that it looks like the official logo, yet it has something more, a flair that isn't in the original. On another wall is a duplicate of the Nike logo in black and red. In fact, all the walls and doors and even the ceiling are painted in various logos: 7-Up, Michelin, Fender, Pacific Bell, Taco Bell, *Los Angeles Times*, Volvo.

'You did all this?' Dixie asks.

267

'Who else would do this shit?' Brandon answers.

'You want to go into art or something? Like doing commercials?'

Brandon laughs. 'Fuck, I hope not. Who wants to sit around all day doing what somebody tells you? Fuck that.'

'You're good,' Dixie says. 'These are very good.'

Brandon shrugs. He is not being modest, Dixie can see. He doesn't really care. He leans his skateboard against the wall and flops down on the bed. Next to the bed is a small refrigerator with a hot plate and electric frying pan on top. A package of Lorna Doone shortbread cookies lies open next to the hot plate. He reaches over and grabs a few. He doesn't offer any to Dixie or Joseph. 'Well?' he says to Dixie.

'What?'

'I thought you had to go to the bathroom.'

'Yeah. Where do I go? In the house?' She starts for the door.

'No. I got my own bathroom,' he says. He points to a doorway in the corner she hadn't noticed before. The doorway has no door but she can see the toilet squatting in the tiny room. 'In there,' he says. 'The Mendlesons built that on when they converted this garage into a rental unit. Jews'll put a crapper in their Caddy if it means renting it out for a few more bucks.'

'There's no door,' Dixie says.

'Don't need one. Don't worry, we've heard it all before. Plop plop, fizz fizz.'

Dixie looks at Brandon. He lies back on his bed, his fingers laced behind his head. His knees are bent so that she can look down the leg of his shorts. He isn't wearing underpants and she can see his genitals. He grins at her, knowing.

'That's it, I'm going home,' Dixie announces. She turns

to Joseph. 'Call me later if you want.' She heads for the door.

'Dixie,' Joseph calls and starts after her.

She spins around angrily. 'I'm tired of this shit. You brought me along and now you let this asshole treat me this way?'

Joseph's face reddens until it matches the shade of the cockatoo on his shirt. Even the tips of his ears are red. His lips move as if he's testing words, but no sound comes out.

'Oh, hell,' Brandon says, jumping off the bed. 'If it means that much to you.' He takes a key off a hook and hands it to Dixie. 'You can use the Mendlesons' downstairs bathroom. They let me use their shower.'

'I can't just barge into their house.'

'They're away on vacation. Canada, I think.'

Dixie takes the key and marches out, yanking the door hard behind her. Once outside she lingers out of sight near the door.

'Jesus, Joe,' Brandon says. 'She's got your nuts in her pocket.'

'Fuck you, man. You don't know anything. All your girls are thirteen.'

'Hey, bro, you gotta get 'em before they grow teeth down there.' He laughs.

'Let's just do business, okay?'

'Sure. Let me take a quick piss first. Hope you aren't too sensitive to listen. You can wait outside if you are.'

'Fuck you.'

Dixie hurriedly unlocks the Mendlesons' backdoor. This opens into the kitchen and she heads straight for the wall phone next to the refrigerator. On the refrigerator are notes held by magnetic fruit. A grocery list that includes Thomas' sourdough English muffins. Sourdough is underlined three times. Fresh squeezed orange juice. Fresh is underlined twice. Another list includes: stop the newspaper, cancel bridge game, set auto timer for lights, take Grover to vet, etc. Each item is crossed out except the last item, call Mother & Father. Either they didn't call or they didn't cross it off their list.

Dixie dials the number to her police station. 'Ed, it's Dixie. I want you to send two cars immediately, and tell them I'm still undercover. The address is 179—'

'Hang up,' Brandon says. He is standing in the doorway with a baseball bat. Joseph, his face grim and puffy, stands behind him. Brandon points at her with the bat. 'Hang it up, lady, before I do a Reggie Jackson on your skull.'

Dixie hears Ed DeMerra speaking her name, asking her for the address, pleading with her. She stares at Brandon, assessing how serious he is, what her chances are of fighting both of them off, of running. Either one alone she could handle, but both of them would be too much. She hangs up the phone.

Brandon taps the bat against his palm and grins. 'This is gonna be fun.'

18

Barcelona pushes her reading glasses higher on her nose with the back of her wrist. She is wearing only underpants and a T-shirt and her butt is stuck to the vinyl chair. Her eyes burn and her back is sore from hunching over the typewriter for the past two hours. Ordinarily she uses the typewriter now only to type envelopes. But the screenplay format is so complicated that her computer can't do some of the required notations and she has to type certain phrases on each page. Using two fingers, she types the final (MORE) under the dialogue to be continued onto the next page, yanks the sheet out of the typewriter, and inserts it in the complete script.

She hefts the script in her hand: 128 pages. A little long by usual standards, according to the books she's read. Figuring each page to equal one minute of film, the producers like to have the script no more than 100 to 110 pages. Any film that runs longer than two hours reduces the number of showings per day in each theater. That means one less paid showing and one less trip to the snack bar. Form fits function.

She takes her reading glasses off, rubs her eyes. She swivels the chair around and drags the phone across the desk. Once again she dials Dixie's number. She has been calling Dixie all afternoon. There still is no answer.

Barcelona stares at the title page of the script. The title,

Live Wires, is in bold and underlined. She tries to imagine it on the marquee, then on the movie screen. Would she be drawn into a movie with that title? She's not sure.

She peels her butt from the vinyl chair and walks over to her little Canon photocopier. She turns the machine on and waits for the green light to stop flashing. Then she begins to make two copies of the script, one for Roger Carlyle and one for Grief. As she feeds each page into the machine, she can't help but think about Lynda Kramer, imagine their first meeting, see herself on the set of the film. She begins reading the script again as she copies it. Not bad. Pretty damn good, she thinks as she feeds another page in. Lousy, she thinks as she sees the copy come out the other side.

Barcelona walks back to the phone and dials Dixie again. No answer. Not even the phone answering machine. Nothing to worry about. It is Saturday, and if Dixie had to work today she probably has to keep on working tonight.

She dials again and halfway through realizes she is dialing Eric's number. She immediately slams the phone down as if it had bitten her. She picks it up again, dials Dixie's number, gets no answer.

She goes back to the photocopier and continues to feed her script into the machine. Afterward she will have to hole-punch it and stick those little brass clasps through the holes. Then it will look just like the scripts Roger Carlyle sent her.

Saturday night. The Holy Night of dating. Harley Buss had offered to take her out to dinner and a movie, but she'd turned him down. Not that she had anything better to do, but since seeing Eric again she's been less interested in dating casually where there is no real interest. Friendly dating and friendly sex was getting a little tiring. She wanted some of that good old teeth-rattling passion. The kind where you change your outfit twelve times and your hair eight before your date shows up. She has not felt that kind of passion in years. Eric is the closest she's come to that since . . . well, since pre-Luna Eric.

She stares at the phone. Eric never comes over on a Saturday night. This is when he and Luna usually go to a play. She loves little theaters, community groups, college shows, the cornier the better. Whenever he speaks of this passion of hers, he gets this stupid little grin that makes Barcelona angry, though she is careful not to show it. What are her grounds for anger?

Barcelona crosses the room and snatches up the phone. She stabs the numbers and listens to the electronic tones. The phone rings and rings. Finally the sleepy German-accented voice of Milan speaks, 'Yes, hello?'

Barcelona bunches her T-shirt over the mouthpiece and, in a throaty disguised voice, whispers a long string of obscenities.

PART THREE

Fault Lines

**In Which Romance
Takes Unexpected Turns**

19

Barcelona tries to stop the bleeding with scented toilet paper.

She tears a thumbnail-size piece from the yellow roll and pastes it against her wound. The tissue paper immediately turns limp with blood. It reminds her of time-lapse photography of a wilting flower.

'Christ,' she says.

She tears off a large hunk of toilet paper, folds it neatly in a thick square, and presses it against what is left of the scab on her ankle. The paper expands, grows heavier with the seeping blood. She can almost feel the blood soaking up into the paper, as if it were eating it layer by scented layer. She stares at the top of the wad, waiting to see the yellow paper melt into bright crimson like litmus. It's like some old black and white horror movie, waiting for the zombies to burst through the locked door.

She is sitting on the edge of the bathtub in her panties and bra. The metal runners for the shower enclosure cut sharply into her buttocks and she shifts uncomfortably. The yellow plastic Lady Bic razor is on the lid of the toilet tank next to the spread-eagled copy of Ann Beattie's *Love Always*. During her shower this morning, Barcelona had forgotten to shave her legs, so she thought a few quick swipes before dressing would be okay. Something had distracted her for a moment as she'd been carefully edging around the ankle and she'd sliced through the scab.

The toilet paper doesn't turn red. The bleeding must have stopped. She carefully peels the wad back and sees the half scab crusted next to the open hole brimming with sticky blood. She thinks it looks like the mouth of a volcano. She risks walking a few steps to the medicine cabinet for a Band-Aid and tapes one over the wound. This gives her a good excuse to wear slacks today. This is just as well because she is driving into L.A. later to have lunch with Trina and to drop her completed screenplay off at Grief's office.

Putting the Band-Aid box back in the medicine chest, Barcelona looks into the mirror for the first time that morning. 'Oh my God.' She frowns. 'What next?'

On her forehead, right above her left eyebrow, is a swollen red blemish. It looks large enough to pick up radio stations. She leans closer to the mirror to examine the monstrosity and discovers it is not a blemish, it is a flea bite. 'Larry, you son of a bitch!' she hollers. She storms into the bedroom and finds Larry sitting on the wicker clothes hamper licking his tail. He looks up as she enters the room, seems unimpressed, returns to grooming his tail.

Barcelona snatches up a pillow from the unmade bed to throw at him but changes her mind and tosses it back on the mattress. Larry looks up again and she notices he is missing yet another patch of fur on his shoulder. For a neutered, clawless cat, he gets in a lot of fights. 'Good, you little shit,' she tells him. 'I hope they scalp you bald.' He lies down on the hamper and closes his eyes.

Barcelona feels a nasty pinch on her toe and ankle and looks down at her foot. A black flea is nibbling on her toe and another is attached to her ankle near the Band-Aid. She hurries over to the toilet, lifts her foot over the bowl, and brushes them into the water. They float like poppy

278

seeds, one kicks toward the edge of the water. She wonders who teaches them how to swim. Meantime, another flea has hopped onto her other foot. She reaches down, plucks it off, and presses it between her two thumbnails until the body pops. A tiny drop of blood squirts across her thumbnails. It makes her shiver to realize that drop of blood is her own, slurped out of her by this bug. She flicks the flattened flea into the sink and washes her hands.

Barcelona goes back into the bedroom and dials the phone. She has been calling Dixie all weekend and no one has answered. She's called Diva and Trina, but neither has heard from Dixie. Yesterday, Sunday, she drove over to Dixie's house but no one was there. So far she has avoided calling the police because she assumes Dixie must still be undercover. When Eric called last night from the neighborhood grocery store, she explained her concern about Dixie. He brushed off her worry, saying no cop goes undercover without informing other cops. They'd know where she was. Maybe he's right. But if Dixie isn't back by tonight, she will rethink that stance.

No one answers the phone this time either.

She returns the phone to the cradle, her hand still resting on the receiver. The plastic is warm. Perhaps its warmth comes from the millions of voices shooting through the wires, all that emotion condensed into electronic pulses. She thinks about calling her mother. Will Milan tell her about last night's mysterious caller?

Barcelona isn't sure why she has been making these obscene calls to her mother. Eric would certainly offer her a few choice psychological theories with nasty-sounding names. True, she didn't start them; she only picked up where the original caller left off once he stopped calling. She quickly jerks her hand away from the phone, as if her thoughts might somehow be transmitted directly to Milan.

Whatever dark reason is snorkeling through the swampy

muck of her id, this one memory comes back to her again and again when she calls:

The summer Barcelona turned eighteen. She worked that whole summer in her parents' deli, waitressing. On the Hebrew National calendar on the wall, she used a red Magic Marker to cross off the days until college started. Her cuticles were red and swollen from pickle brine, her hair smelled of smoke from fried pastrami. Her fingers were nicked from washing silverware.

The deli's customers were mostly travelers, on their way to or from somewhere, stopping off only for a quick bite and to use the tiny rest room. They were all universally poor tippers. Nevertheless, Barcelona tossed their quarters and dimes and nickels into her Styrofoam tip cup, each clink getting her closer to college and farther away from here.

While her father baked fresh goods downstairs in the basement, her mother would sit on the end stool of the small counter, smoke pack after pack of Benson & Hedges cigarettes, and do the crossword puzzle in the New York *Daily News*. The coffee cup and cigarette butts in front of her were branded with her red-brown lipstick, the color of dried blood. And so it went, day after day, the summer burning away toward fall.

Barcelona's nights weren't much more exciting. Dating local boys meant a drive-in, calloused palms groping under her blouse, beer-flavored kisses.

But one day the routine shifted.

A boy—he seemed like a man at the time—of about twenty-two came into the deli, straddled a stool, and, without looking at the menu, ordered a tuna fish salad sandwich on white bread.

'We don't carry tuna fish,' Barcelona told him.

He wore a baseball cap, which he took off and put back on again, smoothing back his hair in between. 'What kind of diner doesn't have tuna fish salad?' he said with a slight drawl. He wasn't angry, just curious. He smiled at her; his teeth were straight and white, but the front one was chipped.

'We're not a diner, sir. We're a deli.'

He looked around the store as if noticing it for the first time. He saw the slabs of corned beef and pastrami in the refrigerated showcase, saw the Star of David on the menu.

'Oops,' he said. 'Tell you what, why don't you make me the best sandwich you all serve. No harm done.'

Barcelona made him a Reuben sandwich, grilling corned beef, sauerkraut, and Swiss cheese between rye bread. When he ate, some of the Russian dressing slid down his chin. She laughed and pointed. He wiped his chin with a napkin and said, 'Man overboard, huh?'

He came in every day that week for lunch. His name was Tim Beufort, from Tea Kettle, North Carolina. He had come to town to play baseball for the local farm team. He played shortstop but was angling for the first baseman's position.

The second week Tim asked Barcelona out. That evening they drove forty miles over to Lewisburg to eat dinner and see *Butch Cassidy & the Sundance Kid*. She did not return home until six the next morning. When she did, her dress was torn in three places, her nails broken, her shoes ruined. Mud was caked across her face. Blood striped her legs from knees to ankles.

Barcelona walked about the back of the house to let herself in the backdoor. Her father would already be at the store, down in the cellar baking danish and doughnuts. He drove down at 4 A.M.; Barcelona and Milan followed at 7 A.M. With any luck, she could sneak into the house and miss Milan altogether. No explanations.

But as Barcelona rounded the house, she nearly tripped over Milan on her hands and knees, weeding the flowers along the walkway. She wore huge leather pads on her knees, thick weeding gloves, and a wide-brimmed straw hat with a green visor embedded in the front brim. The hat was useless since the sun was still not up yet, but barely lit the east mountains directly behind them. Still, this was her gardening outfit and she wouldn't dream of wearing anything less than the entire ensemble.

'*Gutten morgan*,' Milan said without looking up.

'Good morning.'

'Did you have a nice time?' She yanked a weed up by the roots and threw it on the others on top of a spread piece of newspaper.

'Do I look like I had a good time?' Barcelona snapped.

For the first time, Milan looked around. Her eyes were red and tired, as if she hadn't slept well. '*Ach Got*, child. What happened?' She started to rise but Barcelona touched her shoulder, preventing the gesture.

'I'm fine. Tim's car blew a tire and we went over an embankment. The road was pretty deserted, so we had to dig ourselves out. Took most of the night. Believe me, Mom, nothing else happened. I swear, Tim was the perfect gentleman. Nothing happened.'

Milan stood up, wiped her hands on her jeans, and touched her gloved hand to Barcelona's cheek. 'Of course not, dear.' Then she gathered up the newspaper full of weeds and carried it to the garbage can.

Barcelona stood on the walkway alone. She was shaking with anger.

It had been the truth. The flat tire. Digging the car out of the dirt. Nothing else happened. No attack. No sex.

Despite the evidence to the contrary, her mother had believed her instantly. No cross-examination, no disapproving look. Ordinarily, that response would be wonderful, the envy of every teenage girl. But Barcelona knew it wasn't trust that had motivated her mother's statement;

282

the trust for a well brought-up child to do the right thing. No, when Milan had stood up and touched her cheek and said, 'Of course not, dear,' she was making a declaration, not of faith, but of destiny. The trust you have for a blind child who says he did not steal your car and drive it to the next town.

Of course not, dear. How could anything happen? You aren't capable of such spontaneous passion.

Barcelona pushes the phone away and returns to the bathroom to stare at the red bump on her forehead. She is not one who uses much makeup, but this red-eyed dinosaur needs some heavy camouflage. Trina once taught her a makeup trick that she has yet to use. But if there was ever a time for makeup magic, this was it. She runs downstairs to the kitchen, grabs a bottle of mineral water from the refrigerator, rushes back to the bathroom. She dumps some of her Revlon foundation in the palm of her hand, spills in a few drops of mineral water, dabs a little moisturizer on top. She stirs with her finger and begins applying the mixture to her face. The red bump sinks out of sight.

'There,' she says, staring at her reflection. 'Not everything needs to be a disaster today.'

Barcelona is driving to school. She keeps leaning over, checking her forehead in the rearview mirror, wondering if the flea bite has chewed through the makeup yet. She changes lanes and—

Bam!

A sudden explosion causes Barcelona to instinctively duck down in her seat and pull the steering wheel to the right. Instantly she remembers what Diva told her about the kid shot by an irate driver and wonders who she might have pissed off on the four miles from her home to here.

The Geezemobile rolls to the side of the road and the rest of the traffic whooshes past her without breaking rhythm. Fortunately she avoided the crammed freeway this morning and took a back road that wends through the construction sites and farm fields, so it is not too difficult to make it to the dirt shoulder. From the thumping roll of the car, Barcelona realizes now that no one has shot at her; she merely has a flat tire. The second one in her life.

She gets out of the car and walks around to the front right tire. A ragged hole the size of a baby's fist gapes at her. She takes a deep breath and her eyes widen at the lingering odor. This is the same road on which she killed the skunk, though that happened about a mile away. Still, as she walks along the edge of the shoulder, she glances down in the drainage ditch for the body. She sees a couple of squashed rabbits, flat and dry as cardboard. No skunk.

She unlocks the trunk and removes the jack and spare tire, leaning the tire against the back bumper. Her hands are black with dirt and she is careful not to wipe them on her slacks. She has an auto club card, but she doesn't want to hike to a phone, then wait the thirty more minutes or so for the truck to show up. Her class meets in half an hour and she has no intention of being late.

She positions the jack and starts wenching up the car.

'Need a hand?' a voice calls to her.

She straightens to her feet and sees two boys getting out of a beat-up Impala parked behind her car. Their skulls are shaved to the flesh on the sides, the top has a quarter inch of bristle. They are maybe eighteen. She recognizes them as marines from the El Toro base less than a mile away from here. She looks over her shoulder across the condo sites and the strawberry fields and there stands the two monstrous hangars where the helicopters are stored. The hangars are gigantic, shaped like lunch pails. She's read that clouds actually form up in the rafters.

Barcelona has often driven by the base, seen the drab concrete housing where the marine families live, the wet towels hanging off the wooden balconies, the rusted barbecues, the overturned tricycles on the patchy brown and green lawn. The marine families can often be seen in Irvine, a sharp contrast to the affluent families that make up most of the community. Marine families are seen mostly at the fast-food restaurants, sitting noisily at Wendy's or McDonald's or Carl Jr.'s, wolfing fries and burgers, the kids screaming, the father telling them to shut up, smacking sticky fingers that spill ketchup. The marine wives are always young, mostly overweight, with pasty skin and dull eyes, hair always limp and unwashed, looking like children themselves, but always with a child of their own riding a hip or clutching a hand. Sometimes in the movie theaters, she will see marines sitting together in what the locals called Marine Formation: with an empty seat between them, so as not to sit too close to another man.

Relations between the locals and the marines are not very good right now. Many local residents are annoyed by the constant noise of the helicopters, not to mention the threat of them crashing. Also, marines seem to be involved in more than their share of drunk driving accidents. Two months ago, a marine was arrested for robbing a Denny's restaurant.

'Need any help, ma'am?' one of the boys asks again. He is wearing black motorcycle boots, torn jeans, and a green T-shirt. His face is red from a bad sunburn.

'It's just a flat,' she says.

'Yes, ma'am. Me and Bundy seen flats before.' He's not being smart, he's just friendly. He smiles broadly. Bundy lags behind looking vaguely uncomfortable. Stopping was clearly not his idea. 'Wouldn't bother us to change it real quick. Wouldn't do for you to be getting all dirty over a dumb tire.'

Barcelona is torn. She is fully capable of changing the tire herself. There is nothing in the act of changing this tire that requires superior strength. As a woman, she feels some obligation to do it herself, if for no other reason than to prove to these two that she can do it. On the other hand, she is dressed in nice clothing and doesn't want to be late for class.

'Thank you,' she says. 'I wouldn't mind a hand.'

'Name's Carson,' the boy says, holding out his hand to her. 'Not related to Johnny.'

'My hand's dirty,' she warns.

'Mine will be soon enough,' he says and grasps her for a firm shake. 'Let's do it, Bundy.'

Bundy frowns and sighs but finally squats down next to Carson and they quickly go about the task of changing the tire.

'I see by your outfit that you are a teacher,' Carson says, squinting up at her.

'How'd you know?'

He laughs. 'Faculty parking permit on your back bumper. Sand Coast College, huh?'

'Yup.'

'What do you teach?'

'English. Some composition, some literature.' She feels slightly pretentious saying this to him.

'Really?' he says, looking up at her again. His face is so sunburned, Barcelona winces. 'You teach poetry?'

'Some.'

'Now that's interesting because I'm kind of a poet myself.'

'Oh?' she says.

'Yeah.' Bundy smirks. 'He's the Death Squads official poet.'

Carson elbows Bundy in a friendly way. 'Ignore him, ma'am. Bundy's brain don't kick in 'til sometime 'round

286

noon. Only Death Squad we got is the cooks in the mess hall.'

Bundy looks up at her and grins but not in a friendly manner.

'I really dig writing poetry,' Carson continues as they switch tires. 'The rhymes are the hardest part, though, thinking up new ones all the time. I been meaning to get one of them rhyming dictionaries. Think that would help?'

'It might.'

'Damn, I wish I had some of my poems with me now. I could show 'em to you and you could tell me if they're any good.'

Barcelona goes into the car and picks through her purse. She comes back and hands him her business card with the college's address. 'Send me a couple here. I'll look them over, make a few comments, and send them back.'

Carson stands up excitedly. 'No shit? Hey, great!'

Bundy releases the jack and stores it in the trunk. He slams the trunk lid harder than necessary. 'Let's go, Shakespeare. We'll be late. Then you can start figuring what rhymes with latrine duty.'

'Marine cooty,' Carson says, grinning. He reads her card. 'Barcelona? That really your name?'

'Uh-huh.'

'That's cool. That's why I joined the marines, to meet women with names like yours.' He laughs and returns to their rusted Impala. They drive away and he waves her business card at her and smiles.

Barcelona drives to school. She enters her classroom one minute late and gives her students a pop quiz on John Milton just for the hell of it. They moan and complain. Someone asks if she had a fight with her boyfriend and everyone laughs. Barcelona laughs too. The grades are fairly high. One student fails, but he always fails.

*   *   *

'They sent me to talk to you,' the young woman says.

Barcelona is bending over the drinking fountain, slurping up cold water from the tiny trickle that dribbles out. The water is refrigerated and it jolts a nerve in her upper right bicuspid. She's needed root canal work on that tooth for more than a year now but has put it off. She hopes to keep putting it off despite the dentist's warnings and the little drawings of the damaged root he does every time she visits him.

'They said I should see you,' the woman repeats.

Barcelona straightens, wipes water from her mouth and chin. 'Who're they?'

'I'm Crystal Ponce,' the young woman says, ignoring Barcelona's question. 'I'm writing a novel.'

'Ah,' Barcelona says.

'Someone in my advanced comp class said I should talk to you. You've published novels.'

Crystal Ponce looks like a younger version of the rude woman in the BMW the other day. She is maybe twenty-eight and is wearing a short denim skirt, a blowsy white sweater, and flat Capezio shoes. Everything casual and inexpensive. Except for the wedding ring, a knotted tumor of raisin-size diamonds worth at least $5,000.

Crystal seems to sense Barcelona's hesitation, for she says, 'I just want to ask you a few questions. Okay?'

'Sure,' Barcelona concedes. 'Ask.'

Crystal looks around at the milling students. 'Can we talk in your office?'

Barcelona had hoped to avoid that. Once they settle comfortably into a chair, they can't be pried out in less than forty minutes. Out in the hallway, she's usually able to keep them down to ten or fifteen minutes. 'You might be better off seeing me tomorrow during my office hour. I'll have more time then.'

'This won't take long.'

Forty minutes later, Crystal Ponce has worked her way from her troubled childhood in a wealthy Rhode Island family to her current role of wife and mother in a wealthy California family. 'I'm young, I have a great husband, two terrific kids,' she says. 'My husband is a realtor, loves to surf, has the nicest ass of any man I've ever seen. Wants to screw every other night. And my kids. My kids are so loving, so sweet, it makes me cry sometimes. But I want to write, be a writer, a novelist like you.'

'Have you read any of my books?'

'No.'

'Then how do you know you want to be a novelist like me?'

Crystal stares at Barcelona. 'Have I offended you somehow?'

Barcelona immediately feels bad. The woman is serious and deserves to be taken seriously. 'I'm sorry. I just don't know what you want from me. You seem to have everything. Being a wife and mother doesn't have to exclude being a writer. You just have to learn to organize your time wisely, let your family know this is an important priority for you, tell them—'

Crystal waves her hand impatiently. 'No, no, you don't understand.' She crosses her legs, revealing lots of trim tan skin. One narrow ankle is circled provocatively by a thin gold bracelet. 'My family is not the problem. I have lots of free time.'

'What is the problem?'

'What I'm writing about. I'm not sure I'm doing it right. Can you take a look?' Without waiting for an answer, she opens her shoulder bag and pulls out a bunch of papers held together by a pink paper clip.

'I really don't have time right now, Crystal,' Barcelona explains. 'You can leave it with me and I'll try to get to it next week.'

289

'It'll just take a minute. It's the first chapter. I promise you, you won't be bored. I just need to know if I'm on the right track.'

Barcelona sneaks a glance at the last page number. Ten. Not too bad. She can read ten pages, make a few general comments, and be rid of Crystal Ponce. She flattens the chapter on the desktop and begins to read. The novel starts with a woman, twenty-eight, with two adorable children and a hunk husband. She is in their vacation home in Lake Tahoe; she is alone. She has come here without telling anyone. She has brought a gun. She sits in the hot tub with a glass of expensive wine recalling wonderful times with her family. Then she places the gun to her head. Haunted her whole life by a terrible affliction she can no longer live with, she has decided to kill herself. Her affliction: she's too beautiful.

Barcelona stops reading, looks up at Crystal's intent expression. The woman is serious.

Barcelona bites her cheek to keep from laughing and finishes the chapter, which ends with the woman cocking the hammer. Barcelona looks up from the chapter again and leans back in her chair. 'What happens next?'

'The rest of the novel is a flashback that shows how she's reached this point, how her beauty has driven her to this desperate dilemma.'

'Then at the end, she either pulls the trigger or not. That's the hook, right?'

'Yes. Though I haven't decided whether or not I'll show what her choice is. Maybe I should leave that up to the reader. What do you think?'

Barcelona stares at Crystal Ponce now, examining her face, her long thin nose, the tiny flat eyes, the stiff over-sprayed over-frosted hair. She is somewhat attractive, yes, but far from the mind-numbing beauty of her character.

'Do you really think this character's problem is that . . . disastrous?'

Crystal laughs bitterly. 'Take my word for it. No one takes you seriously when you're beautiful. They think you're a ball-buster, spoiled bitch, or dumb. Or all three. They all want you, sure. The women want to look like you and the men want to fuck you blind, but nobody *cares* about you. They don't take you serious. I'm not stupid.'

That last phrase startles Barcelona. It's what Diva had said on Saturday. A chill nibbles on her neck. She has a strange feeling that all the women of the world held a meeting recently without inviting her and in it they all agreed to act weird. Her mother attended, so did Diva. So did Crystal Ponce.

'I don't know what to tell you, Crystal.'

'Is it any good, my chapter?'

'The writing is smooth and clear. It's an interesting premise, though I'm not sure you've made her sympathetic enough that the average reader is going to care about her. We don't readily identify with her problem.'

'What do you mean?'

A loud knock on the glass startles Barcelona. Crystal, however, offers no reaction. She waits for an answer to her question.

Barcelona looks up and sees Harley Buss waving through the glass partition. She waves back. Harley points to his watch, flashes a questioning expression. Barcelona holds up one finger.

'I have an appointment now,' Barcelona lies. 'Why don't you keep working on it and we'll discuss it later.'

Crystal doesn't budge. 'When?'

'Next week.'

'Monday?'

Barcelona rises and opens the door, holding it open. 'Tuesday. During my scheduled office hour.'

291

Crystal gathers her chapter and walks out of the office without a word. Harley gives her an appreciative glance as she passes him and Barcelona wonders if maybe Crystal was right about her beauty after all.

'Do you think she's beautiful?' Barcelona asks Harley when he closes the door.

'Who?'

'Who? The woman who just strolled by.'

'I didn't notice.'

Barcelona laughs. 'You turned your head, you watched her ass wiggle down the corridor.'

'Reflex action. I look, but I don't always see. Was she cute?'

'Jesus.' Barcelona sits back in her chair. She opens her desk drawer and pulls out a packet of Breathsavers. She offers one to Harley, but he shakes his head and settles behind Susan Mesa's desk.

Nothing is said for almost a minute.

'You come in here for sanctuary?' Barcelona asks. Ordinarily she enjoys Harley's visits, but this morning she is in a rush to grade a few papers and hit the road. She still has to meet Trina for lunch and deliver her script to Grief.

'I'm doing the budget.'

'Uh oh.'

'But that's not why I came in.'

'Oh?'

'I came in to ask you if you gave my phone number out to one of your friends.'

Barcelona blushes fiercely. Her face is so hot she presses her palms against her cheeks. The Breathsaver suddenly tastes oily and bitter. 'Well, I, I didn't—'

Harley grins. 'Not that I mind. Actually, it's kind of flattering that you think so highly of me you'd recommend me to one of your friends.' He leans forward, his hands steepled together on top of the desk. He looks like he's

292

praying. 'I know our friendship isn't going to develop along any other lines. Not that that's bad. Hell, I've gotten to the age where I'd rather not screw up a good friendship with romance. When you do, you usually end up losing both.' He leans back in the chair again and laces his hands behind his head. 'So what can you tell me about her?'

Barcelona doesn't know what to say. Only Trina would have the guts to call Harley this way and Barcelona is torn between admiring her courage and resenting her aggressiveness. Somehow she feels as if Trina is stealing a little bit of her life away. She knows that's silly, that she herself gave Trina Harley's name. Still. 'She's very intelligent. She's sexy. Pretty. I don't know, what do you want to know?'

'Is she rich? If this works out between us, can I retire?'

Barcelona throws a paper clip at him. He catches it with one hand. 'I didn't know you were a golddigger.'

'I can learn. Besides, when she told me she was a professional singer, I thought maybe she—'

'A singer? Who?'

'Who are we talking about. Dianne Klosterman.'

'Diva?'

'Yeah. She said that's what you called her. That's cute. How come you never made up a nickname for me?'

'I did. You just don't want to hear it.'

Harley laughs and tosses the paper clip back at her. Barcelona is too distracted to catch it and it skitters across her calendar desk pad and drops onto the floor.

Diva. Barcelona is shocked. When did Diva start to be so aggressive? She did say she was changing her life; maybe she meant all of it, not just the career part. Barcelona looks over at Harley, his sleepy sexuality, tall tanned figure, his secret passion for T.S. Eliot's poetry. She thinks of Diva, chubby beach rat, reads only dumb magazines.

Her philosophy of life is determined by the Top 40. There is no way they will hit it off.

'Just answer me one thing,' Harley asks.

'What?'

'She's not into anything strange, is she? Horseback riding or anything?'

'No, Harley. She likes volleyball.'

He thinks that over. 'Volleyball is okay. I can stand that.'

'Thank you, Mr. Romance.'

Harley gets up and stretches. 'No big deal. It's just dinner and a movie. Maybe a drink afterwards if we can still stand each other.'

'And if you can't stand each other?'

'Then we skip the drink and just have sex.'

Barcelona laughs.

Harley winks and leaves. Barcelona reaches for the phone and dials Dixie's number again. Still no answer. She is not in the mood to grade papers now and stuffs them into her briefcase. She is just stepping out of her office when Crystal Ponce steps up to her. 'I had a couple more chapters in the car. I thought I'd leave them with you. Okay?'

20

Trina walks into The Candidate's office that morning and finds Mary Abrahms trying to set Warren Schuller on fire. She'd heard their hollering all the way from the elevator.

When she first opens the door, Mary and Warren are sitting together on the small leather sofa shouting into each other's faces, their shrill voices a jumble of high-decibel insults. Warren's usually neat beard looks oddly chaotic this morning, as if scribbled onto his chin with a frayed Magic Marker. Mary orchestrates her verbal abuse with a lipstick-smeared cigarette bobbing up and down on the end of her lips like a conductor's baton. Smoke escorts every word from her mouth.

The Candidate is sitting behind his glass desk, watching them without expression. When Trina walks in he hikes up his pant leg and points at his ankle to show he is wearing socks. He grins.

'You don't understand what I'm saying,' Warren tells Mary. Warren is a bony stick figure of a man, emaciated to the point that he sometimes looks as if he's dying from a voodoo curse. Childhood photographs have confirmed that he always looked like that.

Mary is squat and stubby, built like a '50s jukebox. Her face is round as a pumpkin and as homely. Her eyes are pale gray as if stained by her constant smoking. Her black hair is straight and lifeless, chopped unattractively short.

'I understand every word, Warren, I just don't agree.'

'Then you don't understand,' Warren says. 'Maybe my concept is too sophisticated for you.'

'You little shit,' Mary snarls and thumbs her Bic lighter into a high flame. She brushes the flame quickly over Warren's arm. A patch of hair on his forearm shrivels and withers.

'*Hey!*' Warren yells, jerking his arm away. He scoots across the sofa hugging his arm as if he's just been shot by a sniper. 'That burns!'

'No shit,' Mary says.

Warren carefully touches his arm. Several crisped hairs drop off. 'That really hurt.'

Mary chuckles hoarsely.

Trina can smell the sour scent of roasted body hair. She rubs her nose and closes the office door behind her. 'I see you guys started the discussion without me.'

The Candidate nods. 'Warren and Mary were just explaining their new election strategy.'

'I'm always wary of campaigns that involve setting the candidate on fire.'

'I'm a little reluctant myself,' The Candidate says.

'We have troubles, Trina,' Warren says. 'Bad troubles.'

'Deep shit,' Mary agrees. She stubs out her cigarette but keeps the lighter clutched tightly in her hand like a grenade.

Trina sits down in the matching leather chair and sets her briefcase on the floor, a little imitation-leather wall between herself and Warren and Mary. Even when silent, their anger at each other is radioactive. Trina can't get over how much they've changed in the past six months. When this campaign first started a year ago, Warren and Mary were happily married to each other, decorating their new home in Santa Monica. Monday mornings they would come bustling into the office and tell how they drove down to Mexico over the weekend to find just the right hand-painted tiles for the bathroom. Or how they drove to Oxnard and bargained with some rude farmer for an antique grape press. Now they are separated. Trina isn't sure whether the cause of the split was the pressure of the campaign or redecorating their house. A month ago Mary moved out of their painstakingly completed house and into a flashy chrome-and-glass Marina del Rey condo with her new boyfriend, a black relief pitcher for the Dodgers. Trina suspects that Warren, who used to be a rabid Dodgers fan, hates Mary more for taking away his pleasure of rooting for the Dodgers than for her leaving him.

They have always disagreed loudly on campaign strategies, even before the separation, but lately their disagreements have escalated beyond raised voices. Two weeks ago in front of Mary's desk, Warren scissored his own precious Dodgers warm-up jacket he'd worn daily for eight years. Last week Mary threw a pen at Warren, hitting him in the back and leaving an ink mark on his expensive new Ralph Lauren jacket. Enraged, Warren picked up the pen and threw it back. Mary tried to catch it but missed. The sharp point gouged a blue hole in the palm of her hand. There was some blood. The sight of blood seems to have destroyed any civilized boundaries between them. Now, anything goes.

Their bickering has become annoying to Trina, but it is too close to Election Day to replace them. Despite their marital status, they continue to operate as partners in their political consulting firm. Besides, they're very good. Both have worked on many campaigns, most of them for underdog candidates with liberal leanings. Warren, forty-two, the only son of labor organizers, spent his early years after college helping run campaigns within labor unions. One night a couple of beefy goons warned him to quit the campaign, then broke his windshield with a Louisville

Slugger. The next day Warren quit. His father, who in his young union-organizing days had been shot twice and beaten a dozen times, has not spoken to him since. His mother and he correspond secretly.

Mary's route was more conventional. College as a political science major hoping to end the Vietnam War. Warren had been a guest lecturer at one of her classes their first week together. They smoked dope and made love every night; the second week they got married. Mary has a tiny lobster-shaped scar on the back of her neck, which she received when a cop yanked off her seashell necklace during the Chicago Democratic Convention riots in 1968. She has shown the scar to everyone in the office.

'So, how deep is this shit?' Trina asks. Her own voice surprises her, coming out so flat and cynical. As if she didn't really care. She suddenly realizes she *doesn't* really care. She doesn't really care about this campaign, about whether or not The Candidate is wearing socks, whether or not Mary sets Warren on fire. She has a whole day of this kind of crap in front of her and all she really wants to do is go home, slip into a steaming tub, and read a trashy novel.

This attitude scares her. It's not just Monday morning blues. She didn't leave the house this morning feeling this way. She rarely has dreaded her work; in fact she genuinely loves it. Her job is as much her avocation as vocation. She even likes the pressures, the competition, getting down and dirty with the best of them. She's not sure why she feels this unexpected loathing. She feels disoriented, as if she's been ambushed. Maybe it has something to do with watching Mary and Warren's marriage dissolve slowly over the months, like a snake digesting a lump that once was a rabbit. Maybe it's just rampant hormones. Whatever the reason, Trina trembles a little in her seat, senses a sharp panic worming up through her stomach. She feels hot and sweaty. Feverish. She tries to shake it off, concentrate on the business at hand. Act the professional. After all, that's what she is: Trina Bedford, Jr., The Ultimate Professional Woman. She screws her face into a serious businesslike expression and says, 'What's the problem, Mary?'

'We were doing fine in the polls,' Warren says before Mary can answer. 'Better than we'd expected last month. Inching our way up slowly, but rising, always rising. I think in another twelve days we would have been even with Bennington.' He smacks a rolled-up newspaper against his knee. 'Then this.'

'Then what?' Trina says.

Mary sighs and shows Trina a photo of Carla Bennington in this morning's *Los Angeles Times*. She is in a park wearing a headband and jogging outfit, sitting on the grass stretching her legs. The headline is 'Candidate Runs a Different Kind of Race.'

'Carla Bennington is running in that multiple sclerosis benefit marathon in a couple weeks,' Mary says. 'She'll have cameras on her for days before the race as well as during the whole thing.'

'Just the kind of sex-and-sentiment crap the media eats up,' Warren says. 'A candidate, especially an attractive woman, walking around in skimpy shorts and a tight T-shirt.'

The Candidate looks at his copy of the newspaper spread open on his desk and smiles. 'She's got the ass for it.'

'You understand what this means, Cory?' Warren says a little testily to The Candidate.

The Candidate smiles, but his eyes narrow. 'Gee, Warren, I think so. It means—and please help me out if I get stuck—that during the next two crucial campaign weeks Carla Bennington will be on a shitload of local talk shows on TV and radio supposedly publicizing the marathon. She'll probably make a big show of keeping the whole thing nonpolitical. When they ask her about the election, she'll flash that sincere-as-a-nun smile of hers and say, 'I didn't come here to talk politics. I came here to help people with multiple sclerosis.' Voters will admire her commitment to a worthwhile cause as well as her integrity at not taking political advantage of all that free air time.'

'Um, yes.' Warren looks contrite. He lowers his head and tugs his beard.

The Candidate winks at Trina.

'Let me see that,' Trina says to Mary, taking the newspaper. She studies the article on the marathon, spots a disturbing detail. 'Hmmm. Here's an ugly coincidence.'

'Yeah,' The Candidate says, leaning back in his chair. 'Ain't it.'

'What?' Mary asks.

'What?' Warren echoes.

The Candidate props his feet up on his glass desktop. A worn patch of white chewing gum is stuck to one heel. 'The race route travels through several different districts to make sure it's nonpartisan. However, coincidentally, the route cuts through a corner of Carla's own district, specifically the Capshaw area, the one where she's lowest in the polls and we're the highest.'

'Shit,' Warren says. 'I missed that.'

Trina looks at The Candidate and once again is impressed by his sharpness. Despite his casual appearance and manner, not much slips by him. She has the feeling that he could run this entire campaign without any of them.

Mary lifts her hand and thumbs her lighter into a tall flame. Warren flinches and leans away. Mary chuckles and sticks a cigarette between her lips, torching the end. 'What we need,' Mary says, then turns to Trina. 'And this is what we were discussing before you came in. What we need is something new for Cory to make a stand on. Some reason to call a press conference, focus some of those cameras on him. Steal some of the air from her sails.'

'What'd you have in mind?' Trina asks.

'We were hoping something also to do with sports,' Mary says. 'I suggested we arrange something with Cory and some guys I know from the Dodgers. A sports demonstration for disabled kids or something.'

'That's stupid,' Warren says, spit flying from his lips and dewing his beard. 'Nobody gives a shit about the goddamn Dodgers right now. They've lost their last five games.'

'So what? They're still athletes. They project a healthy, vibrant, youthful impression. That's what we need, especially considering how tough Bennington's going to seem after she's finished that goddamn marathon. Like she could eat nails and piss wine.'

'Maybe she'll dehydrate and start puking,' The Candidate says. 'We could get photos of that. Remember when Jimmy Carter swooned during a run, that picture of the Secret Service holding him up. That cost him a few votes.'

Warren and Mary think this over, nodding. 'I wouldn't count on it, Cory,' Warren says. 'She's always finished without any problems before.'

Trina shakes her head. After all this time, they still can't tell when The Candidate is kidding them.

'Well, you're my advisers,' The Candidate says. 'So advise.'

Warren unconsciously strokes his burned arm hairs while thinking. His arm rests in his lap like a pet. 'Maybe something with AIDS. Some rock benefit.'

'We've covered that issue,' Mary says, annoyed. 'Six months ago.'

'The homeless.'

'We already issued a plan for helping them,' Trina says.

'We issue a new plan,' Warren says. 'More benefits.'

'Forget it,' The Candidate says. 'We've beaten that one to the ground. What else you got?'

'Crime?'

'Covered,' Trina says.

'Specialized crime. Drugs.'

'Bad timing,' The Candidate says. 'They'll think we'll want to raise taxes.'

Warren looks depressed; he's rubbing his charred hairs. 'Pit bulls are hot. We suggest a bill to outlaw pit bulls. That will give TV news a chance to whip out their footage of pit bull attacks.'

'That's lame,' Mary snorts.

'Fuck you!'

'I'd rather fuck a pit bull.'

'You probably have.'

'Knock it off,' Trina says. 'What's our weakest area? Which voters are we least appealing to?'

Mary and Warren look at each other, thinking. Instantly gone is their animosity, their hate, as they silently shift back into their role of a successful business team facing a sticky challenge. Their angry outbursts are completely forgotten during these intense stares, as if they were communicating on some psychic level. Their eyes soften, their mouths go slack. Watching them during these moments is as intimate as peeping into their bedroom during sex. They were born to be a team, but *only* a business team. Trina wishes she could tell them that, but she knows it would be no use. She is the Cassandra of human relationships, destined to be right, cursed not to be believed.

'Our weakest area,' Mary says, 'are those people who vote for incumbents, no matter who is in office. They're afraid of any change, good or bad.'

'Forget them,' Trina says. 'We can't touch them. Let's stick with the undecided.'

'Well,' Warren says, 'there are also those who perceive

302

Cory as being too liberal, too sympathetic to minorities. Too soft. Our own polls have pointed that out several times.'

The Candidate laughs. 'I could burn a cross in Dodger Stadium in front of crippled kids. Cover all the bets.'

Trina opens her briefcase and rifles through her file of newspaper clippings in the folder marked District Problems. She doesn't find anything suitable and abandons that file for another one marked So. Cal. Problems. 'I've got something. Hold on . . .' She keeps flipping through them until she finds the one she wants. It's a two-inch story with a six-inch photo. She hands it to Mary, who reads it, looks at the photo, makes a disgusted face, and passes it to Warren. Warren has the same repulsed response. He hands it to The Candidate.

The Candidate reads it, looks at Trina. His face is grim. He is not joking now. 'Christ, Trina. Gutted bears?'

'Gutted bears.' Trina nods. 'These black bears are protected by the state, but they're being killed and gutted with an alarming increase, as the picture shows.' The photograph is of a dead black bear on his back, his stomach and chest sliced open, the blood-matted fur peeled back from his ribs, his internal organs jumbled like the contents of Trina's purse. She points at the clipping in The Candidate's hand. 'All these poachers want is the gall bladder.'

'The gall bladder?' Mary says, wrinkling her nose. 'What the hell for?'

'Powdered gall has been used for centuries by Orientals. It's supposed to relieve arthritis, high blood pressure, impotence, lots of stuff. They grind it into powder and sell it at three hundred forty dollars per ounce.'

'That much?' Warren says, impressed.

'That's about the same as gold,' Mary says. 'Or good Maui weed.'

'So what are you suggesting here, Trina?' The Candidate

303

says briskly, all business. 'We don't have any goddamn bears in this district. We don't have many Orientals either. We're mostly whites and Latinos who don't give a shit about de-galled bears.'

'That doesn't matter. We have you suggest an ordinance or something that will raise the fines for poaching bears. We call a news conference. The newspapers will print it, and it's got a kind of an amusing angle that the TV news will certainly run with some cute footage of bears romping playfully in the woods. The gall bladder stuff is a bit weird and occult, they'll love it. Believe me, I know.'

'So what do we get out of this?' Mary asks. 'Other than some cute footage.'

'Oh yes. Yes, yes, yes.' Warren is nodding, grinning. He understands. 'Jesus, Trina, that's brilliant. It's fucking brilliant.' He sits up on the sofa, leans forward excitedly, stroking his beard. 'The conservative uncommitted voters will think you're cracking down on the Orientals, which they will see as a policy of getting tough with minorities.'

'Of course!' Mary is nodding now too, smiling. 'And the liberals will see it merely as a conservationist policy, protecting wildlife and the environment.'

The Candidate shakes his head. 'All over some bear's gall bladder?'

'Politics is all illusion,' Trina says. 'You know that.'

'Campaigns are all illusion,' he says. 'Not politics.'

Trina is again surprised. Sometimes she forgets that The Candidate is serious, that he really does want to win the election, and not just to have office. He wants to do some version of good.

The meeting disbands as Mary and Warren rush out to start putting the gall bladder campaign in effect. They leave chatting excitedly, like teens on a first date. Mary holds Warren's arm. But soon, Trina realizes, within minutes, something will remind them of the other part of their relationship, the failing domestic half, and they will again begin gnawing on each other's spleens.

'Trina,' The Candidate says, gesturing for her to stay.

She walks over to his desk.

He opens one of the black wire basket drawers and pulls out the folded flyer they recently mailed out. The front displays three unflattering photos of Carla Bennington's face while she is talking. They'd hired a photographer to stalk her for weeks to get those shots that made her look like a bitching fishwife. Above the photo in one-inch letters is the line: TALK IS CHEAP. Beneath the photos of her open mouth is another line: UNLESS YOU'RE PAYING FOR IT. Inside the folder are the usual facts and figures and razzle-dazzle oatmeal of words meant to confuse the issues rather than clarify them. Trina wrote the flyer herself.

'I'm convinced that these flyers are the reason I've been coming up in the polls,' he says.

'I think you're right.'

He smiles. 'Good, I thought you might fight me on that one.'

'What for? I'm damn good at what I do.' She hears her own voice being much too loud, as if she were arguing or picking a fight. Why? For Chrissake he's complimenting you, girl. She is careful to lower it when she speaks again. 'Trust me on this bear thing. I know it sounds silly, but it will work.'

'I'm sure it will. It's just that one day when I'm president of this great country, I hate to think I rode into the White House on a bear's gall bladder.'

'Some have ridden in on worse.'

'True, true. But as much as I appreciate your brainstorm here, and I do recognize its subtle brilliance, Trina, I would still prefer something with more substance to defeat our opponent. What about Carla Bennington? Anything on those mysterious trips of hers yet? Have you connected them to city funds, illegal junkets, anything like that?'

'I'm still chasing down a couple leads.'

'The fuse is lit, Trina. It's only a matter of time before we have to start running for cover.'

'What the hell does that mean?'

'We need it soon. Very soon.'

'Immediately, O Wise and Great Pretender to the Throne of Los Angeles.' She bows formally and starts to back out of the office.

'That's more like it,' he says.

Trina sits at her desk and dials Dixie's number for the fourth time that morning. Ever since Barcelona told her what had happened with Dixie at Fashion Island over the weekend, she's been calling. The phone rings and Trina rests her head on her hand, waiting. The desktop is a mess of wrinkled papers stacked in indiscriminate piles. Three open Diet Cherry Coke cans stand together on one stack. Two of the cans are half-full, opened sometime last week. One is fresh from this morning. She straightens a few papers while listening to the tenth ring. No answer. She hangs up the phone but keeps her hand on the receiver, trying to decide if she should call Dixie's captain.

The phone rings suddenly and she pulls her hand away as if she's received an electrical shock. The phone rings again and she answers it. 'Hello?'

The voice is entirely too cheerful: 'You want it? 'Cause I got it.'

'You bragging, Howdy? Because remember, I've seen it.'

'Ho, ho. Two ho's, that's all you get. And all you're going to get if you aren't nice to me.'

Trina sighs. 'Pretend this is me being nice.'

'That's the best you can do?' Howdy White says. 'Not nice enough, not for what I've got.'

'Okay, dazzle me first, then we'll talk nice.'

'Not good enough, Trina.' His voice is still cheerful, but a serious edge has crept in. 'Remember that raise we talked about, the one when I come to work for you and Cory Meyers?'

'The one we didn't talk about.'

'I want it, Trina. In exchange for what I've got.'

'You sound like a blackmailer, Howdy, the creepy murder victim out of the old "Perry Mason" show.'

'I've always had a theatrical streak. Well?'

Trina thinks it over. 'Is this a firm something or just a maybe?'

'A firm maybe. I got it going through Lila's purse. If she ever found out she'd cut my dick off and throw it in the blender. So I'm running some risk here, sweetheart.'

'A small risk.'

'You get one ho for that.'

'Christ, Howdy, when did you become such a bastard?'

'I've always been one. You never noticed before.'

Trina takes a sip from one of the soda cans, one of last week's she realizes too late. Her mouth puckers from the flat sour taste. She presses her palm against the other two cans, chooses the one whose aluminium is a little cooler, and sips. The sweetness washes away the metallic taste in her mouth. Howdy's disloyalty to Councilman Nicastro was to be expected; that's just political survival. But betraying his own girlfriend suggested an attitude that, should he come to work for The Candidate, might eventually prove dangerous.

'You stalling, Trina?' Howdy asks.

'Okay, you get your raise,' she says. 'Only if what you give me works out to our advantage. I mean, if we chase her mystery days down to find out she's working as an aide in a nursing home, you get zip.'

'Understood.'

Trina hesitates. She's already made up her mind that no matter what happens, she will have to find a way to back out of hiring Howdy. If Nicastro and Lila can't trust him, Cory sure couldn't. 'Okay, James Bond, gimme what you got.'

He chuckles. 'There's more truth to that than you realize. Lila was in the shower while I was rummaging through her purse. You wouldn't believe the shit she keeps in there. Ticket stubs, old grocery lists, enough tampons to plug a leak in the Hoover Dam. Suddenly the shower stops and she's walking down the hall in a towel talking to me about which movie we were going to that night. I swear, I just barely got the damn purse closed by the time she enters the room. I was in a cold sweat.'

'What did you find out?' asks Trina flatly.

'Councilwoman Bennington is due for another disappearance sometime this week.'

'When and where?'

'I don't know where.'

'Do you know when?'

'At two-thirty P.M. She'll be leaving from City Hall.'

'What day?'

He chuckles again. 'Today.'

21

'Ready for lunch?' Barcelona asks.

Trina jumps out of her desk chair as if she's just had a few hundred volts wired through her. Her face looks pale and clammy. 'Is it that time already?'

'Just about.' Barcelona checks her watch. 'I'm twenty minutes early. The freeway traffic was a little light. Can you leave?'

Trina nods absently, stares at her hands, wiggles her fingers.

'You okay, Trina? You're acting kinda goofy.'

'Goofy is in. It's happening, it's now, it's sexy. It's in all the women's magazines.'

Barcelona nods at the telephone. 'You get a hold of Dixie?'

'Not yet. You?'

'Nothing. I'll try again after lunch.'

'Speaking of which.' Trina opens her desk drawer and hands Barcelona a sheet of paper. 'Here's our menu, kiddo. Lots of beef, a couple come with some serious lettuce.' She rubs her fingers together to indicate money. 'Plus one guy I thought of later, Jamison Levy. He's that reporter I told you about.'

'Ah, him.'

'I think he'd be perfect for you. Smart, sexy, talented.'

'What about for you?'

'Too smart, sexy, and talented. I like 'em dumb, homely, and klutzy. They're more grateful that way.'

Barcelona holds the menu in front of her. She's having a little trouble reading the elite typeface without her glasses. 'Diva didn't waste any time. She's already called Harley Buss and arranged a date.'

'I know. I had an early breakfast with her and gave her a copy. She called right from Coco's. I think he was still sleeping.'

Barcelona looks at the typed list of men and their vital statistics, shaking her head. 'I don't know about this. This goes beyond goofy, makes me feel sneaky, like a spy or something.'

'Shit, Barcy,' Trina snaps angrily, 'it's just for fun. We're not trying to screw with your existential dialectical bullshit. Just for fucking fun. You don't want to call, don't fucking call!'

Barcelona is startled by Trina's outburst. Obviously Trina also attended that secret meeting of the world's women, the one she wasn't invited to. She wonders if she went to Trina's house would she find a space pod under the bed. 'What's wrong with you?'

'Nothing. Nothing's wrong. You're just making a big deal out of a simple lark.'

Barcelona picks up one of the soda cans from Trina's desk. She shakes it, listening for any sound of carbonated fizz. Nothing. 'Any of these fresh?' Trina hands her a different can and Barcelona sips. 'Hey, I'm sorry. I'll lighten up if you do. Deal?'

Trina nods. 'Sure.'

The Candidate knocks at the open door and comes in. 'Mail call,' he says. He waves a handful of envelopes and hands them to Trina. 'These are yours,' He turns to Barcelona. 'Hi.'

'Hi.'

'Barcy, this is Cory Meyer, The Man Who Would Be City Councilman. Cory, my friend Barcelona Lee, the famous author of a soon-to-be-released major motion picture.'

He smiles and his lips peel back to unsheathe a magnificent set of teeth that makes Barcelona immediately promise herself to floss and brush more often. His smile is truly dazzling, almost hypnotic. A sense of well-being seems to wash over her. 'Trina has spoken of you,' he says.

'You too,' Barcelona says.

'Yes, I pay her to lie about me.'

His smile dwindles to a grin hiding those teeth and she relaxes a little. He is not at all what she expected. He is not as lifeguard handsome as in the posters, but he is far more attractive. He stands close to both of them, not guarding any personal space that men seem to protect, but neither is he hovering in a sexual way. He's just there. Barcelona has the feeling that she could say anything to him and he wouldn't be shocked. Suddenly she has an image of him in the shower with Trina, standing behind her as she described it, his hips pumping away, steamy water sluicing across their skin, his eyes closed, a low moan at the back of his throat. His hands gripping her hips tightly, pulling her back onto him.

'You okay?' he asks her.

'What?' Barcelona says.

'You look a little flushed. You feeling okay?'

Indeed, Barcelona feels heat across her cheeks and forehead. 'I'm fine,' she insists.

'Look, Barcy, I'm sorry but I have to cancel lunch. Something's come up.' Trina turns to Cory. 'A lead on Carla Bennington's lost weekends. I've got to hurry.' She starts gathering her purse and briefcase.

'Okay,' Barcelona says. 'You want to try for dinner

tonight?' She is supposed to see Eric, but she's concerned about Trina's strange behavior.

'Uh, not tonight. This lead may take me out of town. I'll call you. If you reach Dixie, leave a message on my machine.'

'Yeah, okay.'

Trina hustles out of her office without saying good-bye to either of them.

'Well,' The Candidate says, unleashing his smile again. 'How about I take her place for lunch? You've still got to eat, right?'

22

Diva is locked in the trunk of a 1978 Buick. Her head is resting on the spare tire and every once in a while the car drives over a bump and jostles her. Her hands are braced against the trunk lid to keep from getting too badly bruised. A tennis racket handle digs into her hip, but when she shifts away from it her other hip presses against a baseball bat.

She tries not to think about the stuffy heat and sinister darkness of the place. She has never been afraid of the dark, but this darkness is so complete, so final, she is having trouble swallowing. She smells the unmistakable odor of marijuana. She wouldn't be surprised if she rooted under the spare tire to find a Baggie or two of the stuff. The intense heat of the trunk is cooking it just enough to produce a slight scent, like brewing tea. She wishes she were smoking some of it right now.

The car hits a dip and Diva lifts off the bottom of the trunk and slams her head into the lid. She falls back down and her head bounces off the tire, her hip is gouged by the tennis racket. She is getting tired of this shit.

The car slows, turns left, stops. The motor idles. They are here.

There is some muted conversation. The guard is checking IDs. After a couple of minutes she hears the guard say okay and the Buick drives away, making a lot of sharp turns before leaving paved road and rolling slowly across gravel like crunchy granola. The car stops, the motor is shut off, but no one opens the trunk. Minutes pass. Diva is starting to feel spikes of panic piercing deep into her chest. Sweat thick as glycerine rolls along her nose, down her chin, into her ears, behind her neck. Her legs are drenched, She imagines the bright sun outside, the hot rays that are hitting the metal trunk having traveled millions of miles to get here from the sun. Having come all this way just so it could turn the trunk of the Buick into a tin oven and fry her brain. She wonders if the brain literally does fry, the brain juices sizzling against the hot skull bone, steaming like clam chowder soup.

She kicks the lid of the trunk. 'This isn't funny. Let me out.'

'Sssshhhh,' Forge says, pounding the trunk. 'Lost the damn trunk key.'

She isn't sure whether he is serious or merely saying that for the benefit of a passerby who'd heard him talk to the trunk. Either way, she doesn't like it. She begins to doubt the wisdom of all this.

Finally the trunk pops open and Forge stands over her smoking one of her black cigarettes. 'Left your purse in the front seat. How can you smoke this shit?'

Diva quickly climbs out of the trunk and brushes dirt from her knees. She plucks the cigarette from his mouth, takes a drag, then throws it away. The cigarette rolls under his car. 'You hit every goddamn bump on Melrose, you dumb asshole.'

Forge shrugs. 'Melrose needs some serious work.'

She slams the trunk, grabs her purse from the front seat. She opens her compact and sees a tread mark across her cheek. Wetting her fingertips with saliva, she rubs the black tire smudges from her face. 'Let's get going,' she

314

says, dragging Forge along the narrow sidewalks of Paramount Studios. He follows without protest.

Diva went to high school with Forge. Back then all he did was surf and smoke dope. Now he surfs, smokes dope, and builds sets. In high school she sometimes surfed with him, sometimes she smoked dope with him, occasionally she even had sex with him, usually in his converted VW dune buggy. He is only an inch taller than she is, but he has remarkably muscular arms, thick as telephone poles. He wears a faded black Iron Maiden T-shirt with the sleeves torn off to highlight his bulging biceps. On his right arm is a sloppy tattoo of a swastika on a surfboard and the words 'surf nazi' crudely printed under it. In high school Forge was arrested once for beating up some fifteen-year-old kid from Manhattan Beach who'd come down to Huntington Beach to surf. Locals didn't like outsiders stealing their waves.

As they walk, Forge is explaining his job: 'We're building these cool sets now for some sitcom pilot about this family, only they aren't really a family. There's a father, mother, teenage daughter, and teenage son. Only they aren't really related. They're all in the Witness Protection Program, given new identities because they testified against the Mob. The Mob is still looking for them too. But because of budget cuts, the Feds had to stick these four people together as one family, even though none of them knows the other and they don't like each other. Makes for some really funny gags.' He chuckles and Diva can smell the marijuana on his breath.

'Hey, Forge,' Diva says. 'Thanks for sneaking me in, I appreciate it.'

'No prob, Dianne. We done it a couple times at the drive-in, remember?'

'There's Tommy's building. I've got to go.'

'Sure. See ya. Maybe we can get together sometimes, hit the waves at Doheny.'

'Yeah. Thanks again.' Diva cuts across a couple of lawns to a white building in the back of the lot. She passes the elevator and climbs two flights of stairs because she doesn't want anybody to stop her and ask her any questions. Finally she finds the recording studio. Tommy is sitting behind a pair of SL4000-E mixing boards with hundreds of knobs, dials, switches, and lights. Directly in front of him is a plate glass window looking onto the recording room, which is empty except for half a dozen microphones. Above the glass window is a paneled wall with a dozen speakers built in.

Diva opens the door. Tommy doesn't see her or hear her. His back is turned toward her. He is hunched over the control board with earphones on. Occasionally he slides a knob or twists a dial. He hums a few notes, is silent for a few seconds, then hums another snatch of melody.

Diva pats down her wet bangs. They are stringy and matted, pasted to her forehead with sweat. She fusses with them as she walks toward him but finally gives up. She looks the way she looks. That's how it's always been.

Just as she reaches to tap him on the shoulder, he turns around and stares directly into her eyes. This sudden movement startles her and she jumps back with a gasp. 'Tommy!'

He hasn't seen her in over six months, but he doesn't seem especially surprised to see her now. 'Hi, luv.' Tommy speaks in a fake cockney accent, though he is from Akron, Ohio. He spent his junior year of Kent State in London. That was sixteen years ago, but the accent seems to get stronger with each year. His hairline has receded back to the middle of his head, but what is left is long and heavily waxed, pulled straight back into a black samurai knot. He also spent a year in Japan playing lounge shows with his

316

rock band, Fully Lined. For the past five years he's been dubbing sound tracks to movies.

'How'd you get on the studio?' he asks.

'I snuck on.'

He nods, not pleased. 'Security here has been going downhill. None of us is safe. Some writer last month had his show canceled and he charged into some exec's office during a pitch meeting and urinated on the guy's desk. All over his scripts and everything. In front of everyone.'

Diva laughs. 'Maybe he'll get a rewrite credit on the scripts.'

Tommy doesn't laugh. 'It's getting scary.'

Diva tries to look serious. A year ago Tommy would have told this story with a grin and laughed heartily at the end. He would have said pissed instead of urinated. The fired writer would have been the hero of the story.

'Listen, Tommy, I need a favor,' Diva says.

Tommy sighs and nods grimly as if he's come to expect those words. They've known each other for six years. He used to mix some of the commercials Diva sang on. They became friendly. They went out a few times. He banged her in the men's room at a Gordon Lightfoot concert. She straddled him while he sat on the toilet. People who heard him moaning must have thought he was passing a gallstone. That's how she got the job singing a mock-Bette Midler rendition of 'Do You Want Some Plants' for that chain of florists. Tommy got her the job. It was never stated that she had to screw him to get the job, but she knew, even if he didn't.

Tommy removes his headphones. 'What favor?'

'I'm writing a song. It's almost done. It just needs some polishing, sweetening really. Can you tinker with it for me?'

He looks her over, his heavy-lidded eyes checking her out from tits to toes and back, deciding what's in it for

317

him, whether he even wants it from her again. If he does, Diva will give it. Not because of what he can do for her, but because in some strange way she is flattered that her body, puffed and flabby as it is, still can wield some power.

'I'm busy now, but I might take a look at it if you come over tonight, luv.'

She remembers her date with Harley Buss, the department chairman at Barcy's school. He had such a nice voice on the phone, charming and funny. 'How about tomorrow night?' she offers.

'Busy. Stuff to do tomorrow.' He reaches back and smooths his Japanese ponytail. He looks at his watch. 'We could look it over now, I suppose. We don't have much time.' He reaches over and strokes her bare thigh.

'Sure,' she says. 'Whatever.'

Walking out of the lot, she thinks she sees Tom Cruise. He is walking across the lawn with a young woman executive-type who is at least six inches taller, four of the inches from her black patent high heels. She is doing most of the talking and he nods and sometimes laughs, says a few words, then listens intently. At one point he stoops and picks something off the sidewalk, a coin it looks like, shows it to the woman, then pockets it. Later she shows him a piece of paper, appears to read it aloud to him. Afterward, she leans over and kisses his forehead playfully. He laughs and looks embarrassed.

Diva starts to follow them, but they turn a corner and disappear behind some shrubbery.

She walks the two blocks to her '71 VW van with the imitation Peter Max psychedelic flowers painted all over it. She bought the van from some ex-hippie folk singer who'd moved to L.A. to become the next Donovan and made ends meet by playing backup on radio commercials. He was very proud of the fact that he'd once spent ten days in a Boston jail for wearing a patch of the American flag on the butt of his jeans. He ended up selling everything he owned to open a little health food restaurant with a girl he met in a movie line in Westwood. Now they own a trendy chain of restaurants throughout the Valley.

Once inside, she immediately lights up a black cigarette to burn the taste of Tommy's come out of her mouth. He was the saltiest semen she's ever tasted, like anchovies rolled in salt or something. The cigarette helps.

She takes a deep drag and blows it against the windshield. The smoke curls back on itself like a horizontal atomic cloud. She reaches into her purse and takes her song out. Tommy scribbled a few unintelligible notes in the margins of the lyrics, suggested a few chord progressions, but otherwise wasn't much help. She knew he wouldn't be. But Tommy has always fancied himself a deep-thinking songwriter, especially after his trips to Europe and Japan. His songs suck and everybody knows it except Tommy. However, Diva knew that by asking him to help, she had him hooked. He would try, fail, and then like a man who has just gone limp during sex, try to make it up some other way. And that's what Diva had actually come for. She needed a sound engineer, and that's what Tommy was exceptionally good at. He promised to help her mix her song when she was ready to record, maybe even get her a break on some studio time from a friend of his.

Diva pulled the van into traffic. With Barcy's loan and a few more favors, she should be able to cut a demo by the end of the month. Maybe sooner if she could finish the damn song.

Freeway traffic isn't too bad and she gets back to Balboa in a little more than an hour. As soon as she enters her apartment she dials Dixie's number again. Still no answer.

Even Dixie's phone answering machine isn't on. Diva calls Barcy at school, but she's gone. She calls Trina at work, but Trina has left already too. She calls the police station that Dixie works out of and asks for her, but of course she isn't there. That was dumb. Even if Dixie is okay, she would still be undercover at that high school. And she certainly wouldn't be using her real name. Diva considers driving over to the school and looking around, but that's what started the trouble in the first place. Finally she pushes the phone away and goes to the bathroom thinking about her date. She checks her face in the mirror for any pimples or blackheads.

23

'I never use urinals. Never,' The Candidate says. He takes another sip of his gumbo soup while Barcelona laughs.

'Then how do you pee?' she asks.

'Same as you. I sit. Men's bathrooms are never as crowded as women's, never a line. Guys go to the bathroom, they're in a hurry to get out again. They walk in, step up to the urinal, don't look to the right or left, do their business, and rush out.'

'Like sex,' Barcelona says.

'There's a distinct similarity. More like a grocery store express line. However, unlike after sex, I've noticed here men rarely even bother to wash their hands.'

Barcelona pulls a French roll in half and butters one side. 'Sounds very efficient.'

'Scary is what it is for most guys. The men's room can be traumatic. Guys are afraid that if they take too long, other guys will think they like it in there, and why would they like it in there unless they were homosexual. The big H. A lot of guys think it's something you can catch, like cancer, only worse. An alien force, not of this world.'

'But you're not afraid?'

'Terrified. Not of catching it, but certainly I don't want to be labeled as one. It would ruin my political career on the spot.'

'I had no idea male bowel movements were so

traumatic.' Barcelona shakes her head, grinning. 'I don't usually talk about urinals at lunch. How did we get on this subject anyway?'

'Your fault. You asked how voters can be certain I'm honest. And I told you, I never use urinals. I don't piss standing up.'

'Maybe I'm a little slow today, but I don't get the connection.'

The Candidate takes the other half of her French roll and runs it around the bottom of his empty soup bowl. 'Okay, my reasons for urinating the way I do are purely practical. First, when you stand and pee into a toilet bowel, the urine sometimes hits the water with such force, it splashes out of the bowel on your shins or trousers. Same with a urinal, it hits that hard porcelain and bounces right back at you. Second, when you're done peeing, there's always a few more drops that keep dripping out. You have to shake the thing a couple of times, and sometimes you get those drops on yourself. Both of these problems are eliminated by sitting.'

'That's very interesting,' Barcelona says. 'But how does that make you an honest politician?'

'In prison, the toughest and meanest convicts force the weakest inmates into becoming their sex slaves. They treat them like women, make them dress up like women, act like women, even got to the bathroom like women. They're forced to sit to pee. So if I went to prison and they saw me sitting to pee on my own, they'd be all over me. That's why I have to remain an honest politician. I can't afford to go to jail.'

Barcelona laughs. They have been chatting for almost an hour, during the walk to the restaurant, while waiting to order. He asked her a lot about herself, her writing and teaching, seemed impressed by both. He never looked for an opening to talk about his own achievements. He waited until she asked and even then made a joke of the whole thing. Cory Meyers is as charming as Trina had described him. Smart, witty, and attractive. She doesn't trust anyone that together.

'You want me to lose, don't you?' he says suddenly.

Barcelona is about to make a joke, but she sees by his expression that he is serious. 'Why would you think that?'

The waiter arrives with their orders. Australian lobster tail for Barcelona and soft shell crabs for The Candidate. Both are drinking iced tea.

Once the waiter has finished fussing about, clearing plates and sweeping bread crumbs, wishing a hearty appetite and complimenting Barcelona on the loveliness of her silk blouse, he leaves and they are alone together. This time there is an awkward intimacy to their meal. Like a long-married couple on the verge of a fight.

'You haven't answered me,' Barcelona says. 'Why would you think I want you to lose?'

'That's not a denial.'

'That's not an answer.'

He waves his napkin in surrender. 'That wasn't fair of me,' he says. 'Forget it.'

'Don't pull that "forget it" crap.'

He chuckles. 'You sound like Trina now.'

Being compared with Trina right now is somehow annoying. Usually she'd be flattered by the comparison, but not now. 'Maybe she sounds like me?'

'Okay, okay. Here's my two-bit, pocket guide to psychological analysis.' He leans back in his chair and wipes his mouth with his napkin. 'There are two reasons you want me to lose. First, you want me to lose because I'm a man running against a woman. A woman who is attractive and single like yourself. Highly accomplished, like yourself.'

'So far I like your description, if not your reasoning.'

'Who's roughly in the same age range.'

'Careful.'

He laughs. 'Give or take a decade. Also, Carla Bennington has done a good job in office.'

'You make a pretty good case for her.'

'She's a good person, as far as we know.'

'Ah, the dirt that Trina's trying to dig up. The fuel of politics. Considering what you just said about her, why should I vote for you, if I were in your district?'

'I think I can do a better job.'

'Because you're smarter, younger, manlier?'

'Because I'm more ambitious. Everyone knows I have ambitions beyond this city, maybe even beyond this state. People like to have friends on the rise because they may need a powerful friend later down the road. That makes them a lot more yielding today to proposals I may have, more willing to compromise. And for me to have a shot at higher office, I need to really prove myself in this office. I need results. People know I'll work my butt off to get those results.'

Barcelona has hardly touched her lobster tail. She stabs her fork into it, twists thoughtfully. 'Say you're right about the first reason. Maybe I would prefer to see a woman in there, even if you are more ambitious and therefore a little more effective. What's the other reason?'

He looks straight into her eyes and Barcelona recoils as if he's struck her across the cheek. 'Because you know I made love to Trina.'

Barcelona looks away from him, concentrates on her lobster tail, digging out the meat with an eye surgeon's precision. She can feel his gaze on her, waiting. She doesn't like the way this lunch is going anymore. She speaks without looking up. 'I'm not a moralizer, Mr. Meyers. Trina's a big girl.'

But Barcelona realizes The Candidate is right. Despite his charm and intelligence, she has been disapproving of him, partially for the first reason he mentioned. Going after a woman in a position in which there are already too few women saddened her, made her feel vulnerable. But mostly she disapproves for the second reason: fucking Trina in the shower from behind when he's got a wife at home. She recognizes her own hypocrisy in this matter. She's been humping with Eric while his young wife waits at home for him to finish his run so they can go grocery shopping. But she's not running for public office, she reminds herself. She sighs at her own shallow rationalizing. 'I'm not a moralizer,' Barcelona says again.

'All of us are moralizers. Some of us would rather not be, but we are nevertheless. Judging people is what we do best. I'm not going to make any excuses. Really it's none of your business except that Trina told you and for some reason I haven't figured out yet your opinion of me seems to matter. It shouldn't. You're not even from my district.'

'I-I don't . . .' She trails off, not certain what she was going to say. She shrugs, looks up at his face. He smiles at her, a low-wattage smile that only shows the tips of his teeth.

'Morality is such a slippery thing,' he says. 'Like trying to grab a handful of wiggling eels.'

'You getting folksy on me, old-timer?'

He laughs. It sounds melodic, as if he were humming a tune while laughing. 'We'll keep it mathematical. Let's take two guys, one looks like Warren Beatty . . .'

'Too old.'

'Rob Lowe.'

'A baby.'

'Mel Gibson.'

'Perfect.'

He takes a deep breath and continues. 'All right. One guy looks like Mel Gibson, the other looks like Dom DeLuise. Now, our Mel lookalike has committed adultery twice, but our Dom clone never has. Who's less moral? Numerically speaking?'

'You really want me to answer?'

'Yes. It's a test.'

'I know it's a trick, but for the sake of your test, I'll say Mel.'

'Okay. Mel is less moral because he slept with two women and Dom hasn't slept with any. But suppose Mel, charismatic animal that he is, has had a hundred offers, gorgeous women with shapely legs, firm asses, Ph.D.s, M.D.s, BVDs, every kind of sexy woman you can imagine. They come on to him constantly. They hand him their panties with their room keys taped to the crotch. He's turned down ninety-eight of them, each requiring extraordinary willpower. Now Dom, nice guy that he may be, has only had one offer from a matronly sort with false teeth and gin breath. He turned her down easily. Mel's fidelity has been tested a hundred times and he's passed ninety-eight times. Dom has been tested only once and he passed once. Who's the more moral?'

Barcelona chews her lobster tail and shakes her head. 'You're a lawyer, right?'

'Yes. Is that another prejudice you have?'

'Yes.'

'Rise above it. Come on, what's your answer? Who is more moral? The man who has proven it ninety-eight times, or the man who has proven it only once?'

'Who's the murderer?' Barcelona says. 'The man who is angry enough to kill a hundred times and on the hundred and first time does, or the man who gest angry once and does nothing? The first guy resisted a hundred times. But there's still a dead body.'

The Candidate grins. 'Very good.'

'Not really. It's a little truth with a lot of bullshit, just like yours. But, okay, I see the truth in what you say.

326

Logically, you're right. But sometimes logic is cold comfort to those who get hurt. Mel's wife isn't going to clap him on the back like a hockey goalie and say, "Way to go, honey. Great goal-keeping. Only two scored." She's going to cry herself to sleep for weeks.'

The Candidate looks around, then lowers his voice. 'That's not my situation at all, as I'm sure Trina explained.'

'Look, it's really none of my business. Really.'

Barcelona shovels some rice pilaf onto her fork and eats. She is conscious of each bite, her teeth crushing each rice kernel, mashing them all together with her saliva until they form a starchy lump. She doesn't want to swallow but can see no graceful way to spit the mess out. She swallows.

Damn, everything had been so light and amusing at first; why did it suddenly turn serious? Why did he feel it was necessary to justify himself? Especially to her. She hasn't exactly been Mother Theresa. Yet, she did act superior, let him squirm unnecessarily.

What was going on lately? All her women friends were acting like maniacs. Like sun-crazed survivors of a plane crash who've wandered through the scorched desert for days without food or water. Trina was remote and brusque; Dixie's disappeared; Diva's charging at windmills. And Barcelona's screwing her ex-boyfriend, her *married* ex-boyfriend.

The waiter glides up to the table with a big silver tray filled with pastries. He smiles hugely and bows, offering the tray. 'Dessert?' he asks. 'Everything is guaranteed nonfattening.' Then he laughs and laughs until Barcelona can hear the loose tip change jingling in his pockets.

'There's an epidemic of trench mouth among editors in New York,' Grief tells Barcelona. 'I heard this last week from another agent there.'

'Trench mouth?'

'It's an infection soldiers in the trenches in World War One used to get. I don't know much about it except they've all got bad breath.' She chuckles. 'They're all going around to these power meetings talking movie rights and sucking Breathsavers.'

Grief is sitting behind her desk nibbling on Mrs. Fields cookies. She reaches into the little red and white bag, breaks off a corner of cookie, and eats it with tiny bird bites. When she finishes with one piece, she breaks off a new piece. She never takes a whole cookie out of the bag.

Barcelona's finished screenplay sits on Grief's desk. With the hand that isn't breaking off chunks of white chocolate cookies, Grief leafs through the manuscript. 'Looks good, Barcy. Very professional.'

'Let's hope it reads as well as it looks.'

She waves her hand. 'It will, it will.' Grief is not a worrier, that much Barcelona knows. When they first met years ago, Grief had told Barcelona that her motto in life was the same as Alfred E. Neuman's in *Mad* magazine: 'What, me worry?' She'd had a lifetime of chest-pounding and hair-pulling from her father, an activist lawyer who'd worked on Ethel and Julius Rosenberg's defense right up to their execution at Sing Sing prison. Taking the defeat very hard, he'd moved his family—wife and three daughters, Mary, Laura, and Susan—to a Vermont commune long before hippies began doing it. He legally changed the daughters' names to Felicity, Hope, and Grief, what he considered the cornerstones of a balanced life. After a couple of years of this his wife gave him an ultimatum: either they moved back to New York together or she and the children moved back without him. They moved back together and he began defending writers against Joseph McCarthy's accusations of Communist party affiliations. Which is how Grief came to know so many writers when she decided to become a literary agent. Her sisters changed their names back to Mary and Laura. But Grief liked the attention her name brought her.

Grief brushes cookie crumbs from her desk and reaches for the phone. She flips through the Rolodex, dials, asks for Roger Carlyle. 'Roger? Grief. Barcelona Lee has delivered the screenplay of *Live Wires* . . . I just finished reading it. It's terrific. Tell you the truth, I'm sorry we made an agreement with you before she wrote it. This thing is worth a helluva lot more.' Grief listens, laughs, rolls her eyes for Barcelona's sake. 'Fine . . . Uh-huh . . . Good-bye.' She hangs up.

'So?' Barcelona asks.

'He's sending a messenger over for it. He'll read it tonight, take it over to Lynda Kramer's people tomorrow.'

'What if he doesn't like it?'

Grief's smile is sharp, almost cruel. 'Listen, honey. chances are he won't even read the whole thing before he gives it to them. He'll read just enough to know what the hell we're talking about. Even if he did read it all he wouldn't know if it were any good or not. All he knows is Lynda Kramer is interested. Even if he hated it he'd take it to her. So relax. His opinion isn't worth shit.'

Barcelona looks under Grief's desk and sees the stocking-covered bunion poking out of her agent's foot. A pair of discarded and very expensive beige pumps lie on their sides next to the afflicted foot. She is fascinated by the growth, wants to ask questions, get down on her hands and knees and jab at the thing as if it were a strange reptile. see what it will do. Crazy. But she feels a little crazy after her lunch with Cory Meyers, The Candidate. Everything had been going so smoothly, the height of sophistication. Witty banter, casual flirting, attentive waiter, everything like in a Cary Grant movie. She was Ingrid Bergman, of course. Then he got serious and ruined it all. After that, there was a silent dessert and a stilted, awkward walk back to his campaign headquarters. Why couldn't he have stuck to the script?

'When do you think we'll hear from Lynda Kramer?' Barcelona asks.

Grief shrugs, rubs her bunion against the carpet. 'Never know. Maybe tomorrow, maybe not for six weeks. Depends.'

'Depends. That covers a multitude of sins.'

Grief reaches into her Mrs. Fields bag but finds no more cookies. She crumbles the bag and drops it in her wastebasket. She seems antsy and Barcelona rises to leave. 'I should be going. Don't want to hit the freeway rush hour.'

Grief nods. 'Relax, lamb. We'll hear when we hear. I feel very good about this, very good. I have psychic abilities, did I ever tell you?'

'No.'

'Well I do. Hunches, feelings, they're almost always right. I have a feeling now. About this script.'

'Maybe it's gas.'

Grief smiles. 'I'll call soon as I hear.'

Barcelona gets on the freeway heading south. Traffic is starting to knot up. A few miles later cars have slowed to a crawl and she sees why. An accident. A green Yugo is crushed against the steel railing that divides the north- and southbound freeways. The front end of the car is flattened back to the windshield. The driver is lying by the side of the road. Paramedics have a neck brace on him and are bandaging his head. Both his pant legs are shredded as if he'd been attacked by a tiger. Blood soaks both legs. Barcelona thinks she sees a small hole in the driver's window and she wonders if this is another freeway shooting.

She turns on the radio and listens to the Zombies' 'Tell Her No.' A few yards past the accident, traffic speed picks

330

up and soon she is zipping back toward Orange County and home. The news comes on the radio and the announcer says that the Department of Defense Maintenance Award has been given to Marine Heavy Helicopter Squadron 466, which services 16 CH-53E Super Stallion helicopters. The general making the award reaffirmed his dedication to the helicopters despite the crashes that have plagued them. Also, David Bowie may be getting married again.

The rest of the drive home Barcelona wonders what she will write next. Now that the script is done she should jump right into something new, maybe another script. She has lots of ideas tacked up on her bulletin board. She considers each one in detail as she whisks past the exit signs.

It is early in the afternoon when Barcelona pulls into her garage. She sees Eric's car parked on the curb near the mailboxes. She's pleased. This day has been unsettling and all she wants to do now is crawl into bed with Eric and be held.

As she hurries out of the garage lugging her briefcase, she runs into Dave walking his Lhasa apso, Foxy. He's carrying a brown lunch bag that looks pretty full.

'Hi,' Dave says. He has a strained look on his face, as if he can't remember her name, knows it's something odd, wants to say something like Berlin or Budapest, but just settles for hi.

'Hi, Dave.' She bends over and pets Foxy's moppy head. Foxy licks her hand. His tongue is rough and slimy.

'Just finishing up our little walk, eh Foxy?' Dave says. He reaches into his pocket and pulls out the garage door opener. The big wooden door swings open with a groan. 'How's it going with you?' he asks but keeps walking toward the garage. Barcelona is forced to walk with him or seem rude.

'Fine. You?'

He nods, shrugs. 'Foxy and I manage.' He smiles. He sets the lunch bag containing Foxy's shit down on the floor, and pries the lid off a huge plastic garbage can. Inside the can are dozens of similar lunch bags. The smell hits Barcelona like a bat across the skull. She winces and cups her hand around her nose. Dave dumps the new bag inside and closes the lid.

'Strong stuff, eh?' he says with a grin.

'Potent.'

He stoops down and scratches Foxy's ears. 'This fella eats pretty healthy. Don't ya, boy?' Foxy flops onto the garage floor and rolls onto his back. Dave scratches his stomach.

Having done her neighborly duty, Barcelona turns to leave when she sees something leaning against the wall at the back of Dave's garage that startles her. She walks toward it. 'Jesus,' she says. 'Where'd you get this?'

He follows her. 'Something, isn't it? Must've taken her three years to complete. Everything had to be just right. Everything's to scale, you know.'

Barcelona stands in front of it. 'Jesus.'

'It's in sections now,' he says, gesturing at the different parts leaning against the walls. 'But when it was all together, the thing measured twelve by twenty-five feet. It was a son of a bitch to lug around, I'm telling you. But it's accurate. Totally to scale and looks just like Elvis's real Graceland.'

Foxy sniffs at a pile of boards and a tiny mouse runs out. Foxy watches it without chasing.

Barcelona reaches down and touches the miniature fence that guards the entrance to this miniature Graceland. Woven into the wire design is an outline of Elvis strumming a guitar, surrounded by musical notes. 'It's fantastic,' Barcelona says.

'Over here's the mansion.' He pulls out another board

332

with tiny trees and fake grass surrounding a huge mansion with white columns. 'Darlene spent all her spare time working on this. You'd be surprised how hard it is to find a model of just the right Cadillac that fits into the scale.' He points to one of the red Cadillacs glued to the painted driveway.

'I never knew she did this.'

'She didn't like to brag.'

Barcelona looks at Dave, but he is not smiling. That wasn't a joke.

'She was planning to start in on Elvis's childhood home in Tupelo, Mississippi next. Before she hung herself.' He stoops next to the mansion and strokes out one of the white columns. Foxy comes over and sniffs at his shoes. 'She did it on Elvis's birthday. I like to think that was some comfort to her.'

Barcelona thanks him for showing her the models and says goodbye. She walks briskly along the sidewalk, her heels echoing in the greenbelt. Larry the cat sticks his head out of a neighbor's bush, sees it's her, and ducks back in. Barcelona hurries into the apartment, anxious to see Eric. She hopes he will be waiting by the door.

He isn't.

She opens the door and finds Luna sitting on the couch reading the newspaper. When she sees Barcelona she looks up with a friendly smile and says, 'Hi. I hope you don't mind, I let myself in with Eric's key.'

24

'Can you squeeze me in?' Trina asks, leaning over the counter.

Marlene sits at the desk behind the counter and runs her white and orange striped fingernail along the appointment book grid. Neatly printed names fill every fifteen-minute slot. Marlene frowns. 'May take a few minutes of juggling.'

'I appreciate it. Whoa, Marlene, that's some nail polish.'

Marlene wiggles her fingernails. 'Leopard stripes. Matches my underwear. Whatever pattern my panties are, that's how I do my nails, that way Gary always knows. I read about it in *Working Woman* or something. It's supposed to keep the passion fires alive in a marriage.'

'Does it?'

Marlene shrugs. 'Sure. Especially when we're out with other couples. All through dinner Gary keeps staring at my fingernails. It drives him nuts, as if I were sitting there in front of everybody in nothing but my panties. Makes him hot as a toaster. You should try it.'

Trina shows her own ragged, chipped nails. 'These already reflect the condition of my underwear.'

Marlene laughs. She leans forward and lowers her voice to a conspiratory whisper. 'I'm glad you dropped in, Trina. Doctor could use the break. These kids this morning are a particularly bratty bunch.'

334

'I'll try to act my age then,' Trina smiles.

Marlene chuckles and rolls across the cubicle on her customized office chair. She's been running this office for the five years it's been open and Trina has yet to see her get up out of that chair.

Trina sits in one of the waiting room chairs, Swedish modern design, blond wood and bright red cushions. She doesn't want to think about why she is here so she passes the time studying her fellow patients and their parents. One redheaded girl about seven has a gauze patch the size of a folded washcloth taped to her cheek. A brownish stain has seeped through. She is sitting quietly next to her mother looking miserable. The mother holds her hand and whispers cheerfully to her. Another little girl closer to ten or eleven is chattering away to her father. She wants to know if she'll have to go back to school after the doctor's done or if they can go out to lunch and maybe shopping. The father has his leather brief-case balanced across his knees and reminds her that if she is too sick to go to school, she's too sick to go shopping. Then he leans over and kisses her on the fore-head.

Trina gets up and walks to the magazines spread out on the big circular blond wood table. *Highlights* seem to be the most popular, followed by *Sesame Street* and *Life*. She grabs one of the tattered *Highlights* and returns to her chair. She leafs through it until she finds her favorite puzzle, the drawing crammed with hidden objects you have to find. She locates the stove, the baseball glove, the cow, then loses interest.

She walks back to the counter. 'Marlene, can I use your phone?'

'Sure, Trina. Come on through.'

The door buzzes and Trina walks through. Marlene slides the black telephone across the desk. 'Leave your

335

quarter on the desk,' she kids and rolls away on her chair to file some folders.

Trina dials Rob's office.

'Rob Barre,' he answers. Brisk and businesslike.

'Rob, it's me.'

Cold silence. She can hear the clacking of his computer as he continues to type. Rob is a partner in one of Orange County's fastest-growing advertising agencies. He's the one who came up with the 'Wouldn't you like to sleep with a cold Fisch tonight?' campaign for Fisch air conditioners. After the divorce he claimed he got the idea from sleeping with her. Finally he speaks, sounding like a recording. 'Trina, I'm working.'

'I know, I'm sorry to disturb you—'

'Uh oh, you want something.' The computer clacking stops.

'I'd like you to take Karyn for the evening. I have to go out of town. It's all very sudden.'

'Everything all right?' His voice lowers with concern. She feels that familiar stab of loss in her stomach.

'Yes,' she says. 'It's just business.'

'This is only the second time you've ever asked me to take Karyn when it wasn't my turn. The first time your mother had surgery.'

Trina uncurls a backward kink in the coiled telephone wire. She wouldn't be giving Karyn to Rob now if she didn't think she had to track down this Carla Bennington mystery. Not for The Candidate's sake or anything so noble, but for her own piece of mind. She's been acting like such a flake lately she needs to prove her old reporter's instincts, her old do-or-die professionalism is still there. That she isn't yet ready for menopause and bridge clubs. 'Really, it's just business. Unexpected. If you can't do it—'

'I can do it. Don't overplay your hand. Want me to pick her up from school?'

336

'Yes. Tell her I'll pick her up tomorrow from school. Don't let her fake a bellyache in the morning and stay home.'

'Don't worry,' Rob says. 'I can take care of my own daughter.'

'Right, sorry. I appreciate this, Rob.'

'You can owe me.' He chuckles. 'Anything else?'

'No. Thanks again.'

'Bye.' He hangs up.

Trina clears the line and gets another dial tone. She dials Dixie's home again and still gets no answer. Again she considers calling the police but decides against it.

Marlene rolls up to Trina's feet. 'Doctor said to hide you out in number five. She doesn't want anybody to see you. Kids don't like it if they know their pediatrician is treating an adult.' She winks. 'Giving comfort to the enemy.'

Trina wonders when and how Marlene spoke with the doctor. She hasn't left this little reception area and Trina hadn't heard her even speak. 'I know the way, thanks,' Trina says and walks down the hall. She passes one tiny blue room where one of the doctor's young female assistants is helping a little boy up on the examining table. The little boy holds a rubber sea gull and is pulling at its wings. The wings stretch and snap back in place. The boy has a small scrape on the side of his cheek. 'Looks like you had a nasty fall, Peter,' the assistant says. Peter nods and stretches the gull's wings.

Trina passes another examination room, this one yellow, and sees another teenage assistant weighing a skinny little girl about nine.

'This is wrong!' the little girl says adamantly. 'I don't weigh this much.'

'The scale is the best there is, Lisa,' the teen assistant says sweetly.

'Nuh uh. The one we have home is better. It has a digital display that lights up in red letters. Not stupid weights you gotta slide around. This is stupid.'

The assistant is wearing a pink blouse and blue skirt, the same cheerful uniform as the other assistant and Marlene. She pats the girl's blond head and smiles patiently. 'This is a very good scale, Lisa.'

'It says I weigh too much. I don't weigh this much. It's off three pounds.'

The teen assistant suddenly sees Trina and comes over to the open door. She looks embarrassed, as if she's been caught mistreating the child. She whispers, 'We see this all the time. Parents with little girls sometimes set their scales back a few pounds.' Then she smiles. 'But then, so do I.' She giggles and shuts the door.

Trina continues on to room #5. This room is white with purple stripes. She puts her purse on the examining table and looks out the fourth-story window to the rest of Fashion Island below. She stares between two tall buildings made of white stone like sand and blue glass to reflect the Pacific Ocean half a mile away. The ocean is calm this morning. Spring fog blurs the horizon; she can barely make out a dark shadow in the fog that is Catalina Island. She leans her forehead against the window glass and looks down. Her eyes rake the sidewalks and parking lots, hoping she'll spot Dixie still wandering around. But this is the medical section of Fashion Island. This is where the damaged shoppers gather to be repairéd.

Suddenly the door bursts open and Dr. Whitney Hempel-Oakes rushes in. Her right hand grapples in her white jacket pocket for a pack of cigarettes, sticks one in her mouth, and lights it. She sucks in a deep breath and blows it out slowly. 'Fuck,' she says. 'That's good.'

Trina grins. 'Still trying to hide your smoking from parents, huh?'

338

'First it was my parents, now it's my patients' parents.'

'I think you get off on having something to hide. I always longed to have some dark secret.'

'You and me don't know shit about secrets,' Dr. Whitney Hempel-Oakes says bitterly. She reaches into her other deep pocket and takes out a wire coat hanger that's been pretzeled into a strange squiggly shape. She throws it on the examining table next to Trina's purse. Then she sits down on a metal stool and leans back against the wall. 'Guess where I got that?'

'You lock yourself out of your car?'

'I just examined a twelve-year-old girl who sneaked it in under her sweater. She wanted me to show her how to use it.'

Trina makes a face. 'Jesus, you're kidding.'

'I wish. Turns out she jacked off some boy her age in his folks' swimming pool. Some of his come floated up and touched her face. She's been terrified ever since that she's pregnant. Hasn't eaten or slept for two weeks. Mother thought she had mono or something.'

'I thought the schools taught them about stuff like that now.'

Whitney sucks hard on the cigarette and shakes her head. Smoke leaks out her nostrils and mouth. 'Conservative backlash.'

'More like backwash.'

'The little girl had heard something about using a coat hanger to abort, but she didn't know how to do it. She saw some cop show on TV, some guy picking a lock, so she twisted the hanger into the shape of a lock pick. Thought she'd work on herself the same way.' The doctor stubs out the cigarette on the inside of the trash can. Without getting up, she rolls her stool over to the sink and washes her hand. 'So, what's up with you?'

'You mean generally, or why did I come to see you?'

'Both.' She opens a drawer, removes a small sample bottle of Scope, washes some around in her mouth and spits it into the sink. 'Well?'

Trina begins to describe her symptoms. The forgetfulness. Loss of ambition. Paralysis. She tries not to exaggerate, but as she listens to herself it all sounds so lame, so wimpy. She's worried that Whitney will think she's a whiner.

But Whitney listens carefully, her attention focused on every word Trina says. She has always been that way, since they were college roommates. Trina doesn't have a regular doctor, except her gynecologist. Whenever there's any other kind of medical problem she comes directly to Whitney, despite her friend's specialty in pediatrics. Seven years ago, Whitney wasn't even a doctor. She was a socialite. A tennis-playing, party-throwing member of the elite with a B.A. in art history. She'd married right out of college, a man who was darkly handsome, sexy, and wealthy. He bought her an expensive house in Big Canyon and gave her the full-time job of hostess. They vacationed often in exotic places. In her spare time, of which there was plenty, Whiteney enrolled in the occasional art history class at the University of California at Irvine. On a lark, she took the school's aptitude test which revealed that she would make a good physician. She told her husband, suggesting it might be fun to become a doctor. He suggested it would be more fun if she slept with him and his secretary, the three of them together.

After the divorce, Whitney enrolled in medical school, became a doctor, and opened her own practice. Then she married another doctor in the same building, a neurologist who is every bit as handsome, sexy, and wealthy as her former husband. Not that she ever went looking for wealthy men. Somehow they just found her.

'I'm worried,' Trina says. 'Like maybe I have the

Epstein-Barr virus. The symptoms sound the same.'

Whitney smiles and it is as if someone opened a curtain in a dark room. A smile to rival even The Candidate's. Her blond hair is short on the top, teased up into a feathery heap. The sides are long and straight, hugging her neck to her collar. Her figure is as perfect as her face, both of which remain sexy and youthful. Her eyes and mouth are oversized, her nose undersized. The effect is wholesome, doll-like. During college she managed to earn some extra money modeling, though it was not a career she actively sought. A big-time fashion photographer on campus for a shoot spotted her kicking a broken vending machine and hired her. Early in their relationship Trina had been jealous of Whitney's spooky good luck. She'd even taken to calling her, instead of Jewish American Princess, Voodoo American Princess. There was no other explanation for her good fortune except the supernatural. But after a while Trina got used to it, realized that it wasn't anything special that Whitney did that brought on this luck. It just was. She had a magic aura, the Midas touch.

'I don't know,' Trina says. 'For a couple days I was even convinced I was pregnant.'

'Did you want to be?'

'Not really.'

Whitney raises a blond eyebrow.

'A little,' Trina admits.

'Your period normal?'

'Yes. But I've been feeling this way for more than a month now. I mean it, Whit, I'm starting to get a little scared.'

'Of what?'

'Jesus, you want me to name the possibilities? AIDS for one.'

Whitney shook her head. 'You're okay there. I ran a blood test on you the last time you were in.'

'You did? You didn't tell me.'

'No, I didn't.'

Trina looks into Whitney's large eyes. She isn't sure whether she should be angry at the invasion of privacy or relieved with the results. She settles for relief. 'What about Epstein-Barr? Do I need tests or something?'

Whitney rolls her stool over to Trina and picks at some bran muffin crumbs on Trina's beige blouse. 'You know better than to wear whites. Not with the way you eat.'

'Are you listening to me, Whitney? I'm goddamn worried here.'

Whitney rolls her stool back against the wall and leans back. She fishes out another cigarette and lights it. 'You're overreacting, Trina. It's probably just stress.'

'Stress. Shit, I could've gotten that much from my mother. I want an expert medical opinion.'

'You're getting one. I'll run a blood test if it'll make you feel better. Hell, I'll get your piss and hair analyzed while I'm at it. But it'll probably come down to the same thing. Tension, stress. You're coming to the end of a long and difficult campaign. Your body's put up with a lot of abuse from you over the past year. Now it sees the end coming and it's starting to limp toward the finish line.'

Trina frowns. This is not the kind of advice she's come for. She wanted to be told that there was a definite physical reason for her body shutting down at times; an identifiable physical ailment with a tricky Latin name they could fight with equally Latin wonder drugs. She did not want to hear that it was all due to her own weak mind, her shortcomings. 'Don't you even want to take my temperature or blood pressure? I mean, it could be Epstein-Barr, right?'

'Yuppie Flu? There are some actual cases of something that may indeed be Epstein-Barr, but it's doubtful you're one of them. Every decade has it own disease, just like its own music or slang, dude. The Fifties had iron-poor blood thanks to "Ted Mack's Amateur Hour" talking about it every week to sell Geritol. Then hypoglycemia, low blood sugar, got blamed for everything. For a while after that it was thyroid conditions quickly followed by PMS. Epstein-Barr is the vogue disease now. There's a whole movement of doctors that blames candida for the problem.'

'Speak English.'

'Candida is a yeast that lives on the body's mucous membrane. The next medical witch-hunt will probably be after the human B-cell lymphotropic virus, HBLV, a member of the ever-growing, ever-fun herpes family, like Epstein-Barr.'

'Maybe I have herpes.'

'Have you had any lesions, itching, burning while you urinate?'

'No. What about myasthenia gravis?'

'Where'd you hear about that?'

'Magazine. Some soap star has it.'

'That's a neuromuscular disease. You don't have it.' Whitney smiles. 'Sorry, you're clean. You need to slow down, but I know you won't, not until the campaign is over. Meantime, delegate responsibilities to others. Don't go looking for crises. You used to get this way every semester during finals, don't you remember?'

'No, I don't. I remember studying my ass off while you barely glanced at a book.'

'I had an easier major.'

Trina shakes her head. 'What happened to the good old days when doctors always had a disease or two they were ready to pin you with. And of course a prescription to cure it.'

'I can give you tranquilizers if you want. They might take the edge off.'

'No, I need my edge to get through this.' Trina picks up the twisted wire hanger and twists it more. 'Next time, though, I expect a lot more medical mumbo jumbo. Instrument trays, rubber hammers on my knees, the whole bit. You're not the only pediatrician in the book you know.'

Whitney laughs, the cigarette smoke chugging out of her mouth. 'Look in the book next year and you won't find my name either.'

'What do you mean?'

'I'm thinking of going back to school.'

'Christ, Whit, why?'

'That's what Micky asks.' Micky is her husband. Whitney drags in another lungful of smoke and blows it out while fluttering her tongue against her lips. It sounds like the rotor blades of a helicopter. 'Crash and burn, baby,' she says. She stares at the glowing tip of the cigarette. 'Okay, here's the punch line. Ready? I'm going back to become —drum roll, please—a *psychiatrist*.'

Trina hops up onto the examination table. She scoots back a little and the movement tears the white hygiene paper that runs the length of the table. 'A psychiatrist, huh?'

'You say it as if it's a moral crime.'

'I'm just surprised. I thought you liked being a pediatrician.'

'What makes you think that?' The cigarette is only half-smoked, but she stubs it out on the inside rim of the trash can. 'I hate smoking, but I still do it.'

Trina is truly surprised. She has watched Whitney with her young patients, seen her stop a sobbing toddler's tears, comfort child and parent alike. 'I'm shocked, Whit. Really. I thought you were so good at this.'

'I am good at it. Damn good. I just don't like it. The aptitude tests tell you what you'll be successful at, not what you'll enjoy.'

'Will you enjoy being a psychiatrist?'

'It beats getting puked on by a five-year-old who's just

344

swallowed a bunch of live grasshoppers. Besides, the mal-practice insurance is cheaper.

Trina twists the hanger some more, trying to restore it to its original shape and purpose. 'What about Micky?'

'Micky supports whatever decision I make. He's a doll, Trina. It's just hard for him to understand my ambivalence. He wanted to be a doctor from the time he was eight and examined little Marcy Gruber in the garage. He worked his way through med school bussing tables in the cafeteria. I breezed through on a generous divorce settlement, driving to classes from my condo. He borrowed up the kazoo to open his practice, worked days and nights, moonlighting in emergency rooms to buy equipment. I waltzed in with enough money to start free and clear. I've been successful here from day one. He's never said so, but I can tell he's irritated by my luck.'

'I know I am,' Trina says.

Whitney smiles. 'You're just like him. You think I owe my luck something. Neither of you understands because you both know what you like and you like doing it. I envy your passion. I'm just good at things I don't care about.' She gets up off her stool and takes the gnarled coat hanger from Trina's hands. She dumps it in the trash can. 'You know the one thing I did in my life that I really enjoyed?'

'Yeah, screwing Gordon Effrem in our dorm room while I was in the other bed pretending to be asleep.'

'Gordon thought you were, that's what counted.'

Trina laughs. 'Okay, other than that, what did you most enjoy?'

She looks overhead at the ceiling. 'I expect hidden alarms to go off when I say this, but I most enjoyed being a hausfrau. I feel like some redneck shit saying that. But I mean it, Trina. I liked staying at home, planning menus, playing tennis, discussing having children. Yeah, we were going to have kids. One anyway.'

345

'What about you and Micky?'

Whitney shrugs. 'We talk about it and talk about it, but I think the mood may have passed me. I've decided I'm more the aunt type. Like with Karyn. I love seeing her and talking to her, but I'm probably just as happy to be leaving her at your place.'

'And sometimes I wish you'd take her along.'

'You don't mean that.'

Trina nods. 'Sometimes. But not most of the time.'

Whitney opens a drawer and removes the little sample bottle of Scope. She rinses her mouth again and spits into the sink. 'Some psychiatrist I'd make, huh? A patient comes to me and I do all the complaining.'

'You're entitled.'

'I'll remind you of that when you get my bill.'

'Doesn't matter, I never pay them anyway.'

Whitney puts her arm around Trina's shoulder and squeezes. 'Listen, you take it a little easier for the next couple months and see if those symptoms don't back off.'

'And if they don't?'

'Then you come back here and I'll send you upstairs to Micky for some tests. He thinks you're pretty sexy stuff anyway and would love an excuse to get you naked.'

'Well, that insight will certainly help me relax the next time I see him.'

Whitney laughs. 'What do you think, doctors have no sex drive? When I was a resident, I had to examine a few naked men that got my pulse up to the danger zone.'

Whitney walks Trina out to her private exit. 'Remember, take it easy. You can't be everything to everybody. A career's just a job you've had for a long time. Being good at it doesn't make you a slave to it. There's more out there. Christ, there'd better be. You want children, have children. Change isn't always bad. Don't be afraid of change.' She stops suddenly and Trina can see that

346

Whitney's out of breath. Whitney smiles an odd, troubled smile. 'Say, who are we talking about here, anyway?'

Trina avoids the freeway because last night there was another freeway shooting. A red Gremlin was tailgating a pickup truck. The truck driver fired a .32 slug into the Gremlin's hood. The driver was not injured. She takes Wilshire Boulevard instead where the drivers are crazy but mostly unarmed.

She cruises the parking lot at City Hall until she finds Carla Bennington's space. The other City Council spaces are packed tight with their dark and shiny city-supplied Oldsmobiles. Carla's space is occupied by her own little blue Ford Pinto which she has been driving for ten years. Not accepting a car from the city because it was frivolous government spending earned her a lot of positive publicity. So did her insistence on owning a made-in-America car and her fiscal conservative attitude symbolized by driving the same car for ten years. Trina smiles at the sight of the small perfectly preserved Pinto dwarfed between the larger Oldsmobiles. By driving that car she'd managed to convey her campaign philosophy with more impact than if she'd made a dozen speeches outlining her fiscal policies.

Trina admires the woman's savvy. Carla is shrewd, but she is also vulnerable. During an economic slump, being the incumbent sometimes backfires, especially on a minority or woman. No matter how good a job that person has done, citizens become restless and dissatisfied with their lives. They want change: divorce, new jobs, fresh leaders. When the incumbent is a minority or woman, the voter figures he's done his social duty, now it's time to get back to basics. Time for a white male to set things straight. This attitude is prevalent among minorities as well. Trina's research had shown this pattern to be especially consistent in large sprawling cities like Los Angeles. Carla Bennington is ripe for an ousting this year.

Trina looks at her car clock. If Howdy's information is correct, Carla should be coming out any minute. Then all Trina has to do is follow her to the airport or train station or wherever she is going, buy a ticket to the same destination, find out what she does there, and whether she uses any of her public funds to do it. Hotel bills, theater tickets, anything like that.

Trina opens her purse and finds a couple of loose vitamins among the stamps and paper clips. She pops them into her mouth and swallows them dry. They scratch like lumps of coal all the way down her throat. She feels something strange on her tongue and pulls a long hair out of her mouth. It must have been stuck to one of the vitamins. She rolls open her window and tries to shake it loose from her fingers. No use. Finally she just plasters it against the car door.

A loud gaggle of voices draws Trina's attention back to the building and she sees Carla Bennington hurrying out of the building. She is closely followed by a camera crew headed by local TV anchorman, Griffin Foley. Foley towers over everyone else; he has to stoop a little so the makeup woman can dab at his forehead. Walking beside Carla is Benjamin Logan, her campaign manager. Benjamin is close to seventy and looks and dresses like Spencer Tracy in *Inherit the Wind*. His face is brown and craggy with sailing, his sole passion outside of politics. His hair is buzz cut, white as bleached bones. He wears a belt and suspenders but is always hitching his pants up as if he didn't trust either the suspenders or belt. When Foley approaches, Benjamin steps back in the shadows with a satisfied smile on his lined face. Trina doesn't blame him for smiling. The marathon angle is a sweet one, undoubtedly what they're interviewing her about today.

Even among all those bustling people, Carla Bennington stands out with a certain elegant serenity. Her clothes are hopelessly mismatched, but that only adds to her casual dignity, as if she didn't concern herself with such mundane things while there is a populace to be served. She pushes her long black hair back from her forehead and the two-inch wide streak of gray that ribbons through it gleams like metal in the sun. She still has her bifocals on and Benjamin reaches over and snatches them off her face just as the cameraman sets his position.

Trina watches Griffin Foley ask a few questions which Carla answers briefly and pleasantly. Everyone looks relaxed and friendly. No hard-hitting questions today, just fluff. They must be doing some special feature on sex and politics, otherwise Foley wouldn't be out here in person. The only time he comes out from behind the anchor desk is during ratings sweeps, and even then only if the feature has the word sex in it. Afterward, the cameraman shoots over Carla's shoulder to show Foley nodding. This will later be edited into the interview as if he were listening intently to Carla's answers. Foley looks pleased with himself.

Carla kisses Benjamin on the check and walks quickly toward her Pinto. She seems excited. Benjamin's face looks concerned as he watches her climb into the car. Maybe he doesn't know where she's going either, Trina thinks. The newspeople load the TV equipment into their van. Griffin Foley pulls out a thick cigar from inside his jacket and lights up. Benjamin scowls at Foley and fans the smoke away from his face. Carla waves to Benjamin as she drives past him and out of the parking lot.

Trina follows. She keeps a row of cars between herself and Benjamin Logan as she parallels Carla's car through the lot then pulls out behind her into traffic. She stays a couple of cars behind. Her stomach flutters with excitement at the adventurous nature of what she's doing: following an L.A. City Council member to some unknown destination. The intrigue is thrilling. She flashes back on her old reporter days. She was a hell of a news hen back then, back before Karyn was born. A sudden sadness clamps onto her chest and she heaves a great sigh to dislodge it. She conjures up images of Karyn running home from school with gossip about her friends and teachers, the two of them lying in bed Sunday morning watching TV together, or leafing through the same magazine while sharing a bowl of strawberries and ice cream. The sadness is mostly gone now so she refocuses her attention on Carla Bennington's blue Pinto.

After half an hour, Trina realizes that Carla is not heading for the airport or the train station or even home. They drive north on the Hollywood Freeway up into San Fernando Valley. Traffic is sparse so they move along at a fast speed. The speedometer needle floats past 80 mph. The sense of drama at secretly following someone quickly wears off and Trina gets bored as they approach the Grapevine. She turns on the radio, switches around from station to station but finds nothing she wants to hear. She feels squirmy and restless. She opens the glove compartment and pulls out a handful of tapes: *Love Songs of Jim Croce*, Peter Gabriel's *So*, Genesis. She tosses them aside and reaches back into the glove compartment. She finds her Learn Spanish E-Z tapes. There are ten tapes and she's listened to the first six. She sticks number seven in the cassette player. A man's deep voice begins to converse slowly in Spanish. He has a slight lisp, or maybe that's just proper pronunciation. He speaks a phrase, translates it into English, then asks the listener to repeat after him.

'*El omnibus esta veinte minutos tarde*,' he intones. 'The bus is twenty minutes late.' Trina says the sentence with him.

Spanish is the first on her list of self-improvement projects. Next comes French, then Japanese. Also she intends to take piano lessons with Karyn.

Six months ago she started on her self-improvement kick. She determined that no day would go by in which she didn't learn something new about the world that she hadn't known when she'd awakened that day. She read more magazines, biographies, even encyclopedias. She was thinking about taking calligraphy, fencing, maybe tap dancing through extension courses. She hadn't told Barcy or the others about it because she didn't want them to keep asking how things were going when she'd hardly done anything yet but listen to six tapes. She still couldn't remember most of what she heard.

'*Estas zapatos me pinchan los pies*,' he says. 'These shoes pinch my feet.' He says 'pinch' with a whine as if his feet really hurt. Everyone's an actor.

Someone honks a horn and she looks around with a start. She realizes she'd stopped watching the Pinto while she'd been thinking. She looks all around, can't find it anywhere. She pulls into the next lane where she can see better and spots Carla Bennington's Pinto gliding over to the right lane to exit. Trina has to nudge into a small space between a postal truck and a station wagon to be able to make the exit. The man in the station wagon glares at her. She follows the Pinto down the ramp but gets trapped by other exiting cars in the turn-right-only lane while the Pinto turns left. The lights turn red and she has to wait while the Pinto sprints into a Union 76 station.

'*El padre te puede ayudar con tu problema*. The priest can help you with your problem.'

'Not this time he can't,' she says and ejects the tape. She quickly lowers her window and waves at the kid in the idling car next to her. He is fat and smeared with grease, wearing a mechanic's uniform. He is drinking from a Dr.

Pepper can, rapping the can against the steering wheel while he bobs his head to some music. She motions for him to roll down his passenger window. He does and she can hear Prince's 'Purple Rain' blaring between them. He makes an inquisitive face.

'Can you let me in?' Trina shouts. 'I'm in the wrong lane.'

'Huh?' He leans closer but doesn't turn down his stereo.

Trina expects the cars behind her to start honking because she isn't turning right on the red light, but they are all uncharacteristically patient.

Trina repeats her request and the kid nods. 'Sure. Just don't shoot out my windshield, okay?' He laughs and toasts her with his Dr Pepper can.

The traffic light changes and Trina swerves over in front of him. She passes the service station where Carla is pumping gas into her Pinto. Carla is no longer wearing a skirt, panty hose, and pumps. She must have changed them all during the drive, for now she's wearing shorts and sandals. Only the white sleeveless sweater remains from her previous outfit.

Trina pulls into the Chevron station next door and pumps five gallons of unleaded into her car before Carla finishes and climbs back into the Pinto. Trina quickly pays the attendant and jumps into her car. She gets ready to turn left to follow Carla back onto the freeway, but Carla doesn't go to the freeway; she turns right and drives west toward the ocean. Trina follows her to Pacific Coast Highway where they head north again. Trina tries to imagine various scenarios of where the councilwoman is going, who she is going to meet. A young lover, maybe someone on her staff, a beefy married man with a pregnant wife. A daughter she'd had secretly when she was sixteen who was born retarded when the umbilical cord choked her during birth. Trina toys with possibilities as they drive along the scenic highway, the Pacific Ocean spanking the shore.

In San Luis Obispo, Carla Bennington drives the Pinto into the parking lot of an Alpha Beta supermarket. Trina follows her into the store. Carla steers a rickety cart around while Trina trails with a red plastic basket. Occasionally Trina puts a can of something in the basket, olives, cat food, bamboo shoots. Carla, however, knows exactly what she wants. She wheels past the fresh fruits and vegetables to the frozen foods aisle. She opens one of the frosted doors and rummages inside, rearranging cartons, apparently looking for something specific. When she emerges she's holding a quart of ice cream. Next stop is the cookie aisle where she tosses in a bag of peanut butter cookies which Trina recognizes as a brand she buys too. Potato chips are next, then soft drinks, Diet Slice Mandarin Orange. She stops among the magazines and paperbacks and looks them over, picking up a couple of books, reading the back covers, putting them back. Finally she decides on two magazines and a romance novel. Trina can't make out the title, but she can see the woman on the cover in a turbulent red dress held from behind by a man nibbling at her neck. Now there's a secret to topple governments: Councilwoman Bennington Reads Trashy Bodice-Rippers. Except that Trina used to read them too, three a week, until her recent plan for self-improvement. Since then she has given up on novels of any kind in favor of nonfiction. Just the facts, ma'am. Illusion is useless out here, but knowledge could save your life. *El vestido tiene muchos butones*; the dress has many buttons. Never know when that will save your life.

Carla pilots the cart around the corner and heads for the liquor department. She expertly examines several bottles before choosing a bottle of rum.

Aha, Trina thinks. One lost weekend coming up.

Carla wheels through the express line and pays in cash.

Trina sets her red basket down next to the cereal and leaves the store. Carla drives a couple of blocks to a video rental store. Trina waits outside in the car. When Carla comes out with three tapes, she follows her through town to a quaint Victorian bed and board house. Carla parks in front and carries her groceries and tapes inside. Trina parks across the street and watches the door for a while. Maybe whoever she's meeting is already inside, in his own room. Maybe he's one of the half a dozen men who's gone in since Carla checked in. How would Trina know? She shakes her head. God, this is weird. Trina shoves her tape back in the cassette: *El coche por poco me atropella.* The car just missed running over me.

Carla reappears. She stands in front of the house, shades her eyes from the setting sun, squints down the street, and starts walking. Her hair's wet and pulled back into a ponytail. She's changed out of that terrible sleeveless sweater into a T-shirt with an airbrushed giraffe on it, but she still looks disheveled, as if she dresses without ever checking the mirror.

Trina gets out of the car, thumbs a couple of quarters into the meter, and follows Carla on the opposite side of the street. Carla enters Favio's Pizza My Heart. She sits near the window. A teenage waitress sulks by with a hostile glare that could only mean she is family of the owner. A minute later she sets a glass of wine in front of Carla. Carla sips the wine, puts on her bifocals, and begins reading her romance book.

This doesn't make sense, Trina thinks. Where's the hunk? She drives all the way up here, four hours on the road, just to have wine and pizza at Favio's? Must be a hell of a pizza. Maybe he's late, tied up in traffic, making excuses to his sick wife, visiting hours at the home where she abandoned her retarded love child are over for the day. Trina stops speculating and just watches Carla. She

354

eats the pizza with small bites but chews with her mouth a little open. Sometimes she'll seem especially involved in a page and stop in mid-chew while she reads. Her glasses slip down on her nose and she raises a finger to push them back but sees the pizza grease all over it and uses her wrist instead. She finishes her wine and orders another glass.

Trina is standing on the street, pretending to browse in the window of a hardware store. She tries to show interest in the beach chairs, Smashball paddles, ice chests, and sun visors, but after a while it loses its magnetism.

'Hi,' the voice behind her says. Carla Bennington's voice.

Trina's heart bolts out of its mooring and tries to escape up her throat. She swallows just in time to send it back down into her chest. But it cowers there, trembling. Trina turns around and faces Carla Bennington. 'Hello.'

'We met at City Hall, remember? Howdy White introduced us.'

'Yes. How are you?' Trina pumps confident energy into her voice, offers her hand.

They shake.

Carla smiles without saying anything. She has a cardboard pizza box under her arm. 'How was the drive?'

'The drive?'

'The drive here. I tried not to lose you. Almost did at the off ramp though. You must have been distracted.'

Trina doesn't know what to say. Denying it would only add stupidity to incompetence. Her skin shrivels with embarrassment, but she tries not to show anything. 'I was involved in my language tapes. Trying to learn Spanish.'

'*Sentirse pequeño o insignificante.*'

'I'm not that far along. What's that mean?'

'To feel small.' Her gaze is steady, amusement in her blue eyes. Trina nods. 'Yeah, that's the feeling all right.'

Carla hands her the pizza box. 'Here, this is for you.

I'm going back to my room for the rest of the evening. If you intend to watch my room you're going to get hungry.'

Flabbergasted, Trina accepts the box.

'Say hi to Cory for me. Tell him better luck next time.' She walks away.

'It wasn't his idea. It was mine.'

Carla stops, looks back at Trina. Looks her over from head to toe. 'You must feel pretty clammy in that suit after a hot day like this. Even James Bond takes an occasional break. Come on.'

'Where?'

'My room. You can look it over, check under the bed, in the closet. Then you can either drive back home and get a good night's sleep, or you can camp outside my room all night waiting for the secret lover who isn't coming. I'll introduce you to Lily, she owns the place. She'll show you my bills and my charge slip on my personal American Express card. No public funds are misused. Any other scenarios you had in mind?'

'A long-abandoned illegitimate child, retarded from birth when the umbilical cord choked off her air.'

'Right. Stashed in a home under an assumed name.'

'Something like that.'

Carla laughs. 'Sorry, no such luck.'

Trina shrugs. 'Desperation.'

'You don't need anything else. I saw that new mailer. Talk Is Cheap. That was very clever. Your idea?'

'Yes.'

'You've run a hell of a campaign. I think Cory has a good shot at my job.' Carla starts walking back toward the bed and board house.

Trina falls into step beside her, still carrying the pizza box. She reaches under the lid, tears off a piece of pizza and eats. 'You don't seem too nervous about our chances.'

'I'm realistic. It'll be a photo finish. Cory is a good man, key word here being man. As enlightened as we all like to think we are these days, all other qualifications being equal, a man still has the edge in politics. We prefer the father to the mother in such matters.'

Trina feels creepy and guilty, like the hangman walking the condemned to the gallows, chatting about his newborn baby. She keeps munching the pizza to keep from having to talk and feel worse. They arrive at the house and Carla opens the door for Trina, but Trina doesn't go in.

'I'm not going to search your room,' Trina says. 'I already feel like an ass, no need to feel like a shit too. I think I'll just head back home.'

'Okay.'

'Listen, I'm sorry about all this. I used to be a reporter. I think I just got caught up in the Watergate syndrome.'

Carla smiles. Her smile can't touch The Candidate's. His is life-giving, a small sun radiating warmth and light. Hers crinkles her eyes so the lines bunch up at the corners. The teeth are small and even except for one on the bottom that is crowded a little forward. She looks like a little girl who's just walked into a surprise party. When the smile fades her face rearranges to that of an attractive woman with brains and humor. The contrast of expressions surprises Trina.

Carla reaches into her purse and pulls out a tissue. She steps toward Trina and wipes her cheek. 'I don't know how you managed to get pizza sauce all the way over there.' She shows Trina the red smudge on the tissue.

'Red badge of carnivore. I'm going to devour the rest of this pizza on the ride home. It won't be a pretty sight.'

Carla laughs and wipes tomato sauce from Trina's lapel. 'If the police stop you they'll search the car for a body.'

Trina nods and starts to walk away. She waves good-bye, stifles a yawn. She turns back to Carla, who is just entering the house. 'Listen, maybe this is against the Geneva

Convention or something, but I wonder if you'd let me take a quick shower. I don't think I can stay awake for the four-hour drive back.'

'Five or six hours,' Carla says. 'Rush-hour traffic.'

'Great.'

Carla crooks her head for Trina to follow. They go inside the house and up the winding stairway to the second floor. The banister is highly polished. The hallway walls have dark wainscoting and thick salmon wallpaper.

'This place is gorgeous,' Trina says.

'Isn't it? I've been coming here for years. Actually, since my divorce. Right afterwards I needed to get away from lawyers and my husband and daughters. They were all being terrific, there was no hostility or anything, I just needed to be alone.'

Trina nods. 'I went to San Diego after my divorce. Took my daughter to the zoo every day for three days. Finally she begged me not to take her the fourth day. I don't know, there was just something about the place that made me relax.'

'The caged animals?' Carla kids.

'The anonymity. The crowds of people looking at all those animals, reading signs about how they behave, no one caring about other humans for a couple hours. Fuck the starving masses, refugees from political torture, screw the plight of the farmer. And the hell with your divorce too. You know what I mean?'

Carla unlocks her room door and they enter. 'The bathroom's over there. Don't be shy about the towels, there are plenty.'

'Thanks. Nice digs, Councilwoman.'

'Fuck the homeless,' she says.

Trina laughs and so does Carla, both looking a little naughty, as if they'd just scrawled something nasty on the stall in the girls' lavatory.

Trina goes into the bathroom and closes the door. She strips off her wine-colored jacket, its double-breasted rows of gold buttons gleaming in the mirror. She steps out of the pleated skirt and hangs both on the hook behind the door. The panty hose are next, then the bra. She turns on the shower, but the water is cold. She holds her hand in the stream and feels it slowly turn warm, but far from hot. While waiting for the water to heat up, she stares at herself in the mirror over the sink. Thick billows of steam from the shower curl around behind her like angel wings. The image makes her laugh. St. Trina on a heavenly mission to expose corrupt politician's umbilical-strangled retarded child, hostage to ambitious career. Jesus Christ, Trina, she thinks, shaking her head. She picks up the red toothbrush from next to the sink and stares at it a moment before replacing it. She nudges it a few times to make sure it is exactly where it was. There is nothing else personal in the bathroom. Nothing to spy on.

Trina looks at her breasts' reflection. They are so big they look unreal. The stretch marks are etched in acid. The nipples are circled by tiny bumps that look like pimples. Perfectly normal, but guys always seem to recoil a little when they first see them in the light. This body has no right to be investigating the body of a woman who can run marathons.

She steps into the shower and lets the hot water punish her skin. The magazines warn against hot water, especially against the face. Water ages skin. Trina sticks her face into the shower stream. She soaps herself, underarms, neck, pubic area. She remembers The Candidate in the shower, clamped behind her, his penis crammed deep inside her. And Jamison Levy, the journalist, blow-drying his sheets. She laughs and water from the shower rains into her mouth. She spits it out. Nice men. All the men she's slept with are nice. Some wanted to marry her. Some didn't.

They all seemed to expect something from her and she didn't know what it was. Some seemed to find it with her, others seemed disappointed when they didn't. It was all very intuitive, no one could articulate it, find words to match the feelings. She doubted these men even consciously knew it. Rob had found it with her but later accused her of changing, taking it away from him. She never knew what he meant. Trina couldn't imagine marrying again until she discovered what it was they found in her or didn't find.

Trina shuts the water off, sweeps aside the plastic curtain, and climbs out of the shower-tub. She is thankful the mirror is steamed over. She's had quite enough of her body for a while. She wraps a towel around her body and uses a second towel to dry her legs and arms. When she is done she puts her skirt and jacket back on. She balls up the textured cranberry panty hose and stuffs them into her pocket. The pocket bulges like that of an inept shoplifter. She steps into her pumps.

Trina opens the door and walks into the bedroom. Carla Bennington is sitting on the sofa with her legs curled under her, eating a bowl of ice cream. Three peanut butter cookies stick out of the ice cream. The television is on and a magazine is open on her lap. 'So that's your big secret, huh?'

'I couldn't hide it any longer,' Carla says. 'Junk food, junk magazines, junk book, junk TV. I'm a junkie.'

Trina smiles. 'What flavor?'

'Almond praline.'

'The magazines?'

'*People, US, Cosmopolitan.*'

'The videos?'

'*The Magnificent Seven, From Russia With Love, Private Benjamin.*'

Trina walks over next to the sofa and sees Steve

McQueen talking with Yul Brynner on the TV. 'This is the kind of information that can ruin you, you know?'

'I was counting on the kindness of strangers. That and a bribe.' She points her spoon at the mini-refrigerator next to the dresser.

Trina opens the refrigerator and pulls out the carton of ice cream. She uses the plastic spoon on top to scrape some into the paper bowl. She also grabs a handful of peanut butter cookies. 'I don't come cheap.' She sits on the sofa next to Carla and they watch the movie in silence, eating ice cream, crunching cookies. This is as relaxed as Trina has felt in a long time.

'I don't usually come up here during the week,' Carla says as Charles Bronson chops wood in exchange for breakfast. 'But I campaigned all weekend on the rubber chicken circuit, and then the photo session for the marathon, I just had to get away for one night. At home I feel compelled to answer the phone. Here I don't.'

Trina spoons ice cream into her mouth and squashes it against the roof of her mouth with her tongue. The cold dripping down her throat feels good. 'I feel funny.'

Carla looks alarmed. 'You mean sick?'

'No, I mean funny creepy. Coming up here like some dime-store spy going through your underwear or something. Then you're so nice.'

'I feel a testimonial coming on. I hope this comes with a watch.'

Trina laughs. 'Christ, you are tough, aren't you?'

'Yes, I am. It's no act, no I-am-woman-hear-me-roar crap. I was three. My mother raised seven kids, five of her own and two of her sister's when she and her husband were killed in a car crash. Even today I'm closer to my cousins than to my own brothers and sisters. Maybe I empathized more with their being orphans. I always wanted to be an orphan.'

361

'My parents wanted me to be an orphan too. Except they didn't want to die, so we were at a standoff.'

Carla pushes the magazines off her lap, sets her bowl on the arm of the sofa, and gets up. 'A tough woman is like a mutant breed in most people's eyes. Like a five-legged dog, three-eyed cat. The extra appendage is unusual, even fascinating, but basically unnecessary. A freak of nature.' She laughs. 'Sometimes I even agree.'

'So you come up here to mellow out.'

Carla stoops beside the bed and opens the night table cupboard door. 'The council meets three days a week. Two days a week I spend on district work. I have two district offices I have to watch over. I'm on the Planning and Environment Committee which is trying to rezone two hundred thousand parcels of land. Our meetings sometimes go on for six hours at a time. Fridays is zoo day, when we honor the local citizens with awards of merit. Each one wants a photo of them with the council. Saturday is walk day, during which I walk my district to hand out campaign literature.' She stands up and holds up the bottle of rum Trina saw her buy. It hasn't been opened yet. 'Talk about mellowing out.'

'What about all those rich glamorous guys you date?' Trina tries to keep the envy out of her voice. 'Don't they help mellow you a little?'

Carla grins. 'Sometimes we mellow a little together.'

'Don't you want someone to mellow with permanently?'

'Don't you?'

Trina shrugs. 'Sure. I've just gotten pickier as I've gotten older. I have a mental list of what they can and cannot do. Every year my list of Can'ts grows longer and pickier. Can't use double negatives. Can't like movies with subtitles.'

'Can't brush their teeth right after sex.'

'Can't use the phrase "woman's perspective."'

362

'Yes!' Carla says. 'That's on my list. Can't have a large dog.'

'Can't have season tickets to the Dodgers.'

Carla laughs. 'We should type these up and compare with other women. We could have a checklist to hand out to prospective dates.'

'I don't know,' Trina says. 'A lot of my friends' lists of Can'ts are getting smaller. It's like when you're in college, there aren't any can'ts. Except you can't be hideous or carry a slide rule in your pocket. Then you go out in the world, you're young and sexy and in demand, so you can afford to start your list of Can'ts. Then you get older, married, divorced, have kids, your butt looks like a quilt, you can't afford to have much of a list of Can'ts anymore.'

Carla opens the refrigerator and takes the carton of ice cream out. She brings it and the rum back to the sofa and sits down. She pours a little rum over the ice cream. 'Try this,' she says and pours some over Trina's ice cream.

'Hey, you got some on the cookies.'

'You'll like it. Trust me.'

Trina scoops a spoonful of ice cream and rum and eats it. 'Whoa!'

'Good, huh?'

'Yeah, I think.' She eats another spoonful.

'I always hated booze,' Carla says. 'Which made it tough when you're growing up trying to appear sophisticated and worldly. You tell your date you don't drink and they think you're a goddamn Quaker. Naturally they equate drinking with sex.'

'"Doesn't drink" equals "doesn't put out." The mathematics of dating.'

'Exactly. But I found I could tolerate rum and Coke, so that became my standard drink. After a while, I even got to really like it. A guy I used to date, some state senator,

363

really took his booze seriously. He introduced me to a flip.'

'Sounds painful.'

Carla pours a little more rum on her ice cream. Trina takes the bottle and pours more on hers too. She stirs her peanut butter cookie in the mix and eats it.

'A flip is a drink from back in the seventeen hundreds. It's a combination of rum, ale, and whipped egg whites that was seared with a red-hot poker.'

'Yikes.' Trina laughs.

'Back then American rum was shipped to Africa and traded for slaves. The slaves were then shipped to the Caribbean where they were traded for molasses, which was shipped to New England to be distilled into rum.'

'So we're eating a piece of history here,' Trina says.

'Damn right. Most of today's rum comes from Puerto Rico.' She holds up the rum bottle. 'Bacardi Silver Label. This stuff. But there are some exceptional rums. Dark rums aged in Limousin oak casks. Great stuff.'

Trina finishes the ice cream and cookies and stares at James Coburn shooting a man off a horse from half a mile away. 'Great shot,' Trina says.

'I was aiming at the horse,' James Coburn complains.

Carla and Trina laugh.

They talk through the rest of the film. When the movie ends, they stick in another cassette, *From Russia with Love*, though they talk through that too. During their conversation, they pass the rum bottle back and forth.

'Don't worry,' Trina says, handing Carla the bottle, 'these sores on my mouth are almost gone.'

Carla laughs, tries to drink, laughs again, finally takes a swig, almost choking on it as she breaks out laughing again. A few drops of rum spray onto Trina's skirt.

'Hey,' Trina says, 'I already showered.'

'In ice cream it looks like.' Carla licks the end of a paper napkin and scrubs the dried ice cream spots fron Trina's skirt.

'Someday I'm going to have to learn to eat neater.'

'Or wear rubber pants.'

'I've already been made that offer by one guy.'

Carla laughs again. Her long hair falls forward, the silvery gray streak covering one eye. She laughs so hard that she drops the napkin, which rolls down Trina's skirt and lands on the floor. Trina and Carla both lean over to retrieve the napkin and bonk their heads together with a thunk. Both stagger back from the impact.

'Shit,' Trina says. 'That hurt.'

Carla rubs her forehead. 'I hope it doesn't bruise. That'll be a tough one to explain to reporters. Tipsy Candidate Knocks Heads With Rival Campaign Manager.'

'Actually, I'm just PR. Mary and Warren are the campaign managers.' Trina brushes Carla's hair from her forehead and pushes her hand away. 'It's a little red, but it won't bruise.'

'My God,' Carla says, looking at Trina. 'You've got an egg.' Trina gingerly touches her forehead and feels the lump. 'Doesn't feel too sore.'

'That's because you're drunk.'

'I'm not drunk.'

'You're drunk,' Carla insists. 'I should know.'

'Why?'

''Cause I'm drunk.'

'Oh,' Trina says.

Carla goes to the ice bucket and brings back a few cubes. Water drips between her fingers onto the carpet and sofa. She presses one against the lump. Carla's other hand is cupped behind Trina's head, to hold it steady while she applies the ice. She is so close Trina can feel her breath against her cheek. Trina closes her eyes and lets Carla rub the ice around the bruise. As the cube melts, cold water

365

drips down her brow and eyes and cheek. The drops collect at the corner of her mouth and she licks them.

Suddenly she feels lips pressed against her lips. She opens her eyes and Carla is staring into her eyes, her lips still kissing Trina. Trina doesn't know what to do. Carla is still holding the ice cube to her forehead, the other hand behind her neck. The lips feel soft and wet. They aren't grinding against her, there is no tongue prying them apart. Just lips. Full soft lips a little like Karyn's.

Carla pulls away. She looks flustered. 'I've never done that before.'

They don't say anything. The ice in Carla's hand has melted. She walks over to get more, brings the bucket back. 'That's not entirely true. When I was eight the girl next door tried to teach me how to kiss boys. She was nine.'

Trina doesn't know what to say or do. She can't move. She wipes some of the melted water from her face and is surprised at how hot her skin feels. She looks at the TV. Sean Connery is kissing a woman on a train. Robert Shaw bursts in and tries to kill him. Love is dangerous.

'This is weird,' Carla says, shaking her head as if coming out of a long coma.

'I guess you were right. We are drunk.'

'That's what I said.' Carla hands her an ice cube from the bucket. Trina holds it against her lump. Carla pulls her own hair back from her face and clutches it in a severe ponytail. She stares at the TV too.

'God, he was sexy,' Trina says as Sean Connery slams Robert Shaw against the wall.

'I think he's sexier now, bald and all.'

Trina can still taste Carla's lips on her own, feel the imprint. She picks up the rum bottle and takes a swig. It is almost empty. 'Hair of the dog,' she says.

Carla nods, her eyes fixed on the TV.

Trina puts the bottle down, tosses the ice into the bucket. She leans over and kisses Carla. Carla doesn't move. She closes her eyes and then Trina does too. The kiss is the same kind as before. Chaste. Lips snuggled against lips. Soft and yielding. Trina leans away and they are both breathing faster.

'What do you expect me to do?' Carla asks.

'I don't know. Maybe we should yell fag or something. Maybe that would sober us up.'

'You want to go further?'

Trina shakes her head. 'I don't think so. You?'

'No. This is what I imagined it would feel like to try heroin or something. The guilt and danger pumping my heart.'

Trina is angry. 'I didn't bring photographers if that's what you're thinking.'

'I didn't mean that. Calm down.'

They sit there not looking at each other. The film ends and Carla sticks in *Private Benjamin*. 'I saw this at a benefit screening with Goldie Hawn. I can't remember what we were benefiting, isn't that terrible?'

'Criminal.'

They look at each other and somehow they are kissing again. Trina doesn't really feel as if she is the one sitting there kissing another woman. She feels like a spy witnessing the whole thing from her hiding place in the rafters. Mentally she snaps photos with her miniature spy camera made to look like a cigarette lighter. She will study them later, figure out how two such nice people could have fallen to such depraved depths. She knows that it is not really her sitting here on the sofa hugging this woman, pressing lips together, feeling some tongue now, accepting it into her mouth. She knows it's not her because she would feel worse than she does. Trina would be horrified. Gay rights

367

is fine in general principle, but the act itself is disgusting. Yet she is not disgusted.

While Goldie Hawn marches in circles in the rain, they make their way to the bed. They strip each other naked. Carla's body is much firmer than Trina's and she feels a little embarrassed as Carla unfastens Trina's bra and those huge boulders plop out. Trina is not aroused by the sight of Carla's naked body; she is more curious. Like a child at a petting zoo. The soft touch of Carla's hand on her hip, the fingers on her cheek, the lips against her neck. They touch something that quickens Trina's heart.

Neither touches the other's breasts or pubic area. They stroke each other's back and legs and buttocks. They cling to each other and kiss. Trina feels Carla's smaller, firmer breasts squash against her own. She thinks hers might actually swallow Carla's like giant sponges. Carla's hand is holding firm to Trina's hip, not moving up or down.

After a while they break apart and look at each other. They both laugh.

'I feel like a clumsy kid in a crystal shop,' Carla says.

'You touch it, you bought it,' Trina agrees.

'Silly.'

'We've come this far, I guess we might as well go the rest of the way.'

Trina nods. It's funny to be talking so casually to someone you're having sex with. Not that she wasn't casual with Rob when they were married or with the other men she's slept with. But the casualness seemed a little forced, like they were both trying to prove that sex was no big deal. No commitment. No contest.

She feels Carla's lips on her breast, the tongue lapping the nipple. She watches Carla lick her. Carla looks up and smiles with Trina's nipple between her teeth.

She closes her eyes as Carla moves to the other breast. What does this all mean? That she's a lesbian? She read

368

an article somewhere that psychiatrists had a convention and agreed that one homosexual episode after you're an adult means you're gay. But if she were gay, why didn't she ever lust after any other women? Maybe she should discuss this with Whitney. If she is gay, how will she explain that to Karyn?

Carla drags her tongue down Trina's stomach. Trina peeps at her and sees Carla looking at her spread apart legs. She is studying her vagina like a first-time swimmer told to dive into the pool. Slowly she lowers her head and Trina feels the tongue gently stroking. Carla's hand presses against Trina's pubic hairs. The tongue flicks over the clitoris and Trina's hips spasm suddenly. The intensity of her reaction surprises her. Carla continues and Trina's breathing becomes rapid and shallow. She looks down at Carla and sees her looking back, her chin slicked and shiny. Then both close their eyes.

Trina feels it coming like a locomotive rushing up each leg heading for a collision at her crotch. Carla is using no special technique. The difference is that Trina doesn't have to think about when to say 'slower' or 'gentler' or 'faster' or 'here' or 'there.' Carla just does it and Trina can lie back and feel the locomotives chuffing at 200 mph along her inner thighs, roaring toward each other with whistles screaming, neither willing to give an inch, until finally Trina bucks up at the impact. Twisted hot steel flying everywhere. Steam billowing. Trina crying out like a wounded survivor.

Then it was Carla's turn.

Trina wakes when the toilet flushes. She sits up and sees Carla coming out of the bathroom wearing her running clothes. 'What time is it?'

'Five in the morning.'

Trina rubs her eyes. 'What's going on?'

'Training. I have a marathon coming up. I need the publicity if I'm going to beat your Cory Meyers.'

Trina nods. 'Right. Cory.'

'Besides, I have to get back to L.A. Today's one of my district days. Glad-handing local merchants. Tell them how I'm going to get more customers into their stores.'

Trina looks around the rooms. She sees her clothes neatly arranged on the sofa. The rum bottle is gone, the ice cream debris is gone. Everything is neat and tidy. It is almost as if last night didn't happen. 'We aren't going to talk about it?' Trina asks.

'If you want to.'

'I don't know. I feel funny. Like I should rush right out and seek counseling or something.'

'Before it spreads.'

Trina laughs. 'Something like that. How do you feel?'

Carla lifts her leg onto the back of the sofa and stretches her hands out to touch her toes. She holds this position while she talks. 'Guilty. I never thought anything like that would ever happen to me. I mean, I'm not gay.'

'Yeah, that's what I feel.'

'Still, we did it. So what does that make us?'

'Maybe we shouldn't worry about what that makes us and wonder what we got out of it.'

'Sex.'

'Sure. Anything else?'

Carla smiles. 'You're not going to send me flowers and promise you'll call next week, are you?'

Trina frowns. 'You don't want to talk. Go ahead and run.'

'What's there to talk about? Do you want me to jump in bed and start in again?'

Trina thinks that over. 'No. Not that I'd mind, I guess. I didn't last night. But I think what I really want right now

370

is for us to have breakfast together and talk, not about this. Just talk. Like last night.'

Carla frowns. 'I have to train.' She goes to the door and opens it. She looks back with a grim expression. 'By the way, I told you I was tough. If you intend to use this episode to help Cory, I have some photos of you and he leaving the Travel Lodge together. And a few telescopic shots of you after your water sports. Grainy, but clear enough.'

Trina stares at her. 'You are tough, Carla.'

Carla's eyes lower a second, then return Trina's stare. 'I told you that.' She leaves, closing the door behind her.

Trina sighs. 'The miniseries of my life.'

25

The pain is exquisite.

Like a syringe needle jabbing into the bottom of her foot. Her mouth snaps open so wide her ears pop. The second burning jolt hits her so quickly, so unexpectedly, she's not sure whether she is feeling pain or pleasure. It is like standing knee-deep in the surf with your back to the ocean and suddenly being attacked by a wave. There's a thrilling rush of excitement at impact, a moment when the pleasure of the cool water enveloping you is flash-burned away by the fear that the wave may also pick you up, flip you over, and smash you headfirst into packed sand, leaving you with a fused spine and a lifetime in a squeaking wheelchair. Diva is surprised that she has time to think such thoughts as she falls. She drops to the ground, landing hard on her butt. Sand grinds into the lip of pink skin that protrudes from the bottom of her swimming suit. Her ankle is already swollen grotesquely. The mutant blue skin puffs like an inflatable pillow. The pain is a steady throb now, the syringe needle has been replaced by a rusty corkscrew being cranked into her ankle.

'Fuck, man,' Coma says. He stoops down beside her, the volleyball tucked under his arm. 'You okay?'

'It's sprained,' Diva says.

Coma nods at the information. Sand from his hair sprinkles across Diva's thighs. He presses a finger against the swelling, leaving a white moon imprint that quickly evaporates. He stands up and offers her his hand. She takes it and he yanks her to her feet with a powerful jerk that almost sends her flying past him. She hops on one foot off the volleyball court over to her beach chair and collapses in it. The two guys on the other side of the net haven't moved. Coma is also still standing on the court. They watch her hop to her beach chair, open Coma's cooler, remove some of his ice, and press it against her ankle.

'You okay?' Coma repeats.

'Yeah, I'm fine. Go ahead.'

Coma looks down the beach at the other net. A game is going on there between Cliff and Bart and two guys whose names Diva can't remember. 'Hey, Bart,' Coma shouts. 'I need a partner.'

Bart is about to receive a high serve. When he hears Coma's voice, he catches the ball and drops it onto the sand. Immediately he runs over to this net and stands beside Coma. The three guys at the other net grab some surfer kid who was watching them play to fill in for Bart. They aren't mad at Bart, Diva knows, because it's an honor to play with Coma.

Diva sighs as the ice melts around her ankle. Just her luck, spraining her ankle before her first date with Harley Buss. She grabs more ice from the ice chest and clumps it against her skin. The swelling shrinks back a little. The game continues in front of her. Bart is a harder hitter than she is, but he isn't as steady. His passes and sets are a little sloppy. Coma gets frustrated with him even though the other team has yet to score any points. 'Put me on the net, goddamn it,' Coma scolds Bart.

Diva reaches over to check her watch which is strapped to the handle of her beach bag. 'Shit,' she says, reading it. She has just enough time to go home and shower and change before Harley Buss arrives. She's been nervous about this date all day. She'd only come down here to play a couple of games and work off that nervousness, maybe sweat off a couple of extra pounds before he saw her. Now she is going to limp her way through this date like Piper Laurie in *The Hustler*.

Diva slowly manages to stand, her bad foot cocked back like a flamingo's. She gathers her bag and beach chair and starts hobbling clumsily back to her apartment.

Coma, about to serve the ball, looks at her. 'You okay?'

'Just a sprain,' she assures him.

He nods and serves the ball.

'Hi,' Harley Buss says.

Diva greets him at the door wearing her lucky sand dollar earrings, though she can't remember why she considers them lucky. She is also wearing black silk pants that hide her pouchy belly under a billow of pleats, a beige silk blouse with a Nehru collar, and red pumps for a hint of passion. Her panty hose are also black to hide the elastic ankle brace. She feels dressed for deception, hiding more than she is revealing. He is wearing a beige sports jacket, a cobalt blue polo shirt, and khaki pants. He is carrying flowers.

'Flowers,' she says, taking them. 'I haven't gotten flowers on a date since the prom.'

'I'm very traditional,' Harley says. 'My mother's waiting in the car to drive us.'

Diva laughs. 'Come on.' She steps out of the way to allow him to enter. She follows him into the living room, taking small steps and trying not to limp. Her ankle aches as if a bear trap is clamped onto it, shredding flesh with each step. She forces a smile and tries not to yelp in pain. He is better looking than she had expected. That makes her even more nervous.

He sits on the sofa and looks around the apartment, studying it like a cop. The poster from *Gandhi* catches his interest. 'Good movie,' he says.

'I never saw it,' she says. 'I just hang the poster as a dieting aid.'

He doesn't laugh, even though she meant it as a joke. *Great, now he thinks I'm dumb and fat.* His eyes scan her bookshelves, where a few lonely volumes sit, most of them popular novels, gifts still unread. He frowns as if he's looked straight into her brain, saw some serious dust bunnies, and now wants to scrub his hands and brush his teeth. He seems to be avoiding looking at her. She's been on blind dates before and recognizes this sympton. It's not good.

'Look,' she says, still holding the flowers. 'I've never been on a blind date before. I don't know how I got the nerve to call you in the first place. But we don't have to do this.'

Harley looks at her directly for the first time but doesn't say anything.

Diva continues, 'What I mean is, if you're disappointed, we don't have to go through with this.' She imagines the svelte stick figures he usually goes out with, young slim students, brilliant teachers like Barcy, executive women with appointment books and no tan lines. 'I'm probably not what you expected.'

Harley nods. 'No, you're not.'

The organs inside Diva jumble to switch places like a Chinese fire drill. Her heart is where her stomach was, her intestines are strangling her lungs. She clutches the flowers to her stomach. 'Well, like I said, we don't have to do this.'

'Okay,' Harley says. He gets up from the sofa and walks down the hallway to the door. 'Nice meeting you.' He walks out and closes the door behind him.

Diva is stunned. She limps to the kitchenette and finds a drinking glass big enough for the flowers. The flowers are a mixed bunch, brightly colored petals with sturdy stems. She can't name them, though. One looks like a marigold, but she's not sure. She fills the glass from the tap, sticks the stems in the water. She thinks about getting an aspirin for the water, but she doesn't want to drag her bad ankle to the bathroom. Besides, she doesn't want these damn flowers to last any longer than they have to. In fact, she doesn't want them around at all. She snatches them out of the glass, water dripping from the steps all over the counter and floor, and throws them into the trash can under the sink. They don't fit so she has to mash them down a little to keep them from spilling out.

'Those were expensive,' Harley says.

Diva looks up and he is standing next to the refrigerator. He shows her the receipt from Conroy's Florists. 'I keep the receipt to everything now. I got audited a couple years ago. That IRS woman told me I kept the worst records, everything from the last twelve years in an old suitcase. She said by the time she got to the bottom of that suitcase she was afraid she'd find Jimmy Hoffa.'

'What are you doing here?'

Harley shrugs. 'We have a date.'

'You left.'

'You got what you deserved,' he says. He goes over to the sofa and sits down exactly where he was before. 'What kind of way is that to start a date? "I'm not what you expected. We don't have to do this." Christ.'

Diva limps to the sofa and sits down next to Harley. 'I'm not what you expected, am I?'

'No.'

'You expected someone prettier, right?'

'Yes.'

'And with a better body?'

Harley nods.

Diva stares at him. 'I hate honesty.' She leans back and lifts her ankle up. 'I sprained my ankle today.'

'How?'

'Volleyball. You play?'

He shakes his head. 'Tennis.'

She lowers her foot back to the floor but continues to stare at it. 'This evening isn't going how I'd hoped.'

Harley gets up, stands directly in front of her. 'I've got an ulcer, hemorrhoids, and herpes. Some of my pubic hairs are gray. My chest hairs are all gray. Sometimes when I play tennis, I cheat; I call balls that hit the line as out. I'm lousy at finances, which is why I live from check to check.' He sits back down next to her. 'There. Feel better?'

'A little.' She looks him up and down. 'Except what am I doing going out with a loser like you?'

'I've never seen gray pubic hairs before,' Diva says.

Harley lifts the sheet and stares at his crotch. 'Distinctive, huh? Looks like Peter Lawford.'

Diva doesn't know who Peter Lawford is. She leans back against the headboard while Harley relights the joint they'd been smoking earlier. He takes a drag and hands it to her. She sucks in a small amount, holds her breath, and looks around his bedroom. There are bookshelves covering an entire wall. The books are hardbound and thick. Many are biographies of writers. She recognizes Poe, Melville, Faulkner, Hemingway. Some names she doesn't recognize —Trollope, Carlyle, Goldsmith—but assumes they must be writers too. On both bedside tables are stacks of books and magazines. The magazines aren't like the ones she reads. They are smaller and plain looking, with names like *Georgia Review, American Scholar, Prairie Schooner*. They have torn snips of paper in them to mark pages.

Diva offers him the joint back, but he refuses. He didn't really smoke much of it earlier either, though he was the one who'd suggested it and brought it out.

'Why don't you have any pictures up?' Diva asks, gesturing with the smoking joint at the bare walls. 'Paintings or posters or something.'

'I haven't found the right ones yet. I have to find the exact right one before I'm willing to put a hole in my wall.'

'How long have you lived here?'

'Three years.'

Three years! Diva sees such pickiness as a bad sign. If he's that finicky about a little hole in the wall, imagine how he must be about a girlfriend. Still, she likes him a lot. Dinner was fun. He took her to a new restaurant that served flowers as entrées. 'I'm determined to give you flowers tonight,' he'd said, 'one way or the other.' She was apprehensive at first, even for a vegetarian, but she ate a salad of hibiscus, day lilies, pansies, fuchsias, nasturtium, and lettuce in a raspberry-hazelnut vinaigrette. Diva had read about such restaurants and people who regularly dined on flowers. She'd read about one new bride whose bridal bouquet was made of edible flowers. After the ceremony she'd tossed the bouquet into the salad.

Suddenly Harley whips the covers off both of them. 'I can't stand it any longer,' he announced loudly. 'I'm starving. Pansies just don't stick to ribs.' He jumps out of bed. 'You care to join me?'

'I did that, remember?'

He grins. 'For food, madam. Real food.'

Diva pinches out the joint and climbs out of bed. She looks around for something to put on. She doesn't like the idea of walking around naked in good lighting in front of him. How long can she stand around sucking in her stomach?

'Come on,' he says and takes her hand.

She hobbles beside him, her only clothing the elastic bandage on her ankle. He puts his arm around her waist to give her support. His fingertips lay against her pouch, which was much less prominent while she was on her back in bed. With her arm around his waist, she can feel his flat hairy stomach.

The kitchen is immaculate. No dirty dishes, no counter stains, no crumbs on the floor. No brown ring around the sink drain. 'Boy, you can clean my house anytime,' she says.

'I have a cleaning lady who comes in once a week. During the week I eat most of my meals out, and those that I eat here I eat off paper plates or standing over the sink. This is the cleanest room in the house.' He opens the refrigerator and takes out a lump wrapped in aluminum foil. He peels it open to reveal chopped meat. He sniffs it, pauses, sniffs again. 'I think it's okay. You game?'

'I'm a vegetarian.'

'Oh, right.' He opens the refrigerator, roots through the drawers, comes out with a zucchini and a suspicious-looking tomato. She frowns at them. 'I can make you some soup,' he says.

She looks at the red meat piled on the foil. Her stomach grumbles with desire. But she is determined to keep control of her life now that she's made some major decisions. She can't ease off anywhere or all the rest of it might crumble in on her. 'Toast would be nice.'

'An English muffin.' He opens a drawer with a built-in bread box, removes two English muffins, pries one apart, and stuffs it into the toaster. The other one he sticks in the toaster oven. 'Sit,' he says, pulling out a chair from the kitchen table. 'I'll take care of everything.'

Diva sits and watches him slap the hamburger meat back and forth between his palms until it is flat. He tosses it in an iron skillet and it smokes and sizzles. While it fries, he sidles up behind Diva and puts his arms around her shoulders. His arms rest just above her breasts. She feels warmed by the gesture. He kisses the back of her neck and she crooks her head to offer him more. 'You'll burn your buns,' she says.

'Bragging?' he says. He takes the muffins out of the toaster and the toaster oven. 'Jam?'

Diva hesitates. Jam suggests she's a pig, gives cause to her lumpishness. Plain, no butter, dry as dust. That's how a skinny person eats. 'Nothing, thanks.'

'Yuk,' he says. He takes a paper plate from the drawer and hands her the muffin on the plate.

'I need to use your phone a second,' Diva says.

'Sure. This one, or if you want privacy, there's one in the bedroom.'

'This is fine.' She dials Dixie's number. There is no answer. Anxiety and guilt squelch any appetite she had. She hangs up the phone.

'No one home?' he asks, lifting the charred burger out of the pan with a spatula.

Diva shakes her head.

'What's the matter? Suddenly you look sad.'

'Worried about a friend. I haven't been able to reach her for a couple days.'

Harley sits down at the kitchen table and begins eating his hamburger. He's poured Catalina salad dressing over it. He nods as he chews. 'Good,' he says, chomping happily away. He offers it to her. She shakes her head again.

They sit silently for a while. Harley stares at Diva, smiling. He looks enormously pleased.

'What?' she asks. 'What are you staring at?'

'You.'

'Didn't we go through this earlier? I already know I'm not what you expected.'

380

'No one is ever what the other expects. Maybe expects is the wrong word here. Hopes is the right one. You didn't look like I'd hoped you'd look.'

'How'd you hope I'd look?'

'Like Kim Basinger. That's how I hope every woman will look. That's what fantasies are all about. I'm sure I didn't look like you'd hoped.'

She tears off a piece of English muffin and eats it. 'Actually, you looked better than I'd hoped.'

Harley looks surprised. 'Really? Who were you expecting, Charles Laughton?'

'Who's that?'

'*Hunchback of Notre Dame*, Captain Bligh opposite Clark Gable.'

'Yeah. He had a wart on his nose or something, looked like a bulldog.'

'That's him.'

Diva nods. 'That's what I was expecting.' She laughs. 'I'm kidding.' She tears off another piece of muffin. 'I just wanted someone nice looking, but not so nice looking that he made me look ugly. There's nothing worse than seeing a real knockout guy walking down a movie aisle with a fat homely woman. Everyone in the audience wonders what they're doing together. They assume she has money or some kind of sick hold over him.'

'That hasn't happened to you, has it?'

'No, I'm the one in the audience who always assumes the fat chick is loaded.'

Harley chuckles. 'I'd like to hear you sing sometime.'

'You already have.'

'When?'

'On your car radio.' She sings to the tune of 'Bali Ha'i': '*Ed Landers' Ford is calling you/Four-oh-five free-way/Harbor Boulevard ex-it/Right away, right away. Landers' Ford, Landers' Ford, Landers' Fooooord.*'

'I've heard that,' Harley says, laughing. 'That's you?'

Diva nods. 'That's me.'

'You have a terrific voice.'

'Well, I do requests. Wanna hear "Hold the Pickle, Hold the Lettuce"? Or how about oldies but goodies: "And flush those troubles down the drain. Roto-Rooter!"'

Harley puts his hamburger down. 'Do I hear a note of irony in your melody?'

She picks up his hamburger and takes a huge bite. At first the meat tastes funny, unfamiliar, almost exotic. Then her taste buds remember and she feels the need for more hamburger, fries with ketchup, a strawberry milkshake. She stops chewing and goes over the the sink and spits the bite out.

He stands up and helps her hobble back to her chair. He reaches down and lifts her sprained ankle to his lap. Then he sits back and asks her questions about her singing, her career, where she is going, what she wants. His sleepy blue eyes stay fixed on hers the whole time, as if he were trying to memorize each word. The intensity of his attention is unusual for Diva, but she finds she likes it. Somehow he even coaxes her into singing what she had written so far of 'Cocktail Waitress.' When she's done, he applauds.

'It's not finished,' she says, both embarrassed and pleased by his reaction.

'You'll finish it. You don't know your own strength.' He get up, arranges her foot gently on his chair, and leaves the room. Diva feels funny sitting at his kitchen table nude, her sprained ankle up on a chair. She is about to go back to the bedroom to get dressed when Harley comes running back into the kitchen with a silver picture frame the size of a record album. She can't see what it is in the frame though. 'I used to write too,' Harley says. 'All through high school and college.'

'What'd you write?'

'Poetry mostly. Some stories.' He holds out the frame to her. 'This is my only publication.'

Diva takes it with reverence, like a sacred text. It is one glossy magazine page mounted on royal red paper. The glass is dusty, the silver frame a little tarnished. 'Is this a story?' she asks.

'Read it.'

Diva begins to read aloud: ' "Dear Penthouse . . ." ' She stops and looks up at him. 'You're kidding?'

He grins. 'Read on.'

' "Dear Penthouse, I never believed any of your letters could be true until this happened to me. I was sitting alone in my dorm room studying for my physics midterm the next day when my roommate's girlfriend, Linda, came in with two of her foxy friends. I told Linda that Biff was out, but she just winked at her friends and they all giggled. They'd just come from cheerleading practice so they were all covered with sweat. I could see the drops beaded on their slender thighs. For some reason, sweaty girls have always turned me on. Then Linda locked the door." ' Diva skims ahead silently as the girls all take off their clothes and seduce the studious physics student.

Harley is leaning over her shoulder now. 'There.' He points at a paragraph near the end. 'That's my favorite line.'

Diva reads it aloud. ' "After fucking her two friends until they'd passed out from pleasure, I was ready to come." ' Diva looks up at Harley. They both laugh.

'That's me: Name and Address Withheld By Request. My first byline.'

'Sweaty girls turn you on?'

'That's just a character I created. Although I do like a certain amount of sweat on a woman at certain times.'

She hands him back the silver-framed letter. 'What about your stories and poetry?'

'Dreadful stuff, really. My writing lacked one ingredient to be successful.'

'Encouragement?'

'Talent. I didn't have any.'

'I don't believe in talent,' Diva says. 'I believe in hard work. You work at something hard enough, they'll eventually call it talent. Nobody can agree on what's good and what isn't, so how are they going to agree on who's talented and who isn't?'

'Barcy's talented.'

Diva's scalp tingles with jealousy. 'She's worked at writing a long time. She deserves her success.' Her voice sounds like a public service announcement. She hopes Harley doesn't notice the pettiness in it.

'I had a student a couple years ago,' Harley says. 'He was a double major, English and computer science. He wanted to program a computer that would be able to judge whether a sample of writing was good or bad. He wanted my advice as to what writers to include as the data base for great writing. His idea was that when he was finished, a writer, instead of agonizing whether or not what they'd written was any good, could just stick the chapter or poem or whatever in the computer scanner. It would read the work, compare it against the samples of great writing, then evaluate it as either good or bad.'

'That sounds awful.'

'Not really. It takes the guesswork out of art. Eventually we could do that with paintings and music. Then we'd only like what was good.'

Diva makes a face. 'You don't believe that, do you?'

'It's a tempting idea. Then writers like me have a chance.'

'You're too hard on yourself. That was a hell of a letter

to *Penthouse*. I'm sure you had teenagers across America whacking off in bathrooms everywhere.'

'See, that's the same idea as that kid's computer. You know when you've written good porn because the guy gets a boner. Like a lie detector. No question, no doubts.'

Diva tears off another piece of English muffin and rolls it into a ball between her thumb and index finger. 'So you've stopped writing?'

'Just for the past twenty-one years. I'm waiting to be inspired again.'

Diva tosses the wad of English muffin at him. He opens his mouth and catches it, chews, and swallows. 'You're pretty fast for a guy with a gray crotch.'

On the drive back to her apartment, Harley coaxes Diva to sing her song again. He suggests a couple of changes, a few additional lines. Diva agrees they improve the song. When they reach her door, she invites him in, but she is happy he refuses. They've both had too good a time together to risk anything going wrong now. He leaves and she stays up late writing down the changes in her song.

26

'Don't look so nervous,' Luna says, putting her magazine aside. 'I didn't come here to fight.' The magazine is the *Journal of the American Medical Association*. Since Barcelona doesn't subscribe, she assumes Luna brought it with her. For some reason the magazine makes her even more uncomfortable. She finds it intimidating, implying the reader is one who cares about people and healing them. Only to be read by the pure at heart. No husband-fuckers allowed.

'I'm not nervous,' Barcelona says. 'I'm surprised to see someone in my house who hasn't been invited.'

Luna smiles and her thick pouty lips part to reveal a slight overbite that makes her look like Carly Simon. She is wearing a plain gray sweatshirt and tight Lycra exercise pants that stop at mid-calf. The pants are black with bright blue and yellow slashes diagonally across the thighs. She is also wearing thick white socks rolled down over the tops of her high-top athletic shoes. Her black frizzy hair is held back by two yellow banana clips. The overall effect is of someone extremely gorgeous, energetic, and intelligent. This depresses Barcelona until she remembers that despite all that, Eric still prefers her over Luna.

'Mind if I get some water?' Luna asks. 'I'm dying of thirst.' She holds up her palms. They look stained with blue ink, until Barcelona realizes those blue stains are bruises. 'I taught four aerobics classes today for a sick friend. I haven't done that in six months. My hands couldn't take all that clapping.'

'You want a soft drink or some iced tea?'

'Water's fine.'

Barcelona leads her out to the kitchen, scoops some ice into a glass, and fills it with tap water. The silence between them is damp and warm, like the air before summer lightning. What's there to say? Barcelona wonders. L: Leave Eric alone. B: That's his choice. L: He's my husband. B: He's my lover. She shakes her head at the imaginary conversation. Surely real people don't say those things.

Luna guzzles the whole glass of water at once. She refills it herself at the sink. She drinks again. Some of the water spills down her chin and neck, soaking into the collar of the gray sweatshirt. Luna doesn't seem to mind. When she's finished she unleashes another Carly Simon smile, rinses off the glass, and turns it upside down on the drain board. 'I reread *Live Wires* last week because Eric said it was going to be made into a movie.'

'Well, not necessarily. Right now it's just a script.'

'I understand. Still, it's a terrific book. The women are so cool. How's that for a literary term?' She laughs and the sound is so charming it makes Barcelona smile. 'What I mean is, the reader feels for their dilemma, their need to find some way to give love in a futuristic society that only allows them to receive love. That restricts by law, by pain of execution, any overt expression of love. Yet they are forced to allow themselves to be loved and lauded. All poetry, music, art must have women as the subject. Sex is forbidden except under the most worshipful ceremony.' She shakes her head with admiration. 'It left me wrung out, really.'

Barcelona doesn't know what to say. Is Luna's praise

387

genuine, or is she mocking? When in doubt, be polite, Milan would say. 'Thank you,' she says.

She doesn't offer Luna a chair, she doesn't want her to stay. But Luna wanders back to the living room and sits down on the big white sofa. Barcelona follows, stands between the stairs and the front door, waiting for something to happen. Luna doesn't look violent, but one can never tell whose glove compartment holds a pistol. Barcelona dreads this, she hates confrontation.

'My family is cursed,' Luna says suddenly. 'Truly. My full name is Luna Tituba Sewall. You familiar with those names?'

'No.'

Luna shrugs. 'Not many people are. But back between May and October of 1692, Tituba and Sewall were famous names.'

Barcelona feels a flicker of recognition. 'Tituba was the West Indian slave who went around telling all those voodoo stories that started all that witch hysteria.'

'I'm impressed. Not many people know that. Poor little Tituba got people so scared that a group of young girls claimed they were possessed by the devil and as a result three Salem women were put on trial. Three men were chosen as judges, John Hawthorne, William Stoughton, and Samuel Sewall. People went nuts accusing each other. Eventually public opinion turned against the trials and the legislature adopted a resolution for repentance, including setting aside a special fast day. It was on that day, January 14, 1697, that Samuel Sewall publically admitted the injustice of the trials. Of course, that was after nineteen men and women had already been hanged. Family gossip has it that we're descended from that Samuel Sewall. Some legacy, huh?'

Barcelona is fascinated despite the circumstances of Luna's visit. 'And so your parents named you after the slave girl?'

Luna reaches back and lifts a hunk of her frizzy hair. 'There's also some family gossip that there's some Negro blood in the line. Maybe Tituba incarnating within our family.'

'What do your parents say about all this?'

'They get off on it. My dad thinks it's neat to have this mysterious background, even though we're not sure we're even related to that same Judge Sewall. My mom thinks it's all very romantic. It was her idea to name me Tituba, to break any curse that might be on us in case Tituba really was a witch.'

'Jesus.' Barcelona laughs.

'Hey, a little melodrama never hurt anyone. They feel special and now they don't have to shoot anybody on the freeway to feel that way, right?'

Barcelona sits on the gray-carpeted stairs. 'Why are you here, Luna?'

'Because Eric comes here so much.'

'And you want to know why?'

'I already know why,' Luna says.

I wish I did, Barcelona thinks, staring at the beautiful young girl on the sofa. Luna is smart, sexy, and lively. And young. Why would Eric not want to rush home to her every night?

Barcelona sighs and rubs her face in her hands. 'I'm not up to this today. I'm really not. Can you come by tomorrow and we'll play this scene out.'

Luna stands up and walks over to Barcelona. She hovers like an older sister. 'I didn't come here to make a scene, Barcy. I didn't bring a scarlet letter to staple to your chest. God, I don't blame Eric for being attracted to you. You're terrific. Beautiful, sophisticated, talented. What I don't understand is why you'd want Eric back.'

Barcelona is confused. The conversation isn't going the

389

way she'd expected. She has no reference point from which to determine what she should say. No novel or play or movie with lines she can borrow.

The telephone rings and Barcelona hurries to the kitchen to answer it. She can see Luna from the kitchen. Luna is sitting on the stairs in the same place and position that Barcelona just left. That and the witch stuff Luna told her makes Barcelona feel a little spooked as she picks up the phone. She half expects to hear a heavy breather, violent obscenities.

'Barcelona?' the voice says.

'Yes?'

'It's Cory Meyers.'

The Candidate. Barcelona is relieved that it is someone normal. It gives her a chance to assess what is going on in the living room with Luna, to imagine several scenarios, to write some good lines for herself. But nothing comes to mind. Cory Meyers's voice interrupts.

'I'm down here in the netherworld.'

'Hell?'

'Close. Orange County.' He laughs. 'I've been hobnob-bing with some environmentalist group that is headquart-ered in Newport Beach. They have some wealthy yuppie members in my district in L.A. who might want to make a campaign contribution.'

'The sum also rises, huh?'

He laughs again. 'I have a gnawing suspicion that you're too smart for me.'

'Is your wife?' Barcelona says this with an edge she didn't mean. She can't believe her own gall. She has the wife of the man she's been sleeping with out in her living room and she splashes cold moral superiority in Cory Meyers's face.

His voice is a little brittle when he answers. 'I thought I explained all that to you.'

'You did. I'm sorry. My mouth has a short circuit somewhere. I'll get it fixed.'

'I like your mouth,' he says softly.

She looks through the kitchen door. Luna is leaning back on the stairs reading her medical magazine. She has an intense expression, as if she not only understands it, but also is moved by what it all means to humanity. This makes Barcelona feel even more like the evil stepmother with a hooked nose and long warted chin. 'I can't talk now,' Barcelona tells Cory Meyers.

'Okay. The reason I'm calling is, I have a house in Corona del Mar.'

'A house in L.A. and one in Corona. I didn't know you were rich.'

'I'm not. The house is a family home. My parents are both dead. I keep meaning to empty it and rent it out, but I haven't gotten around to it. Anyway, sometimes I stay there overnight when I'm down here for business. I thought I'd stay tonight, maybe talk you into dinner.'

'Eating it or being it.'

'Have I insulted you somehow?' he asks sternly.

'No, no. I'm sorry, I'm just beat, that's all.'

'When you're tired you turn into Jerry Falwell?'

'Oral Roberts. You got any blindness you want healed, a bum knee?'

'Actually, I do have a torn rotator cuff in my shoulder. Tore it playing touch football a few weeks ago.'

'Sports injury. Figures.'

'What'd I say now?'

'I can't talk, Cory.'

'Then let's talk at dinner.'

'Can't. Maybe some other time.'

'Did I do something disgusting at lunch? Pick my teeth, blow my nose? Blow your nose?'

Barcelona laughs. 'No, lunch was fine. You give great lunch, okay?'

'So, do you want to eat again? Together.'

Without thinking, Barcelona says yes. Then she stops to think about it and realizes that she really would. 'Yes,' she repeats. 'But not tonight.'

'Okay,' he says. 'I'll call you.'

Barcelona hangs up and returns to the living room.

'This is amazing,' Luna says, holding up the magazine. 'They've discovered a way to create a noise that cancels out other noise and results in what sounds like silence. They match peaks to valleys in the decibel readings. The human ear then hears silence. They've already tested the benefits on reducing stress in the average working place. Amazing. Maybe you could use something like that in your next book?'

'Maybe,' Barcelona says. She sits on the sofa where Luna had been sitting before. She takes a deep breath; it's time to get this over with. 'Look, Luna, I appreciate your coming over here like this. It must have taken a lot of courage. But I really don't know what to say to you. If you want Eric to stop, you should probably be talking to him about this, not me.'

'I didn't say anything about wanting you two to stop.' Luna closes the magazine and balances it across her knees. 'That wouldn't solve the problem. Eric's problem.'

'What problem?'

'He's afraid of me. You're a comfortable memory he can relax around.'

Barcelona's neck burns with anger. 'I think I understand Eric a little better than you do.'

'In some ways I'm sure that's true. But not in this way. Surely you must have asked yourself why he's come back to you after all this time. Especially since he's with a younger woman who is also attractive and intelligent. Plus

392

a little less sexually inhibited.' She says all this without malice, just like a lawyer citing the facts of the case.

'Less sexually inhibited.'

'Well, he mentioned there were a couple things you didn't like to do.'

'Christ.' Barcelona is so angry at Eric right now her vision blurs. She had sucked, licked, and fucked in just about every position he could come up with over the years, and even a few new ones since they'd started seeing each other again. She had drawn the line at adding another woman and at jerking him off in the movie theater. She wonders if Luna, being less sexually inhibited, has fulfilled those needs.

'Don't get mad,' Luna says. 'It's not easy for a guy Eric's age to be married to a younger woman. You think it's every guy's fantasy and so you resent me. But lots of time it's better as a fantasy than as a reality. To Eric I'm unpredictable. He's so scared I'll leave him for a younger guy, someone my own age, he's had some trouble keeping it up lately.'

'I haven't noticed any such trouble,' Barcelona says, hoping it hurts Luna as much as she hurts.

Luna shrugs undaunted. 'Of course, not with you. You're safe. His own age, emotionally unattached. He can relax, be his old self again. See, the problem with Eric is that he's finally met the girl of his dreams and doesn't know how to handle it.'

'Jesus, I admire your balls,' Barcelona says. 'Maybe he's met the girl of his dreams and now it's time to wake up. Dreams aren't always so wonderful in the light of day.'

Luna tucks her knees up against her chin. She looks sad. 'I didn't come here to hurt you, though I see that's what I've done. I thought you'd understand.'

'Understand what?'

'Eric can't come back to you. Nothing can come of it any more than it could before. You two didn't split up because you were bored or restless or anything like that. You split up because there was a part of you that Eric could never be part of. He tried to influence every other aspect of your life, right? What you read, saw, listened to. He's very competitive.'

Barcelona nods. 'Lots of men are.'

'But you had that one thing he couldn't understand. You had your art, your writing.'

'Oh, shit, you've been reading too many women's books.'

Luna smiles. 'When you wrote, you excluded him, made him feel unimportant. It wasn't a big conscious thing on his part. That's just his competitive nature. The more you wrote, the bigger your success, the more diminished he felt. That's really what separated you guys, and why you'll never be able to get back together again. He was too much in awe of you.'

'Don't you think you're a little young to be lecturing so much?' Barcelona says.

Luna doesn't answer. She unties her shoelace and reties it.

'Eric was my biggest supporter,' Barcelona says. 'When I got rejection after rejection, he comforted me.'

'That's Eric too. He loved you and didn't want to see you hurt. I'm not taking that away from him. Hell, that's one of the things I love about him. But then I'm not an artist. I can't write, draw, play a musical instrument, or sing. I can study and get A's. I can do four hours of aerobics. I can apply theories, but I can't think of any on my own. That's why I'm so perfect for Eric. He's the same way. Even his thesis is based on someone else's theory. His professor suggested it to him.'

'Really? He never told me that.'

'See what I mean? He didn't want you to think he wasn't creative too. The dissertation is first-rate research, but he would never have been able to think up the idea on his own.'

Barcelona thinks this information over. Why would Eric tell Luna all this and not her? She sighs at Luna. 'After knowing what he's been doing here with me, why do you still want him?'

Luna's smile is without sadness or irony. 'He may not be the best man in the world, but he's the best man in *my* world.'

Barcelona leans back into the sofa. She picks some of Larry's hair off a cushion then glances at Luna. 'Now what?'

'Nothing. I didn't come here to break things up. I just thought we should talk. I don't want you to get hurt.'

'Me? Doesn't it bother you knowing he's been sneaking over here to sleep with me?'

'I'm disturbed that he feels so vulnerable around me right now that he has to retreat into his past. But after a while he'll see that I'm with him to stay and all that anxiety will pass. Then he'll be back.'

'Our having sex doesn't hurt you?'

Luna smiles at the notion. 'Why should I be hurt just because he sticks a fleshy part of his anatomy into a slippery part of yours and rubs it until it squirts?'

Barcelona presses her finger against the refrigerated glass. 'Gimme a pound of the chicken salad.'

'Yes, ma'am,' the blond boy in the white apron says. His hair is slicked back and shiny in the *GQ* style that Barcelona detests. It makes men look like predators, gigolos with insincere smiles. Maybe that's the way men feel today. The numbers were finally on their side.

The blond boy slaps the plastic container on the top of the showcase. 'Anything else, ma'am?'

'A pound of red potato salad.'

'Yes, ma'am.' He slides open the door and begins ladling the potato salad into another plastic container. He weighs it, pastes a computerized sticker on the lid that tells the date, the weight, the price. He stacks it on top of the chicken salad. 'Anything else, ma'am?'

'No, thank you.' Barcelona came to the market for cat food. She was out and Larry was starting to stalk her. He didn't cry or make any sound, he just followed her around, sitting near her, staring, as if he were waiting for her to fall asleep so he could eat her face. This market didn't carry the 9 Lives brand that Larry preferred, but Barcelona was not about to fight the early evening crowds lined up behind their overflowing carts at each check stand at the supermarket. This little market was in and out. Chicken and potato salads for her dinner. Kal Kan for Larry's.

Luna. What to make of her? Barcelona waits at the checkout stand and watches the tall skinny woman checker ring up her total. The woman's hair has been frosted so often it looks brittle enough to crackle in a breeze. Barcelona tries not to stare as the woman bags the cat food and salads.

'Thank you, ma'am,' the woman says and immediately waves to a man in the other checkout line. 'I can help you over here, sir.' He looks at her hair and hesitates.

Barcelona had intended to cook that night. A curried eggplant dish from a vegetarian cookbook that Diva had suggested. It nettles her somewhat to think that Diva is strong enough to become a vegetarian and she isn't. After all, Diva has never been known for her self-discipline. But maybe that's just because her body looks like it lacks discipline. Fuck it, Barcelona thinks, climbing into the Geezemobile. Tonight she will eat the flesh of chickens while Larry eats the minced flesh of cows. They will have a carnivores' party. The climax will be when they eat each other.

When Barcelona enters her home she is surprised to find no one waiting. The house is empty except for Larry who immediately runs in through the cat door and hops up on top of the TV. She turns it on hoping the radiation will quicken his demise. A movie with Charles Bronson is on. A couple of guys are machine-gunning Bronson's crop of watermelons. Actually, that looks like fun.

She empties a can into Larry's bowl. He watches but doesn't move. Not until Barcelona is seated at the kitchen table does Larry jump down and begin eating his dinner.

Barcelona has four containers in front of her. She opens each: a plastic vat of chicken salad, a plastic vat of red potato salad, a jar of chunky peanut butter, a box of Waverly crackers. Some of the crackers she smears with peanut butter, some she uses to shovel up chicken salad. She uses a fork to eat the potato salad. Charles Bronson searches for the men who killed his melons.

It is during a Toyota truck commercial that Barcelona decides not to see Eric again. At least as lovers. She thinks sadly of the lost sex, the kissing, his warm breath in her hair. She will miss the laughing when they both try to take a bath together in her tiny tub. She will miss skipping any conversation and heading straight for the bed because they both just wanted to get naked and slide across each other's bodies.

She will not miss the books he brings for her to read, the records to listen to. The pressure to improve.

Luna was right about Eric. Barcelona had felt that even as she had shaken her head while Luna spoke. There had even been a moment, a flashbulb microsecond, when she had felt closer to Luna because of the truth they shared than she ever had with Eric. Maybe Luna was indeed part witch.

Whatever. The truth remained, Eric was hiding out in Barcelona's bed, hiding under the covers from the woman he really wanted to be with but couldn't handle the way he could Barcelona. And Barcelona knew she was as much to blame for this as Eric was. She had allowed herself to fall back into that same comfortable bed because she had romanticized their former relationship out of proportion.

Barcelona smears a cracker with peanut butter and plops some chicken salad on top. She eats it while Charles Bronson fires a shotgun from the back of a pickup truck. That too looks like fun. Shooting watermelons and firing shotguns from the bed of a pickup truck is much more fun than thinking about relationships, certainly more fun than having them.

She is full but continues to stuff herself with crackers, peanut butter, chicken salad, and red potato salad. It is easier than getting up, switching channels, putting the containers away, rinsing off the fork.

The doorbell rings and Barcelona is confused. There aren't any doorbells in the bed of a pickup truck. Larry, who has climbed back on top of the TV, looks up. That is how Barcelona knows it is her doorbell chiming. She isn't expecting anyone, but she suspects it is Eric. He must've missed his key, figured out what Luna's done, and come here to talk. He will want to sit on the sofa, not within intimate range, just close enough to reach over and touch each other in a comforting way, close enough to look thoughtfully into each other's eyes. Somewhere along the line one or both of them would shed tears. Afterward there would be tender sex, sleeping wrapped in his arms.

Right now that sounds pretty good and as she walks toward the front door, she does not feel the same strong resolve to end their relationship just yet.

She peeks through the peephole. 'Christ.' She opens the door.

'Hi,' Cory Meyers says.

'Hi. Let me guess, there's a save-the-warthog group in this neighborhood that you're soliciting for campaign contributions. So you dropped by.'

'Actually they're a nuke-the-warthog group. But I'm flexible.' He looks over her shoulder into the living room. 'Nice place.'

She smiles, steps aside to let him in. 'I know a hint when I hear one.'

He enters and looks around. 'Still a nice place.' He looks at the two prints on the walls. They are by different artists, but they are both desert landscapes. One is chalky white and pink, the other brightly colored. 'They match the color scheme of the carpeting,' he points out. 'And the furniture.'

'Something wrong with that?'

'No. It's just interesting.' He follows her out to the kitchen and watches her put the containers of food away. 'Have you eaten?'

'Yes.'

'Are you hungry?'

'No.'

He nods, looks around, scratches Larry's head. '*Mr. Majestyk*,' he says.

'His name's Larry.'

'No, the movie.' He points at the TV screen. 'I've seen this one. I like when they shoot his watermelons.'

'This isn't a good time to visit,' Barcelona says, leaning against the refrigerator door. 'I've been feeling crabby all day and it's just getting worse.'

'I can take it. Let's go out to dinner. Take your mind off whatever's troubling you.'

'If I ate another bite I'd puke.'

He shuts the TV off. 'We'll find a restaurant where no one will notice. One with sawdust on the floor.'

Barcelona knows that sooner or later tonight Eric will call or come over to have an intense talk. She does not want anything intense right now. 'Okay,' she tells Cory. 'Let's go.'

'Still no answer,' Barcelona says, returning to the table.

'Maybe she's still undercover.'

'God, I hope so.' She sits down and sips her wine. 'I feel responsible.'

'You didn't do anything. In fact, you probably salvaged the situation for Dixie.'

Barcelona shrugs, unconvinced.

Cory Meyers reaches across the table and touches her hand. 'You want me to call? I have a few cop friends who might be able to find something out, even down here in Orange County.'

She smiles. 'I don't know. Let's see what happens tonight.'

'Okay.' He removes his hand from hers, but her skin retains his warmth. She looks at it as if she expects to see the imprint still there from his hand. 'Why'd you come over tonight after I told you not to?'

'I don't know.' He shakes his head, stabs his blueberry pie with his fork. 'It's not like me.'

'I'm not sure about that.'

'You're still pissed at me because Trina and I had sex a few weeks ago. You can be very self-righteous sometimes. Give Trina some credit; she wasn't being seduced. It was her idea.'

Barcelona drinks her coffee. She'd been too full to eat, but she'd had three cups of coffee while watching Cory polish off a club sandwich, fries, and his pie. They are sitting in a coffee shop in Corona del Mar, a cozy little coastal city where the livin' is easy but the rents are high. Fashion Island looms on the ridge above the city.

Cory and Barcelona sit in silence for a couple of minutes. Barcelona feels like a saboteur, planting verbal mines for Cory to hit as he pilots through the conversation. He hits one, it explodes, stuns him momentarily, but he pushes on. She likes that about him. She hates herself for being so mean to him, but she can't stop herself.

'Trina is not as tough as she acts,' Barcelona says.

'I know that,' Cory says. 'Neither am I.'

'Oh? Strong but tender. Sounds like a campaign promise.'

Cory Meyers sighs, leans back in the booth, and looks away. Barcelona steals a glance at him, sees his jaw tense. He looks back at her and she looks down into her coffee. 'Look, you want to go home, you only have to ask.'

'Let's go.' Barcelona starts to slide out of the booth. She stops, looks at him. His face is grim. 'I'm sorry. I know I've said that before to you. I don't know why I'm acting this way. Stop me before I insult again.' She points at what's left of his blueberry pie. 'Go ahead, throw it in my face. I deserve it.'

Cory picks the plate up and Barcelona is shocked to think he might actually throw it at her. She flinches. He sets the plate down and laughs. 'I'd have been within my constitutional rights to let it rip, you know?'

'I know.'

'But I'm too civilized.'

'I appreciate it.'

He hands her the bill. 'Here, your treat. It certainly hasn't been mine.'

She grins and takes the check. She lays a twenty-dollar bill on top of it. The waitress, a young redhead with a Band-Aid tattooed on her thigh, scoops up the check and the twenty and rushes off.

'What do you think the tattoo means?' Cory asks.

'She breaks easily?'

He looks over at her standing at the cash register ringing up the bill. Her body and face are lean as a greyhound's. 'I don't think she breaks easily.' He looks at Barcelona with a funny expression that she can't read.

'I always wanted a tattoo,' he says, unlocking the front door of his house. 'In college my best buddy and I decided to get our heads shaved and our scalps tattooed. That way when our hair grew back no one would know about the tattoos.'

'Then what's the point of getting them?'

'Our little secret. Like having a secret identity. During the day, mild-mannered students at a major metropolitan university. But at night, party animals with tattooed skulls and super libidos.'

'I never wanted a tattoo, even after Cher got hers.' Barcelona walks into the house.

Cory follows, flicking the light switch. 'It's a little musty,' he says. 'I haven't been down here in a couple months.' He goes over to the window and, after a couple of unsuccessful tugs, yanks it open.

'This is nice,' Barcelona says. 'Quaint.'

'A dump. Two tiny bedrooms and one bathroom. But we're only two blocks from the beach so it's valuable. Actually, I find it hard to believe that my parents managed to raise me in such a little gingerbread house. It didn't seem all that small when I was growing up. Except when I sneaked a girl into my room.'

'It was her idea no doubt,' she says.

He looks at her, sees she is kidding this time, and nods. 'Women can't keep their hands off me.'

Barcelona walks around the living room. It is paneled in white wood, the tan carpeting is worn and stained.

The pictures on the wall are bland landscapes probably purchased at garage sales.

'Pretty dreadful stuff, huh?' Cory says, gesturing to the paintings. 'If it wasn't for bad taste, my folks wouldn't have had any taste.'

'Did you like them?'

'Sure. My dad won the sand castle-building contest three years in a row when I was a kid. He could really make those towers. That was before they brought in all these professional architects with molds and shit. Back then all you were allowed was a pail and a shovel. Period.'

'What about your mom?'

'No, you couldn't use your mom, just a pail and a shovel.'

Barcelona laughs. 'You're too weird to be in politics.'

'Too weird to win, maybe, but just weird enough to try. Sit.'

There was no sofa, just two white rattan chairs. They each sat in one. 'My mom worked part time as a private nurse for terminal patients. I always liked it when her patients died because then she spent more time at home. I didn't realize how grizzly that thought was until later. Once she came home earlier than expected and I said something like, "Oh, good, Mr. Monroe died." She looked at me horrified for a moment, like I was some ghastly bug she'd never seen before. I thought she was going to squash me right then and there. But suddenly she just grabbed me and gave me a big hug. I never said anything like that again.'

'But you thought it.'

He smiles. 'My secret.'

Barcelona moves her head and her earring snags the collar of her blouse. 'Shit.' She fiddles with it, but her neck is crooked at such an awkward angle she has trouble unhooking it.

403

'Here, let me,' Cory offers, coming over. 'I've had some small experience at doing this.' He kneels beside her and gently works the earring free. 'You'll live.'

She looks into his eyes and there is a moment when they are close enough to hear each other breathing. Barcelona feels silly at such moments, clumsy and uncertain. She wants him to kiss her, wants to kiss him. After all these years the rules still aren't clear. It's one thing to believe it's okay to make the first move; it's another to actually do it.

But then he leans over her, his mouth on hers, lips magnetized, pulling against each other. His hands, bigger than she remembers them, hold her shoulders. Her shoulders feel small and delicate in his grasp. She feels each bone shift under the pressure of his fingers. Her breasts brush against his chest and she feels a rush of adrenaline that shoots up to her lips like a shot from the dentist. The effect is so powerful the eyes behind her closed lids ache. She pulls back, breaking contact. He leans further forward, kisses her cheek, her neck. She cups her hands behind his head. She kisses him. Her tongue slides over his.

'I want to ask you a question,' she says, their faces inches apart. 'Truth is optional.'

'Ask,' he says.

'Don't take this wrong. This isn't me being Billy Graham. It's just that I'm coming out of a screwy relationship and I don't want to get into another one.'

'Define screwy.'

'Married.'

He nods. 'Oh.'

She pulls back into her rattan chair and he sits down on the floor next to her. 'Maybe I'm making more of this than I should. It's just a kiss.'

'Not just a kiss,' he says softly.

She leans her head on the back of the chair and looks up at the speckled ceiling. 'This is the hard part. They should have preprinted relationship cards distributed along with condoms to every kid at puberty. The dialogue is pre-written so all you have to do is hand the card to the guy or girl of your choice and they can check the boxes.'

'I don't have any diseases that I know about. I haven't had the mumps though.'

'That's not what I'm getting at.'

He pulls off his deck shoes and rearranges himself so he's sitting cross-legged. Then he pulls off her shoes and squeezes her big toe. 'My wife?'

Barcelona nods. 'Are you sure this isn't just a temporary thing you two are going through? A spat. A dry period. You get over those things.'

'I'm sure.'

She waits for him to go on. When he doesn't she says, 'Well, I'm glad that's cleared up. I feel better.'

He looks at her with a serious expression. 'Can't you just take my word?'

'You're a politician,' she says, smiling.

Slowly he smiles back. 'I see your point.' He strips off his sports jacket and flings it across the other chair. 'Women always want a lot of words.'

'They want to share. They want men to be open.'

'Do they?' he says mysteriously. He shifts around so he's facing her, sitting cross-legged at her feet. 'My wife is a beautiful woman. She got straights As at Stanford in physics. Now she teaches at UCLA. We get along wonderfully, care about each other very much.'

Barcelona's heart stalls. She's waiting for the 'but.'

'But,' he says, 'we have reached an impasse.'

'About what?'

'Sex.'

'Sex?'

'She doesn't want any.'

Barcelona shrugs. 'You mean she doesn't make love as often as you'd like?'

'I mean she doesn't make love at all. Period. No sex. After a couple years of us trying to work it out, scheduling sex, trying different techniques, more foreplay, less foreplay, different positions, different rooms, props, she finally came up to me and said she'd decided that she just didn't want to have sex anymore, ever. Not that she begrudged me my wanting to, she just didn't like it. It saddened her to do it and she'd come to the irrevocable decision to forswear it for the rest of her life. I suggested she seek therapy, but she smiled and said that she didn't feel bad about not wanting sex, only in that it hurt me. She still loved me and we could remain married, I could have affairs whenever the urge was upon me.'

'My God, how did you feel?'

Cory smiles. 'You won't believe this, but I felt good. Not for our marriage, but for Dayna. I could tell that she felt better than she had in a long time. Her decision had freed her in a way. I was proud that she was able to reach her decision.' He leans back on his elbows. 'Of course, I didn't think we should stay married. I'm still trying to get her to seek some therapy, but she says she's the happiest now that she's ever been.'

'Maybe she's gay?'

'She says she isn't. She claims that sex with either man or woman is equally repulsive.'

Barcelona fidgets with the earring that had snagged her blouse earlier. She takes it off, then puts it back on. 'Weren't there any signs when you first were dating?'

'No. We screwed like rabbits. She says she liked it then but somewhere along the line just lost it. Makes you wonder what I did wrong, huh?'

In fact, that's exactly what Barcelona was wondering.

He must have done something weird to turn her off from sex so radically. 'No, of course it wasn't anything you did.'

He stares at her with glowering intensity. 'Now you know why men don't talk much,' he says angrily. 'Women want men to be open, but only if they say what women want to hear. They don't really want to hear the truths in a man's mind. Men sense that and keep quiet.'

'That's ridiculous,' Barcelona says. But she wishes she hadn't heard the truth.

He stands up, slips into his shoes. 'Getting kinda late. Ready to go?'

She is ready to go. She wants to go. The complexities of talking to Luna, then to Cory, of still not being able to reach Dixie have wrung her out. But now she feels insensitive and cruel. She draws painful confessions from a man, then backs off from him afterward. Somehow she knows Luna would have handled this better.

She had made up her mind to sleep with Cory tonight. He is attractive, fun, and very sexy anyway. Besides, she owes him some comfort, she needs to prove she's not affected by his revelation. She wants to blame the problem on his wife, things like that happen to people. She gets up and kisses him. He is surprised at first, but then responds.

'Pity kiss?' he says.

'You complaining?'

'I'm just curious how far you'll take pity.'

'You're too sensitive,' she says. 'Where's the bathroom?'

He points down the hall. 'You can't miss it.'

Barcelona goes into the bathroom, drops her pants and panties, and pulls the tampon out. It is barely pink since she is at the end of her period. She sits down and pees, looking around for a magazine or something to read. There is nothing. She takes the Tampax box out of her purse and reads that: For Light to Medium Flow. 10 Slender Regular. Made of rayon fiber, rayon nonwoven overwrap, cotton cord, and cotton thread. Associated with Toxic Shock Syndrome (TSS). TSS is a rare but serious disease that may cause death.

When she is finished peeing she dabs herself with toilet paper. She decides against inserting another tampon. She expects that she and Cory will soon end up in bed and there was no need to waste a tampon now. She buttons up her pants, flushes, and checks her face in the mirror. The ugly yellow wallpaper surrounding her casts a jaundiced shade on her skin. She passes a brush through her hair twice and lets it go at that. But as she's leaving the bathroom, she notices the toilet is starting to burp and bubble. Yellow water is regurgitated back up the bowl along with her pink spongy tampon. The toilet bowl is almost full and still rising. The tampon is swirling around the bowl.

Panicked, she hits the handle again, but nothing happens. 'Oh God,' she says. 'Oh, God!'

Yellow water is brimming and starting to overflow onto the floor.

'Cory!' she hollers. 'Cory!'

She hears him running down the hall. He twists the doorknob, but she'd forgotten to unlock the door. Water stained with her piss is spilling onto the floor. She unlocks the door.

Cory looks at the toilet and lifts the seat. Barcelona's pink tampon gushes over the plastic toilet seat onto the floor. She cringes with embarrassment. He tiptoes in his socks to the cupboard under the sink and removes a plunger. He shoves the plunger into the toilet, spilling even more water onto the floor. A couple of plunges and water begins to gurgle down the drain. He tosses the plunger in the corner.

'This is so embarrassing,' she says as he leads her out of the bathroom.

'Now we're even.'

'I hope I didn't break anything. They're supposed to be flushable.'

'Plumbing is ancient. It's done that before. Don't worry. Sit down.'

Barcelona returns to her chair, leaving wet footprints on the carpet. Cory returns with a blue bath towel. He kneels in front of her and dries her feet. He stops, hoists up her pant legs, and rolls off her knee-high stockings. Then he returns to drying, even getting between each toe. When he's finishes he says, 'Ready to go home now?'

She grins at him, kisses him on the cheek. 'Yes.'

He drives down the dark roads and they hardly speak. He reaches out to touch her hand; she slides closer to him. She leans her head against his shoulder. He squeezes her thigh.

'I like sex,' she says, staring out the window.

'I figured you did.'

They drive past the university. Over the freeway. Even at this hour the freeway traffic whooshes by.

He pulls up to the curb and shuts off the motor. He kisses her, his hand chastely holding her waist. She presses herself into his body so her breasts flatten against his chest. His tongue licks across her teeth.

'I'll walk you in,' he says.

'No, it's only around the corner.' She kisses him quickly and jumps out of the car.

'I'll call you tomorrow and we'll try again.'

'Your plumbing or mine?' she says.

He drives away laughing, waving his hand out the window. Barcelona walks to her door. She feels happy about Cory Meyers, though she also feels guilty about Eric. She is cheating on him. She recognizes the absurdity of that thought, yet it is real nevertheless. She returns to her resolve not to see Eric again as lovers. Knowing that this

409

resolve is made easier by Cory's interest does not make her feel especially noble.

Larry is waiting at the front door even though he could have entered through his cat door. In the lamplight by her door, Barcelona can see the glint of blood on his scalp. 'What have you done now, you little jerk,' she says, but feels compassion for him anyway. She picks him up, which he rarely lets her do without a fight, and carries him to the upstairs bathroom. She dabs his wound with peroxide. He hisses at her and nips her finger with his teeth.

'You little shit,' she says, but holds him tight. She sprays the wound with Bactine and lets him run.

She goes down to the kitchen to check her messages on the answering machine. There are only two. The first is from Grief: '*Sorry, honey, but the script deal is off. Complications. We're out of it altogether. Call me tomorrow and I'll explain.*'

The second is from Trina. Her voice is uncharacteristically shrill with panic: '*Barcy, Jesus! Call my service immediately. They'll page me and I'll let you know where I am. Jesus.*' Pause. '*Call me. Dixie's husband has been arrested for murder. I can't . . .*' Pause. '*Just call me, I'll tell you the rest.*'

Barcy pulls up a chair and begins dialing Trina's answering service. She misdials twice before getting the right number.

27

Dixie can hardly breathe. She is facedown on Brandon's bed. Her arms and legs are spread-eagled and tied to the separate feet of the bed. The rope is bright yellow and very rough. The skin on her wrists and ankles is already rubbed raw.

Brandon and Joseph stand next to the bed, staring down at her as if she were some modern art exhibit at a museum.

'What do we do now?' Joseph asks. Dixie can hear the panic in his voice.

'I don't know. I haven't decided.' Brandon's voice is oddly calm, somehow more assured than before. But there is a strange edge in it too, like that of a jumper balanced on a twelfth-story ledge toying with the idea of leaping, wanting to savor it all first, imagining the free fall over and over before actually stepping into the abyss. Brandon sounds as if he is looking over the ledge now and this scares Dixie more than anything else.

'Don't do anything stupid here,' Dixie says forcefully. 'I'm a cop, for God's sake. So far all you've done is deal a little dope. No big deal. I haven't even see a buy, so I can't testify to that. That puts you in the clear, Brandon. And Joe, you know my testimony against you has been compromised anyway because of our physical contact. I've got nothing on either of you. If you let me go right now.'

'She's right, man,' Joseph says. 'She didn't see anything go down between us.'

Brandon opens the drawer of his dresser and pulls out a T-shirt and puts it on. It has the logo of Puma sporting goods on it, the name and a leaping cat. Dixie sees the same logo painted on the wall next to the refrigerator.

'We let her go,' Joseph says, 'she's got nothing.'

'What about us tying her up. She could get us for assault, or maybe even kidnapping, unlawful imprisonment. Cops can always get you for something, dude.'

Dixie twists her head around to look directly at him. 'You think I want everyone to know I let a couple teenagers tie me up? Christ, just out of personal pride I'd let this case drop.'

'She makes sense,' Joseph pleads.

Brandon doesn't say anything. He walks over to the bed and sits down, his back to Dixie. She can smell coconut oil from his suntan lotion. 'I don't know,' he says and leans back so his head is resting on her butt. 'I've got to figure this out.'

'There's nothing to figure out,' Joseph says. His voice is angry now. Apparently, despite Dixie's betrayal, he still sees her as his date. Anything Brandon does to her reflects badly on him.

'There's plenty to figure out,' Brandon says, bouncing his head a little on Dixie's butt. 'This mama's harder than a couple granite rocks. Loosen 'em up a bit, babe, I don't like no rocky pillows.' When Dixie doesn't relax her buttocks he suddenly twists around and swats her hard with his hand. Her skin burns. 'I said loosen those buns.'

'Fuck, man,' Joseph says. 'Knock it off. We're trying to negotiate our way out of this, not make things worse.'

'I like things the way they are.' Brandon grins and nestles his head against Dixie's butt. 'Ah, that's better.'

'We've got to let her go.'

'Do we?'

'What else can we do?'

Brandon chuckles. 'Keep her. Like a pet.'

Dixie can't see Joseph as he paces out of her line of vision. She tries to control her breathing, conscious that Brandon can feel any shift in her pattern from his position on her backside. She doesn't want him to know how scared she is. Her only hope is Joseph.

'You're fucking crazy, you know that?' Joseph says. 'We can't keep her.'

'Who's gonna stop us?'

'The cops, that's who. They know she's undercover, she must've told them about me. I'm the first one they'll come after.'

'Just stay cool. Without her they've got nothing on you. You came down to the beach, watched the surf, had an ice cream, and went your separate ways.'

'That won't wash,' Dixie says. 'They'll be all over him until he talks. You two have been seen together, they'll find out and haul both your asses to jail and keep him there until they find me.'

Brandon rolls off her and kneels next to the bed. He lays his head on the bed six inches from her face. 'What if they don't find you?'

'Why take any chances?' Joseph says. 'Just let her go.'

Brandon stands up. 'I've always wanted a slave. I may never get a chance like this again.' He claps Joseph on the back. 'Lighten up, dude. I'll protect us.'

Joseph backs away from him. 'You're nuts, Brandon. I'm not getting involved in anything like this.'

'You don't have any choice, Joey. You buy your shit from me, but I buy direct from some very tense guys who wouldn't want to see their interests threatened. I tell them you're a loose cannon and they'll come over to your house and stomp the shit out of you and your folks, then you'll fuck your dog for dessert.'

Joseph doesn't say anything. He paces back into Dixie's view. She twists her wrists against the rope, but the knots are too tight. She feels the skin on her wrist scrape away. She tries to make a mental list of her options, but she can't think of any. Only Joseph.

'You dumb bitch,' Joseph yells at her. She can see the fear and anger in his eyes. 'How old are you?'

'Thirty-three,' Dixie says.

'Fuck,' Joseph says.

'Twice as old as me,' Brandon laughs. He reaches down and rubs her butt. 'But she's got the tight ass of a thirteen-year-old. We could have some real fun with it.' He bends over and bites her left butt cheek through the jeans. He chomps down hard enough to bring tears to her eyes, but she doesn't cry out. He stands up and laughs. '"Yummy, yummy, yummy, I got love in my tunny." You know that oldie? It's from your generation.'

'Jesus, man, this isn't the time for that shit,' Joseph says.

'You're getting on my nerves, dude.' Brandon sits on the bed and gently rubs the spot he just bit. The flesh is so tender that Dixie winces under his touch. 'Oops, a little sore?' His hands slip down between her legs and he presses his finger against her crotch. 'That better?'

'That's enough,' Joseph says. He kneels down next to the bed and starts untying the rope. 'We're letting her go.'

Dixie expects Brandon to say something, start arguing, but when she looks back at him he is calmly watching Joseph untie her left hand. His face is oddly serene in its concentration, as if he were seeing a knot being untied for the first time. When Joseph frees the left hand, he runs around the bed, kneels, and begins untying the right. Dixie purposely says nothing, not wanting to tip the balance of power or rattle Joseph's resolve.

414

'I'll drop her off at her car,' Joseph prattles to no one in particular. Sweat pearls are lined above his lip. He avoids looking at Dixie. 'She can holler to the cops or anyone after that, it won't matter. She's got nothing.'

The rope drops away from her wrist and she rubs circulation back into the skin, avoiding the raw sores. One wrist has a flap of skin turn loose by the rope. She yanks it off and tosses it on the floor. Joseph is at her right foot now, loosening the rope.

Suddenly Dixie feels a shift of weight on the bed. She turns just as Brandon grabs the baseball bat from against the dresser and swings it at Joseph. Dixie yells 'No!' at the same instant the bat connects with Joseph's head, just above the right ear. The sound at impact is like breaking a board over your knee. Joseph wobbles sideways a moment, his eyes fluttering white. He moans, tries to rise from his knees, staggers against the bed.

Brandon wallops him again.

This time the sound of the bat connecting with the skull is eerie. Instead of a solid thud, it sounds mushy, like jumping with both feet into thick mud.

'Joseph!' Dixie cries out as he slumps across the backs of her legs.

Brandon walks around the bed, cautiously pokes Joseph's jaw with the bat. Warm blood is spilling out of his cracked skull and soaking through the thighs of her jeans. Brandon pokes him in the ribs and jumps back when the body begins to slide off the edge of the bed. Joseph crumbles onto the floor.

Brandon kneels over him, checking for a pulse. 'Well,' he says, looking up at Dixie with a shrug. 'That's that.'

The rest of Saturday was spent tied facedown on Brandon's bed while he played CDs, listened to the radio, or watched TV from a huge overstuffed chair as big as a sofa. For about an hour he tried to learn to play 'Hotel California' on his guitar, following the chords in a guitar book, playing them over and over again. Around midnight, he munched on peanut butter and Ritz crackers. About four in the morning, while watching *Teacher's Pet* with Clark Gable and Doris Day on the Atlanta Superstation, he decided to paint the logo from the Ritz cracker box just below his Perrier and above Miller Lite.

For most of the night, Joseph's body was hunched into a fetal position next to the bed and enclosed in two large black trash bags. One was pulled over his head and torso, the other was pulled up over his legs and hips. Then the two overlapping ends were neatly stapled together. Brandon had gone about the whole thing very methodically.

Dixie feels Joseph's dried blood on the backs of the legs of her jeans. The blood stiffened the denim and it chafes her skin. If she twists her neck around until a sharp pain needles the muscle, she can see Joseph lumped up into the trash bags like a month's worth of newspapers. Surprisingly, the smell isn't bad.

But by Sunday morning, after Brandon has finished his Ritz logo, he drags the body into the bathroom.

'It wasn't as bad as I thought,' he says to Dixie, wiping the yellow and blue paint from his hands with a turpentine-soaked rag. 'But not as good neither. Murder. The big M. I thought it would feel different.'

'Different?' she says, trying to keep him talking.

'I don't know how, just different than it was. More thrilling, I guess.'

'Maybe if you eat his heart,' she says. 'Some tribes do that to give them the strength of their enemy.'

'Nah, too messy. Besides, all I've got is a hot plate anyway.' He sits on the edge of the bed. This is the first he's talked to her since yesterday when he'd killed Joseph.

The scent of turpentine from his rag stings Dixie's nose, but she's happy for the stimulation. Her body aches from being strapped down and unable to move. She concentrates on making her voice calm, nonthreatening. That remark about eating the heart was wrong, provocative. She needs to defuse the situation, try to bring some rationality, convince Brandon there's a way out. 'Look, Brandon, you're only sixteen. Even with Joseph's death, chances are a good lawyer can convince a jury that you were the junior partner to him, that he was the drug kingpin. You were his unwilling accomplice.'

'Yeah,' he says. 'But I still killed him.'

'Involuntary manslaughter. An argument over drugs. He wanted you to keep dealing, you wanted out, you'd come to realize drugs were wrong, blah, blah, blah. A half-decent lawyer can make that work.'

'Except you'd testify otherwise.'

'Without any additional physical evidence, I don't much like the state's chances of winning the case, do you? I figure you'll walk, worse case a suspended sentence or a couple months in juvy.'

Brandon nods. 'You're probably right.' He gets up, unties her left foot, walks around the bed, unties her right foot.

Dixie tries not to show her anxiousness. She moves her legs a little, though they are asleep and it feels as if she is trying to drag two redwoods up a hill. She waits for him to untie her hands, but he stands behind her, not moving.

She is surprised to suddenly feel his hands on her waist, lifting her hips up as he reaches around to unbutton her jeans. She twists against him, struggling to squirm out of his grip, but he straddles her from behind and begins to roughly yank her pants down. He gets the jeans over her butt when he starts to laugh.

'Red panties,' he says. 'Nice.' He pulls them down too

and pokes her cheek where he bit her. She tenses her muscles so she can't feel his touch. 'Fuck, where'd you get those muscles?'

'You don't want to do this, Brandon,' Dixie says calmly. 'You do this and even a smart lawyer won't be able to help you. There won't be any innocent dupe defense. Your age won't matter.'

He leans over so his face is in her hair, his mouth against her ear. 'Who cares?'

He tugs her pants and panties off over her feet and reties her ankles to the bed. He sits on the bed and runs his fingertips along the crevice of her buttocks. 'See, I've figured it out. I just made my buy for the month, so I'm flush with goodies, lots of product to sell, if not around here then somewhere else. This place is getting pretty lame anyway. I'm bored doing the same shit, seeing the same assholes every day, fucking the same tired pussies. My folks begging me to come back home. I'm ready for a change of scenery. All I gotta do is sell some of my shit and then take off for parts unknown.'

'Where can you go? Cops everywhere will be looking for you.'

He shrugs. 'They can look, but they can't touch. Shit, cops aren't that smart. I've been dealing for three years and they never busted me once.' He slaps her ass soundly.

Dixie isn't sure what tactic to use now. Reason hasn't worked and isn't likely to, mostly because he's right. With a few bucks in his pocket he could disappear and probably never be found again. He is smart, cunning, and completely without a conscience. She feels the black hood of despair slipping over her head. He intends to rape her, of that she is certain. The question now is will he kill her afterward?

She relaxes her bladder and begins to urinate.

'Jesus fuck!' he says, jerking his hand off her butt.

The warm urine soaks into the blankets and bed sheets.

Her massive consumption of vitamins gives the urine an especially pungent odor.

Brandon laughs. 'I didn't know I scared you so much.'

That's what Dixie wants him to think. She hopes he will untie her to change the sheets, hopes that somewhere during her being untied she will have an opportunity to jump him, crush his skull with a baseball bat, drag his brains out of his skull, and stomp them into the floor with her feet.

He unties her legs but not her hands. He pulls the blanket and sheets off under her like a clumsy magician yanking a tablecloth out from under a set of fine China. The blanket burns her stomach as it is jerked out from under her. Then he reties her ankles back to their separate posts. 'You piss again, you can lie in it. Don't matter to me.'

She looks around at him just as he is stepping out of his shorts. His penis is already hard and pointing straight up. It is long and thin, pinker than a man's. The hair is finer. He takes a running start and leaps onto the bed landing with his feet astride her hips. He jumps up and down a few times as if on a trampoline, slapping his hands against the rafter overhead. The mattress bounces hard against Dixie's face. It smells of coconut oil, turpentine, and urine. Brandon drops to his knees, one on either side of her hips. He strokes the skin of her ass and says, 'Eeenie, meenie, minie, moe.'

'Can I have some water?' she asks.

'Sure.' He gets a plastic glass from the orange crate next to the refrigerator and goes into the bathroom. She hears the faucet running. He comes back and stands next to her head. 'Nearly tripped on ole Joey. Tilt your head back.'

She does and he puts the glass against her lips and slowly

pours. Most spills down her chin and onto the mattress, but she manages to swallow some.

She is completely naked now. He's cut her blouse and T-shirt off with scissors. There is a nasty bruise around her left nipple where he bit her. The ragged teeth marks look like the outline of an eye with the nipple as the pupil.

In the past three hours he has raped her five times, twice anally, twice vaginally, and once orally. He had trouble getting into her anally so he'd spit on her and rubbed the saliva on her anus. She thinks that was the worst part of the whole ordeal, feeling this sixteen-year-old killer's spit splatting against her skin. She can still feel each spot on her skin where his spit had hit. She's convinced that there are actual physical marks there, like the blisters acid might cause.

She is so tired now she just wants to sleep.

She closes her eyes. She is pretty sure he intends to kill her. Afterward, he'll probably climb on her for one more ride, see if it's better than Space Mountain. Somewhere outside she hears the putter of helicopters and imagines a rescue squad of marines coming after her. The rotor blades sound like a baseball card stuck in the bicycle spoke she fashioned as a child. Thwacka-thwacka-thwacka. The rhythm rocks her to sleep.

The hiss of carbonation fizzing wakes her. Brandon stands next to her drinking a Miller Lite beer. 'You're starting to smell a little,' he says and pours some of the beer on her ass. The shock of cold causes Dixie to jerk, but as the liquid runs down between her legs it actually soothes her a little.

Her mouth is so bitter and dry she has trouble speaking. Her head hurts from the turpentine fumes. 'Stop now,' she says so quietly she can hardly hear herself.

'Can't hear you, lady. Jesus, you're a fucking mess. Smell like a pig.' He laughs. 'Well, hang on, babe. I've got a few more calls to make, some shit to sell, maybe even line you up with a couple dates. Dudes who'd pay extra when I tell them you're a cop. They may play a little rough though.' He heads for the door. 'Be right back.'

He leaves, carrying the key to the Mendlesons' house and a black address book.

The moment the door closes Dixie begins struggling against the rope. She feels weak and dizzy, though, and stops struggling after less than a minute. She starts to cry and her own tears surprise her. She does not cry easily. The tears make her angry. She turns her head and bites her own upper arm. Hard. The pain sizzles through her brain and she feels a rush of adrenaline spasming through her body. She stares at the rope on each wrist. She has not lifted all those thousands of pounds of weights all these years just to lie helpless now, strapped to the bed of a sixteen-year-old while his friends pay to rape her.

She pulls against the rope, at first trying to break it. But that is a Hollywood fantasy. She changes tactics. She wiggles and squirms her wrist against the rope, trying to loosen it enough so she can slip one hand free. No use.

Another tactic. She tries to stretch her head close enough to the rope to get her teeth on it. She'd chew through the rope. But strain as she does, her teeth fall short by three inches. Now she is trying to decide whether she has the courage to chew through her own wrist to get free. Knowing he is going to kill her anyway, wouldn't it be better to sacrifice one hand?

She will try one other tactic first. She flexes her leg muscles. This is the same position she'd be in if she were at the gym about to do calf raises on the weight bench. She had raised over two hundred pounds once. How strong could the legs of this rickety bed be compared to her legs?

She begins to raise them, bend the legs at the knee, curl them backward. The rope goes taut. She tightens her stomach muscles and concentrates all her energy on those legs, imagines them as huge mechanical winches lifting a crashed car out of the river, water pouring out of the smashed windshield, the dead bodies flopping forward, held tight by shoulder harnesses.

The bed shifts suddenly, the bottom half lowers a fraction. The metal legs of the bed are bending. She grits her teeth and flexes her legs again. The bed's legs bend a little more. Her legs spasm with exhaustion and flop against the mattress. She tries to raise them again, but they don't respond.

Dixie thrusts her face toward the rope at her right wrist. Her front teeth barely touch. She had hoped to use her stronger back teeth, but right now she is thrilled to have any chance at all. She begins gnawing at the rope. The fibers are stiff and sharp as boars' hair. Several times the fibers stab her lips and gums. She can taste the blood in her mouth. Still, she keeps chewing. She tries not to think about Brandon or how long his phone calls will take. She just bites into the rope and yanks her head back and forth until the rope slips out of her teeth, then repeats the action. Each fiber has to be severed separately. Two of her front teeth are loose and sore. The pain shoots straight through the roof of her mouth into her eyeballs. She clamps her teeth on the rope again and shakes her head, her teeth sawing through the stubborn fibers.

She is halfway through the rope when one of her front teeth flies out of her mouth. Blood pours out over her lip. She ignores it, using her other teeth to grab hold again.

Then the rope breaks.

Within two minutes she has untied herself. She staggers to her feet, slips on shorts and a T-shirt from a pile on the dresser, and rushes for the door.

Just as Brandon enters.

His hair is wet and slicked back and there is still some soap in his ear. He has taken a shower while he was in the house. He looks at her with surprise at first, then he grins when he sees her raw and bleeding mouth, the gap.

'I guess I know what you'll want for Christmas,' he says. He starts toward her.

Dixie feels light-headed. She knows there are things she learned to do in such situations, things from the Academy, from experience. But she can barely remember the Academy. If pressed, she wouldn't be able to name one police officer she works with. She doesn't even remember the boy's name.

But she does remember she wants to live. She charges at him and as his hands reach out to grab her, she steps sharply into them and swings her elbow into his throat. His hands fly to his neck as he gasps for air. She drives the same elbow into his nose and hears it pop, blood shooting out each nostril. He drops to his knees. She brings her knee straight up into his chin and his head snaps back. He falls over, grabbing her ankle as he falls. She stomps on his wrist with her other foot and the bone crunches at impact.

She runs out the door.

She doesn't look back. Her bare feet whack pavement. Sharp pebbles gouge her soles, but she doesn't stop. She runs as fast as she can. She doesn't have to look to know he is running behind her. She dodges down an alley, across a yard, through a parking lot. She should stop, she knows, ask for help. But he may be armed now. He may have a gun, aiming the sights on her back even as she runs.

Finally out of breath, panting from exhaustion, legs too wobbly to run, she stops at a public phone and dials, punching in her Calling Card number in lieu of any change.

'Hello?' the voice says.

She is surprised. It is not the police station. 'Karl?' she says to her ex-husband.

Karl picks her up within fifteen minutes. He lives in Irvine, ordinarily a twenty-minute drive, which for Karl would translate into thirty or forty minutes. Not this time. When he sees her sitting on the curb in front of the phone, he double-parks the car and leaps out, leaving his door open. Cars honk at him and drivers shout at him. He ignores them. He kneels in front of Dixie. 'My God, are you okay?'

She hadn't told him anything on the phone. Just that she needed him, it was an emergency. She didn't know why she had dialed his number in the first place, and having done so, why didn't she just hang up and dial her cop friends? Or even the local cops? She wondered about that while she'd sat on the curb waiting for him. She wasn't sure. Maybe she needed to see someone she knew was on her side. Cops would be on her side, sure. They don't like it when one of their own is mauled. But they were still men. They'd be sympathetic, but they'd know she'd been raped; they'd look at her wondering, picturing her naked and spread open and she'd have to relive it every time she looked in their eyes. She'd be able to do that eventually. But not with the first face she sees. Maybe that made her a bad cop. Right now she didn't much care.

'I'm taking you to a hospital,' Karl says, lifting her gently to her feet. 'Don't worry, Dixie, I'll take care of you.'

Yesterday those words would have annoyed her. Right now they were just what she wanted to hear.

He helps her into the car. When other drivers see her they stop honking and yelling at him. They just gawk. She slides into the car and he closes the door behind her.

'I was raped,' she tells him when he gets in.

He doesn't say anything. He switches on the turn signal,

424

checks the traffic, and pulls over into the next lane. 'Everything will be fine, Dixie. You're in shock.'

That struck her as funny. She felt tired, sure, but not in shock, not a zombie. To prove to him that she wasn't in shock, she told him what happened, described it, told him the address. He listened with grim concentration on his driving. When she was finished he asked her if she'd call the police to have Brandon picked up. She said she hadn't, she'd forgotten.

He instantly swings the car over in the left lane, cutting someone off. They honk repeatedly. Karl makes a left turn and shoots up the small Laguna street, navigating the car until they are back on the same street where Brandon lives. She is surprised to see Brandon running along the sidewalk. He is dressed in jeans and a leather jacket and has a backpack over one shoulder. She guesses the backpack contains the rest of his drugs and the twenty-five dollars he got from the brothers.

'That's him,' she says calmly.

Karl, who has never had a single scratch on any car he's ever owned, who methodically washes the car every Sunday, yanks the steering wheel and sends the car hopping the curb, over the sidewalk, and across someone's freshly cut lawn. He brakes twenty feet in front of Brandon.

Brandon sees Dixie. There is no cocky grin now. His nose is crooked with blood crusted around each nostril. A dark bruise curls around his lower jaw. He sees the car door opening and Karl lunging out toward him and he turns and runs in the opposite direction. Karl has never been in a fight in his life, but he chases Brandon as if he has done this all his life. Dixie remains in the car watching. Looking at it through the frame of the windshield makes it seem a little like a movie.

Karl tackles Brandon. They both sprawl across the side-

425

walk, but Brandon is on the bottom and his face scrapes along the cement. Karl straddles the boy and begins to clumsily pummel him, fists pounding down with unerring rhythm. He reminds Dixie of the guy on those slave ships who pounds out the rowing boat on a huge drum. Finally exhausted, Karl stops, slumps a moment to catch his breath, then gets up.

Dixie leaves the car and goes over to join him. She bends over and presses her fingertips against Brandon's neck. No pulse. 'Well,' she says to Karl. 'That's that.'

PART FOUR

One Size
Fits All

**In Which Dixie's Rape
Has Unexpected Effects
on Each Woman's Life**

28

Barcelona closes her office door and says, 'You surprise me. You really do.'

'Surprise you?'

Barcelona walks back to her desk and sits down. She lifts the fifty-eight typewritten pages in one hand and hefts them up and down. The edges flap like a sluggish moth. 'I can't believe this is the same book you brought in here a month ago. It's amazing.'

Crystal Ponce seems confused by Barcelona's enthusiasm. 'It's the same book,' she says. 'Except for the changes.'

'That's my point, the changes are phenomenal. Very impressive.'

Crystal frowns as if annoyed at the compliment. 'It's still the same story. I just touched it up a bit, that's all.'

Barcelona leans back in her chair, still holding the fifty-eight pages. Finally she understands. Crystal resents any implication that the changes Barcelona suggested might have improved the book. She wants the book to be all her own, not share any credit.

'I just wrote, that's all,' Crystal says. 'I don't try to intellectualize everything.'

Barcelona sniffs the air. Crystal's perfume is too strong, Opium, she thinks, or Poison. At least it smothers the charred odor that's been hanging in the air the last three days. Brush fires in the foothills of Riverside and Santa Ana Mountains have made the air greasy with smoke. While driving on the freeways she can see dark gray clouds blossom on the horizons like exploded atomic bombs. Barcelona has taken to washing her hands and face several times a day, each time scrubbing away layers of soot and smudge. Her throat is always dry and scratchy. She drinks Diet Cokes constantly to soothe the rough membrane.

Crystal digs through her purse. Her hand emerges with a stick of sugarless gum which she carefully unwraps, folds in half, and sticks in her mouth. While she chews, she folds the silver foil into a little square and stores that back into her purse.

Crystal Ponse is one of the most infuriating women Barcelona has ever met. When she'd first entered Barcelona's office four weeks ago with those dreadful ten pages about the woman whose life had been ruined by her exceptional beauty, Barcelona had wanted to shove her face into a toilet bowl and keep flushing until her expensively frosted hair lost some of its moussed stiffness. Aside from being as cold and humorless as a gutted cod, her novel had been trite, boring, and unintentionally laughable. Why Barcelona let herself be bullied into reading more pages of the awful thing she doesn't know. The first chapter was truly nauseating, but the next chapter was even worse. Endless whining about the burdens of growing up wealthy, having to endure other children's jealousy. And of course the dreaded Face. Too gorgeous for most mortals to behold. Other little girls went screaming to their mothers, crying over why they couldn't be as beautiful. Little boys feared her perfect face, scattering from playgrounds at the sight of it as if it were a visitation from the gods. It all sounded so turgid, like Ayn Rand with cramps.

Barcelona hefts the revised pages in her hand again. For the first time they feel substantial. The beginnings of a real book. Once a week for the past month she's met in this office with Crystal, endured the younger woman's patronizing attitude of a wealthy matriarch listening to a maid explain why the vacuum broke down.

But something happened during those meetings. However vacant or argumentative Crystal acted whenever Barcelona suggested changes, she actually began making some: fixing only grammar at first, then eliminating some of the more obvious clichés. Then she seemed to get into the spirit and made more and more changes, polishing, cutting, creating new, richer characters, until these pages were so well written they were scary. Harley had once asked Barcelona if she'd ever had a student she thought might be a better writer than she was. Not yet, she'd said at the time, confident that she never would, not at this level. There were many students of exceptional ability and keen insight, many whom she had encouraged and advised and even helped get published. Crystal wasn't nearly as smart or educated as they were, nor was she as talented. But of all the writers Barcelona ever had in her classes, she was shocked to think that this woman, *whom she didn't even like*, would be the one who would put it all together in just the right combination. What Barcelona couldn't understand was how such a rich book could come out of such a shallow mind. True, she had worked closely with Crystal, but she couldn't take credit for the raw power in the style, the energy hunkering behind each word. Yet how could a woman with no insight, no self-knowledge write it? It's like having a priest as a pimp.

'I want you to know, Crystal, I think so highly of your rewrite I've talked to my own agent about it. She's willing to take a look and waive her usual reading fee.'

Crystal shrugs. 'Sure. I guess that'd be okay.'

Barcelona knows better than to expect enthusiasm or gratitude. But that doesn't matter. What matters now is the book. Even though Crystal is a shit, her novel isn't. The book deserves to be finished and published and people deserve to read and enjoy it. 'I've written down the address. When you write your cover letter, be sure to remind her that I recommended you.'

Crystal takes the paper from Barcelona and studies it with a frown. 'I'm not under any obligation to her, am I?'

'What?'

'If I don't think she's getting me high enough offers I can dump her, right?' Barcelona stares dumbfounded. 'Besides,' Crystal continues, 'wouldn't I be better off with a New York agent? I hear they can get you more money because they have lunch with these editors all the time. Can't you get me a New York agent?'

Breast cancer. Barcelona concentrates on those two words, on the image of rabid cells clumped into a carnivorous tumor in Crystal's breast. The surgeon's scalpel slicing into the breast as if scooping out the meat of a grapefruit. Only conjuring up such a vile image keeps her from laughing in Crystal's rigid face. There is no point in getting angry. Crystal would not understand such a reaction. But Barcelona must remember exactly what Crystal says so she can tell the others at dinner tonight. This will be their first dinner together since Dixie's release from the hospital three weeks ago. They'll all be a little tense. This should give them something to laugh about.

'I've read all about the Literary Brat Pack,' Crystal says. 'And they all have New York agents.'

'I don't know a lot of New York agents,' she tells Crystal. 'But you can write query letters to a few of the better known ones and see if they're interested.'

Crystal reaches across Barcelona's desk and picks up the fifty-eight pages, tucking them neatly into her leather notebook. She takes Grief's address and begins folding the paper into a smaller and smaller stamp, like the gum foil.

'Maybe I'll do that. I'll have to think about it first. Maybe I'll let your agent take a look. I don't know.'

'Gee, I hate to leave her dangling on a hook like this,' Barcelona says, knowing that Crystal either doesn't understand sarcasm, or chooses not to hear it.

'I just want to be sure. I've put so much of myself in this, I don't want it to end up as just some little paperback. Like your books.'

Barcelona laughs. 'No, I don't blame you. Don't let what happened to me happen to you. Let my life serve as a warning to others.'

Crystal fixes her with that flat stare. 'I'm easy to make fun of. I know. I'm too blunt and aggressive sometimes. Women don't like that in another woman.' She stands up and walks to the door, stops and turns around just as her hand touches the knob. 'But maybe if you'd have been blunter and more aggressive back when you were starting out, you'd have done better.'

Barcelona stares at Crystal's flat eyes, the over-frosted hair whipped into a bad imitation of something vaguely European. She can imagine Crystal with a page torn out of *Vogue* with some Parisian model flouncing near a fountain, Crystal handing the page to her hairdresser saying, 'Make me look just like that.' Crystal turns the knob and opens the office door. The gaudy cluster of diamonds on her wedding ring sparks fluorescent light from the overhead bulbs. Something softens in Crystal's eyes. 'You look tired lately.' It was the first statement of personal concern she'd ever made. 'Your eyes are red, your skin isn't the right color. You should soften your eyes by dotting eyeliner close to the lashes instead of drawing a solid line.'

Is this her way of paying me back for critiquing her manuscript all these weeks? Barcelona wonders. Beauty tips.

'We can't all be beautiful,' Barcelona says.

'I don't take any credit for the way I look. I know it's mostly just lucky genes.'

Barcelona can see the too-thick foundation coating Crystal's cheeks like latex paint. The blush is too bright and clownlike. Her lipstick is too dark for her face. Barcelona wants to start circling the flaws with her red pen as if Crystal's face were a sloppy manuscript. 'I just haven't been sleeping well lately,' she says. Which is true. For three weeks now she's spent most nights wrestling with her pillow. 'But thanks for your concern.'

Crystal nods solemnly and leaves without another word.

'Gawwwd,' Barcelona says aloud and reaches for her Diet Coke. Her hand brushes the Elvis bank on her desk, spinning it around so he's facing the wall. The bank is a black plastic box with a plastic figure of Elvis on top, holding a guitar. This is pre-blubber Elvis, in jeans and open shirt, collar up, one leg cocked off the ground, one hand raised above the guitar in mid-strum. You get the feeling the next strum would be so powerful it would launch him into space. Between his feet was a coin slot. When you put a coin in, the arm came down in a mock-strum, the hips swiveled back and forth once, and the coin was swallowed into the black box. The bank had been a gift last week from her neighbor Dave. Darlene's husband.

Dave had been standing next to the bushes that lined Barcelona's garage. He'd been kneeling over scooping Foxy's shit into a brown lunch bag. Foxy sat in the grass nearby looking appropriately contrite. Barcelona had just come home from school and was leaving her garage, one hand clutching her briefcase, the other balancing thirty-five student essays on Chaucer's *Canterbury Tales*. Dave's garage door was open and five or six women were rummaging about, picking up Elvis items and showing them to each other and discussing them, then packing them into cardboard boxes. They were young women, Barcelona's age

434

and younger. They wore shorts and tennis outfits and jogging pants and makeup. Four of them were blonde and they were all mildly attractive.

'What's going on, Dave?' Barcelona asked as Dave twisted the neck of his lunch bag.

'Oh, that's Darlene's Bible study group. They used to get together once a week. They're having a rummage sale and I said they could help themselves.'

'I didn't know Darlene belonged to a Bible study group.'

'Just for a couple months. She was lonely during the day, just her and Foxy. She wasn't very athletic, so she couldn't join the tennis club. She was lousy at cards, so she couldn't join the bridge club.'

'What about a job?'

He shrugged. 'Yeah, well, she did some volunteer work at the hospital. She didn't want a real job just yet.'

'That left the Bible.'

'I don't think she ever actually read the Bible before. But then, who has?'

Foxy started barking at the sky, running back and forth, yanking on the leash. Barcelona and Dave looked up and watched a plane with a fat square body fly overhead.

'That's a C-138,' Dave said, shading his eyes. 'Air tanker. They're using them to fight the fires.'

It was the first time Barcelona considered the fires a personal threat. 'Are we safe?'

'Oh, sure. They'll have them snuffed before they get here.'

Foxy stopped barking, squatted, peed.

'Too much excitement, eh Foxy?' Dave said, laughing.

Barcelona started to walk away. 'See ya, Dave.'

'No, wait.' He reached out and touched her arm. 'Wait. I want you to have something.' He started toward his open garage with Foxy trotting spritely at his side.

Barcelona glanced toward the refuge of her home.

Through her own kitchen window she could see the African violets on the sill and beyond them the nineteen-inch TV which she'd hoped to plant herself in front of for a few minutes while she drank a glass of wine.

Dave stopped at the entrance of his garage, turned, smiled. 'Come on,' he said, waving the brown bag.

She followed him into the garage. Dave did not introduce the pretty women who were busily filling cardboard boxes with Darlene's Elvis memorabilia. The women smiled politely at Barcelona but didn't talk to her. A couple of them were discussing how to transport Darlene's miniature Graceland.

'We could cut it in half,' one of them said.

'Put hinges on it. My Jim could do that. He's handy with tools.'

Another woman mumbled something and they all laughed.

'I *wish*,' the woman married to Jim said.

'Here,' Dave said, handing Barcelona the Elvis bank. 'This was one of Darlene's favorites. We drove all the way to Phoenix to buy this. The owner was a pharmacist.'

Barcelona stepped back without taking the bank. 'I couldn't, Dave. It's too precious. I'm not even a big Elvis fan.'

'Me neither,' he said. 'I mean I like a few of his songs. I like "Don't Be Cruel" and "Teddy Bear," but that's about it. Tell you the truth, Darlene wasn't that big of a fan of his music either. She hardly played his records. She just liked him. Go ahead, take it. I know she'd want you to have it. She thought highly of you.'

'Me?' Barcelona said, surprised.

'Oh yes. She always told me whenever she ran into you while walking Foxy. She thought you were so together. So modern, she used to say. A writer and teacher, all that.

An Eighties woman. Like Elvis was a Fifties man. She admired you. She read all your books.'

Stunned, Barcelona accepted the bank. Then, as quickly as she was able, retreated to her home while Foxy yapped at the women packing boxes.

Now the Elvis bank sits on her desk and Barcelona thinks about Darlene. *What connection had Darlene imagined between Elvis and me?* Barcelona wonders.

Barcelona finishes the rest of her Diet Coke and drops the can into her wastebasket. Her eyes are a little watery from the smoke-laden air.

Barcelona has a few minutes of her office hour left before she can go home, shower and change, and meet the other women. She has mixed feelings about dinner. Sure, she is anxious to see her friends, but she senses a certain drifting away among them since Dixie's rape. It's been weeks since any of them have seen each other. She promised Trina she'd meet her early so they could talk. The last time she saw Trina in the flesh was in Dixie's hospital room. Since then everyone's been so busy. Finally they all managed to schedule tonight's dinner, an inauguration of sorts welcoming Dixie back. Barcelona had tried to see Dixie several times, arrange for lunch or a shopping outing, but Dixie was always busy.

Barcelona has been busy too. Having been so abruptly dumped on her ass by Roger Carlyle, Lynda Kramer, and Hollywood in general, she decided to return to what she knew best, writing novels of the future. Imagining the world as it will become, a hoary reflection of the way it is now. Casting the bones, reading the entrails, figuring the odds and probabilities. The modern math of soothsaying. Cassandra of paperbacks. She started her current novel last week after receiving the Elvis bank from Dave. In a way, Darlene was responsible.

She has devoted herself to this novel like none of her

others. She works on it every spare moment, polishing every word with an artisan's compulsiveness. Her fussiness is more than artistic exactitude; she feels Crystal Ponce's spearmint-scented breath on her neck, the clicking of her stiffened hair like iced branches in a winter breeze.

Devoting herself to this new novel has also allowed her some distance from her personal life, to put that in better perspective too. Everything in that department is finally under control. Eric is definitely a thing of the past, filed under Old Boyfriends. They have talked a couple of times on the phone, but he has not been satisfied with her explanation of why she won't see him again. She has avoided seeing him in person. She feels good about her decision, though she misses him.

Cory is another matter altogether. After flooding his toilet with a tampon, she needed a little time to get over the embarrassment of seeing him again. He calls every day and they've had lunch together twice but have not ventured near his Corona del Mar home or her house. She wants to see him only on neutral grounds. With only two weeks until the election, his campaign has demanded most of his time, especially now that the polls have him surprisingly but firmly leading Carla Bennington.

She doesn't know what to think of Cory. She enjoys being with him but isn't sure whether he thinks of her as just a diversion from his high-pressure election, or whether there's something else going on there. Maybe she'd ask Trina tonight, see if he's talked to her about them.

Barcelona looks at the big clock on the wall and decides to cut her office hour short by five minutes. She begins tucking papers into her briefcase.

The phone rings. She and her office mate share one phone so she has to reach across both desks to grab the receiver.

'Hello?' she answers.

'Barcelona Lee?' the woman's voice says. 'The writer?'

'Yes.'

'Oh, good. I tried you at home first, so ignore my message on your machine.'

'Who is this?'

'Oh, God.' She laughs. The laugh, oddly familiar, sounds like the first few notes of the Beatles' 'Across the Universe.' 'I'm sorry,' she says. 'There's something strange about calling a professor. I'm having these prickly flashbacks about my own college days. I'm afraid I wasn't a very good student.'

'Who is this?' Barcelona repeats.

'Sorry, I'm doing it again. This is Lynda Kramer. Hi.'

What do you say to an international star of stage and screen? Barcelona wonders. 'Hi.'

'I just took a chance that you'd be in,' Lynda Kramer says. 'I know when I was in college my professors were never in their offices. Maybe that's just Princeton though.'

'Maybe.' Barcelona doesn't feel part of this conversation. She answers only when Lynda Kramer cues her to.

'Well, I'm glad you're conscientious, or we could have kept missing each other for days.'

'I didn't know we were looking for each other.'

'That's what I'm calling about. To explain.'

Rapid knocking vibrates the office door. The sound is angry, urgent.

'Excuse me a moment,' Barcelona says to Lynda Kramer.

'Sure. It'll give me a chance to untangle my daughter's head from the telephone cord.'

Barcelona is silent, pretending to be gone, but listening. She hears: 'Come here, Sarah. Let mommy have the cord. Come on, sweetie.'

The knocking continues. Barcelona puts the telephone

down and walks to the door. She is about to open it when Eric charges into her office.

'What the hell's going on?' he demands. 'Why won't you talk to me, Barcy?' He is wearing a denim shirt with snaps for buttons. It is new, but it looks just like the one he wore in graduate school. So do the jeans, so do the suede hiking shoes.

'Hiking shoes,' she says sharply. 'Just where the fuck are you planning to hike this afternoon, Eric?'

Eric is stunned by her response. His anger ebbs a little in the face of hers. He stands in the middle of the office and looks down at his shoes. 'What are you talking about?'

'Never mind. Just wait outside until I'm through on the phone.'

'We have to talk,' he insists. 'Clear this up.'

'This is my job, Eric. Not the appropriate place.'

'You won't return my calls.' A vague whine has entered his voice. 'I love you, Barcy. I know you love me.'

'Wait outside,' she says like a teacher to a student. It has always been the other way around.

He looks at her sadly and the white scar that cleaves his eyebrow seems to pulse with its own life. The smooth phosphorescent white reminds her of his selfless act on behalf of that woman. How he had stood up for her, protected her against her bully of a husband. Barcelona feels she owes him something for that abused woman's sake, if not her own. 'Please, Eric,' she says softly. 'Let me finish this call. We'll talk afterwards.'

He nods and leaves. She can see him through the wired glass sitting on the sofa in the waiting area. He is sitting next to a Vietnamese girl who is reading *People* magazine. Eric reaches into his back pocket and pulls out a paperback book. Barcelona can't make out the title, but she knows what it is from the familiar shapes on the cover: *The Doctor and the Soul: from Psychotherapy to Logotherapy* by Viktor E.

Frankl. It's one of his favorite read-in-public books.

Barcelona sits down behind her desk, takes a deep breath, and picks up the phone. 'Hello?'

'Sounds like I caught you at a bad time,' Lynda Kramer says.

'Just some unfinished business.'

'I know whereof you speak. I always think of that poem by Stephen Crane. Where he says love is like a burnt match skating in a urinal.'

'Hart Crane,' Barcelona corrects, but she is impressed by the quote nevertheless.

'Oh, right. I don't know why I get those two mixed up. Hart as in hcart as in love. I took a memory course once because I always had trouble remembering my lines.'

'Do they work? I've always thought about taking one myself.'

'Why? You don't have to remember lines.'

'No, just to remember things, I don't know, dates and such.'

'You can't remember when you've got a date?'

'I mean dates of writers, historical movements, that sort of thing. Teacher stuff.' Actually, now that she's had to explain it, it does sound kind of silly. Barcelona is dying to know why Lynda Kramer is calling, but she's afraid to be too direct fearing there might be some mistake. She feels a little childish to be so thrilled at talking to a movie star. She sees Eric staring in at her through the glass and she shifts her head away from his gaze so he won't know how giddy she is.

'First, I owe you an apology,' Lynda Kramer says.

'Oh?'

'About that script you wrote. We never even read it. To tell you the truth, my agent advised against it. Not because of the script, he never read it either. It was because of Roger Carlyle.'

Barcelona fishes the Diet Coke can out of the trash and begins slowly bending the tap up and down.

'After we talked with him the first time we agreed to take a look at the script he said he had. Then he said there was a delay because you were doing a rewrite.'

'Actually, I hadn't even written it yet.'

'I'm not surprised. He wasn't all that interested in your script anyway. He was trying to parlay his loose association with us into a studio job in production. He went around saying he had a deal with us. When we found out about it, we had to cut off any association with him. Unfortunately, that included you too.'

Barcelona twists the tab to the left then the right. 'So he was never interested in my novel or script except as a means to a job.'

'Mostly. Though there was also a chance your script might sell.'

'So why are you calling?' she asks. 'Are you interested in my book?'

'Well, unfortunately, Roger Carlyle optioned your book for a year with an option to renew another year. That effectively ties it up for two years. I can't wait that long to get started on my next project.'

The tab snapped off in Barcelona's fingers. She dropped it into the can. 'You must have hundreds of projects coming at you all the time.'

'True. But I'm anxious to move in a new direction, expand a little. To tell you the truth, I'm a little tired of playing neurotic, hothouse orchids with foreign accents and a Dark Past to hide. I'd like to prove I can do genre work too. But I want something classy and sophisticated, not schlock.'

Barcelona's heart was thumping solidly in her chest. 'Where do I come in?'

'I read *Live Wires* and a couple of your other novels.

There's something about them that really touches me. I'm no big sci-fi fan, understand. Can't usually get past all the technical jargon. But yours are so rich with people, that's what captures my attention. I think you can do a fine script.'

'A script from which book?'

'Well, that's the thing. I haven't read them all and, to be honest, there's not much of a chance I'll get to them either. What I'd like is for us to have a cozy little lunch and hear you pitch the story lines of each book. See where we can go from there.'

Lunch with Lynda Kramer! Barcelona wants to go to the door and wave Eric back in, have him listen to the conversation. She wishes there was a way she could hook this into the public address system.

And yet. Barcelona is very involved with her new novel. She has never been happier writing, more involved with her characters. She's not sure she's ready to risk losing this sense of fulfillment for another iffy project. She explains that to Lynda Kramer.

Lynda Kramer pauses. 'Tell me about your new book. What's it called?'

'*Feasts.*'

'*Feasts*? Just *Feasts*?'

'Just *Feasts*.'

'Sounds a little spooky, like something from Stephen King. There aren't any space creatures in it, are there? I'm not interested in bumping heads with Sigourney Weaver. Nothing with aliens.'

'No, there aren't any aliens. It's about a woman living a hundred years from now. Only in a hundred years they will have discovered a drug, a medicine that will prolong life. Actually double life expectancy. The problem is that the drug only works on men. Has to do with their chromosome makeup.'

'So the men live twice as long as the women?'

'Right. You can see the social problems, especially when it comes to love and marriage and raising families.'

'Yeah. What does a guy do with his wife when she's old and he still has another seventy years to live?'

'Exactly.'

Lynda Kramer sighs. 'Okay, I'm hooked. Tell me.'

'The society has evolved a very sophisticated approach. Women kill themselves when they reach the age of sixty to allow the husband to seek another wife and even raise new children. The "feasts" in the title refers to the ritualized meals the women prepare, their last meal laced with a painless poison. The entire family gathers to watch her eat it and stay with her until she dies. It's all very loving.'

'Sounds faintly Japanese.'

'Yes,' Barcelona agrees. 'It's meant to.'

'What about the heroine?'

'She's a scientist whose mother is a week from her sixtieth birthday. In the week it takes her mother to prepare her final feast, our heroine attempts to find some way into the pharmaceutical lab where the life-prolonging formula is kept. She believes there's a conspiracy by the men who own the company to keep the drug from women, that the formula can be revised to include them.'

Lynda Kramer laughs happily. 'I like it. Suspense, conspiracy. I hope there's romance.'

Barcelona says, 'There's always romance. This time with another scientist who's trying to help her.'

'And they uncover the conspiracy?'

'No. They discover that there is no conspiracy. That the formula really only works on men and that they haven't been able to find one that works on women, though they have tried.'

Lynda Kramer says nothing for a while. Then, 'I don't

444

understand the point. That's kind of anticlimactic, isn't it?' There is a faint hint of disappointment in her voice.

'Not really. The point isn't whether or not there was a conspiracy. That doesn't even matter. The *real* conspiracy is that the men took the serum even knowing that there was none for women, that the women they loved would die. That they adopted ritualized suicide as an okay social event rather than forgo the drug until they had one for everybody. That's the point.'

Again, Lynda Kramer doesn't speak. Barcelona can hear a baby's gurgling, a pen tapping against plastic. Through the glass strip she sees Eric talking with the Vietnamese girl. His home for abused women had started to see more and more Vietnamese women, Westernized enough to decide beatings were not a natural part of the marriage routine. To help them better, Eric had begun studying Vietnamese and now spoke with remarkable fluency. The girl outside the office is laughing and when she looks at Eric, Barcelona recognizes an infatuational glint in her eyes. Barcelona feels a surge of affection for Eric and suddenly wonders if she hasn't made a mistake with him.

Lynda Kramer says: 'If it's okay with you, I'll have my lawyer contact your agent and see what agreement we can reach for me to purchase the film rights for *Feasts*. Naturally I want you to write the script, the first draft anyway.'

'What kind of money are we talking about?'

Lynda Kramer laughs. 'That's for our agents to decide.'

'Ballpark,' Barcelona said.

'I shouldn't be saying anything. My agent, lawyer, and accountant would take turns strangling me.'

'I need to know.'

Lynda Kramer pops her lips a few times as she thinks. 'I'd say $50,000 for the film rights and another $50,000 for the first draft of the script. More if the film actually gets made.'

Barcelona presses her palm against her stapler and squeezes out a couple of crumpled staples. She sweeps them off her desk onto the floor. A hundred thousand dollars. Eat shit, Crystal Ponce.

They say good-bye with Lynda Kramer expressing how excited she is about the project and that they would talk again soon.

After hanging up, Barcelona sits at her desk and stares across the office at Susan Mesa's desk. It isn't as tidy as Barcelona's. She has photographs of her family on it. There's a large rock the size of a turtle. The rock is painted with Apache symbols that her twelve-year-old daughter learned about at summer camp. There are three books open on the desk, each a critical study of *The Great Gatsby*, which Susan will teach this afternoon. Susan has no ideas of her own about the literature she teaches. She acts pretty much as a researcher, looking up various interpretations of the works she teaches, then explaining those interpretations to her students. Barcelona had teased her about that once and Susan, unashamed, had said, 'I never could figure out what my professors were rattling on about with these books. I just liked the stories. But I was hell on wheels in the library. Come class time, I could spout literary bullshit with the best of them.'

Barcelona tries to imagine a hundred thousand dollars in her bank account. She pictures the numerals written neatly in her checkbook where it says current balance. She is torn between redecorating her office and quitting her job. She wants to drive over to South Coast Plaza and buy clothing, any clothing. She can't believe her luck. This is the kind of good fortune that never happens to her. Everything she's ever gotten has been through steady plodding, long-range planning. She prefers dumb luck.

She needs to share the news, tell someone. She remembers Eric waiting, but when she peers through the glass he's not on the couch. She gets up and opens the door. The Vietnames girl is still reading *People* magazine. Eric is gone.

Barcelona pulls a sheet of blank paper from her desk and writes on it with a red marker. On her way out, she tacks the paper to the door. It says: GONE HOLLY-WOOD.

29

Trina bites into her hot dog and ketchup squirts out the other end of the bun and globs onto her blouse. She looks down just as the crowd of parents on the bleachers screams and applauds and leaps to its feet. She looks up and sees Karyn running for a ball spitting across center field. Karyn runs toward the ball on her skinny legs, glove positioned on the ground, ready to scoop the ball up. The ball rolls quickly, hopping and hiccuping along the bumpy ground like an escaping rodent. Karyn closes in on the ball, her glove less than a foot away. She swoops toward it. The ball hits something unseen in the grass and hops over her glove and rolls away from her. Her teammates are yelling at her to get the ball.

'Go, go, go!' Tommy the pitcher yells.

The catcher stands on home plate awaiting the arrival of the runner from second base. He keeps socking an anxious fist into his mitt.

The batter is a slow runner, but she's closing in on second base anyway.

'Get the ball! Get the ball!' Coach Lyle hollers from the bench. He is chewing gum furiously, waving with both hands.

The coach from the visiting team is shouting for the batter to keep going to third.

And Karyn is running after the ball now, trotting behind

it as it continues to skitter and wobble just out of reach. Finally she hurls herself on it, trapping it under her body. She grabs it, stands, throws to the shortstop, Bill Leader, who's followed her into the field.

By the time the ball makes it to the catcher, a chubby kid Trina thinks is named Axel, the runner has scored and the batter is on third.

Karyn sulks in center field, her face red with exertion and embarrassment. She slaps her glove against her leg. That was the first ball in four innings hit anywhere near him. Trina can almost hear Karyn's muttering as she scolds herself, questions the Fates, and curses the stupid bumpy ground. Karyn is a mutterer, wandering the house in times of emotional stress emitting low-decibel grumbling accompanied by exaggerated face-making. Sometimes Trina tries to secretly follow her when she's doing that just to catch her in one of her strange faces, her eyes wide, her nose scrunched, her mouth twisted into a scowl. Eventually, Karyn always talks herself out of these moods. She's not a moper.

Trina dips the corner of the napkin she had around her hot dog in her 7-Up and scrubs the stain off her flannel blouse. The stain rests on her left breast and the scrubbing causes the breast to shake. Out of the corner of her eye she sees a couple of men on the bleachers watching her progress. She smiles at their furtive stares and tries to figure out what's so sexy about a swollen clump of fatty tissues jiggling under a blouse. Why is it you can have an ass that's too fat, legs that are too fat, but men never think tits are too fat?

She has had her hands and lips on Carla's breasts, felt the soft swell, kissed the plucky nipples. But she has never felt lust for them. Actually, she's had her hands and lips everywhere on Carla's body and has not ever felt lust. She has felt affection, strong caring, but never the dripping, sticky, rip-my-panties-off desire she's felt for men. Yet, and this is the incredible part, the actual sex isn't really much different from that with men, even men she'd thought were gods, men she'd loved, men who'd loved her. That surprises her.

'You okay?' Rob asks. He is sitting next to her on the bleacher, his hot dog gnawed neatly to a nub. His has ketchup, mustard, and relish on it and not a drop of any of them has spilled.

'You know me,' Trina says, nodding at her protruding chest. 'The Continental Breakfast Shelf.'

'They catch better than Karyn.' He grins.

They both laugh. He hands her his spare napkin. He always remembers to ask for a second; Trina never does. There was a time when he used to just automatically reach over and swab barbecue sauce from her face, brush bread crumbs from her lap, dab salad dressing from her blouse. There was something especially intimate about that, gestures of love and affection. Now he hands her his spare napkin, gesture of polite friendship.

Trina has come to the last six Little League games in a row. She used to just alternate games with Rob, but since she's been seeing Carla, her guilt quotient has skyrocketed. She sees herself as a perverse role model for Karyn. She worries that Rob will find out and begin court proceedings to have Karyn taken away. The word lesbian will be used a lot. It's a funny-sounding word and Trina doesn't know how she will react to having it used in connection with her.

When Trina had gone into the office the day after she had followed Carla up the coast, The Candidate had walked into her office cheerfully whistling 'The Jet Song' from *West Side Story*. 'So,' he said. 'What'd you find out?'

'Easy, Action. Your turf is safe. No need to rumble.'

He laughed and sat on the edge of her desk. 'Talk or I fart and scatter these papers all over the room.'

Trina slapped hands on two separate piles of papers. 'I'll talk, boss.' She leaned back in her chair and stared into his eyes, looking for something in them she wasn't sure was there. She'd have to find out the hard way. 'I found out she's tough.'

'We already know that.'

'She's also smart, and very savvy.'

'Cut to the chase, Trina.'

Trina sighed. 'What if I told you she was having an affair?'

The Candidate paused, shifted on the desk. 'Does it involve misuse of any city funds?'

'It involves a chicken, a goat, and long flashlight.'

He laughed. 'I'd say she's more fun than I thought.'

'Really, what would you say, Cory?'

'I'd say that's her business. As long as it doesn't involve abuse of her position.'

Trina stood up and placed a hand on his cheek. 'You really are a nice guy, aren't you?'

'You're surprised?'

Trina kissed his cheek and sat back down. 'I'm always surprised.'

'You're a jaded romantic.' He got up and swaggered toward the door, snapping his fingers. 'Tell Tony to meet me at the gym. And walk tall.'

'We always walk tall,' she said, playing along. 'We're Jets, the greatest.'

He turned and winked. 'When you're a Jet you're a Jet all the way.'

Trina bites into her hot dog again. She watches Karyn adjust her hat. Adjusting hats is what her team does best. Playing baseball is what they do worst. They are in last place without much hope of ever getting out. Karyn has been talking about quitting the team. During soccer season she is one of the stars on a first-place team. She doesn't buy Trina's speech about losing being character building. Trina doesn't buy it either.

Karyn's team makes a double play and Rob waves his arms. His leather jacket squeaks with each movement. Karyn told her that Rob has a bunch of hair transplant pamphlets in his bathroom. Trina glances over at him and tries to imagine him with those terrible connect-the-dot patches on his scalp. She wants to tell him he looks just fine, maybe even a little better with those deep bays cutting into his hairline. But it is no longer her place to make those kinds of statements. Too easy to take it the wrong way: Is she saying that because she doesn't want me to look good for other women? Is she saying that even more hair won't make me attractive? Is she coming on to me? Etc., etc.

Actually, Trina has been getting along quite well with Rob lately. They are cordial, friendly, sometimes even tender. More important, her physical ailments are gone. No memory loss, no disorientation, no hot flashes about wanting to get pregnant. Miraculously, The Candidate has pulled ahead of Carla in the polls. Everything's been just great the past three weeks.

Almost perfect.

That first week after spending the night with Carla, though, that had been awful. Dixie being raped and tortured. Trina's own guilt over Carla had chewed her stomach into wormy confetti. And there was still a campaign to work.

That first week, just returning from the hospital after visiting Dixie, Calvin the office gopher holding one hand over the phone, said, 'Line three for you, Trina.'

'Who is it?'

He shrugged his pointy nineteen-year-old shoulders. 'Some guy.'

'What guy? Always get a name.'

Right.' He nodded but didn't do anything.

Trina marched into her office, still trying to shake the image of Dixie lying in the white hospital bed, wincing with pain when she tried to shift her hips. Trina tried not to imagine the damage hidden under those crisp sheets.

'Hello?' she said into the phone. 'This is Trina Bedford.'

'One moment, please,' the man said. There was some clicking as the call was transferred.

'Hi,' Carla Bennington said. They hadn't spoken or seen each other since that night five days before.

'Hi,' Trina said. She kept her voice cool, businesslike. Her skin tingled, like when she was a kid stealing a quarter from her father's pants. That tingle was like an invisible skin sensing danger, warning her that she was about to get caught. Trina flashed on a possibility that the conversation might be recorded, that it might somehow be used against The Candidate. She shrugged that off as absurd.

'Surprised?' Carla said.

'Yes.'

Carla laughed. 'Not as surprised as I.'

Trina said nothing.

'Sorry for the spy stuff. I had an aide call in case someone there might recognize my voice. I don't want to put you on the spot.'

There was a long pause. Neither spoke. The only sound was their breath whipping across the mouthpiece.

Finally, Carla spoke. 'I'd like to see you again, Trina.'

'I don't think that would be a good idea.'

'I'm not talking garter belts and push-up bras. Just lunch or something.'

'I feel uncomfortable. I have a young daughter.'

'Just lunch, Trina.'

'Okay.'

They ate in Long Beach, away from anyone who might recognize them. They talked about their lives. The polls that morning had shown The Candidate nipping at her heels. They had joked about it. Carla had seemed unconcerned. Even later, after Cory had pulled ahead, Carla only praised Trina's work, lamented that she hadn't hired Trina first. Trina feels bad for Carla, but also good for herself. Her own success keeps her on an equal level with Carla, dulls the competitive edge that always hovers between them. They both like that edge.

Two days ago they slept together again for the first time since that night in the hotel. Karyn was at an Angels game with Rob. Trina and Carla rented a room at a motel in Seal Beach, south of the city. They undressed, made love. The whole time Trina felt like a scientist on a secret mission, pretending to be someone else, exploring the differences between making love with a man and a woman. She imagined a diary or notebook in which she jotted down her scientific observations: Smell and feel completely different. Soft, enveloping, meshing as opposed to hard muscles bouncing off each other. Lying in man's arms, safe, protective. Woman's arms, open, honest, no secrets. Talking afterward, no subtext, no hidden meanings.

'Are we dikes?' Carla asked afterward, her arm across Trina's bare stomach.

'I don't know. Technically, I guess.'

'I don't feel like one.'

'How does one feel?'

Carla rolled over and stared at the ceiling. 'I don't know, I've never done this before.'

'Never?'

'Just that time I told you about when I was eight and that neighbor girl tried to teach me to kiss. That's the extent of my dikishness. Dikehood. Whatever. Mostly we giggled.'

'I miss giggling,' Trina said.

The baseball game ends. Karyn's team loses 15-1. Karyn

454

struck out once, walked once, and was thrown out at first. She shuffles over to Trina and Rob but doesn't look at them. Rob congratulates her for playing hard, tells her that having fun is more important than winning, kisses her on the cheek, and leaves. Karyn never looks at him.

On the drive home, Karyn sits staring out the side window, muttering. Trina tries to talk her out of her mood, but nothing works.

'You'll get them next time, kiddo,' Trina says.

'No we won't. We'll never get them. They're better. All the teams are better.'

This is true and hard to respond positively to. 'Even better teams can be beaten. They get cocky and a smart team can use that against them.'

Karyn turns in her seat and glares angrily at Trina. 'That's crap. Maybe if they all were handcuffed together, maybe then we could beat them. But that's all.'

'You can't give up.'

'What do you know about sports? You didn't play when you were a kid. All you did was ballet.' She says 'ballet' as if it were a disfiguring disease.

'Hey, don't knock ballet, kiddo. You try prancing around on your toes for an hour and see how you feel.'

'Why would I want to? That's stupid. What good is standing on your toes?'

Trina doesn't feel like going into it. When Trina was Karyn's age, ballet ruled. Every little girl wanted to go on toe, lift a leg so gracefully that everyone would swoon in envy. Trina had been good, one of the prize students at the Kirkland School. From three until twelve she glided, flowed, twirled, and leapt through childhood, performing little impromptu snatches during recess or for her parents' friends. Then disaster. At twelve her breasts inflated as suddenly and dramatically as a sea vest. The other girls made jokes. Trina slouched, no longer opened her arms

455

with gleeful abandon. Her movements became cramped, stopped flowing as she tried to hide her bulging chest. Finally, she stopped taking classes. She became a cheerleader instead, where big tits were an asset.

'And guys always act like they're doing you a favor letting you play,' Karyn says as they climb out of the car. 'Like they coulda won if only they didn't have dumb girls on their team.'

'The other team had girls,' Trina says.

'Mom, that's not the point.' Karyn huffs into the house, exasperated at Trina's ignorance. Trina follows, smiling and shaking her head.

Trina goes straight into the kitchen and plays back the phone machine while looking through the refrigerator for some possible combination of foods that might make a dinner for Karyn.

Beep. *Hi, Trina. Can I catch a ride home with you after dinner tonight? Harley's dropping me off at the restaurant. Please, please, please. I'll paint your portrait on my fingernails.* Diva. No other messages.

Thinking about dinner with everyone tonight makes her a little nervous. She reaches into the refrigerator and grabs a yellow plastic pitcher with about an inch of sugar-free Wyler's Tropical Punch. She tilts the pitcher and drinks out of the spout. Some of the punch sluices down her chin and drips onto her blouse. She finishes the punch and sets the pitcher on the counter. She wonders how to act around Dixie, what to say, what not to say.

'I'm making dinner,' Trina hollers, 'so hurry up and take your shower.' Karyn doesn't answer, but Trina knows she heard.

She slices some cucumbers, tomato, and an avocado, drapes a few rings of red onion over the top. Salad.

She heats up the iron skillet and dumps the plastic bag of chicken fajitas in. She stir-fries the chicken, bell peppers,

456

onions, whatever else is in there. They come premixed at the Irvine Ranch Market. While they're cooking she lays three flour tortillas between wet paper towels and nukes them in the microwave. Entrée.

A car screeches outside, the brakes wail in a loud primal scream.

'Jesus,' Trina says, stopping to listen for a crash. None comes. The car continues on. Trina wonders about dessert. There's hardly enough time to make anything and still get changed for dinner with the others. Still, guilt pecks at her and she feels compelled to prove herself as Mother of the Year. All this could be used later in court on her behalf.

She laughs at that thought. She is peering into the freezer, relieved to find some Dole blueberry fruit bars that will serve nicely for dessert, when another scream of tortured car brakes shoots adrenaline through her system. She closes the door to listen, hears shouting. A man. And Karyn's voice.

'Oh, God,' Trina gasps, running for the front door.

The street outside hovers in twilight, the street lamps fighting back the night. In the street in front of their house, a blue Lincoln is parked at an angle in the middle of the street. Heavy black tire marks jut out behind the car for three or four feet. A bald man in a business suit is yelling at Karyn. Karyn listens without saying anything. Trina's heart calms a little to see her daughter alive, but there is a deeper horror just under the skin: *How did she leave the house without my knowing*?

'Karyn,' Trina calls as she walks briskly toward them. 'Karyn, what happened?'

'This your daughter?' the man says. His face is red from yelling.

'Yes. What happened?'

'Some piece of work you've got, lady. Some fucking piece of work.'

457

'Don't talk to my daughter that way, buster, or you'll be walking with a hitch in your getalong.'

He glowers at Trina, but when she doesn't back down he just snorts and starts toward his car. 'Maybe the cops would like to get in on this conversation.'

Trina's neck heats with fear. She looks at Karyn, but her daughter doesn't return her gaze. She is no longer dressed in her baseball uniform, but wears shorts and a sweatshirt. Trina follows the man to his car.

The man walks around the front of the car. Lying pinned under his wheel is a dummy made of Karyn's baseball uniform stuffed with sheets and pillowcases, clothing Trina recognizes from the dirty laundry hamper. The head is a small pink pillow from Karyn's room, stapled to the collar of her baseball jersey. 'Your daughter crouched behind that car there'—he points back at a neighbor's car parked on the street—'and when I drove close, she tossed it in front of my car. Naturally I thought it was a child and I slammed on my brakes. Nearly had a fucking heart attack. When I hit it, I thought I . . .' He shakes his head and sags against the fender of his car. He looks terribly shaken.

'Are you okay?' Trina asks him. She purposely avoids looking at Karyn until her anger is under control. 'Can I get you some water or something?'

'No, I, I guess I'm just relieved I didn't kill anyone. I don't know if I could live with that.'

'No, no, of course.' She puts her hand on his shoulder. He is near fifty, overweight. She can smell the sour stench of fear pouring from him. Her touch seems to calm him a little.

'I didn't mean to swear at her like that. It's wrong. I just . . .' He sighs. Trina has the feeling he'd like to cry with relief.

'My fault entirely. I should have listened to you first. Didn't mean to snap like that. Mother's instinct, I guess.'

458

'Sure. You have a right.'

'Don't worry. I'll take care of this. I'll make sure it never happens again.'

'Yes, please,' he says. There is pleading in his tone.

He gets in his car and slowly pulls forward, unpinning the dummy. Trina drags it out from under his car and he drives away, lighting up a cigarette with shaky fingers.

Trina carries the dummy back to where Karyn is and shoves it into her arms. 'First, you're off the baseball team, young lady.'

'Big deal,' Karyn says. 'I'm off a last-place team. I'll deal with it.'

'Good, because you can deal with this too: You're grounded for a month. Straight to school and straight home again afterwards. No playing with Angela, no movies, no TV. And the same will be true when you see your father. Understand?'

Karyn turns away and starts walking toward the house.

Trina is on her in three steps and grabs her arm, spinning her around. 'Answer me, Karyn. Do you understand?'

'Yes, I understand. Big fucking deal.' She throws the dummy down, a black tire pattern across its pink head, and races for the front door.

Trina runs after her, through the front door, down the hallway, and into her room.

'Get out of my room!' Karyn screams. 'This is my room!'

Trina grips both of Karyn's arms and yanks her down on the bed. 'Stop that! You will not yell at your mother.'

Karyn struggles to twist away, shaking her head. Her hair lashes against Trina's face, but she holds tight.

'Stop this!' Trina says.

'Shut up,' Karyn snaps back.

Trina wrestles down the urge to slap Karyn. She is determined to settle this without hitting. 'Don't you see what you did out there was very wrong? That man could have been killed. He might have swerved and hit another car. He might even have hit you. You both could have been killed.'

'I was just doing it for fun.'

'Scaring someone like that, maybe causing someone else harm, that's not fun, Karyn. That's stupid.' Blah, blah, blah, Trina thinks. *I wouldn't listen to me either if I weren't the one talking.*

'You think everything is stupid.' Karyn hollers this as loud as she can for some reason.

'I certainly do not.'

'You do. You think everything is stupid. You and Daddy. You think I care about baseball? I don't care. You don't want me to do what I want to do.'

'What do you want to do?'

Karyn says nothing. Tears start to flood her eyes. Big tears, the size of dimes. Her cheeks are a steady stream. Great sobs hunch her over. 'Daddy thinks I can't play. I did lousy today. You guys aren't proud of me at all.'

Trina finally understands. Kid logic is hard to follow sometimes; the words aren't always good clues. They can be misleading. Karyn thinks Rob is ashamed of her because of the game. Now Trina understands the relentless practicing in soccer and baseball, why Karyn studies so hard for a sixth-grader. Part of her thinks that if she excelled at everything, school and sports, Trina and Rob would be so proud of her they'd get back together again.

'It's just that we're a lousy team,' Karyn says. 'I could be better with another team. I'd make you proud.'

Trina's own eyes tear, her mouth quivers. She fights it. She wants to comfort Karyn, not cry with her. But she can't help herself. The tears bounce off her cheeks, splash into her mouth. She pulls Karyn close and they sob into each other's arms. Trina stops crying after a minute, but Karyn continues on, sometimes with loud sobs, sometimes with just a low humming sound. Trina's blouse is soaked through. She can feel Karyn's heart patter against her own. Slowly, Karyn's crying stops and she drifts into sleep.

This was nothing really, no more than a spat like a hundred before and a hundred to come. But Trina thinks this is the happiest she has ever been in her life.

30

Barcelona asks the waitress what time it is. The waitress has three bright Swatches on her wrist, each a different color and face design. 'Six-fifteen,' the waitress says. 'I can tell you the time in Tokyo too. Or Sri Lanka.'

'Six-fifteen?' Barcelona repeats, checking her own watch, which says six-twenty.

'Seven more months of waiting tables and I'll have saved enough to go to Tokyo. Japan and Sri Lanka, those are the places I've always wanted to visit.'

The waitress beams at Barcelona. She is about nineteen, with short blond hair except for the back which is red and feathers down her neck past her collar. Like all the other waitresses in Forty Carrots, she wears a white blouse and black pants. Her pants are so tight the V at her crotch hugs her pubic mound in revealing definition. 'I heard that Japanese men worship blondes,' she says. 'Is that true?'

Barcelona wonders when she reached the age where she looked like she'd know the answers to obscure questions like that. 'Yes, it's true. They are obsessed with blondes. Especially tall ones.'

'I'm five six.'

'To them that's tall.'

'Great! From waitress to goddess. Only in America, right?'

'And Japan.'

'Oh, right.' She giggles. 'You want to wait for your friend before you order?'

Barcelona checks her watch again. Trina is twenty minutes late. 'Bring me another glass of white wine while I wait.'

'Sure thing.' The waitress rushes off as if late for her plane. Barcelona's table is outside the restaurant, in a section of mall made to look like an outdoor café, with a fence and plants corralling in the patrons. But there is still something funny and uncomfortable about sitting at a table in the middle of an enclosed mall while shoppers laden with packages trudge back and forth next to you, staring at your food or drink with greedy eyes.

This is not the restaurant where they will be having dinner, but this is where Trina agreed to meet Barcelona so they could chat a little, catch up on each other's lives before the dinner with the others. The dinner restaurant is a ten-minute drive, plus the five-minute walk to her car. That doesn't give her much time with Trina, which makes her angry because she had such great news to share. A phone call from Lynda Kramer, for Christ's sake. She'd actually been *hired* by a famous movie star. Her first thought, absurdly, was how this would look at her twentieth high school reunion just a few years away. Sitting by the phone afterward she'd had a sudden vision as white-hot as grease rags bursting spontaneously into flames: she and Lynda Kramer walking into the Muncy High School gym together, standing there amid the spiraling crepe paper and mirrored ball while her old classmates gaped and cooed and wept with envy. Until now the only thing her hometown is famous for is once having spawned the national poster child for the muscular dystrophy campaign. Jerry Lewis sang a song to the kid on the telethon.

Barcelona has already told her parents. Naturally they were thrilled, proud of her. She and Grief had discussed

463

it too, but that was on a strictly professional level, not personal. Grief knew only what it meant to her career, not her self-esteem. She'd tried to call Cory, but he'd been out all day on the campaign trail. Here she was bursting with important news and no one close to tell it to.

Except Eric.

He'd been waiting for her at her home when she'd left school. She drove down the shared driveway between all the garages and saw his car blocking her garage door. He sat behind the wheel reading a book. She honked at him. She saw his head shift slightly to glance in his rearview mirror. At first he didn't move. She honked again. Finally he started the engine and backed it away just enough for her automatic garage door opener to swing the wooden door open. She drove in, parked, and left by the side entrance. He was waiting there for her.

'We have to settle this, Barcy,' he said.

'It's settled, Eric. Really, it's settled.'

'Why are you doing this to me? What did I do?'

She stopped and looked into his face with sympathy. 'You didn't do anything. It's me. I just don't feel right with you anymore.'

He snorted. 'What's that supposed to mean? You feel guilty about Luna?'

'Yes, I do. Some.'

'So that's what this is about. You want me to leave Luna.'

She unlocked the front door but didn't open it. She turned and stood in front of the door, blocking it, making it clear the conversation would not be continued inside. 'I don't want you to leave Luna. She loves you very much. You love her very much.'

'Yeah, I love you, you love me, she loves me, I love her. How come if there's so much love floating around here, we're all so miserable?'

I'm not miserable, she wanted to tell him. *Lynda Kramer called me today and my life is almost perfect. I'm having dinner with my closest friends, I'm seeing a man who is handsome, smart, and sexy. Everything is finally coming together in my life. Don't slop your misery around me.*

She said, 'I have to go, Eric. Think about what I said and we'll talk later.'

Eric stepped back a few feet and looked at her. The afternoon sun was lodged behind the condos near the community pool, shooting just enough bright beams across the grass belt to case a shimmering aura around Eric. For a second he seemed frozen in time, looking just as he had that first time she saw him on campus, standing near the entrance of Sproul Hall arguing with another shaggy student about whether or not Freud was homosexual. His finger had jabbed the air in front of the other boy in such a graceful yet forceful way you had the impression that through this sudden gesture he was conjuring some dark forbidden powers, that any moment black lightning would crackle from his finger and crisp the other boy on the spot.

Standing there on the sidewalk outside her condo, Eric pointed that same finger at her now and began jabbing the air again. 'This is not you. You're not this fucked.' He said it with such assurance that Barcelona wondered for a moment if he was right.

He turned and walked away, his hiking boots scuffing against the sidewalk.

The mall is crowded, but the restaurant isn't. Barcelona listens to an older couple at the next table. They are discussing Kitty Kelley's unauthorized biography of Frank Sinatra. 'Pret-ty Kit-ty Kel-ley,' the man says with disdain. 'I heard she wrote the book because Sinatra wouldn't sleep with her.' The woman dips her fingertips in her water glass and dabs the drops in her eyes. 'Damn smoke,' she says to him. Barcelona thinks she means the smoke in the air

465

from the forest fires, but the woman turns sharply and looks at the two young women at a nearby table who are smoking cigarettes. Even though this is the nonsmoking section, the older woman and her companion pick up their water glasses and move to another table. When they sit down, the man says, 'Frank Sinatra was ruined by women. Yes he was.'

Barcelona watches Trina walking down the mall toward her. There are dozens of other people walking beside, in front of, behind her. Their shoes all clack against the hard floor in a confusion of sound. But Trina's shoes clack louder than anyone else's. She sounds like a metronome keeping time for everyone else, clacking out the right rhythm for the rest of the crowd to follow. Maybe it's Barcelona's imagination, but she thinks that the people surrounding Trina begin to alter their walking rhythm to fit hers. Without interrupting their conversations, shoppers begin to match Trina's stride, legs scissoring in unison, arms swinging with hers. People look like they are marching next to her, like happy troops escorting her to her destination. Trina doesn't seem to notice. She sees Barcelona and waves cheerfully.

'Jesus, look at the packages,' Trina says, sitting. Trina pokes through the cluster of shopping bags under the table, spoils of Barcelona's celebration spree. 'I hope there's something in there for me. A small token of your esteem. Diamond earrings are nice.'

As always, Barcelona's irritation evaporates in Trina's presence. 'Oooh, this is gorgeous,' Trina says. She pulls out a marled cotton knit turtleneck. 'Eighty-five bucks! That's not like you to spend real money on yourself.'

'A new, improved me. I have heard The Word and The Word is Retail. Now put it back before you spill something on it.'

Trina shoves it back into the bag.

The waitress with the three watches stops in front of the table. 'Ready to order?'

'White wine,' Trina says. 'And a dish of frozen yogurt. Vanilla.'

'We're going to have dinner soon,' Barcelona reminds her.

'Gee, Mom, really?' She nods at the waitress, who hurries off. 'You see how tight that girl's pants are? A yeast infection waiting to happen.'

Barcelona is anxious to tell her the good news. But she doesn't want to just blurt it out. She wants to savor it a little. Telling Trina will somehow legitimize the whole thing, make it real. But before she can start the words, Trina leans forward with a serious expression. Bracelona notices for the first time that her friend's eyes are red and a little swollen. She's been crying. 'What?' Barcelona says, a little frightened.

Trina sighs, looks away. 'I'm not sure I can.'

'Can what?'

'Tell you.'

'Oh, Christ, Trina, don't do this. Tell me what?'

Trina stares at the passers by. Barcelona follows Trina's gaze, staring at the shoppers. Their eyes are glazed from seeing too much merchandise. Some look manic, anxious to get home with their purchases; some look vaguely disappointed, uncertain about the wisdom of what they bought. Most look tired. They walk stiffly like witnesses to a horrible accident.

'I'm going to tell you something,' Trina says. 'It's going to shock you. Hell, it shocks me.'

'What, for Christ's sake?'

Trina begins speaking, her head leaning across the table, her shoulders hunched protectively. The waitress comes, delivers the wine, and runs off again. Barcelona listens to Trina's words, concentrating on each one because the whole gist is somehow getting lost. Words pile up like tax receipts. Something about following Carla Bennington, sleeping with her, still seeing her. Suddenly Trina stops talking, leans back, and sips her wine. She stares expectantly at Barcelona. 'Well?'

Barcelona feels dizzy, disoriented. She takes a deep breath, but the air is scratchy with smoke. She tastes ashes at the back of her throat. 'I don't know what to say.'

'You're angry. Jesus, you're angry.'

'I am not angry.'

'Look at you. Your face is clenched, your ears are red. You're fucking pissed at me, aren't you?'

Barcelona thinks about it a moment and realizes that she is indeed angry at Trina. Trina has taken what should have been a perfect moment at a perfect time in Barcelona's life, and screwed it up with some twisted confession about sex with another woman. Barcelona feels as though she should be somehow supportive, understanding of Trina's emotional turmoil. But she isn't. She wants to reach across the table and smack Trina across the face.

'You think I became a lesbian to make you mad?' Trina asks.

'You're not a lesbian,' Barcelona says quickly. 'You don't just become one, like transferring buses or converting to Catholicism. Homosexuality is an inclination, something you're born with, not a conscious decision. Read the fucking literature before you join the club, okay?'

'You act as if I did this to be in vogue, Barcy.'

'Didn't you?'

'I thought you knew me better than that.'

Barcelona doesn't know what to say to that. Anger is replaced by hurt and she decides to hurt back. 'Guess not,' she says.

Trina rolls the stem of the wineglass between thumb and forefinger. The yellowish wine swirls in the glass. It reminds Barcelona of a toilet flushing and she thinks of that quote from Hart Crane that Lynda Kramer used: 'Love is like a burnt match skating in a urinal.'

'I'm surprised,' Trina says quietly. 'I didn't think you'd act this way at all. I thought you'd be more understanding. On my side.'

'Sorry I wasn't so predictable. But I do have a mind of my own.'

The older woman and her male companion at the nearby table look toward them. The woman is eating potato-cheese soup, the spoon is full and halfway to her mouth.

Barcelona lowers her voice. 'Do you really think you're a lesbian?'

Trina laughs. 'What an odd question. I wish I had an answer. I don't think I am, not in the implied meaning. I don't want to leap across the table and stick my tongue in your mouth.'

Barcelona frowns and looks away.

'I do care for Carla. I do have sex with her. The caring is a lot like how I feel for you. Like friends. Mostly we talk, mostly with our clothes on.'

'Don't make fun of me, okay? I don't deserve that.'

Trina sighs, looks across the mall corridor to the toy store opposite the restaurant. Again, Barcelona follows her gaze. A giant gorilla doll sits in the window with a tiny stuffed kitten in its lap. A stack of picture books are displayed around the gorilla. The book is *Koko's Kitten*.

'I'm nervous,' Trina says, looking back at Barcelona. 'I feel guilty and scared about Karyn. I keep expecting to come home and find Karyn gone and Rob's lawyers pelting me with subpoenas.'

'It could happen,' Barcelona says.

'Thanks for cheering me up.'

Barcelona feels rotten. She isn't handling this well. Not as well as Eric would have handled it. Eric would have put his arm around Trina, made her laugh, calmed her fears. Even Luna could have done that much. Trina is her best friend and she's only making her more miserable.

'Let's go meet the others,' Trina says, looking at her watch. Her voice is cold.

'Wait,' Barcelona says. She finishes her wine, taking her time draining the glass, thinking what to say. 'I don't mean to be angry. Maybe I'm just jealous.'

Trina's smile is as cold as her voice. 'You've already seen me naked. You had your chance.'

'You know what I mean. Your friendship with Carla Bennington. I was your best friend, now somehow she is.'

Trina doesn't deny it. 'You wouldn't be jealous if it were a man.'

'Sure I would.'

'Not as much.'

Barcelona nods. 'Not as much. Because sex was never an issue between us. And friendship with a man can't ever be the same as with another woman. I don't want to wonder if we would have been better friends if we'd had sex. That we're no longer best friends just because we didn't sleep together.'

'You're obsessed with the sex. Believe me, it's such a small part of Carla's and my relationship. We've only done anything twice. It was nice, that's all, more like a massage than a fuck.'

'And that's enough for you?'

Trina shrugs. 'For now. I have a close friend I share my life with and I get off occasionally.'

'I don't know, I just feel like you've given up just because you haven't found the right man yet.'

Trina laughs loudly and several customers turn to look. Even passing shoppers look. 'Jesus, Barcy. You idealize your relationships too much, even ours. I have a feeling when we're not around you make up snappy dialogue for us. Real people must be something of a disappointment to you.'

'I know what I want.'

'Do you? I used to, now I don't. Lately I think all I really want is for someone to occasionally pat me on the head and say, "There there, Trina. There there."'

'There are men who will do that. You have to be patient.'

Trina makes a face. 'I'm so sick of all of us bitching and whining about the Perfect Relationship. That's a fucking unicorn. Love is where you find it, right? That's a song, I think. I found someone who I care about and who cares about me. Period. No mystery to it. I don't desire other women and I haven't given up my lust for men. A tight-assed hunk still gets me wet, okay? I'm just not sitting around with that hungry look anymore. And I'm happier than I've been in a long, long time. And if you can't live with it, then I'll have to live without you.' Trina stands up, tosses three dollar bills on the table and walks away.

Barcelona pays the rest of the bill, calculates fifteen percent toward the waitress's Japan Goddess Fund, and leaves the restaurant. She walks among the crowd of shoppers, but no one follows her cadence.

Lesbian.

Such a strange word. It reminds her of something out of a high school science textbook about microscopic organisms: 'The lesbians swim furiously in the pond water unseen by the naked eye.'

Dixie is sitting alone at the table drinking red wine. Barcelona sees her from the entrance and waves. Dixie waves back enthusiastically. Barcelona is surprised by Dixie's appearance. She looks gorgeous. The bruises are all gone from her face and she is wearing clothes that are more stylish than usual. She's actually wearing a coordinating outfit: wool cardigan sweater that stops at the waist over an ivory silk broadcloth blouse with ruffled lace collar, and lambsuede circle skirt with lace trim at the hem. She looks like a model.

'Wow,' Barcelona says, sitting across from her. 'That's some outfit. Where'd you get it?'

'Nordstrom. I met with one of their personal shoppers who helps you select matching outfits.' She opens the sweater more to show off the blouse. 'This is for the trial. I'm testing it out on you guys first.'

'Looks terrific.'

'But does it look virginal? Karl's lawyer wants me to look virginal.'

'It looks good. You look good.'

'Yeah, I feel good.'

Barcelona smiles and tries to study Dixie's face without seeming to. She's so happy, so positive, looks so radiant. Almost like a bride. This is not at all the way Barcelona expected to find her. She expected brave smiles through trembling lips, pale skin, watery eyes, gnawed fingernails, occasional lapses of attention as she relives her horrible ordeal. The woman had been beaten, raped, and sodomized. Barcelona looks for the darkness in the eyes, the hint at Dixie's inner turmoil. She doesn't find any. 'You look good,' she says again. 'The outfit, the hair. Everything.'

Dixie nods. 'Thanks.'

Trina arrives like a whirlwind. 'My God, Dixie! Look at you. Are you undercover again, as a woman with taste in clothing?'

'At least I can keep mine clean.' Dixie laughs.

Trina sits and waves and looks around for a waitress. 'I'm dying of thirst.'

'It's the fires,' Barcelona says. 'Dries out the throat.'

Trina ignores Barcelona, doesn't even look at her. 'So, Dixie cup, how're you feeling? Back to pumping iron yet?'

'Some. Not much.'

'How's Karl?'

Dixie smiles. 'Hanging in there. He's tougher than I thought. We made bail by putting up my house, but he's not moping around or anything. We meet with the lawyers a lot. The rest of the time I'm at work.'

'You're not back on the job already, are you?' Barcelona asks.

'At a desk. Paper Shuffling R Us.'

From across the room, Diva's voice: 'Hey, guys.'

They all look around and see Diva walking toward them with Harley at her side. Barcelona knows from Harley that they've been seeing each other every day since their first date. Harley seems entirely smitten, which Barcelona has trouble understanding. He's dated smarter, prettier, sexier, wittier women. But he acts as if he sincerely loves Diva.

'Oh, you tramp,' Diva says to Dixie, laughing. 'Look how great you look. I come here after having lost fifteen pounds, dying to show off my new body, and you upstage me. I hate you.' Diva leans over behind Dixie's chair and hugs her. Dixie kisses Diva's cheek.

It is true, Diva has lost weight. Her cheeks are a little more defined, her stomach doesn't bulge as much. The improvements are slight, but she does look better.

'Don't worry,' Diva tells them, 'Harley isn't staying. He just dropped me off. That is, as long as Trina can give me a lift home.'

'Trina's shuttle bus at your service,' Trina says.

They all look at Harley. A long silence follows.

'This reminds me of Butch Cassidy and the Sundance Kid,' Harley says. 'Remember that scene where Redford is called a cheater? Newman tries to get him out of the saloon before there's a gunfight, but Redford says he won't go until they ask him to stay.'

473

'Would you like to stay, Harley?' Dixie says.

'Thanks.' He grins. 'Can't.' He walks over to where Barcelona is sitting and rests his hands on her shoulder. 'I just wanted to come in and congratulate Barcy.'

Barcelona looks up at him, surprised.

'What for?' Dixie asks.

'She hasn't told you?'

'Told us what?'

Diva claps her hands. 'Lynda Kramer called her today, wants Barcy to write a script for her. For real this time.'

'Lynda Kramer called *you*?' Dixie says.

Trina doesn't say anything, looks at the menu. Barcelona wants to reach over and grab her hand, squeeze it, hug her, cry on her shoulder and tell Trina their fight was a stupid mistake, everything will be okay. She doesn't. 'How did you find out?' she asks Harley.

'Evelyn overheard some of it through your office door.' Evelyn Logue is the department secretary. Her breasts are slightly larger than the jets on a 747 and she's known among the faculty, men and women alike, as 'Heavy Evy.' She also has a reputation for snooping, though usually people hear her coming because her industrial strength bra squeaks with each step. Her desk is right outside Barcelona's office door. Harley bends over and kisses Barcelona on top of the head. 'Congratulations, Barcy. Long time coming.'

He says good-bye to everyone and leaves.

'This is so exciting!' Diva says, sitting. 'Dixie looks like a million bucks. Trina's candidate is ahead in the polls. Barcy's got herself hooked up with a superstar. And me'—she smiles broadly, holding out her left hand to show her gold ring—'I got myself married.'

There are general cries of surprise.

'Do you wish for a drink before ordering?' the tiny

Japanese waitress asks. Barcelona didn't even see her approach.

'Wine?' Dixie asks the others.

'You know what I feel like?' Diva says. 'Beer. Let's hoist a few in celebration.'

They order a round of Japanese beer.

'Beer is actually better for you than wine,' Diva says. 'There are sulfites in wine. I read where several people have died from that. People our age.'

'Jesus, Diva,' Trina says. 'We're celebrating, okay?'

'Married,' Dixie says, patting Diva's hand. 'When did all this happen?'

'Last week. We haven't told anyone except my parents and his mom. We were waiting.'

'For what?' Trina asks.

'To hear about our song, "Cocktail Waitress." We finished it two weeks ago and sent it off. Yesterday we heard from the record company that they're interested in it for Rod Stewart.' She crossed her fingers.

'Rod Stewart,' Dixie says. 'Fantastic.'

Diva's smile fades; she looks thoughtful. 'We've all been so lucky these past few weeks. It's almost spooky.'

'Lucky?' Barcelona says. 'After all the years we've worked, the odds were in our favor. It's physics. Universal laws of odds.'

Trina shakes her head. 'I don't know. All of us at once. That's more than physics.'

'Maybe the moon's in the seventh house and Jupiter's aligned with Mars,' Barcelona says. 'Come on. We're just hardworking women with stained dress shields to prove it. Finally our hard work is paying off and you want to pass the credit on.'

'Maybe Barcy's right,' Diva says. 'After all, we aren't all lucky. Dixie sure wasn't.'

'Me?' Dixie says, smiling. 'I'm better than you think. I

know you kind of expected me to come here drooling or hearing voices, but I really am okay. Which reminds me . . .' She reaches into her purse and pulls out a hard-cover book by a rabbi, *When Bad Things Happen to Good People*. 'I swear I've gotten five copies of this book so far from friends. Anybody want one?' She tosses it in the middle of the table.

Diva picks it up and begins leafing through it. 'I read about this somewhere.'

Dixie continues, 'My life really has gotten better. I don't mean just better than that day, but it's better than it was before the rape. I'm not suggesting rape as a form of therapy, understand, but it hasn't destroyed me. True, I wish this might have happened ten years ago when rape was trendier to the general public. Back when it would have made a good Movie of the Week. Now it's just a cliché. I was raped. It's like saying I caught the flu or admitting I'm clumsy.'

'Hell,' Trina says. 'Every personal crisis is a cliché now. Elizabeth Montgomery has played them all out on TV.'

The waitress returns with four Kirin beers and distributes them. She takes the dinner orders and leaves.

No one speaks. They wait for Dixie.

'I'll tell you how I feel,' Dixie begins. She looks each of them in the eye and smiles. 'I was molested as a child. Nothing big, no intercourse. Just some serious touching. A doctor friend of my dad's, also Chinese. I was seven. He was supposed to be examining me, but I knew even then this was more than an exam. I could tell from the look on his face, his fast breathing, his smell. It happened just that once.'

'Did you tell your dad?' Barcelona asks.

Dixie shakes her head. 'No point. He wouldn't have believed me. It didn't scar my whole life or anything. To tell you the truth, I hadn't really thought much about it

476

since then. Until the past few weeks. I think back on all my training, all those hours of lifting weights, toning my body, getting as strong as I could. And still when I was tied down to that sixteen-year-old kid's bed, I was as helpless as I had been when I was seven.'

'There was nothing you could do,' Diva says.

'Oh, I know that. I don't blame myself. In fact, this may shock you some, in a way I feel relieved. I imagine what a young prizefighter must feel like getting into the ring with some bone-crushing champ, how his knees must be shaking, his stomach churning, circling, bobbing, but all the time waiting for that legendary punch. When he finally gets hit, even if it knocks him to the canvas, the punch is never as bad as he imagined it. It must be kind of a relief saying to himself, "That's all?" I guess that's how I feel, like I've been in training all my life. If that's the worst punch they can throw and I'm still standing, then fuck 'em. I don't have to be afraid anymore.'

Barcelona pours her beer into the glass. She likes the way the beer foams energetically. Barcelona would like to toast Dixie for her courage, but that would only embarrass Dixie. Plus, she's a little resentful at how well Dixie's adjusted. It makes her feel somehow inadequate.

'Now what?' Trina asks Dixie.

'Now I help Karl with his trial. You have no idea how much work is involved. I've always come at it from the other side, prosecuting. Suddenly my law classes are a hell of a lot more interesting.'

'And Randy?'

'He couldn't handle all this.' She doesn't elaborate.

Trina shakes her head. 'What about that principal who was interested in you? Peterson was it?'

'Kevin Peterson.' Dixie stares into her glass of beer. She looks more Oriental now that she ever has before, though

477

that could be the makeup. 'He's called, sent flowers. He even visited me at the hospital. He's nice.'

Diva says, 'I talked to him at the hospital once. He was sweet.'

'He's in the National Guard. His unit was called up a couple days ago to fight the forest fires. I think he's up in the San Bernardino Mountains right now.'

'And when he gets back?' Trina asks.

'Right now, Karl needs me. I think I owe him a little loyalty during this time. Besides, I couldn't ask another guy to hang around while I'm constantly busy with my ex-husband's court case. Not the most romantic circumstances. Right now my main concern is Karl.'

'And after the trial?' Barcelona asks.

Dixie shrugs. 'First things first.'

Silence descends as they slurp their soup. Spoons clack against porcelain.

'I want to know something,' Trina says loudly, pushing her empty bowl away. 'I want to know right now if we're going to keep up these dinners now that this extraordinary luck has blown our way. Love seems to have touched most of us . . .' She glances at Barcelona. '. . . in some form or other. I'd hate to have that break us apart. I mean, was being single the only reason we hung out together, like some kind of nerd club?'

'Hell no,' Dixie says. 'I just did it for the gossip.'

'I'll keep coming,' Diva says. 'Though you may have trouble recognizing me. Harley's taking me out on a major shopping binge this week. New clothes, new hairstyle, everything. An entire makeover for my act.'

'What act?' Trina says.

She smiles brightly and rubs her hands together. 'I'm putting a lounge act together. Get a backup group, sing at local restaurants and such. Maybe Vegas.'

Barcelona is pleased at Diva's enthusiasm, but a little

irked to hear about the shopping binge. Especially with the $2,000 still owed which Diva has not mentioned since receiving the check almost a month ago.

The food arrives. The waitress quietly and gracefully distributes the large plates of tempura or black boxes of sushi. Rice bowls are placed next to each woman. 'Enjoy,' the waitress says and bows slightly before hurrying off.

Diva clumsily scissors her chopsticks around a chunk of sushi. 'At first Harley tried talking me out of this whole vegetarian thing. He says it doesn't matter what we eat, it's all part of the chain of life, something like that.'

Trina says, 'That's what I told you when you first started this veggie kick.'

'We shouldn't think of ourselves as individuals eating another individual,' Diva continues, ignoring Trina. 'More like a group of kids within the same family trading baseball cards. One kid only owns the card a short time before it gets traded to another and another. And they all stay in the same drawer anyway. He wants me to read some book by Robert Heinlein. You know him, Barcy?'

'I've read him, yes. He's very good.'

'Yeah, that's what Harley said. *Stranger in a Strange Land*. He says it's about the beauty of cannibalism. Is that right?'

'Partly,' Barcelona says.

'God, *Stranger in a Strange Land*,' Trina sighs nostalgically. 'We read that in high school. All my friends passed it back and forth, we had grok groups.'

'Crock?' Dixie says.

'Grok. That's what they did in the book when they were really talking from the heart. Like an alien rap session. Boy, I hadn't thought about that in years.'

Diva seems to sense the conversation slipping away from her. She raises her voice a little and speaks rapidly. 'Well, I'll read it then, but I'm staying a vegetarian. Look what it's done for me. And I feel great too. And you know what?' She leans forward and whispers. 'My pussy smells different too. Sweeter. I'm serious.'

Trina says, 'Yeah, if you like the smell of brussels sprouts.'

Dixie laughs.

'Go ahead and laugh,' Diva says. 'But I read this article that proves that we pick who we love by smell.'

'God,' Barcelona says, rolling her eyes.

'It's true. We've got smell molecules called pheromones and the part of your brain which registers smell feeds into the part involving emotion and memory. See, what we're smelling is the genetic code of each person.'

'How does she remember this junk?' Trina says.

'These scientists ran these tests with mice. Given a choice, the mice select other mice with an opposite genetic code so their offspring will be stronger.'

'I think I read something about that in the hospital,' Dixie says.

'Maybe that's where I read it,' Dixie says. 'Visiting you.'

'Yeah, that article said that studies show couples who mate with similar genes have a high rate of spontaneous abortions.'

Barcelona picks up a piece of tempura shrimp and dips it in brown sauce. 'So we don't really pick who we love, we just respond to their smells.'

'That's what the article says,' Diva replies.

'I guess it depends on where they smell,' Trina says and Dixie and Diva laugh.

Barcelona imagines the shrimp in her hand sniffing out its mate and puts it back on her plate. She has lost her appetite. Also, she's a little annoyed but she's not sure why.

'Speaking of weird,' Diva says, lowering her voice and

grinning. 'Harley's got this giant collection of pornography in his garage.'

Barcelona is surprised. She has known Harley for years, slept with him, stayed at his house, but she didn't know that. She feels a twinge of jealousy at Diva, similar to the way she felt when Trina told her about Carla. 'He's got half a dozen cardboard boxes full of the shit. His ex-wife collected it in some campaign she was running to get dirty magazines out of the liquor stores in Irvine. She used to haul the stuff out at city council meetings and dump them on the tables. Apparently she was quite a character. She campaigned for bike trails and against smut.'

'What's he do with the stuff?' Dixie asks.

'That's what I asked him. He said nothing.'

'Oh, right. He keeps it for sentimental reasons.'

'Well.' Diva grins coyly. 'He did tell me his ex-girlfriend used to read the letters aloud to him to get them both hot.'

Barcelona is again amazed and annoyed. Amazed at the revelation and annoyed at the shared intimacy Harley has with Diva that he never had with her.

'He told me he still masturbates to them sometimes. I asked him why. He said, "What do you mean? To get off, that's why."'

Trina laughs. 'Good answer.'

'I said, "Yeah, but why do they get you off? You know these letters are all made up by some scummy guy with acne scars and yellow teeth and underpants with skid marks sitting in a smoky room that smells like dog puke." He said, "Yeah, I know." So I said, "Is that what gets you off, knowing that?" He said no.' Diva shakes her head. 'I told him I didn't understand. You know what he said?'

Trina nods. 'He said, "And you never will."'

'Yes!' Diva says, amazed. 'How'd you know?'

'That's what they always say.'

* * *

After dinner Trina suggests they hit a couple of bars to celebrate Dixie's recuperation and everyone else's good fortune. Everyone agrees. Barcelona follows Dixie's Mustang down the street though she isn't much in the mood anymore. She hopes some of their high spirits will rub off on her.

This is not at all how she expected to feel tonight. She thought she'd meet with Trina, share the good news about Lynda Kramer, and they would both be overjoyed and giggle like teenagers. She thought Dixie would be withdrawn and she was prepared to spend all evening coaxing her into a good mood. She thought Diva would come in smoking black cigarettes and complaining about her weight/career/love life. Nothing is as planned.

Dixie follows Trina's car into a parking lot next to an old rundown movie theater in the old part of Costa Mesa. Barcelona pulls into the slot next to them. There aren't many cars in the lot. As they get out of their cars, she notices the dark shadow of smoke in the distance, vague flickerings of light from the Saddleback fires. The others don't even look.

Barcelona had never before noticed the bar behind the theater. The building is dark and squat with black windows and a pink neon sign that says THE USUAL SUSPECTS.

'Great place,' Dixie says sarcastically, looking the building over. 'Where's the delousing shower?'

'This place is great,' Diva says. 'I used to come here all the time back with Crawler.'

'Which one was Crawler?' Barcelona asks.

'You know, the one with the eye patch. Thought he was Dr. Hook. Even wore it during sex. Only time he didn't wear it was when he was sitting on the toilet. Then he'd flip it up so he could read better.'

They all laugh, including Barcelona. It's working. She's starting to feel better. She will make a point of pulling

Trina aside and apologizing. Drive up to L.A. and have lunch with her like old times. Whatever it takes. This is going to be fun. She's not even sure why she was so mad before.

Inside the room is long and narrow like a trailer and smells of spilled beer, some small tables are scattered about with neon beer signs for light. The left side of the room has a traditional bar with three faceless customers hunched quietly over drinks. They are not together. Opposite the main bar is a piano bar. A fat woman in her mid-forties sits behind the piano and plays while singing. She is wearing a pink chiffon dress and a pearl necklace. Her hair is a lacquered beehive. She looks as if she was stood up for the prom twenty-five years ago and has been sitting here playing melancholy music ever since.

'*You are the sunshine of my life,*' she sings, '*that's why I'll always be around.*'

'She's good,' Barcelona says, surprised.

'Yeah,' Diva says. 'Jo used to sing radio commercials with me. But her daughter got sick, some rare disease that paralyzes you for a few years. She has to be home during the day to take care of her.'

Jo sings, '*You are the apple of my eye,*' and nods recognition at Diva.

Diva and Trina sit at the piano bar facing Jo. Dixie sits next to Trina and Barcelona sits next to Diva. At the far end of the bar is a woman in her late fifties smoking an unfiltered Camel cigarette and drinking a dark-colored drink. She shakes her glass and watches the ice cubes shift around. She doesn't seem to be aware of the four women, of Jo, of the music. When she finishes her drink, she orders another by shouting over at the bartender. While waiting, she reapplies her lipstick, a bright pink bubblegum color.

Jo finishes her song, reaches over, and shakes a Camel out of the woman's pack. The woman pushes the Bic lighter at her and Jo takes a deep drag. They never exchange words.

'So, Diva, these the friends you're always telling me about?' Jo says.

Diva introduces everyone. Jo nods at all of them without much interest. 'Voice sounds good,' Diva says.

Jo shrugs, 'you wanna take over while I hit the john?'

'No, thanks. I'm resting my voice for the Hollywood Bowl.'

Jo snorts smoke out her nose. She gets up and walks to the back and enters the room marked Women.

'Gee, Diva,' Trina says, 'you know the nicest places.'

'Hey, this joint is a little offbeat, but it's fun.'

Barcelona likes the place. The three men at the bar never seem to move. There are a few couples at the tiny spool tables, but overall the place has the feel of someplace you'd go to start an affair or end one.

Diva goes over to the bar and brings back their drinks, setting each one before the proper person. 'Full service tonight, girls,' she says. 'Tipping permitted.'

'Someone should make a toast,' Dixie says. 'Barcy, you're the wordsmith.'

'And the oldest,' Diva adds with a laugh.

Barcelona holds up her rum and Coke. 'From my lofty years, looking back on when I was your tender age, I remember something my father used to say in times like this . . .'

'Jesus.' Dixie laughs.

'He would turn to me with that sad but knowing look in his eye, perhaps a lone tear clinging like hope to the rim of his eye, and he'd say, "Barcy," with a tremble in his voice. "Barcy," he's say. "Smoke 'em if you got 'em."'
Barcelona raises her glass higher.

'Here, here,' Dixie says.

They all drink. Barcelona looks at Trina who is drinking but avoiding her gaze.

'I want to add something,' Diva says. 'I think we should drink to Luck. I mean, it's kind of spooky how great everything's been going for everybody the past few weeks, I mean since . . .' She hesitates. 'Since Dixie got out of the hospital.'

Barcelona puts her drink down. 'That's nuts, Diva.'

'What's nuts? It's true.'

'You know what you're suggesting?'

'I'm not suggesting anything. I'm just observing.'

'You're being an idiot.' Barcelona feels her whole neck aflame. Her eyes are dry and sticky in her sockets. Her throat is tight as a guitar string. 'You're acting as if what happened to Dixie was some kind of catalyst, that we all benefited from it.'

'She didn't say that,' Trina says.

'Didn't she?'

'Well, it is kind of true,' Dixie says. 'From the day I was raped we've all had some pretty terrific changes. Even me.'

'That's disgusting,' Barcelona says. 'The things that happened to us were long overdue. We're talented, intelligent women who've been busting our asses for years and it's finally paying off.'

'No one's suggesting voodoo here, Barcy,' Trina says. 'We're just saying it's an odd coincidence.'

Dixie nods. 'It is odd.'

Barcelona wants to holler at them, but Jo returns from the bathroom and slides behind the piano. She is so close, to continue the discussion now would be like invading her privacy.

'Gimme that thing,' the woman at the end says, gesturing with her hand.

Jo hands her the microphone. 'You gonna tell me or what, Lila?'

Lila stubs out her cigarette and grins. 'You'll pick it up.' She puts the microphone to her mouth and begins to sing: '*The night we met I knew I needed you so . . .*'

Jo comes in with the piano, smiling and bobbing her head in time.

Lila continues, both hands gripped around the microphone: '*And if I had the chance, I'd never let you go . . .*'

'This is a great song,' Diva says excitedly.

Barcelona looks at Dixie and Trina. They too are caught up in Lila's singing. The three of them are smiling, swaying with the familiar song. Lila's voice is every bit as good as Jo's. For some reason, Barcelona finds this astounding. What is all this talent doing here in the tar pits?

'*So won't you say you love me,*' Lila sings. '*I'll make you so proud of me . . .*'

Jo plays with the cigarette in her mouth. When the ash gets too long, she continues to play with one hand, flicks the ash into the ashtray, sticks the cigarette back into her mouth, and plays again with both hands.

'*Be my, be my baby,*' Lila sings. '*My one and only baby . . .*'

Lila sings another verse and when she's done the four women applaud. Barcelona can't get over how well she sang, or how well Jo sang either. They aren't just good party singers, there was training, technique, style in their voices.

'What's her story?' Barcelona asks Diva.

'What story?'

'Her voice. She's so good.'

'Yeah.'

'So what's her story? Did she sing professionally? What happened?'

'Nothing happened,' Diva says and turns toward Jo. 'Hey, give us that mike, Jo. My buds and me are gonna sing for you.'

'Oh, no,' Dixie says. 'I don't even sing in the shower; my voice rusts the pipes.'

'I'll do the lead, you guys back me up,' Diva insists. 'It'll be fun.'

'Diva Klosterman and the Supremes,' Trina says. 'It does have a certain ring.'

Diva begins to sing and Jo quickly comes in with the right chords:

> 'When I'm with my guy and he watches
>   all the pretty girls go by.
> And I feel so hurt deep inside
>   I wish that I could die.
> Not a word do I say
> I just look the other way . . .'

Diva points at the others and Dixie, Trina, and Barcelona join in on the lines, '*Cause that's the way boys are. That's the way booyyys are.*'

They sing other songs, old party songs that they remember from junior high school. Lila joins in on a few. After singing 'Angel Baby,' Barcelona slides a twenty-dollar bill over to Diva and says she has to leave. She decides that this should be more fun than it actually is. Dixie and Diva try to talk her into staying while Trina remains silent, tearing the edges off her cocktail napkin and staring straight ahead.

'I've gotta go, really,' Barcelona says and walks down the narrow path toward the door. She can feel their eyes on her back, even the eyes of the other patrons, the men hunched at the bar, the couples hiding in the dim light of the neon bar signs. The good-byes were brusque, forced, a little cool. She has managed to alienate her three closest friends in one evening. So much for their theory of good luck.

31

Barcelona sits at the kitchen table making a list. She has
a yellow legal pad with the words Fuck You Women neatly
printed at the top and underlined twice. She stares at the
three words a moment and then underlines them again.
Then she adds an exclamation point.

It has been three days since the disastrous dinner at
Fuji-Kan and the bizarre singalong at The Usual Suspects.
She hasn't spoken to any of them since. Dixie called once
and left a message on the machine to call her back, but
Barcelona hasn't. She promised herself on the drive home
that night that she would call Trina and patch things up.
She hasn't done that either.

At school today, she ran into Harley in the mimeograph
room. He is growing a beard. He scratches his face constantly and his teeth look whiter contrasted against his
dark stubble. For some reason she couldn't name, the
beard annoyed her. She wanted to ask him why he never
told her about his pornography collection, but she didn't
want him to know Diva had mentioned it to them. She
found it hard to be civil to him.

Grief called yesterday and said that Lynda Kramer had
authorized $50,000 to be paid up front and another $50,000
to be paid when the script was done. There were other
escalators involved in rewrite steps, but Barcelona didn't
pay attention to them. This is more money than she has

made in all her books combined. Grief was very excited. Barcelona was now the hot new writer in her agency. Grief was preparing a whole campaign, lunch with producers, studio executives, directors. 'We have to make the deals now,' she'd said, 'while you're still the flavor of the week.'

At school, Foster Malone and Hester Hoffman, who had worked so diligently to keep Barcelona from teaching any writing courses, approached her yesterday with an offer to teach Introduction to Creative Writing the next semester. Foster smiled in what he doubtlessly thought was a charming expression, stroked his reddish beard, and said with an exaggerated brogue, 'Will there be any chance, darlin', of bringin' the lovely Lynda Kramer down here for the students to meet?' Hester added, 'We might even have a dollar or two in the faculty kitty for some sort of reception for her.' Barcelona said she didn't know about Lynda Kramer and she wasn't sure about teaching the class, indeed whether she'd be back next semester at all.

This morning Lynda Kramer called. Her baby cried through most of the conversation so they kept it short. Barcelona imagined her sitting there all in white cotton, bouncing her baby in her arm, a cup of steaming herbal tea next to the phone, a vase of exotic cut flowers on the desk. The furniture would all be rattan, the food would all be pastel colored. Barcelona was surprised to find herself not all that excited this time to be talking to Lynda Kramer. She wasn't even excited by the money, which was still weeks away from actually being paid. The only new thing they discussed was Barcelona's changing the title of the script. '*Feasts* just sounds too spooky, like a vampire movie or something. We don't want to confuse the audience.' Joking, Barcelona suggested they change the title to *The Usual Suspects*. Lynda Kramer loved it: 'It's got wit, yet hints at suspense. The *Casablanca* reference is perfect.

God, this is going to be great. I knew I picked the right person in you.'

Barcelona sits at the kitchen table and draws a hyphen between Fuck and You. The W of Women is round at the bottom of each dip and looks either like buttocks or breasts. She draws nipples in to make them breasts. She just now came up with this idea, the list of Fuck-You Women. Women with that special look, that aura, that way of sitting down, crossing their legs, laughing, sipping coffee, some single aspect of the person that embodies their whole attitude, that says 'Fuck You, Jack' to anyone who doesn't take them seriously. She writes Sigourney Weaver at the top of the list. She has Fuck-You lips, sharply defined and eager to speak. Next she writes Susan Sontag. She has Fuck-You hair, long and black and thick as her intellect.

Barcelona looks at the clock in the stove. Almost ten. Cory will be here any minute. He had a late dinner with some boys' athletic group in Los Angeles, but he said he really wanted to see her tonight. They talk every day on the phone. Since the infamous Night of the Tampon, they managed to have sex once at his Corona del Mar house. It was during the afternoon and both had to rush right off afterward so it was hard to gauge anything more from it than it felt good. Very good. Certainly nothing about it to explain why his wife Dayna had decided to give up sex forever. She suspects that they will have sex again tonight and has therefore changed the sheets and put on new panties.

Joni Mitchell is singing 'Blue' on the compact disk player. '*Blue*,' she sings, '*songs are like tattoos . . .*' Barcelona writes Joni Mitchell on the list. Her lyrics say Fuck You.

She tries to think of other names. Gloria Steinem? No, looks too pampered. Dianne Feinsten? Not really. Jane

491

Fonda? Nope. She writes Lynda Kramer, stares at the name, then crosses it off.

She writes her mother's name: Milan Lee. She underlines it. Yeah, Milan's got it. The way one scythelike eyebrow lifts in a high arc over the eye when she listens to you talk makes you feel like a suspect hooked up to a lie detector. The eyebrow bobs and rears with each answer, etching a graph of your obvious lies that are recorded in the wrinkles of her forehead. Many of Barcelona's breathless explanations for youthful misdeeds from skipping school when she was fifteen to revealing her abortion when she was twenty-two met with this same test, followed by a brisk nod and the deadly words: 'I see. Well, we'd better not tell your father.' Barcelona can remember a dozen such instances, mostly minor infractions of obscure rules, each somehow uncovered by Milan and requiring an explanation. Each sealed with the incantation, 'I see. Well, we'd better not tell your father.' The result was a pact, one Barcelona didn't want, a secret society of the two of them, sharing secrets, secrets she didn't really care if her father discovered. But to tell him after her mother's pronouncement would be worse, an act of betrayal.

Barcelona writes Trina's name on the list. She stares at the name awhile. Her throat starts to itch. The fires in the mountains are all out now, but smoke still lingers. The air is gritty. She gets up and goes to the refrigerator and opens the door. The bitter smell of rotten food rushes her face. 'Jesus,' she says, squinting and holding her breath. She opens the vegetable drawer and finds a plastic bag of zucchini that has melted into a greenish-white slop. She tosses it into the garbage can. Then she takes the garbage bag out of the can, chokes it with a twist-tie and places it outside the backdoor on her patio. By morning the slugs and snails will be crawling all over it, but she's not in the mood to take it out to the garage right now.

She grabs a Diet Coke and returns to the list. She writes her own name on the list, stares at it, tilts her head to the left, to the right. She underlines it. She crosses it out with three heavy lines.

The doorbell rings.

She glances at the clock. Cory is earlier than expected. She pads barefoot across the gray carpet to the front door and peaks through the peephole. Her chest tightens.

'Hi,' she says, opening the door.

Diva and Harley walk in.

'*Angel baby*,' Diva sings. '*My angel baby.*' She does a funky little dance while Harley looks on with amusement and scratches his stubbly beard. 'God, Barcy, it's fan-fucking-tastic!'

'What is?'

'We sold it. We goddamn sold it. The song. "Cocktail Waitress" is going to be recorded on Rod Stewart's next album!'

Barcelona hugs Diva. She feels tremendous warmth for her right then. 'I'm so happy for you, Diva. For both of you.'

Diva squirms like a child, fluttering around the living room with manic energy. 'Jesus, Jesus, Jesus. I can't believe it. I have to tell you, I never really thought they'd buy it, never in a million years. That kind of luck never happens to me. Never. It's like we're all charmed.'

Barcelona hugs Harley. His jacket smells earthy but nice. His beard scratches her cheek. 'That's some cheese grater you've got there, Harley,' she says rubbing her cheek.

'Isn't it?' Diva says. 'He's about scraped all my skin off, and not just on my face.' She laughs heartily and kisses his cheek. Harley smiles and scratches his neck. 'Oh, shit,' Diva says suddenly. 'Almost forgot why we came here.' She opens her purse and dips her fingers in. Her fingernails are green with miniature musical instruments painted on each one. The thumbs have guitars, the index fingers trumpets, followed by french horns, crossed drumsticks, and tiny cymbals on the pinkies. She pinches a folded check between the guitar and trumpet and hands it to Barcelona. 'I can't tell you how much this meant to me.'

Barcelona reads the amount: $2,200. 'I didn't want interest, Diva. This was a loan between friends.'

'I told her,' Harley says.

'I know that,' Diva says. 'But I used it to make a hell of a lot more money. You came through when no one else would or could. I want you to know how I feel about that. Like you invested in a winner for once.'

Barcelona nods understanding. She feels guilty about her previous uncomplimentary thoughts about Diva being a deadbeat. She decides to use the extra $200 to buy them a wedding gift.

'Well, we're off.' Diva hugs Barcelona quickly and opens the door. 'The record company wants to see some more songs so me and John Lennon here are heading back to the drawing board. We bought this neat synthesizer that makes every damn sound but a buffalo farting. We can practically make our own demo with it.'

'This is just the beginning for you guys. I can feel it.' Barcelona stands next to the open door.

'See you at school,' Harley says, walking out into the night. Sprinklers are hissing across the greenbelt. Some of the spray brushes his pants legs and he steps out of the way.

Diva runs out. She is wearing a denim miniskirt and the sprinklers soak her knees and shins. 'Ooooh.' She laughs. 'Feels good.'

They run off toward their car through the gauntlet of sprinklers. *'Cocktail waitress ain't got an easy life,'* Diva

494

sings loudly in the dark. *'Gotta talk like the devil and listen like a wife.'*

A couple of dogs start barking furiously and Diva's laughter drifts back to Barcelona's open door.

'This is nice,' Cory says.

Barcelona nods.

'Isn't it?' he asks.

'I nodded yes.'

'Oh.'

They are lying on top of the bed watching TV, the last few minutes of a remake of *D.O.A.* in which the hero is poisoned and tries to discover the killer before he dies. They are both dressed. Cory has removed only his shoes and jacket. He still wears his tie. His arm is draped across her bare thigh. The pant leg of her shorts is hiked up so that the white material of the pocket peeks out. Barcelona keeps expecting his hand to creep up her thigh and slip under her pant leg. She would be happy if it did, but she has to admit that she is equally happy lying here with him just watching TV. She can tell that they will make love later and she kind of likes the anticipation.

She looks over at him and catches him staring at her with a dopey grin on his face.

'What?' she asks.

'What?' he says.

'What's wrong?'

'Nothing.'

'You're staring.'

'I like the way you look,' he says.

'Oh?' she says.

A minute passes.

'How would you describe my look?' she asks.

He makes a serious face, works his lips around in concentration. 'I don't know.'

'Would you say I have a Fuck-You Look?'

He laughs. 'Jesus.'

'Would you?'

'Not exactly. More like a John Henry look.'

She brushes his hand off her thigh. 'Wrong answer, Toad Lips.'

He kisses her neck and she laughs. 'You know, like in the folk song: "John Henry was a steel-driving man." Remember?'

'Hmm. So I look like a large black steel-driving man?'

'You're going to make this tough, aren't you?'

'Yup.' She smiles.

He takes a deep breath. 'What I mean was, John Henry had to prove something, prove he could drive railroad spikes better than a steam drill. Of course, it's impossible, but he challenged the steam drill to a contest to see who could drive more rails faster.'

'I know the song. Where do I fit in?'

'Well, he beat the steam drill and became a hero. But he broke his heart doing it, and died.'

Barcelona frowns. 'I don't think I like this analysis.'

'What I meant was, you don't have a Fuck-You Look, you have an I'll-Show-You Look. Big difference.' He leans over and kisses her on the lips. His hand slides up her thigh and teases at the edge of her shorts. He leans back, his hand withdraws. 'Okay?'

'I'll think it over,' she says.

'That's the trouble with women,' Cory says. 'No compliment is ever enough.'

'Oh, is this one of those male truisms?'

'Observations. One of many that men share among themselves.'

'Really? Like what else?'

'Don't you get the newsletter?'

She pokes him playfully in the ribs. 'Come on, what else?'

'Like don't ever sleep with a woman who has more problems than you do.'

'That's no problem, there aren't any women with more problems than men. Besides, once a man's in the mood, he doesn't care if she's axed half the city, as long as she doesn't ax him 'til he's done.'

He reaches over and pulls her toward him. They kiss. She reaches down and squeezes his penis. It is hard and straining at his pants. 'I didn't argue the point,' he says.

'I hate that guys say things about women,' she says.

'Why? Women say things about men, don't they?'

'Sure, but we're accurate. Guys mostly talk about young girls, firm tits, thighs that don't touch when she walks. It's all so childish, trying to recapture their youth, which probably wasn't so hot anyway.'

'That's not it at all.' Cory shifts to look her in the face. His expression is serious. 'Men aren't trying to recapture youth. They're thinking back to the time they traveled in packs, like wolves, roaming the playgrounds and parking lots with their friends. Back when the air was thick and potential, when adventure wasn't just possible, it was inevitable. Maybe because they were all together like that, even the smallest action, walking on railroad tracks, took on mythic status. Big screen proportions.'

Barcelona watches his face, fascinated by the intensity in his eyes.

'Someone might say, "Hey, let's beat up someone," and you'd all say, "Yeah, okay," and maybe you'd beat up some kid you happened on or maybe you'd lose interest looking. Didn't matter. "Let's beat up someone" or "Let's find some girls" had the same meaning. The day was filled with unpredictability.' He leaned over and kissed her hair.

'But once you throw women into the formula, it all goes bad.'

She pushes him away. 'Fuck you, John Henry.'

'Girls were organized. Clean. Terrified of dirt. Dirt is the fuel of adventure, the currency of boys. With girls around, "Let's go walk the railroad tracks" would meet with "It's too dirty." That's okay because guys eventually trade adventure for women. But at some point a man misses that. It's not youth exactly, it's not the midlife crazies or any of that shit. He misses the feeling of the pack, the smell of dirt. Not soil, as in mowing lawns and mulching. Dirt. The unpredictable. Somehow Sunday afternoon at the mall doesn't fill that need.'

'We like adventure too,' Barcelona says. 'We're not just house slaves.'

'I know. It's just different. No point in talking about it; every time one side brings up the differences the other side gets defensive.'

Barcelona did feel defensive. Somehow he'd made her feel like some kind of spoilsport, the evil mother calling Johnny in from play to eat his overcooked vegetables and smelly fish sticks. That is not how she saw herself.

The movie ends sometime during their conversation and the eleven o'clock news is on. Cory sits up straight and stares at the TV. 'I want to see this,' he says.

'Why?' she asks. 'You announce your candidacy for president today?'

'Sshh.'

They watch the headline stories: another random freeway shooting, no one injured; a cute side story about a company manufacturing bumper stickers that say 'Don't shoot, I'm only changing lanes,' and 'Don't shoot, I'm going as fast as I can.'

Larry the cat skulks into the room, his head low in a predatory stance. Cory pats the bed, encouraging him to join them, but he just stares a moment, then wanders into the bathroom. After a minute they can hear him drinking from the toilet bowl.

The news does a couple of stories on the fires, showing blackened ground, charred homes, bodies being hauled off in bags. Twenty-four of California's fifty-eight counties have been declared in a state of emergency by the governor. They show old clips of the special fire retardant being prepared for the bombers and helicopters to drop. Ammonia sulfate powder is mixed with water and a pink dye to create a slush that looks like melted strawberry ice cream. The dye allows them to see from the air how accurate the drop was. The ammonia sulfate is a fertilizer. Another story shows how the 22,000 firefighters were fed in those remote areas. The news team interviewed one of the twenty-five caterers hired to serve these men the eight thousand calories a day required by the U.S. Forest Service. There is film of a man making huge cauldrons of mashed potatoes by mixing them with a power drill. There is film of three women cracking eggs into a giant hydraulically assisted tilt skillet that can cook seven hundred eggs at once.

'For this I'm missing reruns of "Taxi"?' she teases him.

'*A surprising announcement today from City Council candidate Cory Meyers,*' the anchorwoman suddenly says.

Barcelona sits up. Film of Cory at a news conference fills the screen. Dayna is standing next to him, smiling.

Candidate Meyers told reporters that he and his wife of ten years, the former Dayna Churchton, have separated in preparation for divorce.'

'Jesus, Cory,' Barcelona says.

'*Mr. Meyers was asked why he chose to make this announcement now, just ten days before the election.*' The camera cuts to a closeup of Cory in front of a gnarled cactus of microphones. '*This is an amiable separation. I wanted the voters to know everything before they voted for me.'* Cut to closeup of Dayna Meyers, her flawlessly beautiful face smiling with confidence. Anchorman's voice-over: *'Mrs. Meyers said she still supported her estranged husband's candidacy and will continue to work on his campaign. They were still best of friends and would remain so regardless of the election or divorce.'*

Barcelona looks at Cory, shocked. 'Why'd you do it?'

'What if I told you I did it for us?'

'I'd say that scares me. I'd say we don't know each other that well yet. That if you lost the election because you pulled a stunt like this for me, I'd feel like shit.'

'Okay,' he says with a grin. 'I didn't do it for us.'

She touches his face with her fingertips, strokes his jaw. 'I mean it, Cory. I like you. There may even be something more going on between us. Something that could be something. Jesus, where are the words when you need them?' She takes a deep breath. 'But we don't know each other that well.'

'Now we can, without hiding all the time. I wanted you to know how much I value this relationship.'

'What relationship?' she says. 'We've talked a lot on the phone, had a couple meals, and made love once.'

'That can be remedied,' he says, reaching for her. His good humor annoys her.

She holds him off. 'I'm trying to tell you that it scares me a little that you care about me enough to risk so much without knowing me better. This is not the action of a stable personality, a man in control of himself.'

'I didn't ask you to marry me, Barcy. I only announced my separation. Now you know this isn't just about a fling. Besides, I'm glad I came clean before the election. I feel better.'

'How's Trina taking it?'

'Something's going on between you two, isn't it?'

'Why?'

'She acts funny when I mention your name. Puts on a show of being unconcerned.'

'We had a disagreement. We'll work it out.'

Cory shrugs. 'Okay. In any event, she wasn't pleased. She even tried to talk me out of it. Ten days can't make any difference, she kept saying.' He laughs. 'She really wants me to win.'

'So do I.'

'So do I,' he says. He rolls toward her and gathers her in his arms. He kisses her and she likes the feel of his lips on hers, his hand cupped under her right buttock, his tongue ricocheting around her mouth. The TV drones on about sports. In baseball, lots of home runs were hit and there's more controversy about why.

They quickly undress. His clothes are stubborn, lots of buttons. She manages to yank his shirt off and pull his pants down. He tugs hers over her hips, pants and panties together, and stares at her body. He kisses her pubic hairs once, then they shed the rest of their clothes.

His hands are gentle but firm, grabbing hunks of her here and there, a thigh, a breast, a buttock. His penis pokes into her stomach and she reaches down to hold it. She likes the feel of it, large and heavy. Its skin is hot against her palm. She squeezes it and he gives a sigh of pleasure. Men are so easy to please, she thinks, but so hard to satisfy.

He lowers his head to her belly button and stabs his tongue into it. She jerks and laughs. 'That tickles.'

'Good,' he says, but he stops. He drags his tongue down between her legs and burrows in there.

Barcelona glances down, watching Cory's head bob and twist, each movement squirting hot lava into her stomach. He knows what he's doing. But he isn't mechanical about it the way Harley used to be: insert tongue A into slot B and rotate a quarter turn. Cory's movements seem to give him as much pleasure as he gives. She grasps his head with both hands and rocks against his mouth. Her eyes roll shut and she sees vast forests on fire, smoke thick as fog choking off the sunlight. She breathes fast, in gasps, gulping air as the smoke grows darker and thicker. She comes in a small spasm, then a bigger one, then one more that causes her to grind her teeth.

Cory climbs on top of her and eases his penis into her. The sensation is something like sliding down a banister, if the banister were inside you. He doesn't move a lot right then, gives her time to catch her breath. He lies on top of her, supporting his weight with his arms, just enjoying being inside. Barcelona's eyes snap open suddenly and she thinks she may have passed out for a moment, lost consciousness. He is still on top of her, his penis is still inside, swollen and hard, so if she did pass out, she didn't miss anything. He starts to move slowly. In and out. In and out. She pulls her legs up to her chest to feel him better. She gasps with each thrust. His hips smack against her ass with a thump. His penis is punching a button that goes directly to her brain, where it honks the horn and flashes the lights, then pulls back and she feels like her guts are being sucked out her vagina each time he retracts a little.

Finally he picks up his pace, hammering at her. She curls her fingers into his back, encouraging him. She wants him to come. He does. His lips slam into her and he grits his teeth. 'Oh, fuck,' she thinks he wants to get inside her even farther, though this is impossible. He sags, panting, finished. Then he starts to laugh. A big hearty laugh, with head thrown back and teeth and gums glistening with saliva.

'What's so funny?' she asks.

He rolls off her and she lowers her legs. Her skin stings

from the sudden rush of air against her sweaty chest. He is still chuckling.

She smiles at him. 'Why are you laughing?'

'No reason. It just felt good. Sometimes I laugh when I'm happy.'

'That's strange.'

'Stranger things are yet to come.' He nuzzles her neck.

They watch TV awhile then make love again. Afterward both fall asleep. Sometime later Barcelona wakes with a start. The TV is still on. She stares at it without comprehension, finally recognizing a rerun of 'Rockford Files.' She glances at the clock/radio next to the bed: 12.37 A.M. Her heart is pounding terribly and she wonders if she is having a heart attack. She can see the thumping under the skin. She thinks about waking Cory, but she doesn't. She read somewhere that caffeine was good for a heart attack. She gets out of bed, her head spinning dizzily, and stands on wobbly knees. She falls back to the bed. Cory doesn't stir.

'God,' she says and gets up again. This time she can stand. She makes her way downstairs by bracing herself against the walls as she walks. She opens the refrigerator and that same rancid smell whacks her face. She grabs a Diet Coke, pops the tab, and drinks. She sits naked on the wood floor in front of the open refrigerator door and lets the cool air pucker her skin. She feels better. No heart attack.

She walks back upstairs and stands over the bed. Cory is muttering in his sleep, though she can't make out any words. He's smiling and that's a good sign. He's kicked the covers off and she stands there a minute admiring his body. It is trim and toned with only a slight hint of looseness at the waist. He is a good, responsive lover. He is warm and wise. He is honorable. He likes her enough to pull a crazy stunt like separating from his wife before the election.

Her heart starts thumping again and she has trouble

breathing. She goes into the bathroom and flicks on the light. Larry is curled up inside the sink sleeping. He looks up when she opens the medicine cabinet. Barcelona studies the row after row of medicines and remedies, but she sees nothing appropriate. Meantime, Larry has roused himself and is poking his head into the cabinet, licking the tube of Ben-Gay. He is very intent, biting the cap, pulling it out. He drops it on the counter and starts to dance around it. He falls to his back and twists and turns as if he were possessed. This is more animated than she's ever seen him. He jumps up again and attacks the Ben-Gay tube, gnawing at the cap in desperation. Barcelona wonders if there's some kind of catnip in the ointment. She pulls it away from Larry and puts it back in the medicine cabinet and closes the door. Larry continues to dance around the counter, knocking over her makeup bottles and scattering her Q-tips. Barcelona picks him up to make sure he's okay, but he writhes and squirms with such ferocity that he leaps free of her arms and falls to the floor. His senses impaired by the Ben-Gay fumes, he lands on his hip with a squawk, then gets up and limps away.

For an instant, Barcelona knows how Larry feels clawing at the damn tube: blood thumping behind the eyeballs, choking off light, yet still scratching away in blindness. That gnawing unspecific need drilling deeper into the stomach sending gusher after gusher of corrosive acid splashing against tender membrances. The temptation to cry out, not for help or comfort or out of desire, just to hear the sound of your own confusion before the fumes crush the larynx, choking off air. And all the time scratching at the tube, trying to get at the source, knowing when you release the cap, what is inside may kill you.

Barcelona leaves the room and wanders down the hall to her study. The room is painted bright red to keep her attentive during her work. Overstuffed bookshelves scale each wall. The overflow is stacked in neat piles on the floor. Barcelona sits behind her computer and stares at the dark screen. She is astounded at her own good fortune. Before tonight everything was wonderful: money, impending fame, Grief's hot new writer, celebrity at school. All she needed for it to be perfect was for Cory to be unattached. Now hc was. Now everything was perfect.

She was charmed.

Yet she didn't feel charmed. She felt as if she'd just been driven home in a police cruiser by two large and silent police officers. As if her clothes were tattered, unrepairable, and her body smelled of dried blood and hospital disinfectant. She could feel the scratches on her face and thighs, where ragged fingernails clawed for purchase. But that wasn't her, was it?

She turns on the computer, punches up the last pages of the script for *The Usual Suspects*, and rereads what she's writing. She picks right up and starts typing a new scene. The cadence of her typing seems to calm the thumping of her heart. It slows back to normal. When she is finished writing the scene, she copies the disk, shuts off the computer, goes back to the bedroom.

While Cory sleeps, Barcelona quietly dresses, packs a few things, gets into her car, and drives all night to Las Vegas.

32

The dealer wears clear fingernail polish. He shuffles the cards gracefully and deals seven card stud. His glossy nails flicker under the bright casino lights. 'It keeps my nails from splitting,' he tells Barcelona, though she didn't ask. The other players ignore his monologue and study their cards. 'All this shuffling, the dry desert air, handling dirty money. Cracks the nails.' He taps his perfect fingernails on the green felt in front of an old woman with a deuce of clubs showing. 'Deuce opens, sweetheart. Deuces never loses.'

The old woman throws in two quarters. Barcelona folds. Others see the bet or fold. The dealer tosses out another card to each player. 'Some people look at the polish,' the dealer says to Barcelona, 'and they think I'm a fag. Just because I wear polish they think I'm a fag. I'm not a fag.' He winks at her. 'At least not yet.'

Barcelona has been playing seven card stud for four straight hours. This is a one-dollar and three-dollar table, minimum bet is one dollar, maximum bet is three dollars. She is ahead eighty-seven dollars. Her car and overnight bag are in the casino parking lot. She hasn't even checked into a hotel yet. She drove all night through the cool desert air in the Geezemobile, stopping once for gas and a Snickers bar from the vending machine. During the entire drive, she listened only to the all-news station on the radio, even though they kept repeating the same stories over and over. This was unusual because she always plays either her tapes or the oldies stations on her radio. But she told herself this was not a pleasure trip, she was on a sort of mission. She needed constant cold splashes of reality to keep her mind focused, help her concentrate on the task at hand. She needed news, facts.

The radio played one science story that Barcelona can't get out of her mind. It was about how the long-horned beetle bites through the poisonous veins of the milkweed leaf before eating the plant. Like a burglar snipping the wires to an alarm. This causes the toxic fluids to drain off and not poison him while he dines. This also allows the woolly bear caterpillar and the army worm, normally not milkweed eaters, to also eat the plant now that the toxins are gone. Of course, the beetle does ingest some of the creamy poison in the process of severing the veins, but not enough to kill him. Barcelona thinks of Dixie. Even the insect world has its charm.

'Where's the nearest pay phone?' she asks the dealer.

He points. 'By the hologram.'

She walks away, leaving her chips on the table. She wends her way through the maze of slot machines to the giant hologram of a leprechaun sitting in a pot of gold that has poured out of a slot machine. It's a fuzzy hologram, hard to see. It's not clear whether the leprechaun is rolling on his back joyously throwing the gold coins in the air, or if the gold coins are raining down on him and have knocked him onto his back.

She finds the phone, calls Orange County information, memorizes the number, and dials her neighbor. He isn't home so she leaves a message on his answering machine: 'Hi, Dave, it's Barcelona. I wonder if you'd do me a big favor and feed Larry tonight and tomorrow. I was called out of town unexpectedly and I'm not sure when I'll be back. I'll phone you later with details. The spare key is outside my garage under the first flagstone. If there's an emergency, you can reach me at Caesar's Palace in Las Vegas. Thanks, neighbor.' She hangs up and returns to the poker table. She imagines Dave's chubby face as he listens to the message, the leash in one hand, the brown paper bag in the other.

Barcelona sits down and discovers a new player sitting in the chair next to her. He is short and rotund, triple chins accordioned at his neck. He is wearing a plastic name tag with the printed words HELLO, MY NAME IS followed by his typed name: Dr. Earl Downey.

'So, Doc,' the dealer says, throwing cards around the table, 'you with the convention?'

'Yes, I am.'

'So what kind of doctor are you? Gynecologist?' The dealer grins and taps his polished fingernails on the felt in front of Barcelona's up card, four of hearts. 'Low card must open, ma'am. What's your bet?'

Barcelona throws in two quarters.

'Fifty cents,' the dealer announces. 'Major wager.'

Barcelona peeks at her cards underneath, a five and another four. Not enough to bet up, but enough to stick around for another card. Her next card is a six. Someone else with a pair of jacks showing bets two dollars; she calls. She ends up with a straight to the eight and wins another twenty-four dollars. She tips the dealer fifty cents.

'Thank you, thank you,' he says. He taps the coins against the metal edge of the coin tray before sticking the money in his shirt pocket. This is done after every tip to signal that they are not stealing casino money. Above each table, the ceiling is a glittery crazy-quilt design of bright lights and mirrors. Behind the one-way mirrors are cameras watching each game all over the casino. Barcelona looks up and stares at the hidden camera. The bright lights

508

reflect off the mirrors into her eyes, blurring her vision. She strains to see the camera behind the mirror, but all she sees is her own reflection which resembles, with her blurred vision, that fuzzy hologram of the leprechaun.

Barcelona sits naked on the bed eating Kentucky Fried Chicken, extra crispy. The bucket sits between her crossed legs and she hunches over it while she eats so the crumbs fall back into the bucket. A few crumbs sometimes miss and drop into her lap, snagged in the thicket of pubic hairs. To her right a *USA Today* lies spread open to the state-by-state news summary. To her left is what remains of a six-pack of Diet Coke. Three full cans are still looped into the plastic holder. Two empty ones lay on the bedspread, one has rolled down and leans against her left buttock. One is still half-filled and she occasionally sips from it, setting it back on the bedspread where it tilts precariously.

The TV is showing a local talk show.

On the dresser is a stack of her winnings: $376.

She reads the newspaper with her reading glasses, intermittently glancing up to watch a few seconds of TV while taking a bite of chicken and a swig of Diet Coke, and then back to reading the newspaper. Her throat is still a little sore, Vegas Throat they call it, an irritation caused by the constant blasting of icy casino air-conditioning combined with the smoke from millions of free cigarettes streaming hourly into the air.

A psychologist is on the talk show. He is sitting on a cushy chair facing the host. The psychologist looks remarkably familiar. Jesus, Barcelona thinks in mid-bite, he looks like that dealer with the clear polish. The show's host is a shapely woman in her mid-thirties with frosted hair and a nose that Barcelona is positive has been fixed. The psychologist is promoting his new book about

509

relationships, *Intimate Inmates: How to Break Out of Confining Relationships*. The cover photo shows a man and a woman bursting through a brick wall of a jail.

'*How, Dr. Novinger?*' the hostess Vicki asks, squinting intently. '*How can we break out, or even know that we want to?*'

'*First thing one needs to do is recognize that the relationship is indeed confining.*' His voice startles Barcelona; it too sounds exactly like the dealer's. She leans closer to the TV, her breasts dipping into the bucket of chicken. '*It's not always easy to see that a relationship we're in is really a prison of our own construction.*'

'*Ah,*' Vicki says, nodding.

'*For example, the clothes women wear often make them coconspirators in their own imprisonment. High heels are designed to alter the natural shape of the leg to a more sexy angle, but at what price? Strained muscles, chronically sore legs, twisted ankles. The concept is much like the Oriental custom of binding a woman's feet. Much of women's clothing is designed to hinder their movements, like the leg irons on a prisoner. Tight short skirts allow only small steps, as do the high heels just mentioned.*'

'*But men seem to like the way they look,*' Vicki points out.

'*Yes,*' Dr. Novinger agrees, '*as long as he doesn't have to walk with her, drag her behind him. See, that's the point. The clothes are meant to enhance a woman's looks, not her functioning ability. This makes her an object. How many times have you worn panty hose on a hot mucky day when you didn't want to?*'

'*You sound like a man who's tried them on.*' She laughs, poking him in the ribs.

Dr. Novinger smiles good-naturedly. '*Why are panty hose preferable to men than the bare leg? Because the panty hose shapes the leg more, hides the flaws, makes them more*

510

*attractive to look at. Even more destructive than clothing is
the cultural pressure for women to shave their bodies.'*

*'Come, now, Dr. Novinger, you're not suggesting hairy
legs and unsightly armpits? Men shave their faces, don't
they? You do.'*

*'There is a difference. Men shave for reasons of comfort
and sanitation. Women shave for aesthetic reasons. We have
told them that it is better to shave their bodies so they look
like little girls than let their hair grow and look like an adult
of their species. Everything we do as a culture is to reduce
women to the confines of adolescence, the restricting clothing, the shaved bodies. Make them look like children so
they can be controlled like children.'*

Vicki looks offstage. *'Our phones are ringing. Dr. Novinger will be answering questions from our home viewers.'*

Dr. Novinger raises his hand to adjust his glasses and
his fingernails flicker under the bright studio lights.

'I saw a guy who looks just like you,' Barcelona tells the
dealer when she returns to the table.

The dealer tosses cards to the players. 'Richard Gere
must be back in town.'

'Not exactly. A psychologist on TV. Looked just like
you, except he wore glasses.'

The dealer taps his glossy nail under his eye. 'Contacts.'

'Two bucks,' a man with a pipe says. He throws in two
chips.

'Two dollars,' the dealer echoes. 'Two dollars to peek
under the fat lady's dress.'

Barcelona sits down at the five-dollar blackjack table.
She is the only one at the table. 'Kinda slow today,' she
says to the woman dealer.

'Kinda.' The woman nods and gathers up the decks
of cards. She shuffles them one stack at a time, hands

511

Barcelona a red plastic card to stick in the deck. Barcelona does so and the dealer cuts the cards and stuffs them into a black shoe. 'Place your bet, ma'am,' she says with a drawl. She has bleached blond hair as stiff as the cards.

Barcelona has won over four hundred dollars at poker. She takes twenty five-dollar chips out of her purse and stacks them on the felt table. She places one chip in the square in front of her. The dealer tosses out the cards faceup for Barcelona and one up, one down for the dealer. Barcelona has a nine and king. She stays. The dealer has an eight showing. She flips over a ten and pays Barcelona.

Barcelona is not discouraged. She places another chip in the square. She wins again. She tries not to lose hope.

'Hi, Evelyn?' Barcelona says into the phone. 'This is Barcelona. I want you to post my class today, I won't be coming in . . . No, nothing too serious.' Evelyn Logue, the department secretary, persists in asking for details, symptoms. Barcelona refuses to give any. 'You can get Ben Lawrence to substitute for me, he knows how I run the class. Thanks.'

She hangs up the phone and walks to the cashier's cage, feeling guilty about canceling her class. She has never done that before except for severe illness. Still, she had to.

She dumps her stack of chips on the counter and pushes them under the window bars. The kid behind the counter starts stacking them and counting.

'Five hundred and sixty-five dollars,' he says. 'How do you want it?'

'Big,' she says.

He counts out five hundred-dollar bills, a fifty, a ten, and a five.

'Thank you,' she says. 'Where's the luncheon buffet?'

He points. 'Past the hologram to the left.'

Barcelona follows his directions until she's walking down

a hallway behind a couple of beefy college-age boys in USC Trojan sweatshirts.

'Have you eaten at the buffet before?' one of them asks the other.

'You mean the *barf*-et.'

They both laugh.

The buffet is served in the showroom where their top entertainers perform at night. Joan Rivers and the Smothers Brothers are billed for tonight. Barcelona hopes it looks more glamorous at night because right now it looks pretty cheesy.

Barcelona browses past the bins, piling food onto her plate: roast beef, turkey, salads, rolls, gelatin molds, fruit, mashed potatoes. She sits in a booth by herself and eats ravenously, finishing everything on her plate. The food tastes bland, but she has never been so hungry. She goes back for seconds and eats that too.

A black girl wearing a short skirt and high heels asks Barcelona if she wants to play $50,000 keno. Barcelona shakes her head and the girl hurries to pick up the keno sheets from other diners.

Keno is not part of Barcelona's plan; the odds are too crazy. Winning or losing at keno won't prove anything. She has worked it all out very carefully. It is crucial to play each game to win, not take stupid chances and buck the odds. The only way any of this will make any sense is if she plays the games she knows with as much skill as possible. The longer she plays, the better the odds fall in the casino's favor. It is inevitable then that they will win. According to all known laws of probability, she will lose all her money. Once she has, she will have proven her point beyond all doubt.

Barcelona tears her bagel in half to mop up some of the tasteless gravy left on her plate. The bagel is dry, not nearly as good as her father makes in his bakery. She remembers the hot Saturdays downstairs in the kitchen, when she was twelve, helping Dad make the bagels. The bagels were the last thing baked and when they were done she was allowed to go off to the movies for the matinee. Her favorite part was squeezing the yeast for the dough. Eight ounces of Fleishmann's yeast in half a pan of warm water. She had to submerge her hand in the water and keep squeezing the sticky clump of yeast until it melted into a tan soup. Sometimes the warm water made her have to go to the bathroom and she'd squirm and dance until she finished and then run off to pee. When she was done, the melted yeast was poured into the huge robot-sized dough mixer with twenty-three and a half pounds of flour. There were eggs and oil and salt and sugar. Then her father would switch on the mixer and the giant metal arm would stir through the gunk. Her father would stand beside the machine, studying the mixture as it spun, adding water at mysterious intervals until it somehow became dough.

Then, after the dough rose, her father would roll it out, cut it into small squares in another machine, and stand next to his wooden bake bench for hours rolling the dough into fat snakes, wrapping one around his hand, then rolling it closed and flopping it on a tray. When the tray was full, the bagels would rise and then be boiled in water and baked. When the first tray was taken out of the oven, Barcelona had her pick. She ate her bagel hot, often burning her mouth, but nothing was ever more delicious, just as nothing was ever quite as sensual as squeezing that yeast in the warm water.

Upstairs in the store, her mother would be waiting on customers, bagging baked goods, pouring coffee, slicing corned beef, smoking cigarettes. Men especially liked Milan, found her deep voice sexy, her easy laughter flattering. Whenever Barcelona carried a tray of Danish up to the store, her mother would be sitting at the end of the counter, smoking a cigarette, laughing with someone, usually a man. Barcelona and her father had a secret joke about Milan. Whenever Barcelona would return to the basement kitchen with the empty tray, her father would say, 'What's your mother doing?' Then he would make an exaggerated face, as if puffing an enormous cigarette the way Milan did, and they would both laugh.

The thing Barcelona remembers most about her parents' store is the door that separated the upstairs from the downstairs. Upstairs was all light and life, with its brightly lit showcases filled with fresh baked goods and delicatessen meats and four tables and Formica counter with six wobbly stools and lively customers. Downstairs was the basement where the freezers and storerooms and kitchen were, where the actual baking was done, the salads made, the platters arranged. Immediately at the bottom of the stairs was the tiny rest room. The door leading downstairs was short and a customer had to bend and hunch to go down the four steps that led to the bathroom. Above the short door was a big sign hand-lettered by Milan, the black letters looking vaguely European. It said: WATCH YOUR HEAD!!! Even so, Milan or Father or Barcelona knew to add a verbal warning whenever a customer was going up or down those stairs. Nevertheless, not a day went by without someone cracking his head on that overhanging beam and stagger around a full minute rubbing his skull, cursing and wincing. Occasionally there'd be blood.

Barcelona thinks of that sign now, of all the people, herself included, who smacked their heads on that beam on their way to and from the bathroom. WATCH YOUR HEAD! she thinks and finishes eating the stale bagel.

Four hours later she is $824 ahead. Sometimes she loses hands, but soon after she wins it all back plus more. She changes seats to avoid the occasional fluke deck that continuously lays winning hands at one seat. Finally she changes tables too. She keeps winning. The cigarette smoke is so bad she lights one up in self-defense.

She decides the problem is that she isn't risking enough. She is betting too small. She needs to put more money on the line. Much more. Her puny bets aren't a mathematical challenge.

She moves up to a higher stakes poker game. Minimum bet is forty dollars, maximum is eighty dollars.

'Fresh blood,' one of the players says to her. He wears his long brown hair in a ponytail and dresses like a Western outlaw, complete with leather vest and boots. He hasn't shaved for a few days.

'Welcome,' the woman dealer says. She is painfully thin with cheekbones as sharp as a pickax. Her eyes are sunk so deep it's hard to tell what color they are. 'I take it you're familiar with the game, ma'am?'

'Yes,' Barcelona says. She's played poker since she was old enough to distinguish the difference between the cards. Her parents are both avid poker players with a weekly game at the house every Friday night. Her father is a steady odds player, Milan is more the reckless intuitive type.

Barcelona stacks her chips in front of her. Compared to the tremendous stacks of the other players, her pile of chips is embarrassingly small.

'That's what I call confidence,' another player says. He's an old man in his seventies. The cheaper tables are filled with old men and women, but there are few at these stakes. Las Vegas casinos seem overrun with old people shuffling around with their bucket of change or single fistful of chips. It's as if they were at a giant amusement park especially constructed for the retired and dying.

There are eight players at the table, including Barcelona and excluding the dealer. The room chatters with the constant clacking of chips being stacked, unstacked, re-stacked, mostly from the players fidgeting.

'Deal 'em, dealer,' the ponytail says.

She does. Cards fly and land in front of each player. Bets are made. Barcelona loses eighty dollars before dropping out of the hand. An Oriental woman in her late twenties wins the hand. She is wearing a blue jogging suit and a ring on each finger. Barcelona guesses the rings' worth to total over $300,000. When she goes to the bathroom, someone says she's married to some ambassador and that she once lost half a million dollars in one night shooting craps. Her husband hasn't allowed her to play craps since.

Barcelona folds early in the next hand. After the fourth card, the only two left in the pot are the old man and the ponytail. The old man throws in eighty dollars. 'Get outta my pot,' he scowls. Ponytail raises eighty dollars. The old man raises another eighty dollars and repeats, 'Get outta my pot.'

The Oriental woman returns, lights a cigarette, and holds it straight up between finger and thumb as if it were a candle. She looks off toward the crap table.

The old man finally drops out of the pot and ponytail rakes it in. 'My pot now, Jim,' he says. The old man shrugs.

Four hours later, Barcelona is $2,785 ahead. She is playing well, but no better than the others. She decides she still isn't risking enough. So far she's been playing only with her winnings. She needs to bet big, *really* big. So big that she can't afford to lose.

At the cashier's cage she is taken to see a credit manager. They are in a private office. He is young, maybe twenty-four, but wearing a fabulous suit. He is also extremely handsome with a large mole on his upper lip. Actually, the mole enhances his looks. He is very polite and respectful to

517

Barcelona, but there is a slight feeling of pity or contempt in his look. Most of the people who work in Las Vegas have that look, as if they can't help but think of you as a born sucker.

He jots down all the pertinent information on a pad, stands, and says, 'I'll be right back, Ms. Lee. Naturally we have to check it through some computers, make a few calls. Then I have to get it approved by my supervisor.'

'Of course,' she says.

'A hundred thousand dollars, right?'

'Yes.'

'Make yourself comfortable, this may take a few minutes.'

'I'm comfortable,' she replies.

He leaves. She picks up a copy of *Esquire* from the table and leafs through it. She gave the young man Grief's home number to verify the deal with Lynda Kramer, and of course she did have good credit, equity in her condo, a salary, and some royalty income.

Half an hour later he returns. He stands behind his desk and says, 'Fifty thousand is the best we can do.'

'I'll take it,' she said. But it's not enough. Not nearly.

'Hello?' the sleepy voice whispers. 'Hello?'

Barcelona listens to her mother's tired voice squeeze through the telephone. She is calling home to ask for money, a loan against the money she will be earning for the script. She has never borrowed from them before, not even for college. They could wire her the cash in the morning. She needs another fifty thousand dollars to make her total of one hundred thousand dollars. Playing with a hundred thousand dollars will settle this issue once and for all. Then the stakes will be high enough.

'Hello?' her mother says again. 'Who's there? It's late.'

Barcelona can't talk. Her lips are stuck shut. Finally she

pulls her sweater lapel over the mouthpiece and is about to whisper an obscenity when she hears a soft sobbing. Her mother is crying. 'It's all right,' her mother says through the sobs. 'It's all right, really.'

In that instant she realizes her mother knows it is her, that her mother has known all along it's been her making the calls.

Barcelona immediately hangs up the phone. Her hands are trembling.

Barcelona sits in the cocktail lounge and sips a dark beer. On the small stage behind her identical twin sisters in matching cowgirl outfits sing 'Desperado.'

The most noticeable aspect of people in Las Vegas, Barcelona decides, is the hair. There are many different styles, all seem carefully constructed, with lots of angles, dips, bumps, then solidified with so much grease, mousse, and spray that they resemble hood ornaments on old cars. The twins' platinum hair is freeze-dried to resemble Patsy Cline's.

'Hello,' a nervous voice behind her says.

She turns and sees the short stout man who'd been playing poker at her table earlier. The doctor with the convention. He is sitting at the next table. She smiles politely.

'They're pretty good,' he says, gesturing with his drink at the twins on stage.

'Yes, they are.'

He gets up and brings his drink to her table. 'I'm Dr. Earl Downey,' he says, sitting next to her. 'We played poker.'

'I remember.'

'Actually, you played poker, I made a donation.' He chuckled.

'My favorite charity,' she says. 'Give 'til it hurts.'

'Are you still winning?' he asks.

'I'm ahead a couple bucks.'

'I'm way down.' He says it in a bragging manner, as if losing were admirable as long as you lost big. 'But that's why I come here.'

'To lose?'

'To gamble. Take chances.' He looks at Barcelona to see if she caught the suggestiveness in that last phrase. She stares back innocently. He stares at the stage while he speaks. 'You here alone?'

'Why?'

He shifts uncomfortably. 'Curious. A beautiful woman like you all alone in Las Vegas. Must make you nervous.'

'Why should it?'

He shrugs. 'No reason I guess.'

'Oh, I get it. You think I might be mistaken for a hooker. Is that it?'

He is clearly shaken by her directness. He looks over his shoulder longingly at his old table. 'N-No, not necessarily.'

'It's all right. I'm sure you meant that as a compliment.'

'Well, of course, I . . . I didn't mean to offend.'

Barcelona finishes her beer. 'Have you ever been with a prostitute?'

He bristles at the implication. 'No, of course not.'

Barcelona looks at her watch. It is past midnight. She didn't sleep last night and she doesn't plan on sleeping tonight. Sleep would ruin the experiment, screw up the equation. She must do this without sleep, keep playing the games without closing her eyes. Stamina is part of this too, physical prowess. But she needs more money. Cash. She has already received cash advances from her MasterCard and Visa that took them to the limit. She cashed a check that wiped out her bank account, and now she has a credit line with the casino for $50,000. Still, it isn't enough, it

520

doesn't risk enough. She needs more money. Only a hundred thousand will do.

Dr. Earl Downey sips his drink, avoiding Barcelona's gaze. He looks over at the twin cowgirls who are singing 'Candy Man.' He taps in time on the edge of the table.

'Still,' Barcelona says, 'I wonder how much a hooker makes around here, don't you?'

He tries to kiss her in the elevator. She has to bend over to meet his lips. They are thick and rubbery and taste of bitter cigars and cheap scotch. He tries to poke his tongue in her mouth, but she pulls away. They are on their way to his room and he is very excited. He has his arm around her waist and he lets it slide down so he can feel the curve of her hip under his pudgy fingers. She lets him.

Barcelona feels a little dizzy as the elevator rushes skyward. Dr. Earl Downey is under the impression that Barcelona is going to have sex with him in exchange for money. Two hundred dollars was mentioned in an oblique way. Barcelona hasn't decided yet what she will do when the elevator door opens. She needs more money to prove her point. She is in the middle of a great chemistry experiment and she's run out of one of the main ingredients, cash. Also, there is something proper about getting the money this way, from Dr. Earl Downey in exchange for a quick jump. Somehow it adds unity and dimension, universality to the experiment.

Dr. Earl Downey kisses her again, pressing his lumpy body up against hers. He tries to force his tongue between her teeth again, but she keeps them clamped together. Meanwhile, he rubs up against her, his crotch thumping against her thigh. He rubs so fast and furiously the denim on her jeans is heating up. Suddenly he makes a high-pitched moan and jumps away from her. His body spasms and she thinks he is having a heart attack. But it is only his hips that are spasming. They both look down at his crotch and she can see the wet stain soaking through the material around the zipper.

'Oh, God, no,' he says, staring.

'Oops,' she says.

The elevator door opens and Dr. Earl Downey runs out without her, one hand groping in his pocket for his room key, the other hand clamped over his crotch. Barcelona presses the Lobby button and the doors close and the car descends. She wonders if the restaurant is still serving.

Barcelona is standing in the shower when she hears the knocking on her door. 'Just a minute,' she hollers. She shuts off the faucet and wraps a towel around her body.

The knocking continues. Firm but not impatient.

'Just a minute, I'm coming.' She quickly towels off and climbs into her panties, jeans, and a sweatshirt. They smell of cigarette smoke, but she only packed a change of underwear. She walks over to the door toweling her hair. 'Who is it?'

'Autrey St. James,' he says.

Barcelona opens the door. 'You're early.'

'I like to be punctual,' he says, entering.

'Twenty minutes early isn't punctual, it's pushy.'

'Sorry,' he says, though there is nothing in his voice to indicate sincerity. He is about twenty-five, the same age as the young man from the casino who gave her the credit line. Autrey St. James is in the same business, extending credit, but without a casino to back him. He is strictly a private entrepreneur. He has a cocky walk, stiff but purposeful, a half march as if he's capturing the room. His clothes are a little too hip: white linen jacket with the sleeves rolled up to his elbows, peach-colored shirt unbuttoned to his sternum. His watch is worth more than her car. So are his shoes. He sits on the edge of the bed and smiles at her. 'So, down to business, okay?'

'Okay,' she says. She lifts her room service tray off the desk chair and sits down.

'You must've been hungry,' he says, nodding at the stack of empty plates.

'Cards make me hungry,' she says. She had eaten a stack of buttermilk pancakes and a three-egg Denver omelette, including juice, toast, and coffee. There was little else to do all night but watch TV, read newspapers, and eat. She refuses to gamble another dime until she has her entire amount, one hundred thousand dollars. Since the casino would give her only fifty thousand dollars in credit, she still needs another fifty thousand dollars. A few chats with several well-tipped bellboys got her a phone number.

'I've done some checking on you, Ms. Lee.' Autrey St. James smiles but his face seems to resent the exercise. 'You're not un-well known.'

'Un-well known?' She smiles at the word.

His face stiffens. He is not sure how, but he senses an insult. 'You're not exactly famous either. But I gather from my sources, you do have some readers. I only mention this because I want you to feel at ease. I have many famous clients, names you wouldn't believe me if I told you. Top TV stars, singers, movie stars. I conduct business with a lot of celebrities.'

'You lend them money?'

'Sure, money. Whatever they want.'

Barcelona watches him. Everything about him is studied and rehearsed, even his smile and the pout of his lips. Every gesture is calculated for effect. He reminds her of all the young goal-oriented executives at large corporations, grooming themselves for their eventual seat on the Board of Directors.

He crosses his legs and tugs the wrinkles out of the knee of his trousers. 'Fifty thousand is a lot of money.'

'You wouldn't be here if you didn't know I can make it good.'

His smile widens. His teeth flicker in the lamplight like the dealer's fingernails. 'Yes, you can make good. But I also know you received a similar line of credit from the casino. If you lose both, you'll be ruined. I know all about your screenplay for Lynda Kramer, but after your agent's cut and taxes, you won't see much of that money, maybe half. You'll lose your house for starters. The casino has legal means to collect. I do not. You understand?'

Barcelona yawns. 'Sorry.'

His face tightens into a grim mask. 'I'm not boring you, am I?'

'No, I'm sorry. Not enough sleep.'

He relaxes. 'You do understand, don't you? I won't make any loan until the client is fully aware of his obligations to me and how serious I am about those obligations. With responsibility, we're no better than animals. Our obligations make us civilized.'

Barcelona finds it amusing that she's sitting here doing business with a man who is basically threatening her life, promising bodily harm if she does not pay, just like in the movies. Barcelona is not really concerned, she has more important things on her mind. Actually, the threats are good because they raise the stakes considerably for her. Make the contest more real. Now she will have her full one hundred thousand dollars to gamble with and if she loses, she loses everything. That's what must be at stake for this to work.

Everything.

'Do you have the money here?' Barcelona asks.

'Not so fast. Do we understand each other concerning the terms?'

'Yes, I understand the interest rates and payment schedule. I also understand the penalties for late payments.'

He smiles approval. 'You're very smart.'

'That's what I'm here to find out.'

He reaches into his jacket pocket and pulls out a stack of envelopes. 'These are stamped and addressed. This is what you mail your payments in. The dates due are written on the inside flap for your convenience. Send a money order, no check, made out to the name on the paper inside each envelope. It's a different name each time.'

'Very efficient,' she says.

'I've been doing this awhile.'

'You're so young.'

'I'm also so rich.'

She unwraps the towel from her wet hair. 'Do you have the money here?'

He leans back on the bed, propping himself on his elbows. He is smiling again, trying to look suave and sophisticated. He manages sharkish. 'You're a writer, so you probably have some ideas about how I do business. You probably imagine I'll send a couple goons around to rough you up and give you another chance. Or maybe that you'll come home and find your cat hanging in your closet, his throat cut.'

Barcelona's skin chills at the mention of Larry. That Autrey St. James knows about him is an intimacy she didn't expect. She told him about her finances, but nothing personal.

'But that's Hollywood talking,' he says. 'I'm much more practical. I don't come around and I don't send anyone around. You miss a payment.' He holds up a finger. 'Just one. You miss one and the next thing you know you will be driving down the street and suddenly in a major car accident. A lawyer defending the victim, my associate, will be suing you and your insurance company for a lot of money because, believe me, the accident will be your fault. Witnesses will testify to that. That's easy to arrange. The tricky part is controlling the injuries during the accident, that's guesswork. Either way, I get paid.'

Barcelona stands up, snatches a stray bite of cold pancake from the room service tray and eats it. 'Do you have the money here?'

He laughs. 'I like a woman who knows what she wants.' He stands up and unzips his fly. 'As long as she knows what I want.'

Barcelona eyes his zipper without expression.

Autrey St. James reaches into his fly and pulls out a roll of cash secured with a red rubber band. He reaches back in and pulls out a second roll. 'Crowded in there,' he says, grinning. He zips his pants back up.

Suddenly someone knocks on the door and says, 'Barcy? You in there?'

Barcelona doesn't answer.

'Come on,' Cory says. 'The maid said you were in.'

Autrey St. James's eyes look feverish as he glances at the door. He snatches up the two rolls of hundred dollar bills and quickly stuffs them in his jacket pocket. 'This better not be a rip-off,' he warns through clenched teeth.

'My boyfriend,' she explains, knowing she sounds like a teenager caught necking with a boy from a rival school. But she doesn't want a man like this to know Cory's name.

Barcelona opens the door and Cory enters. He looks at Autrey St. James who is again leaning back on the bed, grinning with sexual innuendo. 'You okay?' Cory asks her.

'Of course. How'd you find out I was here?'

'Your neighbor with the dog. I was still at your place when he came over to feed Larry. I'd been on the fucking phone all morning trying to find you. What's going on?'

'What's it look like, pal?' Autrey St. James says.

Cory ignores him. 'You okay?'

526

'I told you, I'm fine. This is just business.'

'What kind of business?'

'Research. I'm gathering material for a book.'

Cory turns to Autrey St. James. 'Thanks for dropping by. Ms. Lee will contact you later.'

'Ms. Lee's already *contacted* me,' he says with a lewd grin.

'Then that must conclude her research into microdicked morons who masturbate until they lose all their manners and taste in clothing.'

Autrey St. James stands slowly. His eyes don't blink, don't waver. His voice is lower, throatier, as if filtered through a bucket of water. 'Why don't we just ask the lady who she wants to stay?'

They both turn to Barcelona. 'Christ,' she sighs. 'Cory, can you wait downstairs for me?'

Autrey St. James leans his face close to Cory's and grins. 'Bye bye, baby.'

Cory throws his fist into Autrey St. James's stomach, doubling him over. Autrey St. James drops to his knees clutching his stomach, coughing. 'Son of a bitch,' he gasps. 'Fucking faggot.'

'Jesus, Cory,' Barcelona says, running over to help up Autrey St. James. 'I know what I'm doing. I don't need protection.'

Autrey St. James pulls out a six-inch switchblade and clicks it open. He slowly rises from his knees, pointing the knife at Cory. He doesn't say anything, make threats, growl insults, curse. He just concentrates on his knife like a pool shark about to make a difficult shot.

Cory is backing up, looking nervous. 'Hey, okay, you made your point,' Cory says. 'Now put the knife away.'

But Autrey St. James doesn't answer. He stalks.

Barcelona picks up a nearby plate from the room service tray and throws it at him like a Frisbee. It clips his shoulder

527

and he grunts in pain and spins around to face him. 'Cunt!' he says.

That's when Cory jumps him. Both Cory's hands grip Autrey St. James's wrist, trying to shake loose the knife. Barcelona also grabs the wrist, her hands wrapped around Cory's hands. Suddenly Autrey St. James punches her in the side of the head with his free hand and she tumbles backward over a chair and sprawls on the floor. Her head throbs. Getting punched hurts more than she imagined.

Cory manages to shake the knife loose and kick it under the bed. Autrey St. James punches Cory in the jaw and knocks him into the wall. A painting of a serene Alpine village drops to the floor. Cory rubs his jaw. 'That should about make us even. Right?'

Autrey St. James glares at him, fists held high in front of him. But Cory makes no threatening move, he just stands against the wall, waiting. Barcelona is impressed that Cory doesn't appear scared. Autrey St. James stands in his boxer's crouch for a long time, just staring at Cory. Finally he takes a deep breath, brushes the wrinkles out of his jacket, and walks to the door. 'I'm a businessman, not a thug. I won't do business this way.'

He walks out of the room.

'You okay?' Cory asks Barcelona as she rises from the floor.

'How many times you going to ask me that?'

' 'Til I get an answer I believe.'

She walks over and touches his bruised jaw. 'That hurt?' He winces. 'Yes.'

'Good. That's what you get for poking your face into my business.'

Cory goes into the bathroom and soaks a washcloth in cold water. When he returns he presses the folded washcloth against Barcelona's forehead where she'd been punched. It feels good. Not just the coolness of the nubbled cloth, but the warmth of his caring. She leans against him and feels his arms enclose her. She closes her eyes and smells the jet fuel fumes in his shirt. It's nice. 'You've ruined everything, you know,' she says softly. 'I needed the money.'

'If you needed money you could have asked me. I'd make you a loan.'

She chuckles into his chest. 'Fifty thousand dollars?'

He pauses. 'If that's what you want.'

She considers it but shakes her head. 'No, that wouldn't work. If I lost it and didn't pay you back, you'd just let me get away with it. You wouldn't sue me or arrange an accident.'

'Jesus, Barcy, what are you talking about? What accident?'

'I'm talking about my work, my life. I'm talking about who deserves what. Something like that.'

'You're not making sense.'

'Not to you.' She yawns.

'You need sleep.'

She pushes away from him. 'That would be cheating. Invalidate the whole experiment.'

'What experiment?' he asks in frustration.

She starts pacing the room. It's impossible to explain to him, he wouldn't understand. He takes his good luck for granted. 'I need money.'

'I told you, I'll lend it to you.'

'I told you, it wouldn't count.'

He looks at her with sad eyes. 'You want it to count? We'll make it count.'

Barcelona walks up to the one-hundred-dollar blackjack table. No one is sitting at the table, most gamblers are at the five-dollar tables. The dealer is a tall redheaded woman with pale skin and a small Band-Aid over one nostril. Her arms are crossed across her chest. The cards are spread out on the table in several fans.

'You open?' Barcelona asks.

'Yes, ma'am,' she says, uncrossing her arms. She gathers up the cards and starts shuffling.

'Not too busy yet.'

The dealer, whose name tag says Billie Jo, looks around the casino. 'Still early. In another hour this place will be shoulder to shoulder. You could have five meaningful relationships just walking across the room and never meet one of them.'

Barcelona laughs. She is in good spirits, excited and jittery, but somehow calm inside. Like one of those Mexican high-cliff divers poised on the edge of the cliff looking down. Once you've made the resolve to dive, the rest is easy.

She empties her purse on the felt table. One hundred fifty chips spill out. Each chip is worth a thousand dollars.

Billie Jo glances over at the chips but shows no reaction. She continues to shuffle the cards. 'Not a good idea to be walking around with that much in your purse.'

'I thought the Mob scared all the muggers out of Vegas.'

Billie Jo laughs. 'Yeah, that's what a lot of people think. Only it ain't so.'

'Don't worry,' Barcelona says. 'I'll either be walking away with twice this amount or none of it.'

Billie Jo glances up into Barcelona's face. Barcelona detects that same look of pity and contempt. 'Good luck, ma'am,' she says.

Barcelona begins stacking the chips. It took all day, but Cory managed to raise another one hundred thousand dollars. They went to several banks, he made several more phone calls from her room. He borrowed against some personal stock, against his house, against things he didn't tell her about. But he raised it. During the whole day he didn't try to talk her out of what she was doing. They didn't eat a single meal, they didn't make love, didn't even touch. When he finally handed her the money he touched her arm and said, 'Is this what you want?'

'Yes,' she said. 'It's important.'

'The stakes should be high enough now. If you lose, I'll lose everything. There'll be press inquiries and it will eventually come out that I was in Las Vegas when I did all this. The public will draw its own conclusions.'

'I didn't ask you to do this. I can make my own arrangements.'

He kissed her cheek. 'I don't want to watch,' he said. 'Call me afterwards if you want.' And he walked out of her room.

She didn't stop him.

Barcelona stacks twenty-five chips in the square in front of her. She'll start with a twenty-five thousand dollar bet, just to get her feet wet. To tease.

'Five thousand dollar maximum,' Billie Jo says.

'I could play all six slots,' Barcelona says. 'But I don't want to have to move.'

Billie Jo turns and says something to the man in the suit standing behind her. The pit boss. He is in his fifties with curly brown hair that refuses to be tamed by whatever grease he is using. Various strands poke wildly from his scalp like broken springs in a mattress. He lifts his glasses up to his forehead and looks at Barcelona, sizing her up while Billie Jo whispers to him. When she's finished, he nods approval.

'Okay,' Billie Jo says. She hands Barcelona the red card to cut the shuffled decks. Barcelona sticks it in the middle and Billie Jo cuts and stuffs the cards into the shoe.

A small crowd gathers, attracted by the stack of chips in front of Barcelona. They mutter and fret among themselves.

Barcelona watches the first card float down to the felt in front of her. A three.

The dealer has an eight showing.

Barcelona's next card is a seven.

The dealer's card is down.

Billie Jo waits. 'Take your time,' she says. 'You have ten.'

Barcelona is touched by the kindness in Billie Jo's voice. That kindness gives her confidence. 'Double down,' she says. The crowd buzzes and fusses as she stacks another twenty-five chips next to the first pile. She has bet fifty thousand dollars on the next card.

Billie Jo deals.

Seven.

Billie Jo flips her card: jack.

Barcelona loses.

She smiles. The odds are catching up. Her heart is compressed in her chest to the size of a pea. But she has enough strength to push another twenty-five chips out.

Billie Jo deals: six and two to Barcelona, a six to herself. Barcelona doubles down again, pushing in another twenty-five thousand dollars. Billie Jo flips over her hole card and reveals a five. Eleven. She takes another card. A four. That gives her fifteen. The next card is a seven. Twenty-two.

'Bust,' Billie Jo says, almost relieved. She counts out fifty chips and stacks them next to Barcelona's two piles.

Barcelona stares at the four stacks. She has lost one hand and won one. The next deal would be the tie-breaker. Proof positive of something, though she's lost the train of her former reasoning. She's suddenly not sure anymore exactly what she's trying to prove. Still, she's here, she's gone this far.

She pushes in all of her chips.

The crowd flutters and bumps into each other.

The pit boss wanders over, raises his glasses again, and stares at Barcelona. A stubborn curl on his forehead points at her.

Billie Jo starts stacking the chips into neat piles. Three stacks of fifty thousand dollars each. She glances up and Barcelona sees a warning look, but it's so brief she thinks she may have imagined it.

'The bet's a hundred fifty thousand dollars,' Billie Jo says.

'I'd like new decks,' Barcelona says.

Billie Jo looks at the pit boss. He nods. She brings out four new decks, breaks the wrappers, fans them out faceup, and counts the number in each deck. Then she messes them all in together and starts shuffling.

The crowd has grown even larger. Barcelona doesn't look at them; she resents their marginal participation in her battle. A Greek chorus of bystanders, cattle looking through a fence at life on the other side. They can't possibly understand. And now neither can Barcelona. All that's left now is instinct.

'Would you like a cocktail?' Billie Jo asks. A cocktail waitress stands next Barcelona waiting.

'Gotta talk like the devil and listen like a wife, don't you?' Barcelona asks her.

'You know it, honey,' the cocktail waitress says.

'Nothing, thanks,' Barcelona says but drops a dollar tip on her tray anyway.

'Thanks,' the waitress says and moves away to the next table. She isn't concerned about the outcome of the next hand, Barcelona realizes, but about the next tip.

Billie Jo hands Barcelona the red card.

Barcelona shoves it in the middle of the deck, cuts the cards, and lays the deck into the shoe.

For the first time, the crowd falls silent.

*   *   *

Barcelona sleeps.

She wakes up, looks around. The heavy curtains are drawn so she doesn't know whether it is day or night. She goes back to sleep, not caring.

Barcelona sleeps.

She wakes up, looks around. A tray with orange juice and pastries sits on the floor next to the bed. She doesn't remember ordering this, doesn't know how it got here. She drinks the orange juice and goes back to sleep.

Barcelona sleeps.

She does not dream. She does not replay the past few days.

She wakes up, looks around. On the floor next to the bed is an ice bucket. Inside are three cans of Diet Coke. The ice is almost completely melted. She fishes a can out of the bucket, pops it, drinks. Some spills down her chin onto the sheets. She goes back to sleep.

'Do you remember?' he asks.

She sits up in the bed and rubs her eyes. 'Yes.'

Mostly she remembers watching Billie Jo's hands as they shuffled the cards, cut the deck, laid the decks into the shoe as carefully as if she were handling a newborn infant.

She remembers reaching over to her chips neatly stacked on the felt betting square, her hand cupping the upright towers, and pulling them gently toward her without spilling one. She remembers saying, 'I've changed my mind.'

She remembers the crowd making loud grunts of protest, enraged at her choice. She remembers the look of relief on Billie Jo's face. The pit boss lowered his glasses without changing expression and wandered away to watch another table.

Barcelona remembers walking away from the table with

her purse full of chips, remembers the man in the crowd who grabbed her arm as she passed by, pulling her close and kissing her hard on the lips. She remembers kissing him back, recognizing the taste, the texture of his skin, the piney smell, the pressure of his arms around her without having to look. Afterward, him saying, 'Can I have my money back now?'

Barcelona grabs another pillow and sticks it behind her back. 'I remember everything. How long have I been asleep?'

'Two days,' Cory says.

She nods at this information, thinks about it. 'Am I crazy?'

'Only if you don't hang on to a great guy like me.'

'Oh, really? What if I told you all those orgasms I had with you, I faked them.'

'That's okay. So did I.'

She laughs and and hits him with a pillow. 'Okay, I didn't fake them. But I could have. And you would have risked your whole campaign on a lie. A misperception.'

'To me the truth wasn't in how you felt about me, but in how *I* felt about you. That's what I based my decision on. And that was no misperception.'

She thinks about that a moment. He sits on the side of the bed and lays his hand on the sheet covering her leg. She feels the warmth of his flesh through the stiff sheet.

She leans forward and kisses him. She closes her eyes and relaxes in his arms. In the darkness of her closed eyes she drifts into a place that may be sleep or a dream, though she can still feel the anchor of his arms keeping her from drifting forever. In this place she sees her parents' store, the door leading downstairs to the basement, the kitchen, the bathroom. And the sign over the door, hand-printed, the letters vaguely European, the sinister warning: WATCH YOUR HEAD!

33

'How was Vegas?' Diva asks.

'Vegas was Vegas. Noisy, smoky, you know.' Barcelona digs her fork into her cheesecake.

'Did you win?' Dixie asks.

'Broke even.'

'Broke is the key word when I go to Vegas,' Diva says.

The three of them are sitting in the Garden Café eating dessert. This is not one of their regularly scheduled dinners. Just a spontaneous lunch to celebrate Diva's song being picked up by Rod Stewart. Trina told Dixie she would try to join them if she could get away, but the crunch of the last few days before the election demands most of her time. This may be an excuse, though. Barcelona still has not spoken to Trina since coming back from Las Vegas. She called twice and left messages, but Trina has not called back.

Barcelona spent last night with Cory in his Corona del Mar house. After they made love he waltzed around the room singing songs from various musicals. He knew all the songs from *Man of La Mancha, West Side Story, Camelot, Oklahoma*, and a few she never even heard of. He had a terrible voice but was so enthusiastic that she loved watching him perform anyway. Plus, he seemed totally convinced his voice was just fine.

They never spoke of Vegas, of the money, of why she

went, what she was trying to prove. She only vaguely understood it herself. It had seemed so clear, such an epiphany when she'd been in the manic state on the drive down, the sleepless days that followed. Now it was just something that happened a long, long time ago in a galaxy far, far away. She wasn't sorry, nor did she feel foolish. Just distant, as if it had all happened to a great-great aunt and the story had been passed down generation after generation until it became more myth than truth.

While she was gone, Larry got into the medicine cabinet and dragged out the Ben-Gay. He bit through the tube and ate some of the ointment. Dave took Larry to the vet and the bill was $74.50. Larry welcomed Barcelona home by stepping in his food dish and tracking gravy across the kitchen floor.

'We're going to Hawaii,' Diva announces, chewing her apple cobbler. 'A little surf and sand will give us a chance to come up with some new song ideas.'

'Sounds great,' Barcelona says.

'Yeah, we haven't exactly been reeling them off here. I think all the excitement and everything, plus us still getting to know each other. I mean, we just got married on top of everything else. I think that may be inhibiting us a little.'

'Get away,' Dixie advises. 'That's what I'm going to do when this damn trial is over. Take a river raft trip down the Colorado, something exciting like that.'

'With Karl?' Barcelona asks.

Dixie digs out another piece of carrot cake, avoiding eye contact. 'We'll see.'

Barcelona finishes her last bite of cheesecake and gets up. 'I'm going to the rest room. Could you beg our waitress to give me some more coffee?'

In the bathroom, Barcelona sits on the toilet even though she doesn't have to go. The seat is wobbly and uncomfortable. She is enjoying the lunch, but she misses Trina. Trina was her other half at these meetings. Not just at these meetings, at everything. She reads the graffiti on the stall door. MEN SUCK is scratched into the paint. Underneath is scratched a reply: IF THEY DID, THEY WOULDN'T NEED US. Barcelona stands up and opens the door.

Trina is standing by the sink. 'Don't forget to wash your hands,' she says.

Barcelona stares. 'When did you get here?'

'A couple minutes ago. I saw you come in here and followed you.'

The door opens and two women walk in talking about work. 'The guy's a jerk,' the taller woman says. 'And his secretary is worse. She thinks she's Nixon's secretary, whatshername, the one who erased the tape.'

'Rose something,' the other woman says.

'Whatever. They're both going to get caught if Phillips finds out the way they're operating the department.' The taller one goes into a stall and pees while the shorter one washes her hands and applies makeup. The three of them can hear the tinkle of the tall woman's urine against water. The short one tries to cover for her friend by washing her hands again. The two women give Trina and Barcelona odd looks as they leave.

'Well,' Trina says, 'there goes your reputation.'

'You get my calls?'

Trina nods. She takes out her lipstick and starts applying it. They stare at each other's reflections in the mirror. Barcelona sees her own face and notices how well the makeup covered the bruise on her forehead from Autrey St. James's punch.

'I see Cory's still ahead in the polls,' Barcelona says.

'He's going to win.'

'What's Carla going to do?'

'There are other offices to run for, she may even teach at UCLA. What about you? Quit your job yet?'

Barcelona leans against the stall. 'Not yet. Probably never.'

'Good. These kids need you.'

Barcelona shakes her head. 'No they don't. I need them.'

Trina packs her lipstick away and turns to face Barcelona. 'Are you still worried about everyone's good luck since Dixie's rape?'

'Maybe it wasn't as good as it first seemed. Diva's sold her song, but she and Harley haven't been able to write one since. An obscure cut on an aging rocker's album isn't exactly a state of grace.'

Trina nods and starts to walk toward the door. Barcelona walks toward the door too and somehow they intersect, bump into each other. The bump suddenly becomes an embrace. Barcelona feels Trina's fuller body against her own and wonders what it must be like for Trina and Carla when they hug to feel another woman's body, but to also share that other intimacy. She is still jealous of Carla, but she loves Trina. She smells Trina's neck and hair, shampoo and perfume and something stronger, like wet sand at the beach. 'There there,' she says. 'How's that?'

'About a four on the sincerity meter,' Trina says.

They both laugh, still leaning against each other.

The rest room door opens and Dixie and Diva walk in.

'What the hell are you two doing in here?' Diva asks. 'Dancing?'

'When did you get here?' Dixie asks.

'A couple minutes ago.'

Dixie points at Barcelona. 'We came in to check on Barcy, she's been in here so long.'

'We thought you were sick,' Diva adds.

'I'm fine. We were just talking.'

'Four women in a toilet,' Diva says, looking around. 'There's got to be a hit song in this.'

Barcelona laughs, closing her eyes. Behind closed eyes,

539

she sees the camera pull back and up, rising high above them, and we look straight down and see the four women talking and laughing, getting smaller and smaller until they are indistinguishable, the room shrinking out of sight, starting to spin faster and faster until it bursts into flames and becomes another twinkling star in some undiscovered galaxy. Barcelona feels the warmth on her face from the tiny star. It is comforting to be a star among this constellation, among this universe. Among four women in a spinning white room watching their heads. She looks around at her friends and marvels at them, their beautiful eyes flickering under the bright bathroom lights, like the dealer's polished nails, Autrey St. James's knife, helicopter rotor blades, Eric's scar. Like stars.

Four women in a toilet. Laughing.

Fade out.

JESSICA MARCH

TEMPTATIONS

Once she had been the international jet set's most glittering cover girl. Throwing herself into an ecstatic whirl of love affairs, fuelled by the most potent pleasure drugs of an era of abandon, Stevie Knight had emerged as a rare survivor from her generation's dizzying, devastating trip into decadence. Survived because she was as strong as she was beautiful.

Now, America's richest and most glamorous women come to The Oasis – the haven she has set up in the New Mexico desert. There they are helped to overcome their addictions, repair their shattered lives.

But even as she uses all her strength and her hard-won insights to help her clients, Steve is facing her own greatest challenge. She has fallen in love with a passion greater than any she has experienced before. Fallen in love with a man who demands a commitment she is too proud to make, who demands the one thing to which she has never surrendered. Surrender itself.

A Royal Mail service in association with the Book Marketing Council & The Booksellers Association.
Post-A-Book is a Post Office trademark.

JESSICA MARCH

ILLUSIONS

Marriage was not for Willa Dellahaye.

Love to her was surrender, and Willa would never surrender. Tough, glamorous and successful, still she could never forget the pain and helplessness of her childhood. Never forget her father's brutal betrayal of her mother.

A brilliant divorce lawyer, she had built up an unmatched reputation for fighting and winning for the women she represented.

Now, en route to Saudi Arabia by private jet, she was heading for the greatest challenge of her life – and about to discover that the ultimate battles would be fought within her own heart . . .

'Power, passion and well-reasoned philosophy'
Annabel

'A must if you enjoy Hollywood-style blockbusters'
Manchester Evening News

HODDER AND STOUGHTON PAPERBACKS

ELIZABETH ADLER

THE RICH SHALL INHERIT

'She was the mysterious elegant woman travelling first class on the liner *Ile de France* on her way to New York; she was the beautiful, aloof stranger dining alone on the Orient Express . . . the slender wary-eyed chic woman who spoke to no-one on the cruise from Cairo to Luxor . . .'

Poppy Mallory: hauntingly lovely and unapproachable. Her whole life had been marked by passion, tragedy, scandal – and mystery.

But now that mystery was to be unravelled for Poppy had died rich; very, very rich. And the scramble was on to lay claim to her fortune.

Claudia, greedy for yet more luxury, Pierluigi, desperate to save his financial empire, Orlando, his artistic genius held back by poverty, Aria, enchanting innocent on the brink of life, and Lauren who had sacrificed herself to care for a child – all were obsessed with the need to discover the truth about Poppy's life . . .

'Detective story, thriller, romance and rags-to-riches saga rolled into one vast, glorious read'
New Woman

'A satisfying, sexy saga'

Woman's World

HODDER AND STOUGHTON PAPERBACKS

MORE FICTION TITLES AVAILABLE FROM HODDER AND STOUGHTON PAPERBACKS

JESSICA MARCH

☐	50077 2	Illusions	£4.99
☐	52808 1	Temptations	£3.99

ROSEMARY ENRIGHT

☐	52469 8	Alexa's Vineyard	£4.50

ELIZABETH ADLER

☐	50952 X	The Rich Shall Inherit	£3.99
☐	41551 7	Fleeting Images	£4.50
☐	41369 7	Peach	£4.99
☐	39460 9	Private Desires	£5.99

HILARY NORMAN

☐	49351 8	Chateau Ella	£4.50
☐	41117 1	In Love and Friendship	£4.99

All these books are available at your local bookshop or newsagent, or can be ordered direct from the publisher. Just tick the titles you want and fill in the form below.

Prices and availability subject to change without notice.

Hodder & Stoughton Paperbacks, P.O. Box 11, Falmouth, Cornwall.

Please send cheque or postal order for the value of the book, and add the following for postage and packing:

U.K. including B.F.P.O. £1.00 for one book, plus 50p for the second book, and 30p for each additional book ordered up to a £3.00 maximum.

OVERSEAS INCLUDING EIRE – £2.00 for the first book, plus £1.00 for the second book, and 50p for each additional book ordered.

OR Please debit this amount from my Access/Visa Card (delete as appropriate).

Card Number

Amount £ ....

Expiry Date ....

Signed ....

Name ....

Address ....